A Fatal
Freedom

A Fatal Freedom

An Ursula Grandison Mystery

Janet Laurence

The
Mystery
Press

Dedicated to
Hannah Strong
and in memeory of her parents,
Jeanie and Michael Sayers

Cover illustration: Holloway Prison
at the turn of the century.

First published 2015

The Mystery Press, an imprint of The History Press
The Mill, Brimscombe Port
Stroud, Gloucestershire, GL5 2QG
www.thehistorypress.co.uk

© Janet Laurence, 2015

The right of Janet Laurence to be identified as the Author
of this work has been asserted in accordance with the
Copyright, Designs and Patents Act 1988.

British Library Cataloguing in Publication Data.
A catalogue record for this book is available from the British Library.

ISBN 978 0 7509 6302 2

Typesetting and origination by The History Press
Printed in Great Britain

Chapter One

1903

In the centre of London, just off the junction of busy Tottenham Court Road and Oxford Street, was the jungle. A large carved screen carried images of wild animals: leaping lions, stalking ostriches, giraffes, monkeys, dancing bears, elephants. Ursula Grandison was captivated; surely no jungle could have contained all these animals? She remembered mountain lions back in the Sierra Nevada, where she'd lived in a mining camp. She'd heard one roar on a winter's night, imagined it starving, seeking food, and had shivered in her makeshift bunk. Now she heard another lion's roar, not coming through the silence of snow-covered mountains but rising over the crunch and clatter of traffic on a hot August afternoon in London.

Along one side of an opening in this show-stopping screen Ursula saw the words *Crystal Palace Menagerie*, and along the other, *Patronised by Nobility and Gentry*. A white-faced clown banged a drum in front, calling in the Londoners who thronged around the fair.

'Something, ain't it?' said Thomas Jackman. He slipped a thumb inside an armhole of his waistcoat and sounded as proud of the scene as if he owned all of it himself. 'That's what's known as "the flash".' He waved an arm at the screen. 'In the trade they say "It ain't the show that brings the dough, it's the flash what brings the cash." That's what's attracting all these folk.'

Ursula smiled at her stocky friend. When she had arrived in London, Jackman had been the only person she had contacted. A fresh start was what she needed, she told herself, after her tragic stay in the West Country. She had accepted his invitation for this afternoon with delight and met him at the fairground with real warmth.

Now, though, she saw the way his sharp eyes surveyed the crowds that excitedly pushed towards the opening, paying their entrance fee to view the wild beasts within.

'Thomas Jackman, you haven't asked me along here as a treat, you are on a job!'

He gave her a comradely grin. 'I knew you were a fly one, Miss Grandison.'

She swallowed what she told herself was unreasonable disappointment. 'Come on, now; didn't we agree we'd drop the formalities, that you'd call me Ursula and I'd call you Thomas? After all, I'm a Yankee, not one of your high-falutin' society women.'

'American you are, and maybe not a society woman, but you got style, Miss Grand—, Ursula.' He stood a little back from her and appraised her cream cambric shirt with its small red buttons and brown linen skirt trimmed with a band of darker brown just up from its hem.

'Don't try and soft talk me, Thomas. How dare you invite me here on my afternoon off on false pretences.'

'False pretences?'

'You send me a note suggesting I might like to visit what you call "an amazing menagerie". You do not tell me the famous detective is on a job and needs a respectable companion for cover.'

He looked injured, 'A suspicious mind, that's what you got, Miss Ursula Grandison.' Then he grinned at her again, 'Didn't I say you were a fly one? I should have known I couldn't fool you for more than a minute. How did you catch on so quick?'

Disappointment over, she felt an odd satisfaction that she had seen through his little ploy. When they had first met, it had taken her some time to feel comfortable with this sharp-minded ex-policeman. But he'd earned her respect and for a very short time they had formed something approaching a detection partnership. However, she had no wish to continue the professional association.

'You should have paid more attention to your female companion and less to searching out your mark. Isn't that what you call a person you are trying to follow?'

'That's what a conman calls his potential victim.'

'Not so different, I think.'

He gave a quick sigh and slipped his hand beneath her elbow. 'Miss Grandison, Ursula, shall we proceed to view the menagerie?' he said with exaggerated courtesy.

'By all means, Mr Jackman, I shall be delighted. And at least I can assume that the entrance charge will be covered by your expenses.'

As she and Jackman moved towards the gap in the beautifully decorated screen, Ursula could not help looking around to try and identify who it was that the detective was interested in.

It was a varied crowd, all intent on seeing the wild beasts presented for their entertainment. It was too early in the afternoon for tradesmen and other workers; these were mainly wives and mothers with children. Like herself, they were dressed respectably but not in the height of fashion and from the middle to lower classes rather than the cream of society. Here and there were men as well, some accompanying women, others who looked as though they were idling away the afternoon. Ursula made sure her purse was securely fastened to her belt.

Then she felt Jackman's hold on her elbow tighten. She followed his gaze. A woman and a man were entering the menagerie ahead of them. They seemed rather more stylish than the other sightseers. What, she wondered, was her companion's interest in them?

Thomas Jackman had once been a member of the elite detective division of the Metropolitan Police Force; now he acted in a private capacity, which could mean anything from finding a long-lost relative, through dealing with stolen goods by owners who did not want to involve the authorities, to solving a mysterious death, which had been his commission when they first met. From what Jackman had told her, however, Ursula gained the impression he was most often called upon to obtain evidence of an adulterous relationship.

Once through the entrance, they found themselves in a huge tent supported by poles down its centre. The bright sunshine penetrated the canvas and clearly lit a variety of cages set around three sides. Lazy growls and grunts from bored animals mixed with excited comments from the visitors. Ursula's nose twitched at the aroma of feral beasts, stained sawdust and the more familiar scent of human bodies overdressed on a hot day. By the sounds emanating from where the crowd was thickest, the most popular exhibits were lions.

Jackman steered Ursula towards a less populated part of the tent. A young woman, a dark-haired girl wearing a floppy cream beret over a long plait, studied a somnolent hyena. Her burnt-orange linen jacket and skirt was creased in the manner of that material, giving the impression of someone who cared little about her appearance. Further along the cage stood the couple the detective seemed to be interested in.

The woman looked to be in her late twenties and was stylishly dressed in a well-cut pale green suit trimmed with lace, her blonde hair carefully arranged beneath a graceful hat of fine straw trimmed with green flowers. Her hands, in cream kid gloves, clasped and unclasped themselves, the fingers writhing in a constant pattern of distress as the woman surveyed the trampled ground around them, her gaze moving everywhere except up at the man. He seemed to be pleading with her.

He was tall, with a shock of dark red hair almost hidden by a large hat with a floppy brim. Ursula recognised the look, she had seen it in New York; he was a Bohemian, an artist perhaps. A loosely tailored jacket in brown and beige checks and rumpled light beige trousers reinforced this impression. She could only see a bit of his profile, a straight nose and well-shaped chin, but his shoulders looked broad as he leaned slightly forward, as though imploring the woman to look at him, to listen to his words.

Jackman had positioned Ursula and himself before a wide gap in the three-sided arrangement of cages. Blank canvas hung over what could perhaps be an exit. Beside it was a low table covered with a cloth that reached to the ground. The cage they stood beside contained a couple of stately ostriches, their extravagantly feathered behinds looking dusty and bedraggled. Curiously small heads, held proudly above long necks, bore pop eyes that surveyed the scene with disinterest, then they bent to the floor and pecked at the straw in a desultory way.

Ursula, though, was far more interested in the little scene being played out by the pair near the hyena. The man reached forward to take the woman's restless hands. After the shortest of struggles, she allowed him to hold them, lying limply in his, his solid thumbs caressing their backs. All at once, the girl studying the somnolent animal glanced sharply in her and Jackman's direction and Ursula transferred her attention to the birds.

Where, she wondered idly, did ostriches come from? Africa? She turned to ask Jackman, but he'd moved to the table. From beneath its cloth, he fished out a Box Brownie camera. None of the happy crowds in the tent noticed, they all had their backs to him and were far too interested in the wild beasts.

He seemed to be preparing to take a photograph of the couple. Ursula looked back at them, wondering if there was enough light for a successful photograph; the sunlight was bright but filtered through canvas.

The woman at last turned her gaze up to the man and Ursula was struck by the beauty of her eyes. They were deep violet and had a rare radiance. She said something; her whole face lit up with joy and her hands moved to clasp the man's tightly.

Jackman moved stealthily to his right, trying to position the camera so he could achieve the shot he needed. Before he was ready, though, the girl with the plait abandoned the hyena, raced towards the detective and barged into him. He dropped the camera. The girl somehow scrambled up on to the table, put her fingers in her mouth and produced a stunningly loud whistle.

'Ladies and gentlemen,' she shouted. 'Your attention, please!' People turned to stare. 'Look at these poor animals, living their lives in cages, don't you long to free them? Such a noble word, freedom. But it isn't only animals who need it.'

Ursula could not help admiring the spirit of the girl. The burnt orange outfit commanded attention, tendrils of dark hair beneath the beret had escaped the plait and softened her appearance. She had a full mouth, high cheekbones and fiery eyes that were ablaze with conviction.

People started moving towards her. Their mood hovered between interest and condemnation. 'Well, I never!' 'Extraordinary!' 'Who does she think she is?' and 'Is this part of the entertainment?'

Thomas Jackman was cursing. He had no chance now of catching his subjects on film. Indeed, they seemed to have disappeared from the menagerie.

'Freedom, ladies and gentlemen,' the girl continued, her voice gaining intensity. 'Freedom for us women – that is what we need. Join me now. Call Votes for Women!'

She was shouted down. 'Disgraceful!', 'Shouldn't be allowed' and 'Come away, dear' could be heard on all sides.

Two burly men in well-worn suits appeared, obviously part of the menagerie, and headed for the table.

Ursula hated the idea of this spirited girl being apprehended. No point in trying to stop the men. What she needed was a way of shouting 'fire' without actually using a torch. Looking around, she found her gaze fixed on the lock of the ostrich cage. A padlock that should have been fastened hung open in the door's metal loops. With her back to the bars, working blind, Ursula dislodged and dropped the padlock on the ground, then gently opened the door. Making a cheeping sound such as might attract chickens, she moved towards where the girl was now struggling in the grip of the two men.

It took no more than a few moments before a scream arose above the tent's disjointed noise. 'Those birds – they're out!'

Ursula looked behind her. The ostriches were now stalking across the floor of the tent, their curious heads turning this way and that, the feathered behinds moving with the grace of a music hall dancer, their long, long legs taking them towards some parakeets. A young girl held out a hand as though she wanted to stroke one of them.

'Get away from those birds, they're vicious,' called someone.

People moved hurriedly out of their way.

The two burly men abandoned the girl and hustled after the birds. Jackman tried to catch her but, moving with the speed and slipperiness of an eel, she eluded him, as well as some half-hearted attempts by others to detain her, and ran out of the main entrance. Jackman looked frustrated and furious.

'What happened?' asked Ursula.

'Damnation knows! Begging your pardon, Miss Grandison. But that's the very end of enough.' Holding his camera, Jackman looked around the tent hopelessly. 'They've gone. She was in cahoots with them, no doubt about that.'

Down at the other end of the tent the ostriches had been rounded up. The sightseers drifted back to look at the lions, the bears and the monkeys, all interest lost in the girl and her message, if, indeed, it had been a message.

'But who were that couple? Why were you trying to photograph them? And how did you manage to hide your camera underneath that table?'

A man hurried up. Surely, thought Ursula, he had to be the proprietor of the menagerie. His costume was magnificent,

Mexican bandit crossed with Spanish grandee; black hair was slicked down, thin moustache twirled up either side of his face, dark eyes flashing with anger. 'Tom,' he boomed. 'You swore to me there would be no disruption; instead you cause uproar. The animals will take hours of calming.'

Ursula looked around. The occupants of the cages hadn't seemed to pay much attention to any of the disruption, but perhaps the smaller ones did seem a little more lively than before. Certainly the hyena seemed to have woken up. At that moment two lions let off mighty roars; those standing in front of their cages fell back.

'You see? Now I shall have to delay my show. I'm not putting my head into one of their mouths when they're in that state.'

Jackman placed a hand on the man's arm. 'Pa, I apologise. I had no idea that girl would pull such a stunt. Don't know who she is, where she came from. Did someone catch her?'

The splendid showman shook his head. 'Gone – the men were too busy catching the birds, no one was on the door. And that's another thing, how in heaven's name did that cage get opened?' He strode over to where the ostriches were being persuaded to re-enter their home, picked up the open padlock and waved it at the assistants. 'When I find who was responsible for this, he will wish he'd never been born.'

'Warn't us,' both assistants said. 'Dunno how those varmints could've opened the door,' said one.

'Been some little kid, I bet,' said the other. 'Thought it was fun to have us chase them all round the place.'

'I'll have 'is guts for garters, whoever it was.' Pa inserted the padlock into its loops. 'Wicked bite those birds got; ostriches can kill. Bert, find the key and make sure the cage is properly locked this time.'

Ursula could not help feeling guilty. The padlock had not been her fault, but the birds could not have opened the door themselves. If she had known ostriches could be so dangerous, she wouldn't have encouraged them. But to confess would cause even more trouble for Jackman.

'Let's get out of here,' the investigator said. 'I'm sorry about the fuss, Pa. There's some money for your men, thanks for your help.'

★ ★ ★

Some fifteen minutes later Ursula and Jackman entered Regent's Park.

'Take a pew,' said Jackman, waving at a bench.

Ursula was happy to accept the invitation. 'Now,' she said, 'I think it's time you told me what all that was about.'

Jackman set down his Box Brownie, wiped his brow with a cotton handkerchief and slumped hopelessly down beside her. 'I don't often fail but I'm out to the wide here. If I'm not careful, Peters is going to call me a right Bengal Lancer.'

'Bengal Lancer?'

He straightened himself with a curt laugh. 'It's rhyming slang: a Bengal Lancer, a chancer. Forgot for a moment you're a Yankee.'

'Ah,' said Ursula. 'Lancer, Chancer; that's neat.'

'Neat? What's tidy about it?'

Ursula laughed. 'Didn't someone say the English and Americans are divided by a common language? It's a bit of slang. To us "neat" can mean that something is fit for its purpose.'

'Ah,' said Jackman. He sat silent for a moment and Ursula let him gather his thoughts while she admired the swathes of green grass and graceful trees stretching up to a magnificent terrace of stuccoed houses. They had some of the grandeur of Mountstanton, the house she had stayed in at the start of her visit to England. She didn't want to think about what had happened there, so she prompted Jackman, who finally took a deep breath and launched into an account of his current assignment.

'I was approached by Mr Joshua Peters of Montagu Place, Marylebone. Mr Peters is worried that Mrs Peters …'

'His wife?'

'Who else?'

'His mother? No, I'm sorry, Thomas, of course it is his wife.'

'He was worried his wife, Mrs Peters, is, as he put it to me, "straying from hearth and home". He commissioned me to follow her for a spell to see if she was meeting up with some fellow.'

'And it was Mrs Peters who was at the menagerie today? And the man with her was, I take it, not Mr Peters?'

'You have it. She's been meeting him regularly, putting on a show, making it seem that they have run into each other accidentally.'

'An act just in case anyone who knew her caught sight of them?'

'You got it. And she's good at it; could get a part on the boards I reckon. Now, I managed to chat up Mrs Peters' maid. Nice little thing, innocent as a newborn kitten. Told me how unhappy her mistress was with the master ...'

'My, you did chat her up well.'

'It's my manner,' said Jackman smugly. 'Charm the birds off the trees, I do.'

'One moment she's a kitten, the next a bird,' said Ursula, straight-faced. 'What is the name of this dear little girl?'

'Millie. And Millie tells me how her mistress is to visit the menagerie today. Says how fine it's supposed to be. I reckoned she was angling for an invitation from me for her afternoon off. I reported the matter to Mr Peters, without disclosing my sources ...'

'I'm glad you didn't betray Millie's indiscretions.'

'Without disclosing my sources, as I said, and asked Mr Peters if he didn't want to go along to confront them.'

'In public?'

'That's exactly what he said to me. And he told me how tricksy Mrs Peters could be. She looks like an angel, he said, but he swears no schoolboy can lie as she can. Which is why he wanted a sworn statement of the different occasions I'd seen her with this man. And then he asked if I couldn't arrange for a photograph to be taken of them at the menagerie. Said she would not be able to explain that away. I said he didn't know what he was asking. Could hardly get them to pose for me, could I? And I couldn't set up flash photography. I told him I'd have a go with a Brownie, but I doubted there'd be enough light to develop a recognisable image.'

'Yet another one of your talents, photography?'

'Always been interested. And it comes in useful from time to time.' He unslung the Brownie from his shoulders. 'Such a clever little box this. Got a rotary shutter, takes snapshots and timed exposures as well. Three stops and two finders.' He turned the camera around to show Ursula. 'This one's for upright exposures, like portraits, and this one's for horizontal, landscapes they call them. All very straightforward.'

'I've seen advertisements for them,' Ursula said. 'They seem aimed at the young.'

'They're much more than a toy,' said Jackman. 'Anyway, Mr Peters said he would make a snapshot worth my while.'

'But what about the girl? Who was she?'

Jackman groaned. 'I reckon she's Mrs Peters' sister. Millie told me about her, said they were very close. 'I'd fixed it with Pa earlier, Charlie Maddocks I should say, but he's always known as Pa, and his wife's Ma. We go back a long way; I've run into Charlie and his menagerie – and the circus that's part of the set-up – all over the country. Anyway, he'd agreed I could leave the camera in the tent. I know how visitors spend their time looking at the beasts. And I reckoned that Mrs Peters and her fancy man would be a little apart from the main crowd, seeking a bit of privacy, know what I mean?' He looked at Ursula.

'Indeed.'

'When I saw the two of them standing close together, so still, with him holding her hands, well, I thought it might work after all. Then that wretched girl pulls her stunt.'

'Is there any chance Mrs Peters could have suspected that she was being followed? Oh, I know you're very skilled, and you've told me some of the tricks you use, moustaches, wigs, different hats and style of clothes, but Mr Peters' comment about her being able to explain anything away suggests she is much sharper than she looks. So, she asks her sister to come along with her to meet this man. Do we know his name?'

'Mr Daniel Rokeby.'

She wondered how he'd found this out. 'She may well have thought putting someone on her track was the sort of dirty trick her husband was capable of. I think she put her sister completely in the picture. So while she speaks with Mr Rokeby, or allows him to speak to her,' she added, remembering how silently the woman had listened to the man, 'the girl pretends to be looking at the hyena but is actually keeping an eye out for someone who could have followed them.'

'Watching me?'

'If Mrs Peters has noticed you, she will have described you.' She surveyed Jackman. 'About five foot nine inches, well built, looks around forty years old, has a fine head of light brown hair, sideburns, thick eyebrows that almost meet, brown eyes, a slightly beak-shaped nose, wide mouth.'

He looked astonished. 'You reckon she could have clocked me that well?'

'If she's really cheating on her husband, and she's as bright as he suggests, yes. And could you perhaps have underestimated her? How many times have you followed Mrs Peters?'

'Six.'

'And where have they met?'

'The first time was this park, the second an art exhibition, then there was some sort of literary society meeting, I had a little difficulty getting into that, not being a member ...'

'I expect that's where Mrs Peters noticed you. And once she had, she would have kept a very sharp eye out. Her description might not have been quite as detailed but enough for her friend or sister to know who to look out for.'

For the first time in their acquaintanceship, Thomas Jackman looked chastened.

'That speech about freedom for the animals and the cry for Votes for Women was a marvellously judged piece of distraction.'

'It's a cry that's becoming more and more familiar,' said Jackman gloomily.

'Votes for Women?'

He nodded. 'Your sex has a lot to answer for.'

'It's a cry we are hearing in America as well. I think it's only fair for women to get the vote. Why shouldn't we have equality with men?'

Jackman hardly seemed to hear this. 'Now I have to go to Mr Peters tomorrow and explain just how I have failed. No doubt Mrs Peters is currently back at Montagu Place sipping a glass of wine and making eyes at her husband.'

Ursula thought about the maid who had told Jackman that her mistress was unhappy and she remembered the radiant look that had come over the face of the woman with the wonderful eyes, as though she had at that very moment made a decision.

'What is Joshua Peters like?'

'Hard business man. Not the sort of man I like to cross.'

Could such a man make a good husband? 'And would you say he loved his wife very much?'

Jackman gave her a sharp glance. 'What you're asking is, does he look on her as a prize he would hate to see given to someone else?'

Ursula nodded.

'I'd say that would about sum him up.' He sat fiddling with the chain of his watch. 'I wish I knew how those wretched birds escaped.'

'Yes, that was unexpected,' said Ursula. 'Do you think the girl opened the cage before she leaped on the table to give her speech?' She felt even Mrs Peters could not have improved on the innocence of her look as she said this.

Jackman, though, took a deep breath. 'You, it was you, Ursula Grandison. You couldn't see a supporter of Votes for Women get her comeuppance, could you? Never mind about loyalty to me!'

'Loyalty to you? How about you not telling me anything about why you had issued your invitation?' Ursula rose. 'Enlisting my help but keeping me in ignorance! Not to mention giving all your aid to a self-serving husband instead of helping an unhappy wife. And you wonder why women want the vote!' She drew on her cotton gloves. 'My boarding house will shortly be serving supper. No doubt cabbage will be a prominent dish but maybe we shall be fortunate enough to have brisket on the menu as well.' She held out her hand. 'Goodbye, Mr Jackman. It has been an interesting afternoon.'

She left him sitting there, staring after her in stunned silence.

Chapter Two

Ursula Grandison had arrived in London that July with a small amount of savings and no contacts.

It was her choice. After three months spent in a stately home as companion to a young American girl, she had been offered every help in establishing herself in the capital. Instead, bruised and disillusioned by the disastrous events at Mountstanton, she preferred to strike out on a new phase of her life relying on nothing but her own resourcefulness and a single reference.

Her train had brought her to Paddington Station. Consigning her case to the Left Luggage, Ursula had rapidly found any number of small hotels of reasonable cost and some that provided adequate cleanliness and comfort. She chose one, handed over her passport and sent for her luggage. At the local library she scanned the periodicals provided.

Soon she had a list of agencies that offered their services in finding staff for respectable households.

'A lady's companion, is that the position you are seeking?' The interviewer was a brisk woman who looked to be in her late forties. Her solid body was encased in a well-cut but conservative dark grey shirt and skirt. The shirt sported a thin black tie. On the dust-free desk in front of her were neat piles of buff-coloured files and a glass vase with a single cream rose.

'Now, Miss Grandison, perhaps you will be good enough to give me details of your experience.' Mrs Bundle sat straight-backed, pencil poised, taking in her applicant's appearance:

the neatly swept-up chestnut hair underneath the black straw hat with its very small brim; the rather fine grey eyes; the black linen suit, freshly ironed that morning, that was no more than neat.

Ursula gave a carefully edited account of her suitability to offer companionship to a lady who might need someone to cope with correspondence, run errands, perhaps deal with servants and generally make her life easier.

'You are American,' Mrs Bundle stated looking at her notes. Both her tone and her expression said this was unfortunate. 'You do not know London and have only been in this country a few months.'

'But that time was spent in the highest society circles as companion to a young lady of great wealth,' Ursula said steadily. 'I am familiar with how social matters are handled in England. Reaching the end of my time there, rather than returning to the States, I have decided to remain in England. I am anxious to discover London.'

'It is slightly surprising that the aristocratic family you have been residing with have not provided the sort of contacts that would yield suitable employment.' Her tone said this circumstance was suspicious.

Ursula forced herself to forget exactly how her employment as companion to Belle Seldon had ended. 'You will perhaps be aware of the family's tragic circumstances. They, and I, are in mourning.' With the smallest of gestures, Ursula indicated her outfit. 'However, the Dowager Countess was kind enough to provide me with a reference.'

Mrs Bundle picked up the sheet of paper with its ornate crest and fierce black handwriting. 'The Dowager appears to have been completely satisfied with both your skills and behaviour,' she said slowly.

Ursula dipped her head in acknowledgement of the encomiums which had been provided. 'I am a quick learner; I am used to dealing with difficult circumstances and to mixing with a wide variety of people.' She smiled inwardly as she thought of her life amongst silver miners in the Sierra Nevada. 'I am confident of being able to fulfil any tasks I would be set,' she added persuasively.

'Are you, indeed?' Mrs Bundle regarded her closely. 'It is no doubt your American background that allows you to sell yourself so strongly.'

Ursula said nothing.

'It is in your favour that you do not seem to have one of those nasal and, frankly, ugly American accents,' the interviewer added thoughtfully.

Again Ursula said nothing.

Mrs Bundle leafed through several files and Ursula felt a tiny seed of hope.

★ ★ ★

Three days later, the seed of hope had withered. Four appointments with elderly women who required a companion had led nowhere.

'You seem a very nice person,' one had said apologetically after a short interview. 'I do not feel, though, that you will allow me to be comfortable in my ways.' The lashes of the tired eyes had fluttered sadly. 'Agnes was so quiet, she, well, she *melted* into the background. Just always there when I needed her.' A handkerchief was produced. 'A wasting disease has taken her from me.'

After all the interviews had been concluded, Ursula once again sat in Mrs Bundle's office while the employment consultant went through the results.

'I am afraid, Miss Grandison, you appear to prospective employers as too independent of mind.' She picked up the last letter. 'Is it that independence of mind which did not allow you to take up the offer of a position as companion to Lady Weston? She appears to think you could have been suitable.'

Ursula shifted a little uncomfortably in her chair. 'When I asked if I would be permitted to practise on her piano, a fine Bechstein,' she added. 'Lady Weston said, quite coldly, that there was an upright in the servants' hall that would be available for such spare time as I would have.'

Mrs Bundle removed her spectacles, placed them on the desk and sighed. 'Miss Grandison, you do understand the nature of the position you wish to obtain?'

Ursula nodded. 'I do, Madam. And I was conscious that Lady Weston and I would not do well together.'

Mrs Bundle replaced her spectacles, flipped through her manilla folders, then laid a hand on the pile. 'I am afraid there is no other position for which I can arrange an interview,' she said briskly. 'However, I have your address and will let you know if a suitable vacancy becomes available.'

Ursula left the office with little hope that one would. Her visits to other employment agencies proved equally unproductive.

Tired of rejection, she sent a note to the one London contact she was willing to get in touch with and was cheered by the immediate response she received. Thomas Jackman, ex-policeman and now private investigator, visited her the next morning and Ursula was surprised to find how very welcome his appearance at her hotel was; she remembered how, working together as they had at Mounstanton, initial distrust had gradually been replaced by respect on either side.

'Shall we go for a walk?' he suggested, looking around the unattractive hotel hall.

'It's very clean,' Ursula said apologetically. 'I am afraid I cannot afford the charges of a fine hotel. And I have known much worse than this.'

It was a sunny day. Jackman walked her into Kensington Gardens and across a bridge over a stretch of water she was informed was the Serpentine. 'A popular place for swimming; frequented, I believe, by the Bohemian set of Pimlico,' Jackman said.

They passed two nurses pushing highly polished perambulators, chatting merrily while their charges in sweet little lace-edged bonnets waved rattles at each other.

'Kensington Gardens is very popular with society nannies,' commented Jackson. 'You will always find them on parade here. Now, why don't you tell me why you are in London and what your intentions are.'

Ursula was happy with the bluntness of his approach and the way his square, craggy face had listened intelligently, his bright eyes full of amusement at her description of the society ladies who had interviewed her.

'My, Miss Grandison, they have had a narrow escape,' he observed at one point. 'You would have organised them into oblivion almost as soon as you commenced your employment. I am feeling quite sorry for the luckless lady you finally accept.'

She sighed. 'I am afraid I am not having much success in that line.' There was a little pause, then she added, 'I have to hope that something will come along soon. But,' she rallied, her tone bright, 'I need to find a suitable boarding house. The charges at that hotel, mean though it is, are too much for me. Would you be able to help me find one?'

He gave her a wry smile.

She quickly put a hand on his arm. 'Please do not think that is the only reason I contacted you. When we parted in Somerset, you were kind enough to say that if I did come to London, you would be happy to continue our acquaintance. I was hoping you might introduce me to some of London's sights.'

'I shall be delighted, Miss Grandison,' he said, then produced a notebook and pencil and scribbled down several addresses. 'The proprietors are all known to me personally and I have no hesitation in recommending them.'

They spent a little more time walking through the pleasant environs while Jackman entertained Ursula with an account of a recent case he'd been involved with, then he returned her to her hotel with a promise of future contact. 'But let me know your new address,' he said, tipping the curly brim of his bowler hat as he left.

The second of the recommended addresses was a terraced house just west of Victoria station. It only accepted female boarders. Mrs Maple, a bony woman with a severe face, showed Ursula a second-floor room. Reasonably sized, it contained a bed with a firm mattress, a comfortable armchair, a small table with a bentwood chair, a hanging rail shielded by a curtain, a chest of drawers and, behind a small screen, a washbasin. Mrs Maple's stern expression lightened as Ursula expressed her delight at this feature.

'Mr Maple insisted that every room be provided with running water,' she said. 'Poor man, he knew he was not long for this world and was determined that after his demise I should be provided with the means for a reasonable income.'

Ursula announced that she would be very happy to take the room and pay two weeks' rent in advance. As she counted out the coins, she silently hoped that before it was due again, she had obtained employment.

She moved in the next day and posted a note to Jackman thanking him for his help and confirming her new address. Arriving back at Mrs Maple's after another fruitless interview, Ursula was met by Meg, the lanky maid-of-all-work. 'Oh, miss, Mr Jackman's here. He's with the mistress and she says you're to go to her parlour.'

Mrs Maple was laughing as she handed the investigator a cup of tea in the room at the back of the house she reserved for her private use. 'Ah, Miss Grandison, Mr Jackman has called to see you are settled. Mr Jackman is a good friend, I don't know what Mr Maple would have done without him sorting out that crook of a builder he had the bad luck to employ. Sit down and have a cuppa, won't you?'

Ursula was happy to oblige. Her feet were tired from another day of walking around London in her hopeless quest.

'How pleasant to see you again, Mr Jackman,' she said, sitting down. 'Tell me more about the crooked builder.'

Soon Ursula was enjoying an account of various difficulties Mr and Mrs Maple had had setting up the boarding house. Under her severe demeanour, Mrs Maple gradually revealed humour and warmth and it was evident that she and Jackman had a companiable relationship.

'And how has your day been, Miss Grandison?' Mrs Maple asked after it had been explained how the crooked builder had been warned off by the investigator.

'Without result, I am afraid,' Ursula said brightly. 'However, I have hopes for an interview that has been arranged for tomorrow.'

'I wonder,' said Mrs Maple slowly. 'I ran into an old friend yesterday. We knew each other a long time ago. She moves in different circles these days. Mrs Bruton she is now, quite the lady.' The dry way she said this told Ursula that Mrs Maple's friend had patronised her. 'She told me,' Mrs Maple continued, 'that Mr Bruton passed on two years ago and she is now out of mourning. She also mentioned that she has need of some sort of secretary. I didn't give it attention at the time but with you looking for a position, Miss Grandison, I wonder … now, what did I do with the card she gave me?' Mrs Maple started investigating her pockets. 'Here it is!' She handed over a piece of pasteboard.

The card was stylishly printed, the name 'Mrs Edward Bruton' printed in flowing italics, with an address in Wilton Crescent in smaller typeface on the bottom left-hand corner.

'Now you write to her, Miss Grandison, and say you are available.'

'Can't do any harm,' said Jackman. He rose. 'Must be on my way, just dropped by to say hello to Mrs Maple and see you were settled, Miss Grandison.'

Ursula remembered how they had agreed down in Somerset that they would use each other's first names. Somehow this didn't seem the right time to remind him.

★ ★ ★

Two days later, Ursula met a fluttery woman in her forties who seemed happy to relate her circumstances. Mr Bruton had been considerably older than herself, there had been no offspring of the union, and the widow had been left well provided for. Now out of mourning, she was beginning to involve herself with various activities.

'I wish to enlarge my circle of friends. Edward was a very private person, Miss Grandison.' Mrs Bruton rearranged the wayward chiffon scarf that was draped over her pale pink crepe de chine blouse, prettily tucked and inserted with lace, the sleeves slightly puffed at the shoulder and anchored in lace-bedecked cuffs, each fastened with a row of tiny pearl buttons. A dark grey slubbed silk skirt, its cut pronouncing that it came from no ordinary dressmaker, managed to suggest that its wearer was slimmer than close inspection revealed.

The interview took place in the morning room of a fashionable home in Knightsbridge. Sun lit Mrs Bruton's pale gold hair, artfully arranged in a sort of pillow with escaping tresses that suggested a mind free from too many formal restraints.

The face was softly plump with only a few lines around the eyes. The mouth had none of the stern qualities Ursula had discerned in those older ladies she had recently met who required companionship – or a genteel slave. The eyes were a gentle blue with heavy lids. Hanging from her neat ears were pearls whose sheen declared they were genuine, as was the long string around her neck. Her hands were soft; diamond rings flashed brilliantly on plump, white little fingers as their owner fiddled with her scarf.

'As long as he had me to keep him company in the evenings, Edward was perfectly happy, he did not require social activity,' Mrs Bruton continued, lightly touching a Lalique dish that sat on a small round table beside her chair. 'Occasionally we would have one of his legal friends to a luncheon.'

'Legal?'

'Edward had been a solicitor. By the time we met, he was retired. He said I had been sent to enlighten the last years of his life. There was nothing he liked more than to play cards with me.'

It sounded a somewhat humdrum existence. Ursula wondered how captivating a companion Mr Bruton had been.

'Did you travel, visit friends at weekends?' she enquired.

'Edward adored abroad.' Mrs Bruton's blue eyes suddenly spar-kled as brightly as her diamonds. 'He said the weather was so much better. We would stay in Nice in the spring, and we went to Berlin and Vienna; we loved Vienna almost as much as Nice. We would visit the opera, dine in restaurants and occasionally we would meet people. I always had to take new dresses and hats. He would buy me jewels, tell me how lovely I looked.' She gave a musical little laugh. 'I longed for the times we would travel, it was as though a door had been opened from a dull room on to one filled with light and gaiety.' Mrs Bruton gazed out of the window that gave on to a small garden filled with soft greens and a variety of pink and white flowers. 'Life has been very dull for me since his passing away.' She reached a hand towards Ursula's wrist in a confiding gesture.

'While he was moving towards his end I hated to see him suffer. But, do you know, Miss Grandison, after he had gone, after the first relief that he was no longer in pain, I missed not only Edward but my efforts to turn his mind from his illness. I would read to him, relate little incidents I had noted in my afternoon walks to take the air. And I missed the activity of the sick room, the doctor's calls, the nurses, the occasional visit from one of his legal friends. Was that dreadful of me?'

The soft blue eyes seemed anxious.

'Mourning drains the spirit,' Ursula said gently. 'You must now welcome the opportunity to take up a social life again.' Then she wondered at that 'again'. It did not sound as though the woman had had much of a one before.

'I want to involve myself in good causes,' Mrs Bruton said earnestly. 'There are so many who suffer in life and so many splendid women who organise relief for them. I wish to join their number. Also,' she added quietly, 'I am sure my dear Edward would not want me to bury myself away wearing widow's weeds for all eternity. I have no children to occupy my thoughts or my days and I think I deserve some entertainment; do you not think so, Miss Grandison?'

Ursula hastily reassured her that that was so.

'Now, let us turn our minds to why you have so kindly attended on me. With my social life expanding, I shall need someone to organise "At Home" cards, send out invitations, keep my diary, and advise on what should be served at such little *thés*

and even *soirées* as I shall hold, shall I not? Also, I will need someone to assist at such events, for I am woefully unaccustomed to
social matters in England. You, Miss Grandison, have such an air
and with so splendid a reference from the Dowager Countess of
Mountstanton, I can be perfectly at ease knowing that all is safe
in your hands.'

It seemed that the position was being offered. Just as Ursula was
about to say she would be happy to work for her, Mrs Bruton asked,
'I do not think you mentioned how you knew I was in need of a
social secretary?'

'Mrs Maple, who I understand is a friend of yours, told me of
your requirement.'

'Mrs Maple?' It seemed Mrs Bruton had difficulty recalling
the name.

'I understand she encountered you unexpectedly a week or so
ago and that it was some time since you had last met.'

The blue eyes fixed a contemplative gaze on Ursula. Then light
seemed to dawn. 'Why, of course, Mrs Maple! Such a long time …
and we had once been quite friendly. But, you know, the paths
our lives follow can diverge. Poor Maisie, once she settled for
Mr Maple, and I met my beloved Edward, we moved in totally
different circles.' Mrs Bruton looked around her immaculate room
as though conscious its silk upholstered chairs, antique occasional
tables, attractive water colours and porcelain ornaments were a
world away from Mrs Maple's functional boarding house.

'If indeed it was Maisie Maple who sent you to me, I have a
feeling I shall owe her a debt. Tell me, when could you start?'

★ ★ ★

'Mrs Bruton seems so disingenuous, so unused to the ways of the
world,' Ursula said to Thomas Jackman a few weeks later. 'Yet she
is very shrewd. The position is only two and a half days a week
and not live-in. However, the pay is not ungenerous and I may be
able to find someone else who also requires a part-time secretary.'

'It must be a relief to have some income,' Jackman said. 'Even
if it is not as much as you need.' It was one of Ursula's half days
and they were in a small eating place near Victoria station enjoying a pot of tea for two. 'Tell me more about your employer, she
sounds an interesting woman.'

'I find her so. As I said, she is really much shrewder than she appears on the surface. Two women called on her the other day. She had a slight acquaintance with one but was meeting the other for the first time. They wanted to interest her in donating to some charity for orphan children. Mrs Bruton made them very welcome and wanted to know everything about the "poor little children", as she continually referred to them: where the foundlings came from, where they lived, who cared for them, and particularly what sort of education they were being given. At the end of the tea, she said very sweetly that she would think carefully about all she had heard and would be in touch.'

'Did she think they were trying to milk her?'

'Afterwards she was quite angry and said fancy imagining she was unaware that the state provided education without charge for the poverty-stricken.' Ursula gave a gurgle of laughter. 'The women had been very stupid, for at one stage Mrs Bruton introduced the name of Froebel but they seemed unaware of who he was or his kindergarten principles.'

'Did she not think they could be perhaps ignorant but still charitably inclined?'

Ursula shook her head. 'She thought they were using every possible ground to convince her large sums of money were required to care for and educate the poor orphans.'

'So, the poor little children will not be receiving any of the Bruton funds?'

'Not through those agents.' Ursula checked the pot and poured them both more tea. Soon, though, Jackman had to leave and she made her way back to Mrs Maple's.

She was finding working for her new employer was both pleasurable and challenging. Mrs Bruton had a way of dealing with several subjects at the same time, interweaving the description of a new friend with plans for an entertainment and the necessity for enlarging her wardrobe of tea gowns. Ursula would find herself making confused notes that later had to be sorted out and sometimes required applying to Mrs Bruton for confirmation she had understood her wishes correctly.

'Oh, Miss Grandison, what a silly woman you must think me. I meant that Mrs Trenchard was to attend luncheon with me on Thursday this week; I did tell you I met her through the church, did I not? Why, look at that dear little kitten in the garden, do chase it away, I saw it kill a bird the other day.' After Ursula returned to the morning room, it was as if no interruption had taken place, 'Then the tea party I wish to arrange, with Mrs Trenchard's help, is to be the week after next. Now, where did I put the list of guests to be invited?' Searching her desk, Mrs Bruton's attention was caught by several samples of blue silk. 'Which do you think, Miss Grandison, matches my eyes?'

The list found and Mrs Trenchard consulted, Ursula sent out the invitations. She memorised all the names and enjoyed trying to work out from the addresses and her scant knowledge of London where in the social hierarchy the various guests belonged, but she soon gave up.

Mrs Bruton's cook was used to providing simple fare; apparently that was what Mr Bruton had preferred. For a formal tea more would be expected and Ursula spent much time consulting a well-worn edition of *Mrs Beeton's Household Management*. Remembering the delicacies the chef at Mountstanton had produced for tea, Ursula had long discussions with Mrs Evercreech in the well-appointed kitchen, convincing her that miniature chocolate éclairs and tiny iced sponge squares were well within her capabilities and would be ideal beside the wafer-thin sandwiches with either cucumber or egg fillings and Battenberg cake she was used to producing.

'A nice jam tart, that was what Mr Bruton liked,' Mrs Evercreech said with a sigh as the book was closed. 'Still, it will be nice to do something different for once, long as they turns out all right.'

'You will do everything perfectly, Cook,' Ursula said firmly.

On the day itself, her employer was, perhaps understandably, nervous. 'I do so hope Lady Chilton will attend.'

'She has accepted your invitation,' said Ursula, consulting her list of guests to make sure her memory had not failed her.

'And Mrs Bright, she is such a leader in political matters.'

'Indeed,' murmured Ursula, wondering how far her employer was determined to enter that arena.

Mrs Bruton adjusted the lace jabot of her powder-blue chiffon afternoon gown, then fussed with her enamel and sapphire bracelet. Ursula had managed to persuade her that single pearl earrings were more suitable for the afternoon than sapphires, but Mrs Bruton had insisted on the bracelet. 'Edward so liked to see me wearing my precious things,' she said sadly, laying the earrings back in her jewel case. Huckle, her maid, closed it with a snap that said she disapproved of anyone else advising her mistress on her appearance.

The delicate chimes of the little clock on the bedroom mantelshelf reminded the hostess she should be downstairs to receive the first of her guests.

Soon the drawing room was alive with fashionably dressed women managing to avoid accidental encounters with other hats and greeting acquaintances with every appearance of delight.

'So pleased Mrs Bruton is taking up the cause, I am sure you were responsible, Mrs Waterside ...'

'Such a failure on the political side over the years, you have to agree, Mrs Parsons ...'

'Rachel Fentiman was so brave the other day ...'

The voices came and went in Ursula's ears as she supervised the maid serving the tea. Enid was every bit as nervous as her mistress and needed gentle encouragement.

'Is they all here, Miss Grandison?' Enid looked doubtfully at the last few cups on the side table.

'I think so.' Ursula tried to make a headcount of the room. Just as she decided one guest was still to arrive, the doorbell rang. Enid almost dropped a cup and saucer as she tried to decide which needed her attention more, the tea or the door.

Ursula rescued the china and said, 'I will answer the bell, Enid; you continue serving.'

Standing on the doorstep was a girl with an alive face and though the plait had given way to a fall of dark hair beneath a cream beret, Ursula had no difficulty in recognising her.

'Rachel Fentiman,' said the girl. 'Am I horribly late? My omnibus was so slow I think it would have been faster to walk.'

'Please, come in, Miss Fentiman. Mrs Bruton will be so pleased to see you.' Ursula opened the drawing room door for the girl who had made the freedom speech at the menagerie.

Chapter Three

Miss Fentiman gave Ursula an apologetic smile. 'Afraid I'm a little late. I do hope Mrs Bruton will forgive me.'

She was wearing a cobalt-blue, short-sleeved shirt with a narrowly cut matching skirt; it was a severe design and yet it did nothing to dim the girl's attractive aura of energy. Everything about her seemed fresh: the clear, peach warmth of skin, the shine of dark hair, the sparkle of vivid blue eyes.

Ursula led the way into the drawing room and announced Miss Fentiman's name.

Mrs Bruton immediately came forward, as did Mrs Trenchard.

'Rachel, my dear,' said the woman. 'Let me introduce you to our hostess. Mrs Bruton, this is my niece, Miss Fentiman.'

'It is so kind of you to invite me,' said the girl after apologising for her tardy arrival. 'I do admire you for holding this event.'

Mrs Bruton purred. There was no actual sound, but Ursula could think of no other word to describe her employer's satisfied expression or the way she laid a soft hand on the girl's arm.

'My dear Miss Fentiman. Your aunt, Mrs Trenchard, described you in such admirable detail that I have been longing to make your acquaintance. Now, how many of my honoured guests have you met before?'

A woman, well dressed but with hair scraped back unbecomingly beneath a plain straw hat and skin the colour and appearance of parchment, said, 'Why, Miss Fentiman and I are old friends. She has been good enough to assist me in the East End hospital of which I am the chairman. Alas, she does not seem to have time for such activities these days. Other interests appear to have taken over.'

Such was the force of the woman's antagonism, Ursula expected Miss Fentiman to be abashed. Instead she said, quite cheerfully, 'How nice to see you Mrs Mudford. I hope St Christopher's is faring well. Now that I am back from Manchester, I shall try and assist again, if that will suit.'

The slightest incline of Mrs Mudford's skull-like head. 'That pleases me, Miss Fentiman. Mrs Bruton, I trust I can interest you in joining our little committee? We do most valuable work.'

Before Mrs Bruton could respond, Mrs Trenchard said swiftly, 'And I have been telling our hostess about the Society for Women's Suffrage I am so closely involved with. Now that you are so sadly widowed, my dear Mrs Bruton, I am sure that you will support our Movement to achieve the vote for our sex.'

'Mrs Trenchard,' a small woman bustled into the little group, her generous curves beautifully contained in tightly tailored, bright pink linen. She said with determination, 'It is votes for spinsters and widows we fight for, not all women.'

'And,' said Mrs Mudford, looking as though she chewed on a lemon, 'you, Miss Fentiman, did the cause no favours by your behaviour the other day. Quite disgraceful. If your father were still alive, he would be ashamed of you.'

Miss Fentiman, her eyes sparkling, opened her mouth but, once again, Mrs Trenchard took the initiative. 'I thought what Rachel did was splendid. That is what our Movement needs: action.'

Ursula, refilling cups of tea while Enid passed round the cucumber sandwiches and exquisite pastries Cook had produced, saw a rustle of interest pass through the others at the party. Up until that point, groups of two or three had enjoyed exchanging conversation with one another. Now it was as if the curtain had gone up on a stage.

Had all Mrs Bruton's guests come on the recommendation of Mrs Trenchard? Ursula wondered, giving a recharged cup to a slight woman in a stylish grey silk outfit. She had not seemed on easy terms with any of them.

'Mrs Mudford, will you not ask our hostess how she would feel if, having received the vote, she had it taken away from her on the occasion of a remarriage?'

The other woman bridled. 'You go too far, Mrs Trenchard. Next you will be saying there are women who will vote differently from their husbands.'

'Surely,' Rachel Fentiman said in a most reasonable voice, 'no woman of intelligence would allow herself to be instructed on how to place her vote?' She turned to her hostess. 'Mrs Bruton, I have only just met you and we have hardly exchanged more than half a dozen words, but you have the look of a woman of intelligence. Tell us, if you will, did you allow your husband to monitor and guide all your thoughts?'

Mrs Bruton took a sharp intake of breath and for a moment Ursula saw something flash in her employer's eyes. Then she smiled warmly. 'Why, Miss Fentiman, you are too kind. My intelligence could never match that of Mr Bruton and I was therefore happy to accept his views. I have always held that it is a wife's duty to defer to her husband. Of course,' she added, 'there were small matters, concerning the household for instance, where he allowed me to make such decisions as were required.'

There was an appreciative little rustle amongst the other women.

'But,' continued Mrs Bruton hastily as Mrs Tenchard seemed about to speak, 'I think the point about a widow on remarriage having to give up the vote, should we women be fortunate enough to be granted such a privilege, well, that is something to be thought about indeed.'

Another little rustle of approval.

Mrs Mudford looked as though she was gathering herself together for a determined assault and Ursula, fascinated by the arguments being displayed at what she had thought would be a purely social occasion calling for chitchat of the most inconsequential kind, waited for what came next.

The doorbell rang.

Enid was at the far end of the drawing room with two women hovering undecided over a plate of pastries, so Ursula went into the hall, a little curious over who the visitor was. All the guests had arrived and this was not an hour for the leaving of cards.

The moment she opened the door, a heavy man pushed past her. 'I know she is here, useless to try and stop me.' He threw the words at her and charged into the drawing room, still wearing his bowler hat.

Ursula, astonished, followed preparing to apologise to Mrs Bruton for not being able to stop the intruder.

She was given no opportunity.

The man went straight to Rachel Fentiman. 'Where is she? You have no right to withhold such information from me, her lawful husband.'

'What do you mean?' Miss Fentiman said haughtily. 'What information do you think I'm withholding?' Then her attitude suddenly changed. 'Are you saying that Alice has left you?'

'Don't pretend ignorance. Don't pretend that my wife doesn't tell you everything.' He grabbed her by the shoulders; they were much of a height and his gaze locked with hers. 'You must know where she has gone.'

For a moment Ursula thought he was going to shake the information out of the girl. But Mrs Bruton said, 'Sir, I do not know why you should intrude in this rude manner but you have no business molesting my guests.' Her tone was every bit as icy as Rachel Fentiman's.

The rest of the guests were silent but Ursula could feel an electricity running through the group, as though it was a cord that bound them in suspension. If the stranger actually tried to attack the girl, she was convinced the waiting women would swoop on him like a pack of vengeful Furies.

The man dropped his hands and turned to his hostess, his face a mask of anger.

'And who are you, Madam?'

His solid face, with its heavy jowls and strong cheekbones, seemed designed for confrontation. Pouches under small eyes and broken veins in the fleshy nose hinted at dissipation. A large black moustache failed to hide a mean mouth.

'If you will not introduce yourself,' Miss Fentiman said coldly, 'then I shall have to make you known to Mrs Bruton. First, though, remove your hat.'

Additional hate flashed over his countenance as he snatched off his bowler. Ursula smoothly removed it from his grasp, earning her one of his vengeful looks.

'This gatecrasher,' the girl's voice dripped scorn, 'this remnant of humanity, is Mr Joshua Peters of Montagu Place. My sister, Alice, has the misfortune to be Mrs Peters.'

Ursula realised with astonishment that the man must surely be the client Thomas Jackman had told her about after his quarry had disappeared from the menagerie.

'Mr Peters, this is Mrs Bruton and it is her tea party you have invaded,' continued Miss Fentiman.

Joshua Peters glared at his hostess. Confronted with his hostility, she backed away, a hand at her lace collar, her face pale.

For a long moment it seemed as though the intruder was searching for a method of attack, and his hostess for some course of action that would defuse his anger.

'If Alice has brought herself to the point of leaving you, I can only congratulate her good sense,' Miss Fentiman said.

He rounded on her again. 'Your sister was a well-behaved wife until you taught her to forget her duties.'

'You mean encouraged her at last to stand up to your bullying.'

His eyes narrowed. 'Where is she? It is my right to know.'

Miss Fentiman laughed derisively. 'An abusive husband should have no rights.'

Ursula admired the girl's ability to maintain her composure in the face of his anger. She also wondered how it must feel to be married to such a husband. The man she had married in America, and followed across the prairies to a silver mine in the Sierra Nevada, had had many faults and she had suffered in his company, but Jack had also been charming and fun and from time to time made her feel loved and wanted. He had been nothing like this bully.

Joshua Peters let out a howl of frustration and lunged at his sister-in-law. Several of the watching women leaped forward and grabbed his arms.

'Shall I send for the police, Mrs Bruton?' asked Ursula.

'I ... I ...' Mrs Bruton seemed too flustered to speak. She looked at the man struggling against the restraining force of four women who were visibly challenged by the effort needed to keep him under control, their faces anxious but determined. The hostess took a deep breath. 'I think Mr Peters would rather leave with a certain amount of dignity instead of being handcuffed to a police constable.'

The colour faded from the man's face, leaving it a sickly grey. He stood quite still and gazed at the hostess with a stricken expression. The women released him, stepping back and looking at their hands as though they had touched something disgusting.

Joshua Peters ostentatiously brushed down the sleeves of his jacket and fought for self-control. When he spoke, his voice was steady and vindictive. 'Mrs Bruton, you will hear from me. You

will regret inviting that viper into your society.' With a last venom-
ous glare at Miss Fentiman, he walked out of the drawing room.

Ursula hurried after him. He snatched his hat and wrenched
open the front door. She grasped the handle, frustrating any
intention he might have of slamming it shut, then watched as he
stalked down the steps, cast one last look of hatred at the house
and stormed off down the road.

Ursula closed the door and turned to see Mrs Bruton standing
in the hall looking after her uninvited guest. Then she moved
back into the drawing room and said in a voice that was once
again under control, 'Ladies, that ill-mannered intruder has
departed. Enid, please ask Cook to make fresh tea.'

There was a collective sigh of relief. But Joshua Peters' unpleasant invasion had destroyed the carefully cultivated atmosphere.

Mrs Mudford, her lips tight with distaste, was the first to say
goodbye.

'So kind, Mrs Bruton,' she said as though she could hardly bear
to utter the words. 'I must leave now.'

Ursula accompanied the departing guest to the door.

Mrs Mudford declined to offer any thanks as she drew on
white gloves with sharp, angry movements. Instead, without
glancing at Ursula, she said, 'What a hussy. No wonder that man
was half demented.'

Did she mean Miss Fentiman or Mrs Peters?

Ursula found herself manning the door as guest after guest
followed Mrs Mudford with apologetic murmurs of thanks.
They gathered on the pavement, then walked with heads bent
together, no doubt discussing the extraordinary way the tea party
had ended.

Ursula closed the door behind the last of them with a decisive click.

In the drawing room Rachel Fentiman was sitting down, her
head bowed, her face white, her hands clasped tightly together.
The composure she had displayed in front of Joshua Peters had
finally cracked.

Mrs Bruton collapsed into a chair, her face almost as pale as
Miss Fentiman's. 'What a disaster,' she muttered as Ursula came in.
'What a disaster.'

Mrs Trenchard looked around the room and spied a side
table with spirit decanters. 'Brandy, that's what's needed,' she
said cheerfully. 'Such a shock as we have all had.' She found two

glasses, charged them from one of the decanters, and supplied Mrs Bruton and her niece.

'This, I think, will help to calm your nerves.'

Miss Fentiman drank half the glass, choked slightly, then seemed to pull herself together. 'I am so sorry, Mrs Bruton,' she said. 'That was an appalling display of bad manners you and your guests had to witness.'

Ursula moved quietly around the room collecting up discarded cups and plates.

'How did Mr Peters know that you were here?' Mrs Tenchard asked, sitting beside her niece on an upright couch. 'I told no one I had suggested to Mrs Bruton she sent you an invitation for this afternoon. Did you?'

'Only Martha.' She gave half a laugh. 'You know how interested she is in all my movements.' The girl turned to Mrs Bruton. 'Martha was my mother's maid and now looks after me, more of a house-keeper than a maid. Mr Peters must have gone to my apartment.'

'Do you really not know where Alice is?' Mrs Trenchard asked.

Miss Fentiman set her half-finished glass down. 'I know she has been trying to summon up the courage to leave that brute; she should have done so a long time ago. It was only after ...' she broke off, then said in an agitated voice, 'but she promised to let me know before she acted. I ... I was afraid Mr Peters would use force to prevent her.'

'Hmm.' Mrs Trenchard smoothed down the skirt of her linen suit. 'My dear sister, your mother, told me before she died that she did not think the marriage was proving a success. She regretted not persuading your father that Joshua Peters would be an unsuitable match for Alice.'

'I pleaded with Papa,' said Miss Fentiman. 'But he was obdurate.'

'Why did your Papa think Mr Peters should be married to your sister?' broke in their hostess. She caught herself. 'Forgive me, I have no right to pry into your family matters, but having seen what happened here, in my drawing room ...' She lifted a hand, then let it fall back in a gesture of helplessness.

'Mrs Bruton, it is we who should apologise for bringing our worries into your delightful surroundings,' said Miss Fentiman. 'As to why Papa wanted Alice to accept Mr Peters' proposal, it was because he is rich.' She rolled the word round in a way that made it sound disgusting.

'Rich?' said Mrs Bruton faintly.

'I know money should never be discussed in polite society,' Miss Fentiman said. 'But it has to be stated. Joshua Peters has made a fortune out of import and export. Alice has lacked for nothing material. In all other areas she has been poor indeed.'

Placing the last cups and saucers on a tray, Ursula wondered if the gentleman the girls had been with at the menagerie would be mentioned.

Mrs Trenchard rose. 'Dear Mrs Bruton, I do apologise for the ruination of your delightful tea party. Come, Rachel, we must leave our hostess to peace and quiet. Will you come home with me?'

Ursula saw them out, then took the tray downstairs and told Enid and Cook that the guests had departed.

Mrs Evercreech sighed and removed a large kettle from the stove. 'Just as it's coming to the boil. Isn't that life?' She lifted it up with sinewy arms and placed it on the side.

Ursula laughed; she and Cook had quickly established an understanding, each respecting the other's place in the household and enjoying their brief contacts.

The drawing-room bell rang and Enid hurried upstairs. Ursula followed more slowly and found Mrs Bruton sitting with her eyes closed, an expression of intense concentration on her face.

She looked up as Ursula entered. 'That was not quite the tea party I had planned,' she said, her tone ironic. 'Thank you for your help.'

'I'm afraid there was not much I could do, Mrs Bruton. Is there anything you need just now?'

'No, Enid is just about to get me more tea and it is time for you to leave. Tomorrow is one of your days, I think?'

After assuring her employer she would be there the next day, Ursula returned downstairs, said goodbye to Cook and Enid and left via the basement entrance. As she emerged from the steps up on to the pavement, she found Miss Fentiman waiting for her.

'It was you at the menagerie, was it not?'

Ursula nodded.

Miss Fentiman remained standing in front of her. 'You seemed to know the man who tried to take a photograph. My sister is convinced he has been following her.' It was an accusation.

'He is an old friend,' Ursula said slowly. 'He used to be a police inspector and now he's a private investigator. I didn't know he'd been hired by Mr Peters in the matter of his wife, and when I found out, I told him I was shocked.'

'You did?'

'I said he should be helping an unhappy wife not aiding a self-serving husband. And that we women should have the vote!' she added, hoping this would persuade Miss Fentiman she was on her side.

For a moment the girl looked at her as though assessing her sincerity, then she broke into a smile. 'Which way are you going?'

Ursula told her.

'Oh, good, I live not far from there. May I walk with you? I would dearly like some conversation.'

Now filled with curiosity, Ursula willingly agreed.

For the first few moments, though, the two women walked in silence.

'The thing is,' Miss Fentiman said after they had crossed a busy road, 'that brute has made me very worried about my sister. You saw us together at the menagerie and it was your quick action that enabled us to escape that awful man.'

So Thomas Jackman had not been sufficiently skilful to avoid being noticed!

'You say you are a friend of his. So what made you release those birds?'

What indeed?

Ursula stumbled as the lacing of one of her shoes came loose. 'A moment, please,' she said and bent down to retie it. As she did so, her attention was caught by a figure melting into a shop entrance some little way behind.

It was Thomas Jackman.

Was he following Miss Fentiman now?

Chapter Four

Thomas Jackman was taken aback to see Ursula Grandison emerge from the Wilton Crescent house. He had not seen her since the unfortunate episode at the menagerie some ten days earlier.

Since then he had tried several times to work out why she had reacted so badly to discovering he had been on a job. They had worked together on that extraordinary matter at Mountstanton House. He thought they had made a good team. When she had contacted him to say she was in London, he'd thought … well, what had he thought?

When they'd first met she had been living in aristocratic surroundings; they had seemed her rightful background. Then he had found her in that seedy Paddington hotel. When she'd asked if he knew of a suitable lodging house – well now, who had been using whom then? – it had seemed to mean that he and she were on a level. He hadn't hesitated to ask her to accompany him to the menagerie. Had he, he suddenly wondered, had he maybe even thought she might be happy to help him in his assignment?

What if it had been just the pleasant outing Ursula Grandison had obviously expected? For the briefest of moments, Jackman enjoyed a warm sensation that a handsome and intelligent woman would welcome social contact with him. Would like to be, instead of a reluctant investigator working alongside him, a friend.

'Friend'. The word rang melodiously in Jackman's mind. Friendship was a rare commodity in his world. His wife had died several years earlier. Such friends as they had enjoyed together seemed to melt away when she was no longer around. His work, first as a detective with the Metropolitan Police Force and latterly as private investigator, by its very nature precluded close contact with those he met.

Not, he told himself, that there were many he'd be happy to spend time with. Petty crooks, frightened witnesses, people trying to cope with the sordid detritus of London lowlife, plus every now and then the mind-numbing business of dealing with the upper classes who relegated such as Jackman to cockroach status.

Then there were the business men such as Joshua Peters. The ones who feared they were being cheated: by confederates, by tradesmen, by wives. Who expected Jackman to prove their suspicions and meanwhile patronised him. There were many times he disliked the life he had to lead.

Trying to understand the contempt in Ursula Grandison's voice as she left him in Regent's Park after the menagerie, the following day Jackman had attended on Joshua Peters at his home in Montagu Place.

He was shown into a dark room next to the front door by a scared-looking maid. Heavy net hanging within swathes of thick brown velvet curtains cut out light from the window. Wallpaper in brown, with touches of cream, compounded the gloom. On top of a large desk, on an expanse of gilt-edged leather, sat a small pile of papers. An elaborate brass inkstand sat at the back, a green shaded lamp on one corner. A marble fireplace was corralled by a padded seat-cum-fender. In the otherwise empty grate was a brass stand that emulated peacock's feathers on full display.

A side table against the back wall carried a large bronze of a rearing horse. Two huge engravings of the Fire of London Monument and Ludgate Hill either side of a bookcase holding books with elaborately tooled leather bindings did little to lighten the stultifying effect of the room, which was compounded by a dark brown carpet half covered by a Turkish rug in purples and murky reds. Jackman's previous interviews with Joshua Peters had taken place in his city office, a workmanlike place with ample light. If asked, Jackman would have claimed not to be a man affected by atmosphere but he knew he would find it impossible to work effectively in this room. Standing waiting for his employer, he found himself uncharacteristically nervous.

The door was thrust open and Joshua Peters strode in. He sat heavily in the leather upholstered swivel chair behind the desk.

His formal suit suggested he had just returned from his place of business. 'So,' he said, emphasising the word. 'You have the photograph you were to take yesterday?'

'Unfortunately, Mr Peters, there was an incident which made it impossible to capture Mrs Peters and her friend.'

'Incident? What sort of incident?' The man's voice was filled with menace.

Jackman gave a brief account.

Peters' small, brown eyes gazed at him scornfully. 'You allowed some birds and a girl to prevent you performing your job.'

Jackman said nothing.

Peters continued to look at him for a long moment, then pressed a bell beneath the desk. Jackman could just hear a remote jangling in the nether regions of the house. It did not take long before the same maid who had opened the front door to him appeared.

'Tell Mrs Peters to attend me here.'

'Yes, sir.' With a quick bob of the head, she was gone.

Joshua Peters picked up the little pile of papers from the middle of the desk and quickly shuffled through them. Jackman recognised the reports he had sent in.

'A great pity you have not produced the photograph but these should be sufficient.'

The door opened again and there stood Alice Peters. During his surveillance of her activities, Jackman had had plenty of opportunity to study the woman. The charm of her personality had grown on him, as had the effect of her marvellous eyes. From considering her to be no more than 'a sweet face', he now thought of her as beautiful. He had seen the warmth of her smile, the way those remarkable eyes lit up as she looked at the companion she had met on those carefully orchestrated 'unexpected' meetings. He had almost felt the touch of her small hand on his arm as she laid it on her companion's.

This afternoon her face was unnaturally pale, the eyes veiled behind lids that were almost transparent. Her mouth, usually so sweetly shaped, was tightly closed.

'You wish to see me?' It was as though she could not bring herself to utter her husband's name.

'Yes, I do.' Again that tone of menace. 'Sit.'

She flinched, recovered herself, walked steadily towards the desk and sat on a chair to one side, arranging her hands neatly in her lap. Then, as if for the first time, she noticed Jackman and her eyes closed for a moment.

'Who is this man you have been meeting?' The question was thrust at her, and he pushed across the little set of papers.

'What do you mean?' Jackman could hardly hear her nervous voice.

'Don't try to come the innocent with me, Alice. I have had you followed,' he waved a hand briefly at Jackman. 'This has been the result.' Again he thrust the papers at her, leaning forward so that his heavy face was inches away from hers. 'You will tell me who you have been meeting and why.'

Looking at the aggression in every line of her husband's body, Jackman thought it was no wonder that Alice Peters wanted to spend a few hours in the company of a man who could make her feel life was enjoyable.

She passed her tongue over her lips and glanced helplessly at the investigator. 'You had me followed?' she said, her voice breathless. 'Why?'

Peters rose, his heavy body seeming to hang over her frailty like a bear that has tasted human blood. 'Because I wanted to know who you were meeting.'

She turned her white face to Jackman. 'If you have indeed been following me,' her voice was suddenly steady, 'then you will know that I have a wide acquaintanceship and meet a great many people.'

'Tell her,' Peters suddenly roared at him. 'Tell her who she meets.'

Jackman took a grip on himself. 'Mrs Peters,' he started slowly. 'As instructed by your husband.' He realised he had put the slightest of emphases on the word 'husband', as though to remind her that the man had every right to know what she did and where she went. 'As instructed by your husband,' he repeated without inflexion, 'I followed you for just over a week. You met the same man on five out of eight days. His name is Daniel Rokeby.'

She flushed. 'We move in the same circles,' she said, her voice gaining strength. 'Daniel is a friend of my sister, Rachel. If you were following me yesterday, you will know that the three of us visited the menagerie at Tottenham Court Road together.' Her hands clutched tightly at the arms of her chair.

Jackman nodded.

Joshua Peters' face darkened. He flourished his handful of papers. 'Yesterday perhaps. But here,' he leafed through them, picking out first one and then another. 'You met Rokeby by himself at the British Museum. And again walking in Hyde Park. And then at some art exhibition. You cannot deny this.'

Bombarded by her husband's words, Jackman saw Alice Peters find courage. 'They were accidental meetings,' she said, looking him straight in the eye. 'I may have told my sister where I was going and perhaps she mentioned it to Mr Rokeby. As I said, he is her friend.' She swallowed hard. 'What is it you accuse me of, Joshua? Meeting an acquaintance and passing a little time with him?'

She managed to make the suggestion sound ludicrous and Jackman inwardly applauded her spirit.

Suddenly Peters rounded on him. 'Have you reported everything to me? There were no assignations, no meetings in hotels you have failed to note down?'

'Mr Peters, I am not in the habit of cheating on those who employ me.'

All at once, the man looked like a bear who had lost his way.

As though the changing of her husband's target for a moment had given her additional courage, Alice Peters rose. 'If you have nothing else to say, I will be in the drawing room. I am expecting my aunt to call for tea.'

Jackman managed to open the door for her. She went through without a glance at him.

Peters flung himself back in his swivel chair. 'Bitch!'

The word shook Jackman. He wished he could tell this overbearing man what he thought of him. If only he didn't need the fees …

'Do you wish me to continue surveillance on Mrs Peters' movements?'

The man sat, his heavy head bowed, chewing on a thumbnail. It was as though he hadn't heard. Jackman waited. Finally Peters glanced up. 'Call at my office 9.30 tomorrow morning.'

Jackman nodded. 'I'll be there. I'll let myself out, sir,' he added.

Once outside, he felt lighter, as though in that gloomy room he'd sloughed off a skin.

The next morning's meeting was short. Peters announced that he had accepted his wife's word that nothing unseemly had occurred between her and Daniel Rokeby and that he had promised to withdraw Jackman's surveillance.

'For the moment, anyway,' he finished. 'I'll soon know if she's up to her tricks again.'

Peters reached into a drawer and drew out an envelope and looked at him with hard eyes. 'You wrote in your notes that the man Rokeby is some sort of poet but supports himself selling scurrilous stories to low magazines, right?'

Jackman nodded. It hadn't taken long to establish who the attractive stranger was. After the third meeting, Jackman, instead of ensuring Mrs Peters was returning home, had followed the young man into a public house, where he had greeted another. They fell into an easy-looking conversation, drinking beer, laughing and joshing together. Then Jackman's target punched the other lightly on the upper arm and left.

Jackman had approached the bar, slipped, clutched at the other man, and apologised. After that it didn't take long for Jackman to pretend he'd wanted to catch an old friend, only to discover that the man who had just left was called Daniel Rokeby.

'You don't say! I could have sworn it was my old mate, Alfie Brooks. Alfie's a solicitor's clerk, says he's going to be rich one of these days.'

The young man had given a hoot of laughter. 'More than Dan will ever be.' Half an hour later Jackman had everything he needed to know about the fellow who had captured Alice Peters' heart. For Jackman was sure that this is what had happened. And who could blame her, married to a man like Joshua Peters?

Peters handed the envelope to Jackman. 'That clears my account with you. I'll be in touch if I need you again.'

★ ★ ★

For some ten days after that Jackman heard nothing more from Joshua Peters. He had long ago learned not to become emotionally involved in any of the investigations he undertook, or to make moral judgements on those who required his services. In this case, though, it had become increasingly difficult to maintain his distance and perform the job he'd been hired to do.

Then he had received a scribbled note that looked as though it had been written under extreme stress, commanding him to meet Peters immediately and gave an address in Bloomsbury.

Jackman had looked at the note. It ignored any possibility the investigator might not be available, and, like the man, conveyed aggression. He felt a strong urge to disregard it, he could always claim he had been otherwise engaged.

Yet, he found he wanted to know the next stage in this story.

Arriving in Bloomsbury, he found Peters waiting in a hansom cab. 'Get in, man. The aunt isn't there. The maid said something about a tea party but didn't know where. Can't get the staff these days.'

As Jackman got in, Peters rapped on the roof and gave the driver an address in St George's Square, Pimlico.

As the cab fought its way through dense traffic, Jackman waited to hear what had brought the summons.

'She's gone, the bitch has gone,' said Peters eventually, beginning to gnaw on his thumb.

Jackman felt a flash of admiration at her courage. 'Are you sure?' he asked, then inwardly cursed himself. Of course the man was sure, Peters didn't deal in uncertainty.

His face dark with rage, Peters passed him a letter. 'Found that when I came home for luncheon.'

Jackman had learned that Joshua Peters was a man who regularly spent a long day at his office. What had brought him back to luncheon?

He opened the piece of paper.

> I am sorry, I cannot bear life with you any longer so I am leaving.
> Do not try and follow me, it will be of no use.   – Alice.

Jackman folded the letter neatly and handed it back to Peters. 'She left this morning?'

The cab slowed to a crawl in dreadful traffic; a few motor vehicles interfered with the horse-drawn buses, carriages, cabs and carts, making the everyday road tangle worse. Jackman was in two minds about the enduring quality of motor transport. Breakdowns, punctures in tyres, noisy, requiring ample amounts of petrol, they seemed to him little improvement on horses.

Peters shifted uneasily. 'Last night. I ... I was out at a Masonic meeting. When I returned home yesterday evening to change, I was told Mrs Peters had a headache and was not to be disturbed. I left early this morning and did not think of checking on her before I left.'

Hung-over more like, thought Jackman. He wondered about the sleeping arrangements at Montagu Place. Did Peters normally share a bed with his wife, retiring to a dressing room if she required peace and quiet, or did they keep separate quarters?

'At the office I thought I should come back for luncheon and see how she was. That was when I found the note. She could have gone last night or this morning.' He looked down at the piece of paper he held, his jaw working. Then he suddenly crushed it in his hand.

'Are we checking where you think she might have gone?'

'She's gone to that bastard, Rokeby. I want you to find his address. In the meantime I thought her aunt or her sister would know.'

'And now we are going to the sister, right?' Jackman remembered the girl with the beret who had ruined his photographic efforts and made that passionate speech at the menagerie. He wouldn't mind meeting her again.

'Rachel Fentiman. She's at the bottom of all this nonsense. Ever since she went to university in Manchester she has been an evil influence on my wife. Didn't Mrs Peters say yesterday that the bastard Rokeby was a friend of her sister's? Miss Fentiman must know where to find them.' He looked out of the cab, a muscle working in his heavy jaw.

Eventually the hansom arrived in a long square just off the Thames Embankment, full of tall, respectable-looking houses with a church at one end.

Peters flung himself out of the cab as it halted. 'Wait there,' he cried and charged up the steps to ring the bell. The door opened and he disappeared inside, only to reappear a few minutes later.

'She's not there! Nor is my wife. But I've been told where Miss Fentiman has gone!'

Once again Peters rapped on the cab's roof and gave a new address. As they moved towards Knightsbridge, Jackman tried to estimate how long it was going to take him to find out Rokeby's address. Unless luck went his way, it could mean a long and tiring trawl enquiring after a freelance writer amongst the offices of the lower class of publication. Failing that, a search for poetic societies.

Peters showed no inclination to say anything further. Jackman tried to work out if the man was nursing a broken heart or if it was just that his pride was damaged. He thought of the way Peters had called his wife a bitch and told himself the answer was dead plain. Peters needed to reinforce his authority over his property.

Their destination this time was a crescent of stylish houses just off Belgrave Square. Once again Peters alighted. 'Wait for me,' he commanded Jackman. 'If she's there, I may need your help to bring her home.'

He was out of the cab before the investigator could query why a man as strong as Joshua Peters needed help subduing a small woman.

Then he realised that Peters thought Rokeby might be there as well. He got down from the cab, told the driver to remain where he was and moved towards the house Peters had disappeared into.

Jackman decided to wait a couple of steps down the basement entrance. No need to advertise his presence.

It wasn't long before Peters emerged, clutching his bowler and charging off up the road. Jackman followed. Peters turned on him. His face was livid with rage, his eyes pig-tiny. 'That Fentiman bitch knows something, I'd bet the business on it. You can recognise her again?'

Jackman nodded. Rachel Fentiman was someone he would never forget.

'Stay here, follow her. She'll lead you to my wife.' Peters now sounded full of confidence. 'Then let me know where she is. I'll make her regret the day she was born,' he added almost beneath his breath. He swung himself into the cab and it moved off.

Jackman watched it and felt an urge to throw Peters' business back in his face. Then he remembered the bills waiting for payment. Peters' last cheque had only cleared the worst of them. He moved to a position where he had a good view of the house's front door but was out of the direct line of vision of anyone on the steps.

From there he watched a number of women leaving the house. The way they huddled together, then moved off in twos and threes, throwing words between themselves, resembled a murmuration of starlings. Jackman liked collecting odd words.

There followed a long period when nobody came out of the house. Jackman began to think Miss Fentiman might have left from the rear and cursed himself for not having checked whether there was an exit there. But if he'd done that, he could have missed her departure by the front door.

He whiled away time by thinking again of Ursula Grandison. If she was in his place, he knew exactly what she would do: ensure that Alice Peters escaped her brute of a husband. What, though, would she think of Daniel Rokeby, poet and scandal-sheet writer?

Then his eye was caught by the opening of the front door. Rachel Fentiman stood for a moment on the top of the steps, then walked down and turned to the right. Jackman prepared to follow her, only to find she had taken up a position by the basement steps.

Even more surprising a little while later was to see climbing those steps and being accosted, nay, claimed by Miss Fentiman, Ursula Grandison.

Chapter Five

When Ursula looked again, Thomas Jackman could no longer be
seen. She tied her shoelace, then rejoined Rachel Fentiman.

'Now, where were we?'

The girl slipped her arm through Ursula's. 'I want to know
why you opened that ostrich cage.'

Miss Fentiman looked to be in her mid-twenties, a few years
younger than Ursula. She had an openness that was heartwarm-
ing. Ursula realised how long it was since she had had a friend.
Was that one of the reasons Jackman had so disappointed her?
Had she thought he could be a friend? Initially a reluctant
partner with him in the investigation that had involved her so
insidiously, she had grown to enjoy their sometimes acerbic discussions and to value his judgements. Ursula acknowledged to
herself that she really had thought that in London they could
meet as friends. Instead, he had tried to involve her in the sordid
investigation he was carrying out for a despicable man.

However, it was through Jackman that she had met Rachel
Fentiman. 'You were so brave,' Ursula told her honestly.
'You could see your sister was in trouble and needed help. And
the way you got everyone's attention was inspirational. I, well,
I thought an additional distraction was needed.'

Miss Fentiman smiled happily and squeezed Ursula's arm.
'It was all we needed to make an escape. The moment I saw that
man with his camera, I knew it was something to do with Alice.
Several days before we went to the menagerie, she mentioned

having an odd feeling of being watched and Joshua is just the sort of man to hire a detective to follow his wife. Can you imagine a worse act? So to distrust your wife?'

Ursula was silent and after a moment Rachel said ruefully, 'I know, she was spending far too much time with Daniel but, even so,' she added robustly, 'wouldn't you have thought Joshua would try harder to succeed in her affections?'

An image of Daniel Rokeby's charmingly informal looks swam insistently into Ursula's mind, followed swiftly by a picture of Mr Peters as he had appeared that afternoon. Then she remembered her glimpse of Thomas Jackman. Was he actually following Rachel now, expecting her to lead him to her sister? If so, she must warn the girl.

Why on earth had Jackman got himself involved with that unpleasant man and his marriage difficulties? Then Ursula wondered. It had only been the swiftest of glimpses; could she have been mistaken?

Rachel was continuing. 'Alice is the sweetest of souls but you have to understand, Miss Grandison, that she is happiest surrounded by those who love her. It was such a tragedy ...' she broke off, disentangled her arm from Ursula's, stopped and, pulling at her white cotton gloves in a nervous gesture, said, 'All Alice's life I have tried to look after her. She is such an innocent, and she does not think ahead. That is why she allowed herself to be given in marriage to that ... that quite appalling man. Oh, if she has left him, despite the scandal that will follow, I shall be so pleased! But why didn't she tell me where she was going? Let us hurry on, Miss Grandison. Maybe I will find a note waiting for me.'

She seemed to assume that her companion would come home with her.

Ursula allowed herself to be swept along the busy street. Workers were going home and several times she found herself jostled by hurrying passers-by. The question as to whether or not it was Jackman she had seen had to be answered. She glanced behind but it was impossible to make out whether he was following them or not.

'Miss Fentiman,' Ursula pointed to a small general store on the corner of a street. 'Do you mind if I obtain something for this evening?' Without waiting for a response, she pulled the girl in with her, then pretended to be studying a display of tinned meats next to the window. She had a clear view up the street.

'Are you not supplied with an evening meal where you are living?'

'Oh, yes, but I was late the other night and missed it. I need to guard against having to starve for a second time.' Ursula picked up the first tin her hand found. 'This will do,' she said, took it to the counter and apologised to the assistant for helping herself.

'Oysters!' exclaimed Rachel. 'You have strange tastes, Miss Grandison, if that is how you sup.'

'They bring back a happy time I spent on Chesapeake Bay,' Ursula said brightly, wondering how she was going to make them into a meal if the need ever arose. But she had not seen any sign of Thomas Jackman. Feeling her heart suddenly lighter, she led the way out of the shop, clutching a paper-wrapped parcel.

Rachel Fentiman lived near the Embankment, in an elongated square with a church at one end. The sides were lined with terraced houses, tall, with classical columns at the front of each. Ursula was led into one somewhere near the middle. Inside was a narrow hall, with a tiled floor in black and red. It had the anonymous look typical of an establishment that let out rooms. A door on the right led into a living room.

'I'm back, Martha,' Rachel Fentiman called, taking off her hat.

Alice Peters appeared and flung herself into her sister's arms.

'Oh, Rachel; I have been such a fool,' she said and burst into tears.

'Please, Alice,' said Mrs Trenchard wearily. Ursula was surprised to see her sitting in a straight-backed chair beside a desk. Rachel's living room was large and well proportioned, furnished with a minimum of pieces and dominated by a well-stocked, breakfront bookcase. Beside it, upsetting any semblance of symmetry, was a set of open shelves crammed with more books and a pile stood on the floor threatening to overtip. There was only one picture on the walls, a portrait of a sweet-faced woman with fair hair who bore a great resemblance to Alice Peters. A tall window gave on to the square and a round table stood before it. There were only two chairs that looked at all comfortable and the room had a look that said here lived someone concerned only with practicalities.

'Come and sit down, my sweet.' Rachel guided her sister to one of the comfortable chairs and settled her in it. 'Now tell me what has happened.'

'I will take my leave,' said Ursula, feeling a great reluctance to go but knowing that she was an intruder. 'Perhaps we may meet up another day?'

'No,' said Rachel Fentiman decisively. 'You have already seen so much, we have no secrets to hide. Do you not agree, Aunt?'

Mrs Trenchard gave a hopeless shrug. The woman who had dominated Mrs Bruton's tea party seemed older and her air of command seemed to have slipped from her like a too-heavy cloak.

'And you may well be able to help us once again.' Rachel crouched down beside her sister. Alice tried to wipe her eyes with a small handkerchief that already looked quite sodden.

An elderly woman brought in a tray of tea and set it on the table in front of the window.

'Thank you, Martha,' said Rachel. 'I was just about to ask you to bring some. As usual, you read my mind.'

Ursula smiled at the woman. 'Why don't I pour the tea?' she suggested.

The little ceremony seemed to calm the atmosphere in the room. Ursula cut large pieces of the excellent-looking seed cake.

While attending to this task, Ursula had a good view of the square with a heavy curtain protecting her from being seen. A postman was delivering letters to houses on the other side. Two men dressed in formal business attire descended from a cab. A middle-aged woman hurried past the window. There was no sign of Jackman.

'I found her on my doorstep,' said Mrs Trenchard, taking the plate with a slice of cake Ursula handed to her. 'About to ring the bell. Dear Felix is not at all well and must not be disturbed, so I bundled her into a cab and brought her here. I am afraid she was quite unable to give me a coherent account of her activities.' She drummed her fingers irritably on the desk. 'Apart from the fact that she has left her husband.'

Alice Peters was shivering, her huge violet eyes swollen and red, her mouth quivering. 'I could not stay,' she moaned. 'I could not stay one more minute. Not after I knew my feelings for Daniel.'

A hand banged down on the desk. 'I never thought to hear my sister's child abandon her duty!' The words seemed wrenched from Mrs Trenchard, her face a cold mask. Alice Peters visibly flinched.

'She owes no duty to that brute,' Rachel Fentiman said angrily. She rose. 'How can you talk like that, Aunt? What about the equality for women that you fight for?'

'Achieving female suffrage has nothing to do with the duty a wife owes to her husband.'

'Balderdash!' Rachel once again crouched beside her sister. 'Tell us everything, Alice,' she said gently. 'When did you decide to leave Joshua?'

Alice sat pulling at the sodden linen of her handkerchief, took a deep breath and found her composure. 'Joshua faced me with a private detective. He told me I had been followed. He had a whole list of times and places where Daniel and I had met.' She gave a small gasp. 'Rachel, you would have been proud of me. I don't know how I held myself together; Joshua was outrageous and I found myself so angry.' She looked round the room. 'I think that's why I'm here. Somehow, facing Joshua and that detective, I found I was stronger than I ever thought I could be. And I determined that from now on, I would not let Joshua rule my life.'

Rachel patted the now still hands. 'But didn't you tell me you thought someone had been observing you?'

'Oh, that! But I only thought maybe a young man was trying to find an opportunity to meet an unaccompanied female. I wasn't used to going around on my own; I felt vulnerable. But I never imagined I was being followed by a detective.'

'What did you tell Joshua?'

'I said Daniel was a friend of yours, Rachel. Well,' Alice glanced quickly at her aunt then looked again at her sister. 'It's true, isn't it? Didn't we meet at a poetry afternoon you took me to? Didn't you introduce us?'

'Quite right. Daniel and I have been friends for several years,' Rachel said soothingly. She removed the sodden handkerchief and handed her the plate with a slice of cake that Ursula offered.

'When we went to the menagerie, I hadn't told you he would be there, had I?'

Rachel shook her head. 'But I was not surprised to find him waiting for us.' She smiled at Alice.

Her sister dropped her gaze. 'He'd been pleading with me for weeks to leave Joshua. He said we could live on the continent, that it was cheap in the South of France. I have the income that Mama left me. It should be enough if we live simply. That is until Daniel becomes a famous author.' She looked passionately into Rachel's eyes. 'He is so clever and yet he loves me; loves me as Joshua never has.'

'We all love you, darling.'

Alice ate a little of the cake in an absent-minded way. 'It was at the menagerie that I realised how much I needed Daniel, that I couldn't live without him.'

'Pshaw!' exclaimed Mrs Trenchard. Her hand resting on the desk clenched but she said nothing further.

'I didn't tell Joshua that, though, when he faced me with his detective,' Alice said proudly. 'I couldn't tell him then that I was going to leave him; I had to make sure that, when I went, I wasn't followed, because if Joshua found me, he'd force me to return.' She gave a big sigh. 'You will never know how hard it was to keep my true feelings secret, to make him think I was still an obedient wife.' She smiled proudly and ate more of the cake.

Ursula watched the way Alice leaned confidingly towards her sister. The girl seemed young for her years. How long had Jackman said Mr and Mrs Peters had been married? Five years? Alice could have easily passed for eighteen and yet she had been married to that brute of a husband for five years.

'Yesterday I discovered that Joshua would be out that evening, a Masonic affair. I knew he would be late home and that he would sleep in his dressing room. So I wrote to Mrs Rokeby. Daniel had said his mother would be happy to take me in until we could leave for France. I told her I would come today. Then I wrote and told Daniel the same.' She gave her sister another of those confiding looks. 'Usually I would have given the letters to Millie, my maid, to post. But lately I have suspected that she has been too free with details of where I'm going. I told myself I was too suspicious; Millie and I have always been close.' She gave a little gasp and put down the now empty plate, 'I've always relied on her; in that dreadful house, she's been my support, but how else could that detective have been able to follow me?'

'So you didn't tell Millie you were going to leave?' Rachel said.

Alice shook her head. She'd taken off whatever hat she had been wearing and tendrils of fair hair hung down beside her cheeks. 'I posted the letters myself. Last night I hardly slept. I rose very early, long before it was Millie's time to come and wake me, and I dressed myself.' She gave a little laugh. 'I had trouble with my corsets and then could hardly do up my waist band; it was such a relief to have Martha pull the strings properly tight.'

Ursula could not help wondering at the girl's anxiety about the size of her waist, then told herself she did not care enough about her own. As long as she looked neat, she was happy.

'I left a note for Joshua and took a small bag with necessities. Nobody saw me leave.' Another little gasp. 'Millie will have had such a shock!'

Martha reappeared. 'Thought you might need some hot water,' she said, filling the teapot. 'Are you all right now, dear?' she said to Alice. 'Your poor mother would be so upset to see you in this state.'

Alice smiled at her. 'If only I had taken you as my maid after Mama passed away.'

'There, there, my little dear. Who would have looked after your sister? Now, you let me know if there's anything else I can do.' She looked across at Rachel Fentiman. 'Will there be anything else?'

'No, thank you, Martha, that will be all.'

The woman patted Alice's shoulder and left the room.

'I do wish you had let me know what you meant to do, Alice,' said Rachel, handing her cup to Ursula for a refill. 'I could have told you that Mrs Rokeby was unexpectedly called away. Her mother is very ill in the Lake District. I met Daniel at a friend's house three days ago and he told me he was to take her there the following day. Did you go to her house?'

Ursula offered more tea to Mrs Trenchard, who waved her away with an impatient gesture.

'No one was there,' Alice wailed. 'So then I went round to Daniel's rooms and no one was there either. I didn't know what to do. I didn't dare come here because I was certain this was the first place Joshua would look for me. I couldn't think where to go.' Tears came again and Rachel found a clean handkerchief for her. 'I wasn't far from Regent's Park. Daniel took me to the Zoological Gardens there a little while ago; he wanted me to see the new idea of bringing the animals out into the open instead of keeping them inside. I was amazed that camels and lions and monkeys, which are used to such hot climates, could survive our cold weather, but they do!' Her eyes were wide with surprise. 'And they looked so happy to be in the fresh air. Daniel said I mustn't think they have emotions like us but they really did look happy.' It was as though she felt it important they believed this. Gradually she had become much calmer, as though she had once again found that inner strength she had talked about earlier.

'So you went to the Zoological Gardens just now? Did you expect to see him there?' Her tone suggested this would have been a vain hope.

'Not really but they have tea rooms and I thought I could get some refreshment and work out what I should do. Even though I took cabs, I was exhausted from all the travel and carrying my bag, and everything seemed so hopeless.' She looked like a child who had been dragged around beyond its strength. 'I thought that perhaps Mrs Rokeby had been so scandalised by my letter she had decided not to open her house to me after all.' She closed her eyes. 'I tried not to think that Daniel might also have regretted encouraging me.' Then she looked straight at her sister. 'But I knew I could not return to Joshua. So finally the only place I could think to go was to Aunt Lydia's. I didn't realise that Uncle Felix was ill. I am so sorry.' She sounded hopelessly sad.

A capacious Gladstone bag stood by the entrance door to the living room. Ursula thought of the fragile-looking Alice trailing around London with it. No wonder she was exhausted. The radiance the girl had displayed in the menagerie had vanished; she was drained of colour, a waif.

No one wanted more tea and Ursula went to sit down by the window table but a movement outside caught her eye. Thomas Jackman was unobtrusively descending the basement steps of a house across the square.

Ursula shrank back against the window curtains. Once again the man had placed her in an invidious position. She had thwarted him at the menagerie. If only he hadn't revealed his chauvinistic attitudes, his belief in male superiority.

Alice Peters was a woman being forced to remain in an unhappy marriage. Should she continue to support her own sex or must she allow her former comrade to fulfil his contract?

'What am I to do, Rachel?' asked Alice.

Mrs Trenchard rose. 'You must return to your husband, that is what you must do.' She seemed to recover some of the authority she had shown at the tea party. 'I am very sorry, child. It is not a marriage I would have wished on you but you agreed to it and now you must follow your duty. If you cannot do that, I suggest you go to an hotel. I cannot help you.'

'I cannot afford an hotel,' Alice said desperately. 'Daniel's mother might not return to London for some time. What am I to do?'

Rachel Fentiman looked around her living room. 'If you stay here, Joshua Peters will find you. Let me try and think of a friend you could go to.'

Ursula made up her mind.

'I know my landlady has a free room, Mrs Peters. Her charges are far less than an hotel's. Would you like to come back with me for a night or two? It is not far away, just the other side of Victoria station. Your sister could contact you there when she has arranged other accommodation.'

'Miss Grandison, you have found the perfect solution. You will not mind that, Alice, will you?' Rachel Fentiman sounded greatly relieved. 'I am sure in a day or so either Daniel will be back or I shall have found somewhere more … well, a friend you can stay with.' She asked Ursula for the address of her lodging house and scribbled it down. Then she picked up a chic straw hat from the top of a pile of books. 'Now, let me put this on you.'

'Miss Grandison, I am sure you mean well but I am not at all sure this is the right solution,' said Mrs Trenchard.

Ursula picked up the Gladstone bag. It was heavy but she felt well able to carry it as far as her boarding house.

'Is there a back way, Miss Fentiman, that you could show us? I think it would be circumspect for us not to use the front door. And perhaps Mrs Trenchard could leave with us in the same way?' For if Jackman believed it was only Ursula that Rachel Fentiman was entertaining in her rooms, he was unlikely to continue his surveillance for much longer and would never know she had left earlier than he.

Miss Fentiman showed no surprise at this suggestion. 'What a good idea. Follow me.'

'I will leave the way I came in, via the front door,' Mrs Trenchard said coldly.

'Aunt Lydia, for once, please just do as someone else wants.'

Mrs Trenchard stood rigid for several seconds. 'Rachel, I can hardly believe what I have just heard. To think that … well, what my dear sister would have said. After everything we have done for you.'

Miss Fentiman coloured painfully. 'Aunt Lydia, I apologise. I had no right to speak to you like that.' She took a deep breath. 'At the moment, though, Alice has nowhere to go and this idea of Ursula's is the only solution that will do. And as for your leaving with us, it's just, well, if Joshua is in the habit of engaging detectives, would it not be best to evade any possibility one is even now watching this house?'

Ursula's belief in Rachel Fentiman's intelligence was strengthened.

Mrs Trenchard looked horrified and glanced towards the window.

'Come with me,' Rachel said firmly. She took a key from the mantelpiece and led the way out of the room. After a moment's hesitation, Mrs Trenchard followed Alice and Ursula.

They were taken through a courtyard at the back of the building and at the end, a door in a wall was unlocked. They emerged into a mews. Ursula swiftly assessed its occupants. A farrier was reshoeing a horse; a groom led a saddled and bridled horse into its stable; and two motor vehicles stood on the cobbled way. One had its bonnet up, its engine being inspected by a sturdy, fair-haired young man; jacket abandoned, he was wearing breeches, with braces over a collarless shirt. The competent manner with which he removed a sparking plug convinced Ursula he knew his business. As the little party drew level with the machine, he raised an intelligent-looking face and nodded to Rachel. She half raised a hand in acknowledgement but turned to Ursula.

'If you walk through that arch at the end and turn left, you will almost certainly find a cab,' she said. 'Thank you again, Miss Grandison. I will seek you and Alice out tomorrow. What time are you due at Mrs Bruton's?'

'It's not one of my days with her, so come any time.'

Ursula took a firmer grip on the Gladstone bag, said farewell to Mrs Trenchard, then turned to Alice Peters in time to see her raise a hand to her forehead.

'I don't think ...' Alice said in the faintest of voices. She swayed and Ursula dropped the bag in time to catch hold of the girl as she lost consciousness.

Chapter Six

Mrs Bruton surveyed the plate of deliciously dainty cakes, brushed a few crumbs from the front of her chiffon afternoon gown, and selected a pink iced one; it was her third.

'Please have one yourself, dear Miss Grandison, and will you attend to our empty cups?'

One of the most pleasant aspects of working for Mrs Bruton was her insistence that Ursula should take afternoon tea with her.

As Ursula handed Mrs Bruton her refilled teacup, Enid brought in the afternoon post.

'Do look through it, Miss Grandison,' said Mrs Bruton. 'But do not show me any with brown envelopes, they always contain unpleasant bills. Is there anything that looks more interesting?'

Ursula flipped through the half dozen or so letters and handed over the envelopes that bore educated handwriting. 'Two look to be invitations and surely that one is in a continental hand?'

Mrs Bruton gave an excited little cry and eagerly ripped open the envelope. 'Please, Miss Grandison, while I read this, perhaps you will attend to the other letters?'

Ursula helped herself to another cup of tea and looked longingly at a chocolate éclair, but she could not afford to have her clothes remodelled. She resolutely started opening envelopes.

Mrs Bruton lowered the letter, her eyes sparkling. 'This is delightful, Miss Grandison. Edward and I met Count Julius Meyerhoff in Vienna on one of our last visits before Edward passed over. What a good-looking man, and always in such demand,' she gave a faint sigh. 'I wondered, indeed I once discussed the matter with my Edward. "How," I asked him one day. "How does that delightful man remain single when so many beautiful women pursue him so relentlessly?" Do you know, Miss Grandison, Edward laughed and said that the count obviously preferred to sample a variety of feminine charms than to anchor himself to one! So then I had to ask my dear Edward if he felt "anchored" as he put it, rather coarsely I told him, to me! I was only teasing him and he soon made amends by buying me my lovely sapphire bracelet. Don't you think sapphires are the most beautiful of all gems?'

'If you have blue eyes, certainly,' said Ursula, smiling. 'With grey eyes, like mine, I think diamonds might be the best choice.'

'Ah, diamonds! They do, I agree, enhance any woman. I hope, Miss Grandison, you have a set of them?'

Ursula could not help laughing at the idea. 'Alas, I have very few items of jewellery and certainly no diamonds. But one can dream! Is Count Meyerhoff in England? I noticed that the envelope bore a London postmark.'

'That is why he has written to me.' Mrs Bruton picked up the letter again. 'He says he has launched a new venture and is inviting me to visit his showroom.'

'Showroom? What sort of venture is it?'

Mrs Bruton frowned slightly and looked at the letter again as though there might be some information she had missed. 'He does not say.'

'What business did he carry on in Vienna?'

The letter was waved in a vague way. 'I think it was banking. So many bankers in Vienna. Not that he kept office hours, you understand. He always seemed available for social activity.'

Mrs Bruton looked again at her letter. 'The address is *Maison Rose* in Mayfair. It sounds like a couture house. We will plan a visit together, Miss Grandison. I shall value your opinion.'

Ursula laughed. 'Mrs Bruton, you must know by now that my acquaintance with fashion is of the slightest.'

'Granted you have very few clothes, my dear, but you wear what you have with style. One can tell so much about a person, particularly a woman, by how much they care about such matters, can one not?'

Ursula nodded, intrigued. This Count Meyerhoff seemed to have made a great impression on her employer. And even without money to spend on couture clothes, the proposed visit promised to be most interesting.

Mrs Bruton toyed negligently with one of her softly frilled cuffs. 'It is time I made an addition or two to my wardrobe. So delightful I no longer have to wear black. You will make notes on what we see. I am quite excited about our little expedition. Now, is there anything else interesting in my mail?'

'There is a note from Mrs Trenchard.' Ursula handed over the opened letters with that one on top.

'Indeed!' Mrs Bruton held the missive a little way away from her. 'I wish her writing was as clear as yours, Miss Grandison. I think "scrawl" is the only word for it. I must ask you to read this to me.'

Ursula did indeed have to scrutinise the letter carefully before she could announce, 'Mrs Trenchard is asking if you would care to attend a meeting of members of her Women's Suffrage Movement on Thursday of next week. She believes Mrs Pankhurst will be speaking and that you will find the event most interesting.'

'Oh, dear. I don't know that I care to associate myself with that Movement. I found my tea party last week quite upsetting.'

Ursula said nothing.

'I cannot help thinking about the vanished wife of the man who gatecrashed our little assembly, and wondering where she is and what she is doing.'

Thinking about Mrs Trenchard's reaction to Alice's rejection of her marriage, Ursula said, 'You seem to be sympathetic to her predicament.'

'Who could not feel for her? Chained to that odious fellow.' She thought for a moment. 'Perhaps I should go to that meeting. As a woman, and as a widow, one values the aim the Movement is working towards. To be able to cast one's vote for a Member of Parliament must be advantageous. We need a voice to represent us, to give us some power to right our wrongs.' She gave a little deprecating laugh. 'Did I not hear the phrase "to take control of one's destiny" spoken somewhere?'

'Never mind the vote, Mrs Bruton, you will be standing for Parliament yourself,' said Ursula mischievously.

Mrs Bruton raised her hands. 'Miss Grandison, I think that is going a little too far! One would never want to make speeches in public!'

★ ★ ★

A little later, as Ursula walked briskly back to her lodgings, she thought about Mrs Trenchard. As far as she was aware, Alice's aunt had not seen her since the afternoon of the tea party, six days previously. It seemed as though the woman had damned the girl for fleeing from her marriage.

She had, though, seemed as concerned as any of them when Alice had fainted.

Ursula had asked everyone to stand back so that the girl could have some air. The young man who had been working on the motor vehicle came up, wiping his hands on a clean rag.

'Shall I lift her up into my carriage?'

'Oh, what a good idea, John,' Rachel said.

'Do be careful,' Mrs Trenchard warned and she felt in the size-able bag she carried. By the time Alice was placed on the motor's generously upholstered passenger seat, she had found some smelling salts and waved them beneath the girl's nose.

Alice sneezed, opened her eyes and looked in a puzzled way at the little party gathered around her.

'You fainted, darling,' said Rachel, taking her hand. 'You should come back inside and eat something; why did you leave that piece of cake? And you need your clothes loosened.'

The girl raised herself in the motor's seat. 'I am sorry. What a nuisance for you all, but I am fine now.' Her voice gained in strength as she spoke. 'There is no need for me to return to your rooms.'

'Where are you going?' the young man asked. 'I am John Pitney, a friend of Miss Fentiman's. I would be honoured if you would let me drive you there.' His voice was unexpectedly cultured; it matched the educated tones Ursula had grown used to hearing when staying with the Earl and Countess of Mountstanton.

'Oh, John, that would be famous, said Rachel. 'This is my sister, Mrs Peters. Miss Grandison, what is your address?'

'Who is this young man?' Mrs Trenchard demanded.

Rachel sighed impatiently but said, 'May I introduce Lord John Pitney? You may know his parents, the Duke and Duchess of Walberton, their London house is not far from yours.'

Obviously taken aback, Mrs Trenchard took a moment to say, in a stilted voice, 'We have met.' She held out her hand to the young man. 'I am happy to make your acquaintance, Lord John. I take it you have not known my niece long?' She was obviously finding it difficult to understand why Rachel had not told her about such a highly suitable young man before.

'May I introduce my aunt, Mrs Felix Trenchard?'

'Delighted,' said Lord John, stuffing the rag into a back pocket and shaking Mrs Trenchard's hand.

'And this is Miss Ursula Grandison.'

'Delighted,' said Lord John again. Ursula liked the feel of his hand, it was steady and firm, did not crush hers, and his skin was warm and dry.

'And now that we have fulfilled society's requirements, perhaps Alice and Ursula can be driven home?' Rachel said impatiently.

Ursula, too, was anxious they should be on their way. She was worried about giving Jackman any opportunity to pick up on the girl's whereabouts. Any moment he might decide to investigate if the building had a back entrance. 'I shall take good care of her,' she said to Mrs Trenchard and gave Lord John the address.

'Alice will be in good hands, Aunt,' said Rachel firmly. She kissed her sister. 'I would come with you, see you settled, but there's the possibility that investigator could be watching the building. He must think Miss Grandison and I are still in there.'

'We do not want him coming round to check on a back entrance,' said Ursula firmly, once again impressed by Rachel's quick wits.

Mrs Trenchard looked horrified. 'Well, in that case ...'

Alice shrank back and looked on the point of fainting again.

Ursula was guided into the little seat at the back of the motor and given Alice's Gladstone bag. Lord John swung the starting handle and climbed into the driver's seat, then they bumped over the cobblestones and out into the main road.

Alice seemed to revive in the open vehicle and on their arrival was able to thank their driver prettily.

'Will she be all right?' Lord John asked Ursula in a quiet voice as she alighted and slipped her hand beneath Alice's elbow. His ruddy, open face looked as worried as Ursula felt.

'Once she's inside. I'll make sure she eats something.' She turned to Alice. 'Let's go and find Mrs Maple,' she said, steering her towards the front door. 'Thank you, Lord John, that was very kind.'

'I'll keep in touch with Rachel,' he said and started his motor.

Guiding Alice up the steps and into the house, Ursula could not help wondering about the exact nature of Rachel's relationship with him. The ease they showed in each other's company said they knew each other very well. Yet Mrs Trenchard had been told nothing about the young aristocrat.

Mrs Maple was in the hall and only too happy to show Alice one of her rooms. 'It's at the back and so very quiet, Mrs Peters. It's a nice size, only just become vacant, and it's almost next door to Miss Grandison's.'

It was much the same as Ursula's, spartan but bright and clean. Alice only gave it a cursory look. She sat down on the bed, a sad, drooping figure. 'I think I have a headache. I'll just lie down for a little while.'

Ursula turned to Mrs Maple. 'Mrs Peters would like to take the room for a few days. I'll see her settled then come down and sort out any details you need. If she could have a little something to eat, that could help.'

'Of course. I'll get Meg to bring up some buttered eggs.'

During the days that followed, Mrs Maple had seemed as worried about her new lodger as Ursula was.

Alice was charming to everyone and spoke if spoken to at the communal dining table each evening. The other women who lodged at Mrs Maples' greeted her courteously but respected her reluctance to maintain a conversation. At first, after the meal she would disappear to her room, rejecting Ursula's offer of an evening walk or a game of cards, saying sweetly that she needed her sleep.

'I have been so tired recently, I think it has been the strain of deceiving Joshua. Now I am enjoying solitude; I think it is the first time in my life I have not had to answer to someone for their comfort. First it was dear Mama and Rachel, then … then Joshua.

'Please, do call me Alice, and may I call you Ursula? I find your company very restful, so I hope you will forgive me for wanting to be selfish. I am enjoying reading the book you lent me, Mr Trollope's *Barchester Towers*.'

It was a volume Ursula had picked up from a second-hand bookseller. She had loved its ironic picture of life in a bishopric and thought it one Alice might appreciate.

After a few days, Alice seemed to recover a little and was willing to sit with Ursula and discuss books or play some card games.

Rachel had not dared to visit in case Mr Jackman was keeping a watch on her, but she wrote daily letters.

Alice Peters may have seemed to recover a little but she remained pale and languid and Ursula thought that, whatever she said, the girl was not happy. But, then, how could she be? A wife who had abandoned her husband; a woman in love who had lost sight of her lover.

★ ★ ★

Reaching the lodging house at the end of her working day, Ursula went down to the kitchen to say hello. 'How is Mrs Peters today?' she asked.

'Much better.'

Mrs Crumble, the middle-aged but seemingly tireless cook who was always willing to exchange a word or two, bent to roll out a sheet of pastry obviously destined for a large pie dish standing at the back of the table. 'But she went out this morning and looked ever so determined when she came back. And she told Mrs Maple she would be leaving tomorrow. Meg saw her post a letter.'

Meg was the maid-of-all-work.

'Leaving? Tomorrow? Where is she going, did she say?' Had Daniel's mother returned from the Lake District?

Mrs Crumble fetched a large bowl of meat from the larder. 'No, but she didn't sound too happy about it. She said being here had saved her life!' A china bird was fitted into the centre of the dish. 'Just now, though, she had a visitor.'

'A young man,' said Meg, peeling potatoes. She looked dreamily at Ursula. 'You should have seen her run down the stairs to him. Her face – like something out of a fairy tale it was: Cinderella and the prince!' She sat rapt for a moment, knife held motionless. 'Ever so handsome he is.'

'Would that be Mr Rokeby, by any chance?'

'That was the name he gave,' said Meg. 'He was very polite; asked if he could take her out to the square.'

'Meg, if you don't hurry with those tatties,' said Mrs Crumble, shaking flour over the chunks of meat then piling them into the vast dish together with slices of carrot, 'tea won't be served 'til midnight. And have you riddled the range?'

Ursula went upstairs to her room wondering just what would happen now that the young man Alice had left her husband for had reappeared. She threw her straw hat on the bed, shrugged off her linen jacket and went to the window that overlooked the garden set in the middle of the square. The properties around it were furnished with keys to its gate and could enjoy the trees and shrubs that offered greenery and shade in the heart of London.

It was not that Ursula wanted to spy on the lovers but she could not resist the opportunity for a look at the tall young man she had seen with Alice and Rachel in the menagerie.

Thickly leaved trees guarded the privacy of those in the garden but from her second-floor window, Ursula had a view of the grassy interior. Almost immediately she saw the couple walking slowly along the path that ran round the garden. If Alice had flown rapturously into her lover's arms on his arrival, it seemed that passion had now been put aside. She stared straight ahead as she walked with her arms wrapped around herself. Her body seemed rigid, as though she feared allowing feeling to escape. The young man walked with his hands clasped behind his back, listening with his gaze on the ground but glancing sideways every now and then.

Both of them were hatless and Daniel Rokeby's red hair brushed the collar of his jacket. As Ursula watched, he ran a hand through it in a hopeless gesture, then took hold of Alice's shoulders, forcing her to stand and face him. She looked up and shook her head in a despairing gesture. He tried to draw her into his arms. She resisted, pulling back, then suddenly crumpled against him and stood for a moment as he wrapped her in a tender embrace, resting his head on hers.

A moment later Alice tore herself away and flew out of the square. Daniel followed.

Ursula heard frantic steps pounding up the stairs. She left her room and tried to catch Alice.

'My dear, what is it?'

Alice evaded her grasp, threw herself into her room and slammed the door. Ursula heard the key turn in the lock and then the sound of passionate weeping.

Daniel Rokeby came to a stop on the landing. 'Which is her room?' he said urgently to Ursula. 'I must speak with her.'

Ursula put a restraining hand on his arm. 'She has locked her door. You cannot be up here. Please, come with me.'

She led him downstairs and into the boarders' parlour, thankful that it was empty. 'What has happened?' Ursula asked urgently, ignoring any necessity for introductions.

Daniel thrust his hands into his trouser pockets and looked blindly round the room as though seeking answers. 'You must be Miss Grandison,' he said in a moment of revelation. 'Rachel told me about you. You were at the menagerie that afternoon.'

'And you are Mr Rokeby,' said Ursula impatiently. Please, what has happened with Alice? We are all so worried about her.'

Daniel thrust a hand through his untidy hair again, his expression desperate.

'She says, oh, Miss Grandison, I don't know how to say it. She declares she has to return to that evil son of the devil, Peters. It will kill her!'

Chapter Seven

Martha brought in the midday post and set it on the desk. 'There's one in Miss Alice's hand,' she said. Martha could never be brought to use Alice's married name.

Rachel abandoned the legal document she had been commissioned to comment on; she might not be allowed to practice as a lawyer but she could use her legal expertise in other ways.

Immediately her sister had left with Ursula in John's automobile, Rachel had waved goodbye to her aunt and returned home to write a letter to Alice telling her that they must not meet until after Daniel had returned and taken her under his protection; it could be too dangerous. The investigator might very well be watching her, Rachel, hoping she would lead him to where Alice was staying.

She had received one letter from her sister since, saying Rachel must not worry about her, that she was comfortably settled and hoping she would soon be with Daniel. There had been no more letters from her. Rachel had written to her every day, light notes describing what she had done, trying to maintain contact between them. But what Alice had been doing, her sister had no idea.

During the last few days, Rachel had considered visiting Mrs Bruton's house in Wilton Crescent with the idea of meeting up with Ursula Grandison. She had liked the American woman very much. Not only for the help she had given at the menagerie but also for her openness and intelligence. No coy social chitchat with Ursula. And her actions had shown she might be acquainted with the investigator but she was not going to give Alice away. But the possibility of having to confront Mrs Bruton with the memory of the chaos Joshua Peters had caused at her tea party still so fresh had stayed her.

Now, at last, there had come a letter from Alice. Rachel eagerly ripped open the envelope. It was only short but the news it contained was devastating. Rachel shouted for Martha. 'I'm going out, be back some time,' she said, hastily securing her beret on top of her head with a couple of long pins and grabbing her gloves.

'Right, Miss Rachel,' said Martha, who had long ago given up questioning anything she did.

Arriving at Mrs Maple's, Rachel hammered on the front door. It was opened immediately by a skinny maid.

'My sister, Mrs Peters, where is she?'

'Don't know, miss, but Miss Grandison's in the parlour ...' a hand was waved at a door.

Rachel rushed into the room. 'I'm so glad to see you,' she said to Ursula. 'I've had a letter from Alice saying she intends returning to that, that *brute!*' Then she saw who else was in the room. 'Daniel, you have returned, thank heavens. She will listen to you.'

He shook his head hopelessly. 'She says we must never see each other again.'

Rachel looked at Ursula.

She nodded and said, 'She will not speak to me.'

'I got back from the Lake District to find a letter from Alice waiting for me. No, not one, but two letters.' Daniel flung himself into a chair and covered his face with his hands. 'To think of darling Alice actually having the courage to leave that monster and then finding she had nowhere to go. Oh, what she must have been through!' He looked up at Rachel. 'I rushed round here. At first she flew into my arms – but when I told her not to worry, everything would now be all right, she wrenched herself away and said she was returning to, to, oh, I cannot say it.' He rose and strode over to the window, his hands thrust deep into his trouser pockets. 'Now she has locked herself into her room and says we must never see each other again.'

Rachel looked again at Ursula. 'Is this really so?'

'I am afraid it is.' She added, 'I think if Mr Rokeby were to leave, your sister might talk to you.'

'I won't go,' Daniel said, still staring out of the window. 'Not until I speak to her again.'

Rachel rubbed her forehead in despair. Underneath that air of fragile sweetness, her darling sister was one of the most obstinate creatures she knew. Then she said, 'Daniel, go! So long as you are here, Alice will not communicate with us.'

More protestations followed. Eventually he took his hat and said, 'Rachel, she needs me. She has only to send word and I will come, though it be from the ends of the earth!'

Why did Daniel always have to be so dramatic? thought Rachel.

As soon as he had departed, Ursula took her upstairs and she knocked on Alice's door, 'Darling, it's me. Daniel has gone; please let me in.'

A key turned and a moment later Alice was in her arms.

After half an hour or so, Rachel accompanied her sister to the parlour; she carried Alice's bag. Ursula was waiting.

'I can talk no sense into her,' Rachel said despairingly.

'You do not listen to me,' said Alice, equally despairing. She sat down and looked at Ursula. 'Perhaps I can make you understand?'

Rachel saw the other girl sit beside her sister and take her hand. 'Please try.'

Her breast filled with a ferment of strange emotions. She went over to the window and stood as Daniel had. It looked as though Alice had become very friendly with Ursula. Rachel told herself it was ridiculous to feel jealous. No one could come between her and Alice. But nothing of what her sister had said to her upstairs explained her decision.

'You see,' Alice said to Ursula. 'Joshua and I had a son, Henry. He died of scarlet fever two years ago.' Her voice wobbled. Rachel knew what saying this was doing to her and had to force herself to listen. 'He was nearly three, such a darling, so funny, so loving. Never was there a lovelier child than Harry.'

Rachel could see the boy now in her mind's eye. Fair curls, blue eyes with such a sparkle, and so mischievous. Even Joshua had been in thrall to him. With his son, he had shown warmth and a softness Rachel had not known he possessed.

'When I fainted the other day, I suspected I might be with child again. I visited my doctor and today it was confirmed.' That much of what Alice had said to her, Rachel had understood. She turned and watched the two girls.

'Is …' Ursula started and then stopped as though uncertain how to continue.

'Yes, Mr Peters is the father and … and I cannot deny him this second chance for a family. He was as distraught as I when Henry went to heaven.'

Rachel could not stand it. 'By his behaviour to you, he has forfeited any right to such happiness,' she said bitterly.

'Darling, you must understand,' Alice pleaded.

For a moment there was silence.

Ursula rose. 'You have to do what you believe is right,' she said quietly. 'I will go and find a cab.'

Rachel felt she had had the initiative removed from her and was filled with helplessness. In this mood Alice was unreachable.

Before they arrived at Montagu Place, Rachel said, quietly, 'Are you certain Joshua is the father of this child?'

Alice looked at her with a curious expression. 'Why do you doubt it? You cannot imagine that Daniel and I … that we …'

'But you say you love him?'

'I do! I never knew I could feel this way. I fought it, I knew it was wrong; then I came to believe that something that felt so right could not be wrong. That afternoon, amongst all those wild animals, I knew I had to be with him.' She fell silent for a moment and Rachel envied the look she saw on her face. Then Alice added, 'Even then, though, I knew we had to wait until I had left Joshua.'

'But even loving Daniel you allowed Joshua in your bed!'

'He is my husband,' Alice said quietly. 'I could not refuse him.'

Rachel just stopped herself from saying that she doubted Joshua had asked. He would have taken what he saw as his right. As in law it was.

Rachel was not a virgin. She had seen it as her duty as a modern woman to understand the act of 'making love'. Gossip and wide reading told her that it was not something that had to be confined to marriage. The man she had chosen was attractive, she had approached the act with both curiosity and excitement, found it curiously unmoving, and soon severed the relationship. Her lover had been affronted. 'You have no soul,' he'd said. 'No heart. You are frigid.'

'How will you persuade Joshua to take you back? You know how vindictive he can be.'

'I will tell him the truth. That I had to escape his cruel behaviour towards me. But that now we have the chance, if he is willing, of once again being a family.'

'You cannot believe that he will change, not after you have humiliated him by leaving his roof.'

'He can say that I am in a delicate condition and lost my mind for a little, that I have required medical treatment. The servants will accept that. And so will everyone else.'

'Daniel won't.'

'Please, Rachel, that is over – it must be over. You must not mention his name again to me ever.' Alice gripped her sister's arm with fierce force. 'Promise me you will persuade him that that is so.' Her eyes looked compellingly into Rachel's.

'Oh, darling, he will never believe me.'

'He must!'

They had arrived at Montagu Place. Rachel helped Alice down and prepared to follow her into the house.

'Please, go home. I am very grateful to you for coming with me but I need to be on my own now,' Alice said.

Rachel looked into her pale face and knew there was nothing she could say that would sway her obstinate sister. 'I don't understand how you can come back here.' She'd wanted to be loving and supportive; instead her words sounded cold. With despair, she watched her sister's small, stiffly upright figure disappear into the house.

★ ★ ★

Back in St George's Square, Rachel could not find Martha. Instead she went through to the mews.

John's automobile was not on the cobblestones and the doors to the converted stable where it was kept were closed. She stood on tiptoe and looked through the windows set high in the doors. With relief, she saw that the vehicle was inside. She banged on the door that led to the living quarters above. Almost immediately there came the sound of footsteps on the stairs. As he opened the door, Rachel fell into his arms. 'Oh, John, John,' she moaned. 'She's gone back to him.'

He held her close. 'There, there; come and tell me all about it.'

The comfortable thing about John was that he did not believe in dramatic gestures. They'd made friends when she had come into the mews one day and saw him fiddling with that auto-car or automobile. These vehicles were becoming more and more common. There was even an Automobile Club. But up until that point, Rachel had had no chance to experience one at close quarters and immediately went over.

She had at first taken the young man for a chauffeur, employed by one of the St George's Square residents. She had had no hesitation in approaching him and exclaiming with wonder at the machine. With its paintwork beautifully polished, the spokes of the wheels painted to match and the brass work gleaming, the vehicle was a compelling sight.

He'd been only too eager to explain the mysteries of the engine. 'It's internal combustion, two cylinder, can achieve almost thirty miles per hour, runs on petroleum spirit. I've only just bought her,' he added.

It was not only this fact that had told Rachel she had been sadly mistaken in his situation, his voice said that here was a member of the upper classes, educated at a public school.

'I should introduce myself. Rachel Fentiman,' she said, holding out her hand.

He wiped his hands on his breeches and then clasped hers in a warm grip. 'John Pitney, at your service.'

'Are you visiting or have you moved into the square?' Rachel thought he could not have lived there long, she would surely have noticed his tall, well set-up figure and attractively open features.

'I, well, I live up there.' John Pitney waved at the windows above what had once been a stable but now seemed to have been converted to house the automobile.

'Really?' The accommodation was designed to house one or more grooms; it hardly seemed suited to a young man of means.

'Just out of the army and wanted to be independent, don't you know, Miss Fentiman? Would you like a demonstration ride?'

Rachel was thrilled and allowed him to settle her on the padded leather seat. Then she exclaimed at the way the engine caught as he cranked it up with a handle inserted below a honeycomb-style metal screen she was told was the vehicle's radiator. She laughed with exhilaration as he climbed in beside her, took hold of the steering wheel and told her to 'hold tight'.

Then she was jerked violently back as he wielded what he told her was the 'gear shaft' and the vehicle plunged forward. 'Good heavens!' she said, clutching nervously at the side of her seat.

'Sorry,' her chauffeur said cheerfully, 'the clutch is a bit fierce.' The vehicle bounced over the cobblestones towards the end of the mews.

'Oh, this is such fun!' Rachel cried. 'Where can we go?'

'I am afraid neither of us is dressed for a sally on to the higway,' he said, bringing them to a halt. 'How about a proper spin tomorrow?'

'Come and have a cup of tea and tell me all about yourself,' Rachel said recklessly.

'Miss Fentiman, you do realise we have not been properly introduced?'

She looked at him, surprised at his reaction, then saw that he was smiling.

'Your automobile has surely performed all the introduction necessary.'

By the time they had consumed Martha's tea and gingerbread, Rachel had elicited from her guest that he had resigned his commission as a captain in the Coldstream Guards at the end of the Boer War and was currently working for a company recently set up to produce and sell automobiles. It was the start of an enjoyable friendship. Much later she learned that he was the younger son of a duke, and was formally known as the Lord John Pitney, but he'd fallen out with his family when he'd insisted on leaving the army and going into what they considered to be 'trade'.

Rachel didn't care about his title, his background or what he did for a living; as far as she was concerned, John was her friend and he seemed to see her in the same light. He'd shared in her concern over her sister's plight and nothing had seemed more natural now than that she should go to him in her distress.

John led her up the stairs to his living area and settled her on to the large sofa that took up most of the room.

'Cup of tea or something stronger?' he asked and went over to riddle the stove.

It was not a cold day but Rachel was shivering. 'Tea, please.'

He filled a kettle, placed it on the stove, then found a rug and arranged it round her shoulders. 'Now, tell me all.'

She told him everything that had happened, spilling out the words without thought, desperate to make him understand how terrible Alice's situation was. John quietly listened, made tea, found cups and milk. He said nothing but she knew he understood her distress and his calm presence was comforting.

'He'll kill her, I know he will! Oh, not physically perhaps, but she'll collapse, he'll put her in an asylum, refuse to let her see her child and then she'll die!' Tears started to pour down her cheeks.

'Rachel, dearest, you can't know that.' John sat beside her, took out a handkerchief and tenderly wiped her eyes. 'I'm sure you can prevent any such event happening.'

'There'll be nothing I can do,' she said bitterly. 'You don't know Joshua Peters.'

'But surely if he behaves so badly to her, she'll leave him again.'

'He'll make sure he keeps the child, he'll have a legal right. You don't know Alice either. She's fixated, says it's her *duty* to stay with him.' Rachel burst into passionate sobs.

'Hush, hush,' he said, gathering her into his arms, holding her close.

After a little, the sobs grew less and he wiped her eyes again. She closed them, the tears gone but hiccupping breaths worked through her body. 'Rachel, Rachel,' he said softly. She felt him kiss her eyelids and tidy damp strands of hair away from her face. The shivers running through her felt different and she found herself pressing against his body, lifting her face to his and slipping her arms around his neck. His hair was unexpectedly soft and she gave a little gasp.

He clasped her tightly, his breath came faster, and his mouth found hers. After a moment both their lips opened and she strained against him as the shivers ran through her more and more strongly. Never before had she experienced anything like this.

Then she felt him draw back. 'No,' she cried, unable to bear the removal of his arms. 'Please!'

'Oh, Rachel, you don't know what you do to me,' he breathed. 'A man can only take so much.'

She ran her hands up into that soft hair and dragged his head down to hers again, pressed her mouth against his, forced her tongue between his lips. 'I need you.' It came out as a moan. 'Please, please.'

Their clothes went everywhere, thrown off as each gazed at the other as though they were under some form of spell. Then the last piece of interfering fabric was discarded and they could entwine bare limbs on the deep sofa's welcoming embrace until both their bodies seemed one.

Afterwards she lay against his chest, playing with the fair curls that grew there, while he stroked the long tresses that had come loose in her abandonment.

Rachel gave a deep sigh of pure contentment. 'I never knew it could be like that,' she murmured.

He kissed her nose. 'It isn't always, my darling.'

Rachel gave a gurgle of delight and kissed his left nipple. 'So I'm special?'

'Very, very special.'

Rachel could not imagine that Alice had experienced any-thing approaching so sublime a moment with Joshua but this was surely what she should be sharing with Daniel. She hated the thought that her sister should be so deprived; worse, that she should have to endure the caresses of such a man as Joshua Peters. There must be something Rachel could do to help her.

John pulled the rug over them both, tucking it in around their bodies. Another thought popped into Rachel's head and she could not help laughing out loud.

'What is so funny, my darling?'

'I was thinking how horrified Aunt Lydia would be if she knew of my behaviour. She's always saying how dreadful the Bohemian set are, that they've got the morals of alley cats.' She pulled herself up and looked down at his blunt face with its warm brown eyes and kissed the scar above his right eyebrow. 'Miaouw!'

Chapter Eight

Ursula missed Alice. While the quiet girl had been at Mrs Maple's boarding house, she had had a friend to share her evenings with. The difficulty of Alice's position, her listlessness and obvious distress at Daniel Rokeby's continued absence from London, none of this had prevented her from being a pleasant companion. She didn't have Rachel's energy and intelligence but Alice was closer to Ursula in age and, despite the difficulties of her situation, could manage to see the humour in some of her tales of life working for Mrs Bruton.

There was the afternoon her employer had held one of her 'At Homes', with Ursula helping to serve the teas, and had announced in wondering tones how taken aback she had been by a performance of *Hamlet* she had attended the previous evening with friends. 'I expected something out of the ordinary but to me it seemed as though the author had merely cobbled together a whole stream of quotations.'

There had been a moment's stunned silence, then an elderly gentleman seated in a wing chair had stamped his cane approvingly upon the floor. 'That's the wittiest remark I've heard in a long while,' he wheezed. Relieved laughter broke out.

'My employer looked puzzled but gratified,' Ursula said to a laughing Alice. For a moment she had sounded almost carefree.

Then there had been the King Charles spaniel puppy Mrs Bruton had acquired. 'He can be my little guard dog,' she said to Ursula. 'And you will not mind taking little Robbie for walks,

will you.' It had not been a question. But Ursula did not mind
at all, she was very fond of dogs and the animal was great fun.
Mrs Bruton equipped herself with a dog whistle. 'Only Robbie
can hear it,' she said and demonstrated, blowing through it and
watching how the dog's ears moved and his head went on one
side, as though wondering what his mistress wanted him to do.

Ursula found the whistle a great help when she took the little
dog into Hyde Park for a run. Then one day Robbie managed
to get hold of Mrs Bruton's finest nightdress, the one with the
Brussels lace, pulling it downstairs behind him while he tossed
the bodice in his mouth as he descended.

'So I'm afraid I was instructed to return Robbie to the breeder
who had supplied him,' Ursula told Alice ruefully. 'Now she
keeps the dog whistle in her handbag as a reminder of him.'

Alice had laughed at that as well. What seemed to please her
most, however, was questioning Ursula about America and the
possibilities for employment on both the east and west coasts.

'You see, Daniel talks about us going to live on the continent,
it being so much cheaper there. But Mr Peters says that all the
Europeans are liars and cheats. He does business with them, you
see, and has lived there as well.'

'I was educated in Paris,' said Ursula gently. 'We found the
Parisians were very proud. They seemed to look down on us for-
eignors, but I don't think we were cheated.'

'Mr Peters was quite adamant.' Alice looked at her with wide
open eyes. 'He said quite the worst were those in Cairo.'

'Ah, well, my only experience of Egyptians was a girl who was
very lovely but not very intelligent. She could never manage the
French subjunctive.'

'Oh, nor me,' said Alice mournfully. 'Mr Peters also said that he
fears the Germans.'

'Fears?'

'Well, he says they want to be, as he puts it, "top dog".
The Kaiser is very jealous of the British Empire, he says.'

'I'm afraid I know nothing about that,' said Ursula, who
disliked talking about Mr Peters. 'But there are plenty of opportunities in America for a man with drive and ambition,' she
added, getting out the playing cards that were always with her
for a session of the two-handed patience she had discovered that
Alice enjoyed.

After the girl had returned to her husband, Ursula fought a feeling of loneliness. It had been a long time since she had been able to enjoy spending time with someone so close to her in age, especially one who seemed to share her taste in books.

Ursula had hoped to hear how Alice was faring back with her husband. But there was no news. A note to Miss Fentiman, politely hoping that her sister was in good health, had not been answered. Ursula could not help being worried: how had Mr Peters reacted to his wife's return? How was Alice managing without Daniel? On the surface, the girl seemed gentle and malleable, the last person, in fact, to make the scandalous decision to leave her husband for another man. A scandalous decision, yes, and one that Ursula was sure had required considerable courage – and she was equally sure that Alice had needed to summon up even more courage to abandon her new love and return to the thoroughly unpleasant bully that was Joshua Peters.

Ursula almost considered approaching Thomas Jackman to see if he had any news. But she still could not forgive him for taking employment with such a horrid man as Peters.

★ ★ ★

Some ten days after Alice had left the boarding house, Ursula arrived at Wilton Crescent to find Mrs Bruton handsomely attired in a new outfit of pale grey crepe elaborately designed with pleated panels on skirt and sleeves offset with a large number of moulded gilt buttons.

'We are to take up Count Meyerhoff's invitation to visit the *Maison Rose*,' said Mrs Bruton. 'You look most handsome, my dear,' she added, surveying her secretary.

As Ursula had left the previous evening, Mrs Bruton asked her to pay particular attention to her appearance the next day, 'For I have a little plan in mind,' she'd added mysteriously.

Mrs Bruton was always full of 'little plans' and occasionally warned Ursula that the following day she should dress as 'a woman of leisure'. Ursula had accompanied her employer to Kew Gardens, to various exhibitions, and to sample tea at Fortnum and Mason's, which had proved a great treat.

It was for these occasions that Ursula was grateful for several cast-off outfits given her by the Countess of Mountstanton.

'By the time I can discard my mourning,' Helen had said in bitter tones, 'these will all be out of fashion.' Today, therefore, Ursula had abandoned black for a pale blue shantung costume that matched Mrs Bruton's for style.

They were bound for Mayfair. The distance from Wilton Crescent was not far; Ursula would have been happy to walk but this did not suit Mrs Bruton. So the young lad who performed a number of menial duties in the Bruton establishment had been sent to find and bring a hansom cab to the house.

'I would not like my new footwear to suffer,' Mrs Bruton said while they were waiting. She stretched out a slim ankle in a small soft grey suede bootee. 'Particularly since we are to visit a fashion house.'

It was nearly two weeks since Count Meyerhoff's note had arrived. Thinking that it might be her duty to remind her employer of the invitation, Ursula had mentioned the matter.

'Oh, my dear, I cannot seem to be too eager. No, we shall go in a little while.' Today it seemed the 'little while' had arrived.

'Now,' Mrs Bruton said as they settled themselves in the hansom, her white-gloved hands clasped over the stem of a dainty parasol. 'I met Mrs Trenchard yesterday at a charity event – do you know, I had no idea there were quite so many worthy causes chasing one's money – well, I asked Mrs Trenchard if she had heard anything more of that extraordinary man who gatecrashed my tea party. And she told me that her niece, his wife, was now home with him It seems that she had not left but was in a delicate state that required medical attention. In other words, she is with child. Would you not have thought her husband would have known that?'

Ursula murmured something non-committal and wondered again how Alice was surviving in the Peters' household.

'Mrs Trenchard told me that the girl is in good heart. Is that not also surprising? To be in "good heart" married to such an unpleasant fellow?' Mrs Bruton did not wait for a comment from her companion. 'Obviously this is some story concocted to cover Mrs Peters' desertion. Well, that is no surprise. For a wife to leave her husband! Such social ruination. To hear, though, that Mr Peters has accepted her return is interesting. But, then, such passion as he displayed in my drawing room. I could almost forgive him for ruining my little party.'

For once Ursula found herself lost for words.

Their cab had been halted in traffic at Hyde Park Corner, now the way was suddenly cleared and the horse whipped into something approaching a trot.

'I wonder what difference the advent of the motor car will make to London traffic,' Ursula said firmly.

'Why, I cannot believe that anything so crude and uncomfortable will be around for very long.' Mrs Bruton sounded astonished that anyone could think differently. 'So noisy, so inefficient and the mess it makes of one's appearance with the wind and the dust, and the inconvenience to other road users! No, I am confident we shall not see the reliable horse vanishing from Piccadilly.' She waved a hand up the broad thoroughfare they were making their way along in fits and starts.

At that moment the horse, brought to another stop by the traffic, defecated, the result falling in a steaming pile just below their feet. Mrs Bruton's nose twitched but she said nothing.

The cab eventually drew up outside an imposing mansion.

'I would have expected nothing less of the count,' murmured Mrs Bruton as they climbed a gracious flight of stairs that would not have looked out of place in a stately home.

On the first floor a heavy, dark mahogany door bore a shining brass plate that declared: *Maison Rose*. Ursula pressed the bell.

A pleasant girl attired in a white coat that exuded a clinical aura, greeted and invited them into a large, well-appointed salon and took their names. 'Please seat yourselves,' she said. 'I will tell Madame Rose that you await.'

'It was Count Meyerhoff who invited me to visit,' Mrs Bruton said with just a hint of disapproval. 'Is he here?'

'If you will be seated, Madam, I will enquire.' The girl disappeared.

'What a strange uniform for the staff of a couture house.' Mrs Bruton said, seating herself. 'Hmm, it seems no expense has been spared,' she added in tones of deep satisfaction.

The salon was furnished in the style of Louis XVI; the paintings on the wall, though, were modern, colourful and impressionistic. A table covered in a white linen cloth stood near the window with chairs on either side, looking as though it waited for two diners to be seated; there was, though, no cutlery nor glassware, indeed, the surface was quite bare. Two large vitrines set against the walls held a variety of bottles and jars on their glass shelves.

'Surely this cannot be a pharmacy?' exclaimed Ursula.

At that moment a man entered. 'My dear Eugenie, you are here!' he exclaimed, coming over and taking both Mrs Bruton's hands in his. 'I had almost despaired of *Maison Rose* ever being honoured with a visit from the beautiful Madame Bruton.'

Mrs Bruton blushed as Count Meyerhoff, it could only be he, raised first her right and then her left gloved hand almost to his lips, stopping in the correct manner before actually making contact.

'What a delightful picture you make,' he said, dropping her hands and stepping away as though to survey her from head to toe. 'It has been too long.' His English was very fluent but he had the slightest of continental accents that was immediately attractive.

Ursula found herself staring at the count. A compact figure of average height, aged, she thought, in his mid to late thirties, he was dressed in a devastatingly tailored dark suit with a heavy gold watch chain stretched across a silver-grey brocade waistcoat. His face showed a good bone structure but was perhaps a little too fleshy. He had a straight nose and well-shaped mouth. What, though, drew and held her fascinated gaze was his head of thick, glossy, and prematurely white hair. The contradiction with his no more than middle-aged physical appearance gave him an almost unearthly air and underlined a sense of easy sophistication.

Mrs Bruton sat enjoying his attention.

Count Meyerhoff clapped his hands. 'But you must meet Madame Rose!'

As though she had been waiting for her cue, a statuesque female entered. Blonde hair was severely drawn back from a sculpted face with high cheekbones. Flashing, tiger-gold eyes compensated for a beaked nose and thin mouth. A well-cut white linen coat skimmed an Amazonian figure.

'An honour to meet you, Madame Bruton,' she said, advancing with her hand held out. 'I hear from the count of your style and elegance. Also how Mr Bruton was such a man *comme il faut*. I mourn for your loss.'

Madame Rose had a much stronger accent than the count's and it was not Austrian. Ursula cast her memory back to her Parisian finishing school with its collection of girls from different countries for one that matched.

'Come, please to sit for my examination.' Madame Rose's tone was pleasant but firm. She guided her visitor to the white-clothed table, placed her in one of the chairs, and sat opposite.

'The *chapeau*, it shall be removed, yes?' Mrs Bruton was wearing a charming, wide-brimmed hat in grey straw decorated with scarlet roses. The assistant had returned and now efficiently removed first pins and then hat. 'Now, we shall see.'

The table was not wide and Madame Rose was able to take Mrs Bruton's face in her hands and turn it gently towards the light, examining it with serious attention.

The count approached an interested Ursula. He gave her a small bow with a click of his heels. 'Count Meyerhoff at your service, Fraulein.'

'Ursula Grandison, amanuensis to Mrs Bruton.' She offered her hand.

He held it for a moment. She was amused to realise he was not going to raise it to his lips, the way he had Mrs Bruton's, and that his eyes were an unusual, very pale olive green.

'I am most pleased to make your acquaintance, Fraulein Grandison. You are, I think, from America?' The pale eyes were fixed on her face and something in the way he looked at her sent an involuntary shiver down Ursula's back. She told herself not to be ridiculous. This was a charming man, a friend of Mrs Bruton's; not some sinister foreigner. Yet, beneath that suave demeanour there was something that reminded her of the lions she had seen in the menagerie: dangerous power rippling unseen through relaxed bodies. She smiled pleasantly.

'Yes, I have been in England only a few months,' she said in an amiable voice, then glanced across at her employer, who seemed to be totally absorbed in what Madame Rose was saying. 'Mrs Bruton thought that the *Maison Rose* was a couture house but I think this is a *Salon de Beauté,* is it not?'

He smiled back at her, all harmless charm. 'Ah, I see you are a woman of intelligence, Fraulein.' He gave a wave towards the laden shelves in the vitrine behind her. 'These are some of Madame's formulations for the care of the skin. She is having a great success with London society.'

Despite herself, Ursula was intrigued. 'Madame Rose is an expert?'

'Indeed; she has studied in Paris and Vienna with leading dermatological specialists and creates her own creams and lotions for the individual skin.'

He leant forward, peering at her face, and Ursula had to force herself not to take a step backwards. 'You have a most excellent complexion, Fraulein. However, may I ask if you have been used to spending time outdoors in the winter and the summer? I would not normally ask such a personal question but Madame Rose has taught me to see the damage that weather can do to the skin's tender fabric.' There sounded such concern in his voice, Ursula could not take exception to his words; no one was more aware than herself of the damage done to her complexion by several years spent living in a Californian silver mine.

'But Madame is a genius with her formulations. She will find the perfect cream for you.' His voice caressed the words.

Ursula smiled weakly. She wanted to say she had no faith in such formulations. Instead she asked, 'Where is Madame Rose from?'

'Ah, you can tell she is not Austrian?'

'I attended a school in Paris; it was international and there was a girl there, Olympia Estouffa, who was Egyptian. When she spoke English, her accent was very similar to Madame Rose's.'

Something flickered in the count's eyes. 'Madame Rose left Cairo when she was quite young,' he said smoothly. 'Already she could speak several languages and had her great interest in dermatology. But, please, tell me what an American girl is doing in England, working with the charming Mrs Bruton? I have visited New York and its vibrancy and life were, as I believe the English have it, meat and drink to me.'

At last the count had found a subject Ursula could be enthusiastic about. 'I think New York has excitement in its very air. Even when life is perfectly ordinary, you feel it could be turned into champagne at any minute.'

He laughed, 'That is it exactly!'

It was as though a layer of calculated charm had been abandoned and she was meeting the real man. For a moment Ursula felt a sizzling excitement.

Then Mrs Bruton was brought over to the vitrine. 'Now, dear Madame,' said the beautician, opening one of the doors and taking out a jar. 'This is my *crème de printemps*.' The assistant produced a chic carrier bag made in glossy, heavy duty paper decorated with a flamboyant signature; the jar that was placed inside carried a label similarly decorated. Madame Rose now took a bottle from the shelf. 'And here is the astringent lotion that will correct your slight tendency to oiliness, it is this which can bring on the occasional eruption. The lotion will tone your skin. But first you must cleanse.' Another bottle went into the carrier. 'Every day follow the routine I have explained: cleanse, tone and nourish. Come back to me in three weeks' time so I can see the improvement in your complexion.'

'I am so excited, Madame Rose. I shall faithfully follow all your directions.' Mrs Bruton took the carrier bag as though the potions it contained were magic.

'Perhaps, Madame Rose, you could examine Miss Grandison's complexion while I renew my friendship with her employer.' The count placed a possessive hand on Mrs Bruton's arm and she gave him an excited glance as he led her from the room.

Without the count's powerful presence Ursula could breathe easily again. However, 'I am afraid, Madame, I have only accompanied Mrs Bruton to your salon. I am not a potential client.' How could she be? The whole atmosphere of *Maison Rose* oozed expense.

'But, Miss Grandison, an assessment of your skin does not entail an obligation. Come, sit.' She led her to the table.

Ursula could see no alternative. Who knew how long Mrs Bruton would be closeted with the count?

Her skin was subjected to a searching examination, the magnetic, golden eyes carefully assessing every aspect of her face, a firm hand gently turning her head so that the light would fall on every side. Thorough though the beautician seemed to be, Ursula thankfully realised that her care was impersonal.

Finally Madame Rose sat back with a little sigh. 'My dear Miss Grandison, you have been blessed by the Almighty with a beautiful complexion, with colouring most attractive. I can see, though, that it has suffered extremes of weather. The natural oils have been lost; if they are not soon replaced, you will develop wrinkles. These add years to a face that does not deserve them.' For the briefest of moments, the beautician seemed to be genuinely caring. 'I shall give you my *Crème de l'Eté.*'

'But …' Ursula started.

Madame Rose held up her hand. 'I cannot see a fine complexion such as yours remaining ravaged by weather when I, Madame Rose, can aid its recovery. You will not pay, but maybe you find it does what I say — I can see that you do not believe this — but if it does then maybe you tell Madame Bruton's friends, yes?'

'In San Francisco,' Ursula was determined to take control of the situation. 'In San Francisco some cheapskate pharmacist sold me a cream he said would do the same. It brought out a rash that itched to drive me mad. I'll not go through that again, not for all the dollars in Fort Knox.'

Madame Rose stood up, stately and unmoved, went to the vitrine, took out one of her jars, unscrewed the lid and gently applied a little of the cream to the inside of Ursula's wrist. 'You wait until tomorrow, yes? Then, if no rash, you apply to face. Use upward motions of the hands.' She demonstrated with her hands on her own face, carefully smoothing the skin up towards her temples. 'Gentle massage, like this. So, now you have confidence in Madame Rose, yes?'

Strangely enough, Ursula found she did. The pot of cream and another two products were placed in a carrier bag.

'You follow the routine I explain to Madame Bruton. So now I see if Count Meyerhoff and Madame are finished their talk.'

A relaxed and delighted Mrs Bruton emerged with Count Meyerhoff, who bade her goodbye with his special, continental charm.

Then he bowed over Ursula's hand as well. 'A most unexpected pleasure to meet such a stimulating American.' The olive green eyes gave her an intense and unsettling look.

'It has been a most interesting morning,' Ursula said steadily.

A minion had been despatched to find a hansom and by the time they reached the mansion's front door, the cab awaited them.

'Is the count not the most charming man, Miss Grandison? You can see, can you not, how he had all of Vienna at his feet?'

'Continental men do have a certain something,' Ursula managed to say as they set off for Wilton Crescent. 'But, Mrs Bruton, Madame Rose has given me some of her preparations.' She raised the chic little carrier bag. 'I hope she does not think I have rich friends.'

Mrs Bruton patted her hand. 'Do not worry, my dear. The creams and lotions I was supplied with were another gift. The dear count is always so generous.' She paused for a moment then added, 'Of course, the hope is that we shall be so delighted with the effects of these formulations, that we shall send a stream of friends to *Maison Rose*.' The idea did not seem to worry her.

'It will be interesting to see if we notice any difference in our complexions,' Ursula said thoughtfully. 'But Madame Rose is rather splendid, isn't she? She seems to have so much knowledge and confidence. To be running her own business must be quite a thing.' She wondered if she could ever manage to achieve anything similar.

'Of course she has to rely on the dear count,' said Mrs Bruton. 'It will be he who organises all the business details. Madame is very fortunate to have him at her side.' She peeked inside her carrier bag. 'I wonder ... can Madame Rose's creams really benefit our complexions?'

'The count said she had studied with dermatologists in Paris and Vienna. Our mirrors will show us whether her products can fulfil her promises.'

Mrs Bruton raised the glossy little carrier bag. 'I shall commence my treatment the moment we return.'

★ ★ ★

A pile of letters awaited Ursula's attention when they arrived back at Wilton Crescent and the morning's encounter with Count Meyerhoff and Madame Rose was pushed to the back of her mind. However, at the end of the day she carried the little bag carefully back to Mrs Maples'.

There another letter awaited her.

Dear Ursula,
Please come immediately. Alice has been arrested.
Your friend,
Rachel

Chapter Nine

Ursula read and re-read the message, turning the piece of paper over as though there might be something more on the back. It seemed to make no sense. Why on earth should Alice have been arrested? Surely this could not be Joshua Peters' way to make her pay for leaving him? Not after she had returned, surely!

The note had been sent from Rachel's address. Ursula slipped out of the blue shantung costume, flung on a linen shirt and skirt, jammed her ordinary straw hat on her head and set out for St George's Square.

She had to struggle to make quick passage though home-going Londoners. The streets, though, lacked the buzz, the shouts and badinage, of New York. Her brief exchange with the count that morning had brought back the excitement of that vibrant city.

The question as to why Alice had been arrested would not go away. If it had been Rachel, she would have assumed it to be in connection with the Movement for Women's Suffrage. Hadn't there been talk about the need for more militancy? More militancy surely meant breaking the law in one way or another.

But Alice! Surely she could not have done anything illegal. That shy exterior, though, undoubtedly hid passionate depths and once the girl had decided on a course of action, it was unlikely a little matter of breaking the law would stop her.

Useless to speculate. Better to wait and hear from Rachel herself.

The front door was opened by Martha.

'Miss Fentiman is not receiving visitors,' she said, her face tight with controlled emotion.

Ursula produced the note. 'Miss Fentiman has asked me to call.'

'Then you'd better come in.' Martha stepped back and showed her into Rachel's rooms. There she found Daniel.

'Prison! Alice is in prison!' he was shouting as she entered.

He stood, arms waving, his red hair as wild as his expression.

Rachel stood opposite him, an aggressive figure with her head held back, her hands on hips, feet slightly apart and a face full of anger.

'Yes, she's in prison and, yes, it's an outrage.' She saw Ursula, came over and grasped her hands. 'Thank heavens you've come. It's a terrible situation.'

'What has happened?'

'Did Alice write to you? She wrote to me!' Daniel said, slightly calmer but sounding petulant.

'Of course she wrote to you,' Rachel said with a touch of exasperation. 'But it was I who sent a note to Miss Grandison. Alice needs all the help she can get.'

'Why has Alice been arrested?' Ursula sounded sharper than she'd intended. She felt bewildered. Whatever the situation, how could she, an American without money or influence, be of any assistance?

'Joshua Peters is dead,' Daniel threw himself into a chair. 'And Alice is in prison. She'll be hanged.' His Irish accent was suddenly more noticeable.

'Don't say that!' Rachel rounded on him. 'We'll get her out of there.'

'How?' he cried despairingly.

Joshua Peters dead! So Alice was free of him. But at what price? Everything Ursula had heard and seen of the man had revealed someone ugly and brutish. No doubt the world was a better place for his passing but it would be churlish to celebrate the fact.

Ursula took off her hat – she always thought better bareheaded – placed it on a table and sat down. 'Tell me the whole story,' she said calmly. 'How did Mr Peters die and when?'

'Three days ago,' said Daniel.

'In the late evening,' added Rachel. 'He wasn't discovered until the next morning. Alice sent me a message as soon as the doctor had been.'

'And to me,' said Daniel stubbornly.

Rachel walked jerkily around the room. 'I found her in a terrible state. Kept saying she didn't understand, that Joshua had
been perfectly well when she went to bed. Then, in the morning,
Sarah, the under-housemaid, discovered him dead in his chair –
in the drawing room.'

Rachel looked very tired and her summer gown was badly
creased. She sat down next to Ursula. 'Alice sent me a scrawled
note that I could make no sense of, so I went round immediately.
I found the doctor there. He had given her some laudanum and
she was asleep on her feet. There was no getting any sense out
of her in that state, so I put her to bed. Then I went and found
Millie, her maid.'

'And why wasn't she at Alice's side?' Daniel demanded. 'I've
never trusted that girl. She doesn't look you in the eye.'

Hadn't Thomas Jackman said he'd got close to Alice's maid?
Ursula thought. And that she had been very forthcoming with
details on her mistress's movements?

'The girl seemed as shattered as Alice,' said Rachel. 'And the
cook wasn't any help. The only servant who was in any state of
control was Emily, the senior housemaid. She told me she'd asked
Millie to inform her mistress of the master's death but the girl
had collapsed.' Rachel smiled grimly. 'Emily did not seem at all
sympathetic; she said she'd hauled her up, slapped her face and
made her go to her room. Then she went herself to tell Alice
what had happened.'

Daniel roamed restlessly around the room, his hands plunged
into the pockets of his trousers. 'My poor, darling girl,' he muttered. 'I should have been there.'

'How could you have been?' Rachel said sharply, then caught
herself. 'I wish you had been. I didn't know what to do. I asked if the
doctor had signed a death certificate. Emily didn't know, nor did the
cook, though she said she could recommend a local undertaker's.'

'Undertakers!' Daniel muttered.

'I thought Joshua's business partner might want to take care of that
matter so I sent Albert, Joshua's man, to him with a note. He needed
to be advised what had happened in any case,' said Rachel.

'Which is more than you did to me,' Daniel complained.
'It took two days for Alice to send me a note. Shouldn't I have
been informed immediately?'

'It was a matter for Alice,' Rachel said, finality in her voice.

'I suppose Albert was as upset as Millie at his master's unfortunate end,' Ursula intervened. She had a vivid mental picture of the turmoil there must have been in the Peters household.

'Albert does not display his emotions,' Rachel said wryly.

They were getting nowhere. 'But on what grounds has Alice been arrested?' pressed Ursula.

'That damned doctor …' started Daniel.

'He informed the police,' cut in Rachel. 'He thinks Joshua was poisoned.'

'Good heavens!'

'The police arrived and took away Joshua's body. This morning, three days later, they came to question Alice and then arrested her for Joshua's murder. Now she's being held in prison.'

Ursula was stunned. The idea that gentle Alice was in prison for murder was too awful to contemplate. 'That's terrible.'

'I cannot bear to think of that fragile flower in prison's deadly grasp.' Daniel threw the words out with a dramatic flourish.

'Have you contacted a lawyer?'

Rachel drew a bitter breath. 'I am a qualified solicitor but I cannot practice because I am a woman! I am no use to my own sister.'

'I'll go in there and force them to give her up.' Daniel waved his arms in wild and futile gestures.

Rachel sighed wearily.

'Why do the police think Alice killed Peters?' Ursula thought it impossible she could have done so, however beastly he had been to her. The very idea, indeed, that the man had been murdered was incredible.

'It was the chocolates.'

'Please, Daniel, let me tell the story.' Rachel turned to Ursula. 'There was a half-full box of cherry liqueur chocolates by Joshua's chair. He is particularly partial to them. So partial in fact that he forbids any one else to share his. He shouted at me once when I sneaked one out of a large box he'd been presented with.'

'So the police think he was poisoned by the chocolates?' said Ursula. 'Had Alice given him them?'

'Of course not. No one knows where they came from. But the investigating officer in charge of the case is convinced that Alice has the most to gain from his death since she will inherit his estate and that is enough for him to make the arrest.' She rose, walked rapidly to the window and stood looking out. 'He wouldn't listen to any of arguments I put forward. In his eyes my words are useless because I'm a woman.'

'Does he know that your sister is with child?'

The lines on Rachel's broad forehead deepened. She looked as though she had aged ten years. She folded her arms across her chest as though trying to contain her feelings. 'I told him her condition but he refused to believe me.'

'But has not Alice told them?'

'She seems incapable of thinking straight.'

'Give me this fool's name. I'll make sure he understands he can't treat her like this,' Daniel's voice shook. 'There must be influences we can bring to bear on the man.'

Rachel shrugged hopelessly. 'Aunt Lydia is trying her best and Uncle Felix recommended a lawyer he says will be suitable. Suitable! What word is that to describe someone who has to release a girl from prison? The man has proved to be useless. Oh, would that I was allowed to practice.'

Ursula looked at her in dismay. The situation sounded more and more serious. 'Why did you think I could help?' she asked quietly.

'Rachel has some monstrous idea …'

'It is not a monstrous idea,' said Rachel furiously. 'Ursula, that investigator who was following Alice and you say is a friend of yours, well, I thought perhaps we could hire him to find who killed Joshua, or, at any rate, could want him dead so we can tell the police.'

'Hardly a difficult task,' snorted Daniel. 'Ask around and you'll hear several names that could qualify.'

'Starting with yourself,' shot back Rachel.

Ursula wondered at the underlying tension between the two of them.

'But you must see,' Rachel said to her. 'The only way we can get this terrible charge lifted from Alice is to prove her innocent, or show that there are others with more reason to kill Joshua.'

'And you think Mr Jackman can do that?'

Rachel nodded vigorously. 'Surely if he knew how to discover so much about Alice and Daniel, he could look into Joshua's life … and, well, and his end.'

Ursula remembered the efficient way Thomas Jackman had investigated the Mountstanton death she had so recently been involved with. Maybe Alice's best hope of release would be for him to take up her case. 'Do you wish me to write and inform Mr Jackman of the situation and ask him to call on you?'

'No, I want us to go to him now, and put the matter before him. We can afford to pay whatever he charges. Alice will not inherit until she is freed but Aunt Lydia has promised us financial support. Do you have his address?'

Ursula nodded and gave Rachel the details. 'It's in what I believe is known as the East End.'

The girl rose. 'Then that's where we shall go.'

'To be sure we will,' said Daniel, reaching for his wide-brimmed hat.

'No need for you to come as well.'

'Rachel, you know nothing about this man. He could be a mountebank. The very fact Peters hired him to follow Alice should make him unacceptable. If you insist on seeing him, I demand to be there as well.' He jammed his headgear on his wild hair.

Ursula slowly drew on her gloves. 'What if Mr Jackman is not at home? Should I, perhaps, write a letter we can leave there?'

'Of course! Why did I not think of that?'

Rachel found notepaper, a pen and ink and set a chair at her desk.

'While Miss Grandison writes her letter, I will find us a cab,' said Daniel. He thrust his hands into his pockets and strode out of the room with the air of a man glad to have an errand.

Rachel sighed, found her own hat and followed him.

Ursula sat and wrote,

'Dear Thomas,' she started, then put down the pen and tried to collect her thoughts. Finally she had to admit to herself that she did not want to contact the investigator. She still could not rid herself of the dislike his taking on of Mr Peters' commission had raised in her.

Could he now accept another that asked him to clear of murder the very woman he had been hired to follow and find guilty of adultery? Would he not consider that, bearing in mind her behaviour in leaving her husband, she could well now be guilty of killing him?

Ursula shivered as she remembered her discovery of a nurse-rymaid's body, which had first brought Jackman and her together.

She had to admit that the detective had been as concerned as herself that Polly should have justice. And without his experience and support, Ursula doubted that the investigation would have been successfully concluded.

Giving herself a mental shake, Ursula picked up the pen again and wrote an account of the situation without further hesitation.

'All I know,' she ended, 'is that Alice Peters has been charged with murder and is in prison. Rachel Fentiman is convinced she had nothing to do with the death of Mr Peters and wants to hire you to investigate and find the evidence that will prove her innocence. We hoped to find you at home but if not and you read this letter, please contact Miss Fentiman at the above address to discuss the matter.'

At this point, Ursula paused. Should she state she had no intention of playing any part in his investigation?

No, better not to touch on the possibility. With a steady pen, Ursula finished with a formal salutation and signed her name.

She blotted and folded the letter. As she inserted it into an envelope, Daniel returned to say a hansom waited outside. 'Rachel wanted to take an omnibus but I persuaded her a cab would be faster.'

Ursula scribbled Thomas Jackman's name on the envelope and sealed it. Did she want him to be at home, or would she prefer it if he wasn't there? As she went off with Rachel and Daniel, she realised that she honestly did not know.

Chapter Ten

'Hello?' a cheery voice called.

There was a rap on Thomas Jackman's doorknocker and the visitor came straight in.

Thomas was sitting at his desk in the corner of the small living room, doing his accounts, an upsetting business at the best of times; never enough money to cover his outgoings, however small they were, and his dream of opening an office in the West End, where it could attract a better class of client who could afford higher fees, no nearer. Joshua Peters had responded to a small advertisement he had placed in the *Morning Post*. Now this! He put down his pencil and rubbed the back of his neck.

In from the narrow little hall came Betty Marks, a round, cuddly woman, smiling as though confident of her welcome. One hand held the handle of a small metal pail, its lid slightly askew, steam and delicious smells rising from within.

'I brought you some eel and oyster stew. Made it for the pub and thought you could do with some.'

That was Betty. Always trying to make his life a little more comfortable when, truth was, ever since she arrived at the next door *Bottle and Glass*, the recently widowed sister-in-law of mine host Schooner Marks, Jackman's life had become more and more uncomfortable.

'I'll put it out the back, all ready for your tea. Unless you'd like to eat it now, with me?' Her brown eyes smiled at him, brown hair curling from under a mob cap. Thomas sighed inwardly. Half the male customers at the *Bottle and Glass* thought Betty was prime meat; she'd flash those saucy eyes at them and if it hadn't been for fear of Schooner they'd have pawed her curvy body, taken her down the lane that ran alongside the pub, narrow and dark, thrust her against the ancient brick and had their wicked way with her. But flirt though Betty did, she was secure in the knowledge that Schooner would see off any that dared to go too far.

So why, Thomas asked himself, wasn't he delighted with her gifts of food, her desire to spend time with him? Why didn't he issue the invitation he was certain she was waiting for, to climb the stairs to the bedroom he'd shared with Rose, his wife who'd died some two years ago?

Because she wasn't Rose, that was why.

And because she presumed too much.

He didn't want to accept the eel stew but couldn't think of an easy way to refuse it. And the aroma was delicious. 'Very kind of you, Mrs Marks,' he muttered and wondered how to say he didn't want to eat the meal with her.

She stood looking up at him with bright, confident eyes. Thomas Jackman wasn't a tall man but she was a short woman. 'I'll lay the table for us,' she said, and headed for the kitchen. Unless he stopped her right now, she would bring cutlery and plates and place them on the small round table in the window.

Thomas panicked. People would pass by, see them sitting there, eating together. It would be as bad as being caught *in flagrante delicto*. Schooner would expect him to make an honest woman of her.

Someone pounded the door knocker.

'You expecting a visitor?' Betty asked, unable to hide the curiosity that fought with disappointment.

Thomas breathed a sigh of relief. 'Never know when folk are going to call. It can be any time if they need my services. That's what being a private investigator is all about.' He reached the front door and hesitated. Betty hovered, obviously hoping whoever was calling would go away again.

'I have to thank you for your kind thought,' Thomas said, his hand on the doorknob. 'I'll return the pail tomorrow, if that's all right?'

She had no option but to smile.

He opened the front door for her, causing the young man about to beat another rat-a-tat to stumble.

Betty walked past him and the two other people standing on the pavement. 'Bye, Tom. See you tomorrow.' She didn't wait for a response but headed for the pub.

'So,' he said, turning his attention to the group on the pavement.

He recognised Ursula Grandison first and for a moment felt a jolt of pleasure that she had come to see him. Then he saw the young man Alice Peters had met so many times when he'd been following her. There was no mistaking the broad-brimmed hat, or his height and breadth of shoulders. Finally, standing beside Ursula Grandison, and almost as tall as her, was the girl who had been with Mrs Peters and the young man at the menagerie. The last time he had seen either of them was when he had tailed the girls to Miss Fentiman's apartment, and then waited outside for far too long before realising they must have exited through the mews. Which had meant Ursula must have caught sight of him at some stage. Well, he knew she was smart.

His contract with Peters was at an end. What business could they want with him?

'Come in, please.' He stepped back from the door and waved them inside.

A few minutes later they were all in the front room. The two girls were sitting either side of the little table, exactly where Betty had hoped she and he would be eating eel and oyster stew. Rachel Fentiman looked sternly intelligent, almost belligerent; Ursula had a very closed look on her face. Daniel Rokeby, the man Alice Peters had left her husband for, stood in a protective manner behind Miss Fentiman. He looked very tall in the small room.

Thomas moved the chair he'd been sitting on at the desk so that it faced into the room. 'Mr Rokeby, why don't you sit here?' he said.

The man looked startled. 'How do you know my name?'

Thomas said nothing, merely waved his hand towards the chair.

'Oh, go and sit, Daniel,' said Miss Fentiman. 'We don't have time to waste.'

Rokeby gave her a quick look but obeyed, placing his hat on the desk, sitting in the chair and crossing one elegant leg over the other. At least Jackman could now look down at him.

Thomas leant against the sideboard running along the back wall. He didn't look at Ursula. If she was in charge of this little party, she would have spoken up before now. 'Suppose you tell me why you're here,' he said to the girl who had knocked him over in the menagerie.

Rachel Fentiman took a deep breath. 'My brother-in-law, Joshua Peters, is dead. The doctor believes he was poisoned. My sister, Alice Peters, has been arrested for the murder of her husband.' Her voice, steady until now, suddenly quavered and she closed her eyes for a second. Then she continued, once again in control of herself: 'The charge is ridiculous. The lawyer our uncle has hired is useless. We want you to investigate Joshua's death.'

It wasn't often Thomas Jackman was taken aback but at that moment he was astounded. Joshua Peters dead! Poison suspected! Alice Peters arrested! 'Whoa!' He held up his hands then looked across at Ursula. She gave the tiniest shrug of her shoulders. He could expect no help from her. Thomas took a deep breath.

'You say your brother-in-law was poisoned?'

Rachel Fentiman nodded.

'How?'

'The police, and the doctor, believe it was with cherry liqueur chocolates.'

Cherry liqueur? Thomas could think of an obvious candidate to be concealed within those luscious interiors.

'Prussic acid?'

She nodded. 'That is what the doctor believes.'

The chocolates would have been taken away by the police to be tested.

'When did this happen?'

'Three days ago. At least, that's when his body was discovered.'

'Who by?'

'Sarah, the under-housemaid, when she went into the drawing room first thing in the morning to lay the fire.'

Thomas had a moment's sympathy for the poor girl. A body that had died in agony would not be a pretty sight.

'What happened then?'

'My sister was told and she sent for the doctor.'

'After viewing her husband's body?' Thomas knew Alice Peters was twenty-five years old but she looked six or seven years younger, and fragile. The thought that she had had to undergo such a horrible experience was shocking.

'She knew he was dead but also that a doctor would have to sign the death certificate.'

Did she indeed? Maybe not so fragile as she seemed. He remembered the way she had withstood her husband's verbal attack on her that afternoon in Joshua Peters' study.

'Did she know poison was involved?'

Rachel Fentiman lost some of her self-possession. 'No! Of course not. She thought it was a heart attack.'

'And you say she has been arrested?'

'This morning, on suspicion of murder. But it's ridiculous. Alice could not have killed Joshua.'

'Never,' said Daniel Rokeby suddenly, uncrossing his legs and placing both feet solidly on the floor. 'Alice could not do such a thing.'

Thomas looked at the man he had seen Alice Peters meet so clandestinely so many times.

Daniel rose. 'Enough of this. We're here because we need you to prove she didn't kill Peters.'

'Daniel, please,' said Rachel. 'If Mr Jackman is to help us, he needs to ask questions.'

'Rachel, leave this to me,' he said furiously.

The girl gave him a cold stare and after a moment he sat down again.

'On what grounds was the arrest made?' Thomas asked.

'That my sister knew about her husband's predeliction for cherry liqueur chocolates. But so did lots of other people. I did, for instance.'

She did, did she?

'And on what other grounds?' There had to be other grounds.

Rachel looked down at her hands, clasped tightly in her lap. 'According to Inspector Drummond, her desire to end her marriage as evidenced by a diary.'

Thomas saw Ursula look sharply at the girl; this information must be new to her.

'Inspector Drummond?' said Thomas. 'Tall chap, fair hair, with a beard and moustache?'

Rachel nodded. 'You know him?'

Oh, yes, Thomas knew Everard Drummond. Bright, ambitious, with a reputation for building a case on flimsy evidence. 'And you say he cites a diary written by your sister?'

She stared at him defiantly. 'The fact that she wrote down how unhappy she was is not proof she killed him.'

'Any other grounds for suspicion?'

The stare remained steady. 'I believe her maid said something ...'

'Millie Rudge?' roared out Daniel, leaping to his feet again. 'I told you there was something suspicious about her.'

Rachel said nothing, her basilisk stare seemed to be enough. Rokeby sat down again, a sullen look on his face.

But his vehemence stirred a reaction in Thomas. Millie Rudge had seemed a sweet, innocent girl, fond of her mistress, afraid of her master's temper, and unsuspecting of his own relationship with her. Surely she could not have said anything to incriminate Alice Peters?

'An expert on servants told me only recently that they know everything that goes on in a house,' said Ursula calmly.

Thomas thought about the size of the Mounstanton stately home and the number of servants there and quickly compared it with the Peters household. If the Mounstanton staff knew everything that went on with their employers, how much more must those who worked in the much smaller household.

'Will you investigate my brother-in-law's death?' Rachel Fentiman asked him, fixing him with her compelling gaze.

He looked searchingly at her. 'Suppose I find that your sister did kill her husband?'

She made a dismissive gesture. 'Impossible. I know Alice could not have done it.'

Daniel Rokeby rose and took his hat. 'We're wasting our time here,' he said jerkily. 'There's got to be some other way.'

Jackman looked at Ursula. 'What do you think? Is it impossible that Mrs Peters killed her husband?'

Ursula started to pull her gloves back on. She mightn't have said anything so far but Thomas knew she had taken in every aspect of the little scene. She stood up. 'You asked what would happen if you found Alice Peters was guilty. You seem to be confident that you can discover the truth. Rachel is convinced her sister cannot have killed her husband. I trust both of you. Please, say you will do what she asks and investigate Joshua Peters' death.'

A little worm of excitement stirred in Jackman. He knew he wanted this case. Joshua Peters had been a bastard, as mean a bastard as he could remember meeting. He had grown ashamed to work for him. If Alice Peters hadn't been involved, he would have been happy to allow the bastard's killer to go free. But Thomas

agreed with the others. He did not believe Peters had been murdered by his wife and it sounded as though Everard Drummond
had decided that was exactly what had happened. However, best
not act too quickly. He had taken the job Peters had offered far
too lightly and look what had happened.

'I need to think about this,' he said slowly. 'All right if I come
round tomorrow morning and let you know?'

Rachel looked him squarely in the eye. 'You know where
I live so, yes, please do. What about your fee, though?'

'I'll let you know what it is if I accept the case,' he said.

Five minutes later they had left. On her way out, Ursula had
gripped his hand. 'Accept,' she said. 'I'll never believe Alice could
kill that awful man.' Then she followed the other two out.

After he had shut the front door, Thomas sat down and
reviewed what he had been told. It wasn't much. Did he believe
he could investigate the case? He wasn't in the police force any
longer. He had no official standing.

How much had Drummond managed to uncover over the last
three days? Had it really been enough to justify arresting Alice Peters?

Thomas rose, took his jacket and cap down from the coat rack
and put them on. Then he pulled his shirt cuffs clear of his jacket
sleeves and set out.

★ ★ ★

Every detective had his favourite pub and Everard Drummond's
was the *Coach and Horses* in the Strand, on the corner of a narrow
flight of steps down to the Embankment. Thomas walked
through Shoreditch and Holborn, moving rapidly along mean
streets he had once pounded as a uniformed constable; now he
needed to guard his pockets as he moved steadily amongst dubi-
ous locals until he reached the Strand, its wide street thronged
with slow moving traffic.

It was several months since he had visited the pub, not since
he had left the force, but it seemed little had changed. It was
crammed with a variety of drinkers, the air so thick with smoke
fumes and alcohol it was difficult to make out who was there.
Thomas could see nobs, no doubt on their way to the Savoy
Hotel, or maybe the next door Savoy Theatre, mingling with
clerks and salesmen reluctant to return to mean little homes, plus

lowlife on the watch for easy pickings, provided the pub was clear of constables and plainclothes detectives.

Thomas worked his way through the noisy crowd towards the back corner that was Drummond's favourite niche, tucked away so that snitches could have a private word.

There he was, right enough. Half-empty pint glass on the table in front of him, the fancy bowler with its curly brim on a hook just above his head; bright yellow hair slicked back, his lean figure resting easily against the padded banquette, cigar held negligently in hand, bold eyes surveying the bustle surging around him.

Fighting his way to the bar, Thomas bought a couple of pints, carried them over, placed them on the table, one in front of Drummond, and sat down, side on to his former colleague.

The bold eyes looked him up and down. 'So, back to your old stamping grounds is it, Jackman? How goes it with you?'

Thomas grinned. 'Can't complain. Trade's building nicely, thank you.' He raised his glass. 'Here's to you, old mate.'

Drummond finished off one glass and picked up the other. 'Here's to us both, me old codger.'

Thomas drank, lowered his beer and ran a finger round the rim of the glass. 'Gather you've gone up in the world, dealing with murder. It'll be Chief Inspector before we know it.'

A finger smoothed away beer foam from the yellow moustache and beard. The inspector's lips were astonishingly red against his facial hair. Someone had once pronounced that a moustache and beard added gravitas and Drummond had said he believed this. He smiled happily.

'Nice little case,' he said.

'Had dealings with the victim at one time; not the most pleasant of fellows.'

Drummond's eyes narrowed. 'Dealings, eh? Anything pertinent to my case?'

'Looking at his business, are you?'

Drummond gave a growl of laughter. 'Business? Nah, this is a domestic situation. Resentful wife does away with husband she's grown tired of. Wants to replace him with her lover.'

'Poison, wasn't it?'

Drummond puffed his cigar, the very picture of confidence. 'My, word does get around. Prussic acid it was. In chocolates. Woman's weapon.'

'Chocolates? Risky way of dealing death, ain't it?'

'Not if the victim puts the fear of God into any who sneak one from his box. That's how I know it's an inside job. Inside knowledge, you see. That and the fact odds are always on the nearest and dearest.'

Thomas drank thoughtfully. 'Remember that case in Islington? When all that prime silver got pinched? Everything seemed to point to an inside job there. Remember us arresting that dodgy footman and putting him inside?' He shot a sly look at Drummond. 'Then all the goods turned up in a stash at Jesse Johnson's, Jesse the West End grabber.'

'And didn't we get a slap on the back for nailing that cove!' The detective gave his cigar a congratulatory wave. Then he took a deep draught, wiped his moustache again and leaned confidingly towards Thomas, placing a fat finger against the side of his nose. 'This time there's proof.'

'Proof?'

'Can't argue with the written word. The wife put it all in her diary.'

'What, how she was going to rid herself of the husband? Every detail?'

Drummond placed both his hands against the edge of the table, fingers crab-like, his head leaning a little to one side, the very picture of a man who knows elements of his account aren't as watertight as he's making out. 'There's enough in it to hang her, I'd stake my reputation on it. And,' he added, pointing his cigar at Thomas, 'there's the evidence of the maid. Chapter and verse on the lover she's given us. Double timing her husband, Mrs Peters was. We got more than enough to clap Mrs-butter-wouldn't-melt-in-her-mouth-Peters inside.'

'Always need to consider the lover as the killer. Have you looked at him, Everard?'

Once again Drummond narrowed his eyes. 'What you on about, Jackman? Still trying to put one over on me, is that it? Always did want to put me down.'

Thomas adopted a hurt look. 'Only taking a sincere interest, nothing more, old mate. And no one could be more pleased with your success,' he added generously. 'After all, it shows I trained you well. Bet you had a fine old time interviewing all the staff.'

But the man had turned cagey. Thomas abandoned any attempt to obtain more information and spent twenty minutes or so asking about former colleagues and cases, careful to issue congratulations where they were called for and commiserate over shortfalls on the part of other officers. By the time he left the pub, relations between the two of them seemed satisfactorily warm again.

★ ★ ★

Back home, over reheated eel and oyster stew, he summed up the impressions he'd gained from both the trio of visitors and his chat with Detective Inspector Everard Drummond. Just as he'd suspected, the man was over-confident and the current case he had built against Alice Peters was leakier than a sieve. Joshua Peters had been a man who must have lined up more enemies than the Boer. To concentrate solely on his marriage was, in Thomas Jackman's opinion, a clear case of negligence.

The more he thought about the situation, the more Thomas wanted to get involved, to investigate. At the very least it would make him feel better about having worked for Joshua Peters, at best he might be able to prevent a miscarriage of justice.

Was he, he then wondered, convinced that Alice Peters was innocent? And what about Daniel Rokeby? Accessory? Murderer? He might have charmed Mrs Peters, but not Thomas Jackman. What he needed, Thomas decided, was a chat with Ursula Grandison. She was a woman of sense, one who seemed to have struck up quite an acquaintance with Alice Peters' sister. It was more than probable that she could provide a dispassionate view of Daniel Rokeby.

Satisfied he could get no further that evening, Thomas finished the last of the stew and lit a cigarillo (at least the fee Peters had paid him meant he could afford the odd luxury), puffing at it with deep contentment, feeling replete after one of the tastiest dishes he had had in a long time. Perhaps he should overcome his reservations about Betty Marks; a woman with her culinary talents had definite attractions as a companion.

Chapter Eleven

Once outside Thomas Jackman's small house, Rachel said there was no need to go to the expense of another hansom cab, if indeed they could find one in this part of London. There was a stop for an omnibus on the other side of the road.

As they waited, a crowd of drinkers erupted from the *Bottle and Glass* pub next door to the investigator's house. Dressed in workmen's clothes, with heavy boots on their feet, they were rowdy but unaggressive. There was much back slapping, calling of names and friendly insults.

'I am surprised at Mr Jackman residing in such an area,' Rachel said as they waited for their public transport. 'He cannot expect to attract much middle-class business. I am familiar with such areas through my work with the East End Charity hospital, but not many others will be.'

For the first time since meeting her, Ursula recognised how solidly middle class the girl was. She dropped a little in her estimation. A ragamuffin approached them, holding out a hand, his dirty face pinched with hunger. Rachel drew her skirts away from possible contact, then opened her purse and found a sixpence. Ursula added a few pennies she could barely afford but she knew what it was not to have enough food. Rachel looked at Daniel and, after a moment's hesitation, he too found some coins. The urchin's face lit with delight as he inspected his haul. 'Cor! It'll be pie tonight!' He ran off as though the money might be snatched back if he hung around. Rachel brushed her gloved hands together as though to remove dirt.

'No doubt,' Ursula said quietly, 'when Mr Jackman was a member of the police force, he found living here a fertile field for information.'

'And just why is he no longer with the force?' Daniel sounded suspicious and tetchy.

Ursula's explanation was interrupted by the arrival of an almost empty omnibus.

After they were settled along one of the benches, Daniel, hanging on to a strap in front of the two girls, said, 'We need a top lawyer, one conversant with criminal cases. Darling Alice must not remain in that terrible prison. I really do not think Jackman will be any help.'

More passengers embarked at the next stop, removing the little privacy they had enjoyed and conversation faltered and died.

Their journey terminated at Victoria station, ideal for Ursula. She turned to take her leave of Rachel and Daniel.

'You must not think I lack gratitude, Miss Grandison,' Daniel said with an obvious sincerity, taking her hand. 'It may be that your Mr Jackman will be able to uncover at least part of the mystery surrounding that beast's death. I really do hope so. Now, we cannot leave you to make your way home alone. Rachel and I will escort you. I believe it is not far from here.'

Ursula was touched. As the trio walked towards her boarding house, Daniel regaled them with details of a story he was working on for a monthly magazine. It was an historical fiction involving smugglers led by one Richard Wellbeloved, a Robin Hood type, pursued by Customs men as they try to land a cargo of brandy and lace. With the story unfinished, they reached Ursula's destination. He looked nervous and almost shy.

'Oh, Daniel, you are such a romantic,' said Rachel with a touch of irritation.

'You must let me know if it is printed, for I am sure I would enjoy reading such a story.' Ursula said, hoping she sounded sincere.

He smiled and for an instant she recognised the charm that had captivated Alice Peters.

Rachel turned to her. 'All my hopes are with Mr Jackman.'

Ursula nodded. 'Let me know if he takes your sister's case, won't you?'

Ursula waved goodbye and went into the boarding house. She was far too late for communal supper. Downstairs in the kitchen, Mrs Crumble was clearing up the last of the dishes.

'Where've you been, then?' she asked cheerfully, setting a large iron pot on its customary shelf. 'Mrs Maple was that worried, seeing as how you dashed off without saying you wouldn't be in for the meal.' The dark curls escaping her mob cap were damp with sweat but the strong arms handled the heavy pots without difficulty.

'I got involved in something that took much longer than I had foreseen, Mrs Crumble. I do apologise.'

Ursula hovered, wondering whether she could ask if there were leftovers.

In the rocking chair by the stove sat Meg with the kitchen mouser on her lap, her bony fingers gently stroking its tortoiseshell fur. 'Gorn upstairs. 'Ad a headache.'

Ursula murmured her regrets. The aroma of a beef stew hung in the kitchen air and hunger gnawed at her.

'I could find you a plate of something,' offered Mrs Crumble. 'That is, if you was hungry, Miss Grandison?'

Ursula nodded eagerly. The girl went to the larder and returned with a bowl of that night's beef stew, piling a goodly portion on a plate. Ursula refused the offer of it being warmed up; in her experience cold cooked beef was delicious.

'Shall I lay you a place in the dining room, Miss?'

'Would you mind if I ate it in here?' Ursula said, hesitantly. She didn't want to intrude on the maids' gossip.

'In the kitchen, Miss? We'd be honoured, wouldn't we, Meg?'

The woman nodded. 'Sit down there, Miss. I sits here with Tiddles.' Meg stroked the tabby cat, who screwed up its eyes in pleasure and twitched a lazy tail.

Ursula pulled out a chair and sat with her plate of beef. It had carrots, potatoes and small onions in with the meat and the gravy was thick and glossy. Mrs Crumble fetched cutlery, supplied some thick chunks of bread, a dish of butter, and a piece of cheese, then a glass of water.

'Sorry there ain't no cabbage left, Miss. Ate it all they did this evening.'

Ursula was not sorry. Vegetables were not the girl's strong point; they were usually overcooked and watery. Meat was a different matter.

'This is wonderful, Mrs Crumble. How do you get such a shine to the sauce?'

Mrs Crumble heaved the last of the cooking pots on to the shelf and wiped her hands down her apron. She beamed. 'Got to keep skimming the stew, you have. My nan taught me that.'

She removed her stained apron, filled the kettle and placed it on the well-blacked range. 'We'll have a nice cup of tea. Where you been, Miss?'

Ursula thought for a moment then decided there could be no harm in telling the truth. 'Do you remember Mrs Peters, who stayed here for a little while?'

Mrs Crumble, busy fetching the tea caddy, nodded. ''Course I do.'

Unexpectedly Meg said, 'Lovely, Mrs Peters was.' She stroked the cat more vigorously and it jumped down. 'Aw, don't do that, Tiddles.' The cat ignored her. 'Always writing, Mrs Peters was,' Meg added, her hands collapsed in her lap.

Ursula finished a mouthful of stew, her mind suddenly alive. 'You saw her writing, Meg?'

A decided nod.

'In a diary? A book, that is?'

An equally decided shake of the head. 'Naw, on paper. Letters.'

Ursula wondered who Alice had been writing to. The obvious answer would have been Daniel, but she hadn't known where he was. Perhaps the girl was writing to close friends. 'It's convenient to have that postbox on the corner,' she said slowly.

'Aw, she didn't post 'em.' Meg said.

'She didn't?'

'She burned 'em.'

'Burned them?'

'In her grate. Used matches, she did. Then she'd cry.'

Ursula wondered why the girl would go to the trouble of writing letters only to set fire to them. Had she been writing to Daniel after all, hoping she would find out where he was so she could send them? Then perhaps burned them when no address was forthcoming, in case they fell into the wrong hand.

'You saw her when you cleaned her room, is that it?'

Meg gave another vigorous nod. 'Left when I started cleaning. Put letters in drawer. Always writing she was,' she repeated. A sly look came over her face and she scrambled in a pocket of her crumpled dark grey cotton dress. 'Found this in her grate, I did.' She brought out a scrappy piece of paper, its edges singed brown.

'Lovely she was, Mrs Peters.' Meg smoothed the paper over her knee and peered down at it.

'What's it say?' asked Mrs Crumble, filling a teapot with boiling water and bringing it over to the table. 'Writing to her young man, was she?'

Meg looked closely at the paper, bending her head so she sat hunched. 'Can't read.' She held the paper out to Mrs Crumble. 'You read it.'

Mrs Crumble took the paper and held it carefully, scanning the words as though they were difficult to make out.

Ursula felt she should intervene. This was as bad as eavesdropping, especially as Alice had meant whatever she had written to be destroyed.

'I don't think …' she started.

But Mrs Crumble wasn't paying attention. '"you, my darling, I have worked it,"' she read in a monotone, each word given equal weight. 'The next word looks odd,' she said in a normal voice. 'I think a bit's been burned away. "aniel, I can do it, I know I can. It readful" – is that a word? Something to do with reading?' she asked Ursula.

Ursula thought for a moment. 'It might be "dreadful",' she said. 'The "d" could have got lost.'

'"aniel, I can do it, I know I can, dreadful, but then we can be free for" there's another bit must have gone. "He will be gone." That's it.' She turned the bit of paper over. 'Nothing on the other side. What do you think it means?' she handed Ursula the piece of paper.

'Here, it's mine,' said an agitated Meg. 'You had it to read, not give away.'

'You shall have it back,' Ursula said soothingly. 'I just want to see how much was burned.' The writing that was there was educated, the letters clearly formed, controlled but flowing attractively. No difficulty in reading them.

'Don't make much sense,' complained Mrs Crumble.

'Mrs Peters was planning to leave her husband and run away with the young man who came here, Daniel Rokeby.'

'Ooh, is that where she went when she left?' The cook sounded excited.

'No, she went back to her husband. She found she was …' Ursula paused for a moment as she sought for the right phrase.

'With child' sounded too biblical, and she was averse to 'in an interesting condition'; it was a ridiculous way of describing such a natural event. 'In the family way,' she came up with at last.

At least both women had no difficulty understanding what she meant.

'That's nice,' said Meg.

'Cripes!' said Mrs Crumble. 'And gone back to her husband? I thought she was escaping from him.'

Ursula swallowed an involuntary smile. Servants did indeed know everything that went on in the house where they worked, or nearly everything. Then she wondered what Mrs Crumble and Meg knew about her. But what was there to know?

'As he was the father, she thought it was her duty.'

'Treat her right, will he?' asked Meg, frowning in concentration and holding out her hand for the return of the piece of paper. 'Mrs Peters is nice.'

Ursula quickly memorised the few words on the scrap of paper and handed it back to Meg, watching her return it to her pocket.

'Wasn't burned,' Meg said. 'So it's mine.' Her tone was matter-of-fact rather than defensive.

Well, if Alice hadn't ensured all her pieces of paper had gone up in flames, then she had to accept the consequences.

Ursula thanked Mrs Crumble for her supper and went upstairs.

Up in her room, she found paper and pencil and reproduced as well as she could the words as they had appeared on the unburned portion of the letter. The first word did not start with a capital letter, which meant the first phrase was only part of a sentence:

'you, my darling, I have worked it'
'aniel, I can do it, I know I can. It'
'readful, but then we can be free for'
'He will be gone.'

She tore the left-hand side of the paper away, trying to copy the singed bit of the original. How much had been burned? Had the other part of it been wider than her piece, or narrower? With the missing words in place, could it be part of a letter explaining to Daniel that Alice could leave her husband and run away with him, so that they could be free to enjoy their lives together? But what did that last little phrase mean: 'He will be gone'?

★ ★ ★

Ursula had a largely sleepless night, tossing and turning as she tried to make sense of that scrap of paper. It was hopeless, and that last sentence haunted her.

Breakfast was almost over. The last of the other boarders left, finishing her tea standing up before uttering a muttered farewell.

Ursula wasn't due at Mrs Bruton's for another hour and was happy to enjoy some more toast and another cup of tea. She was beginning to appreciate this English habit. The brew was a great deal better than the stewed coffee she had had to endure in California.

There was a knock at the door and Ursula looked up in surprise as Thomas Jackman entered, very smart, wearing a brown suit with curved corners to the jacket and a starched wing collar to his blue shirt. His brown shoes were highly polished. His bowler in his hand, he looked pleased with himself.

'Good heavens,' she said, smiling. 'Mr Jackman. Will you sit down and take a cup of tea?'

'Thank you.' He placed the hat on the sideboard.

There was a spare clean cup on the table and Ursula poured the tea, adding milk and offering him sugar. He watched her with a slightly puzzled expression. 'Do you always add the milk after?' he asked, taking the cup.

Ursula nodded. She had seen the other boarders pour the milk into their cups before adding the tea but she had watched it being done the other way using cream at Mountstanton and it seemed a sensible procedure to her, allowing the strength of the brew to be assessed so the right amount of milk could be added.

'Are you on your way to Miss Fentiman's?'

He nodded.

'And you look as though you are going to accept the commission.' There was something about the confident way he lifted the cup and drank his tea that told her this. But maybe he always acted in this way. It struck Ursula how little she actually knew Thomas Jackman.

'Well, now, Miss Grandison, I would be grateful for a little information from you before I take the step of accepting the case.' He put down the cup and leaned back in his chair, sitting almost sideways on, one arm resting on the table.

Ursula raised an eyebrow at him. 'If there is anything I can tell you, please ask, but it is unlikely. You know the situation better than I, surely?'

His gaze remained level. 'Daniel Rokeby,' he said. 'What is your impression of that young man?'

'Ah, Daniel!' She paused for a moment. 'What, Jackman, are you actually asking me?'

His hand moved slightly as though her use of his surname disturbed him. It did make her sound as though she thought of him as a servant. She wondered why she had not called him 'Mr Jackman', or used his Christian name, as she had started to do at Mountstanton. It would have been more polite and more friendly.

'Do you, Thomas, think Daniel might have murdered Joshua Peters?'

His bright eyes gave her a sardonic look, as though he understood exactly why she had used his given name. 'Well, Ursula, Daniel Rokeby had everything to gain by Peters' death. What I am asking is, do you consider him capable of the deed?'

She looked down at the half piece of toast left on her plate. 'He's a bit of a puzzle,' she said slowly. 'One moment he seems a charming, intelligent, quite sophisticated young man; the next he's arrogant, unthinking and immature. But you must have seen more of him than I during your tailing of Alice Peters. What is your opinion?'

He eased the set of his wing collar. Ursula had always thought there could be few more uncomfortable items of male clothing than those collars, starched and fashioned into a knifelike sharpness.

'Before last night, whenever I have seen Mr Rokeby, he has been lavishing charm on Mrs Peters, who is a very pretty woman.'

'Would you say he was genuinely in love with her?'

Jackman gave her a sidelong look. 'Perhaps,' he said slowly. 'Together they seemed to inhabit a bubble, cutting out everything around them, no matter where they were.'

Ursula remembered the mention of Millie Rudge during the meeting at his house. 'You told me you'd made friends with Alice's maid? Did you ask her what she thought her mistress felt for the man she was constantly meeting?'

'I did indeed. She thought Mrs Peters was in love in a way she had never been with her husband.' He leaned slightly towards Ursula. 'So, do you think Rokeby capable of murder?'

She sighed. 'How is one to tell? He hasn't given the impression that a killing instinct lurks beneath the surface. But, maybe, if he

wanted something strongly enough ...' She thought of something else. 'Didn't you think it odd how he took against you so
immediately?'

'If I was a man full of myself, which I assure you I am not, I'd
be tempted to the conclusion he was guilty of the crime and
afraid I would nobble him.'

Ursula had thought the same.

'Do you think he could be that devious?' Jackman asked.

She gave the question careful thought. 'My instinct says it is
unlikely but, then, I really haven't seen much of him.' She remembered his passion the afternoon he had returned from the Lake
District and taken Alice out into the square's garden. 'I think that
devising murder through poisoned chocolates requires a much
more malevolent character than Daniel's.'

Should she tell him about the scrap of singed paper Meg had
found? No, she decided, not until she had figured out the exact
meaning of what was there. For Alice seemed the least malevolent person she had ever met. There had to be some other reason
than the obvious for the words that had been written.

Jackman picked up his bowler. 'Ursula Grandison, my thanks
for your opinion. I shall now visit Miss Fentiman and tell her
I shall take the case.' He put his hat on his head, slightly too far
back. It gave him an oddly rakish look.

'Thomas Jackman, I hope what I said can be of use.'

He gave her a slight bow and left.

Ursula sat at the table for a few more minutes, then realised
she ran the risk of being late for Mrs Bruton. Running upstairs
to ready herself, she found not having told Jackman about the
bit of paper was becoming increasingly difficult to handle. Why
hadn't she told him? Was it because she thought he would jump
to the wrong conclusions? That would mean she did not trust
him. But would they be the wrong conclusions? Was she trying
too hard to believe Alice Peters could not be guilty of her husband's murder?

Chapter Twelve

Millie woke with a start. For a moment she thought she'd heard that horror-filled scream that had broken into her sleep ten days earlier.

She had sat up in bed, every nerve quivering. Surely it must have woken the whole household. She rose, pulled on her cotton dressing gown and her slippers then ran down the stairs to the drawing room.

Outside the door, she had hesitated. What if burglars had broken in and were stealing the silver? But it was six o'clock in the morning, and any self-respecting burglar would be long gone. Quietly she entered. Sarah stood rigid in the middle of the floor, the bucket of coal on its side, nuggets and dust all over the carpet.

'What's happened?' Millie cried.

Sarah pointed at the wing chair by the fire, the chair that Joshua Peters always sat in. And there he was, his face contorted with pain, his body flexed into an extraordinary position, his eyes – oh his eyes! Millie thought she would be haunted by the agony in those eyes to her dying day.

She had had hysterics.

★ ★ ★

Millie Rudge was born ambitious. Her mother had encouraged her. 'You're bright, you can go far. Perhaps even end up house-keeper to a large household,' she said.

Millie, though, soon singled out the position of lady's maid as her aim. It had status, was apart from the general household servants, meant you didn't have to wear a uniform, and brought perks such as beautiful clothes casually donated by a mistress to a loyal maid, who could wear or, more usefully, sell them.

She had always been good with her needle and she set herself to learn the accomplishments needed to make her a skilled lady's maid: hairdressing – the other maids she worked with proved willing models – the care and washing of special materials such as silks, lace, cashmere and others. She discovered which magazines reported on the latest fashions, made friends with a seamstress and learned how to create patterns that would capture a particular look.

By the time Millie was twenty-four, she reckoned she was fully equipped and took herself off to an employment agency for household staff. They had just received a request from Mrs Joshua Peters for an efficient lady's maid.

'I think we shall deal well together,' Mrs Peters had said at the end of the interview. Millie thought so too. Softly spoken, sweet-faced, with a sympathetic manner, this seemed a mistress from heaven. No doubt the woman had little ways that could make her difficult but Millie reckoned she could deal with them.

Mr Peters also interviewed her and she was not so sure about him. He had dark, brooding eyes and a cold, incisive voice that questioned her qualifications. He wasn't a tall man but his compact body exuded a sense of power that was unsettling.

'Fail my wife in any department and you're out,' he said, looking at Millie in a way that made her feel like she was up for sale in some slave market. 'She has the impression you will be the perfect lady's maid. Prove it and you'll be rewarded. Understand?'

Millie had dipped a little curtsy and told him she did, hoping she was not, after all, making a major mistake.

The Peters household was not as large as the one Millie had imagined herself joining, and her room was small, but at least it was her own. She never wanted to have to share with another maid again.

'Hope you'll be an improvement on your predecessor,' sniffed Albert after Mrs Peters had introduced her to the other staff.

'Heard she'd proved unsatisfactory,' Millie offered, summing him up with one look: too pleased with himself and not much to be pleased about. Medium height, too-close-together pale eyes, sharp nose and carefully slicked-back dark hair. Nor did she think much to his red and orange striped waistcoat. Did he think he was some sort of dandy? She twinkled at him, 'Shall try my best.'

The female staff were less challenging. Chief was Mrs Firestone, the cook; there was no housekeeper. Her food wasn't the best Millie had eaten but it was a long way from the worst. And she was efficient and a worker. She organised her scullery maid with a rough kindness that ensured Abby understood what was expected of her and did her tasks to Mrs Firestone's high standards.

Emily Barker was the senior upstairs maid. Her face might be plain but her character was warm and friendly. Millie felt it was important she maintained her dignity with her, though she was willing to chat in a way that demonstrated she regarded Emily as almost on her level – but not quite. Sarah, the under-housemaid, was another matter. With her, Millie enjoyed paying back the slights she had received at the start of her career in service.

Sam, 'the Odd Man', though he was little more than a boy, Millie paid no attention to at all.

Out running an errand for her mistress one day, Millie had tripped in a busy street and someone had run off with her purse. Before she'd had time to shout 'stop, thief,' the ruffian had been tackled and her property returned to her. She gave her rescuer a sweet smile.

'Joe Banks,' he introduced himself. 'It seems to me as you need a little looking after, pretty girl like you out on her own.'

He had a twinkle in his eye that was very attractive. Millie had spent a long time fending off fellow staff members in various households, together with disdaining approaches made by such members of the opposite sex as she came into contact with from time to time. Now, though, almost without realising, Millie found herself dropping her guard and accepting Joe Banks's invitation to a walk in the park on her afternoon off. After all, no harm could come to her in such a public place.

It was not only the delicious combination of Joe's twinkling brown eyes and the way he married an obvious admiration of her looks with proper respect for her person that was attractive; Mrs Peters had recently stopped taking her maid with her when she went out shopping for fashion accessories, visited charity sales, exhibitions, or just for some exercise. This meant Millie had time to herself and a feeling she was being slightly ill done by.

'Makes me wonder if she's not up to something,' she confided to Joe when he persuaded her to visit a music hall with him a couple of nights later. He was so easy to talk to and it wasn't as though he had any contact with the Peters household and could pass on any information she gave him. Between the acts he kept her in constant hilarity with jokes and gossip about the performers. Normally Millie didn't drink alcohol but somehow a glass of champagne was produced and it seemed only polite to drink it.

'What time's your lady expecting you on duty this evening?' he asked as another glass of champagne appeared.

She giggled. 'She hardly ever wants me to wait up for her, not unless she's got masses of back buttons. She and the master have gone to a dinner tonight and then on to a ball. Mrs Peters said it was a Guild affair. Said she had to look her best for the master and though I say it as shouldn't, she looked a picture when I'd finished with her. Her gown fastened in the front so she said she wouldn't need me when they got back.'

Joe had wanted to know what her master was like.

'I've been there nearly a year but I don't see much of him. Leaves the house early in the morning, back after I've got Mrs Peters ready for the evening. She's a pleasure to dress, nice figure and knows how to wear clothes. 'Course I guide her over what new fashions will suit her. She told me Mr Peters said as how she looks much more fashionable since I came.' She drank a little more of the champagne, liking the way the bubbles teased at her throat.

'Well-matched couple, are they?' Joe asked.

If it hadn't been for the champagne, Millie mightn't have been so frank. 'He's much older than she is. She always seems to do what he says but there are times when I think she doesn't like it.'

'Rough with her, is he?'

Millie was shocked. 'Oh, no!' Then she thought for a moment. 'There was that time she told me she'd tripped on the staircase and bruised her cheek on the banisters. Almost a black eye she had.'

'Had she cheeked him?' Joe joked, then said, 'My big mouth; shouldn't have said that.'

'No, you shouldn't,' agreed Millie. Joshua Peters was a daunting master yet somehow exciting as well. 'He's always polite to me,' she added.

Then, suddenly, it seemed to Millie, events moved so fast she could hardly keep up. First, Mrs Peters disappeared without a word, Mr Peters spent the afternoon looking for her, then Millie had to undergo a blistering interrogation from him. He seemed unable to believe she didn't know where her mistress was.

'Please, sir. I promise you Mrs Peters didn't say a word to me.' Millie looked at him imploringly. 'You have to believe me.'

He put a finger underneath her chin and forced her to look at him. She stood with her hands clasped behind her back, staring him in the eyes. And suddenly he laughed and spoke in quite a different voice.

'No, you wouldn't lie to me, would you, Millie?'

Two days later it was as though he'd forgotten all about Mrs Peters and for some dazzling days it seemed as though Millie's ambitions need know no bounds. She hardly noticed that Joe Banks was no longer around.

Then, no sooner had her world been transformed than everything changed once again. Her mistress walked in and said she had had to have some medical treatment.

Millie was staggered by the way Mr Peters seemed to accept this story, and how Mrs Peters managed to stick to the details she'd given. Almost immediately, though, it became clear what she had been talking about.

Tightening her mistress's corset every day as she did, it was not difficult to notice a thickening of a waistline she knew as well as her own.

The woman's effrontery almost struck Millie dumb. Persuading your husband the child you were expecting was his when all the while it had been fathered by a lover! Alice Peters, she decided, was a bitch of the first water. And Joshua Peters not nearly as bright as she'd thought. How could he be so gentle with his wayward wife? It was as though he had flicked a switch. You'd think his attention had never strayed to another woman.

Filled with bitterness, Millie started to search for the diary she had so often seen her mistress writing in. If she could find that and show it to Joshua Peters, then surely he would have to accept what had been going on.

Then had come the dreadful morning when she had been faced with the sight of her master in a death agony. She had been so upset, Emily had had to take on the task of waking Mrs Peters and giving her the awful news that her husband had died of what looked like a heart attack.

★ ★ ★

Chaos had ensued. It had taken the arrival of Mrs Peters' sister, Miss Fentiman, and her aunt, Mrs Trenchard, for some sort of order to emerge. Mrs Peters had been given a hefty dose of laudanum by the doctor and slept the day away.

Late that afternoon, still numb with the events of the morning, Millie had tried to tidy up Mrs Peters' boudoir but found she was too clumsy to do much good. So clumsy that she knocked over the chair that stood by the desk. Righting it, Millie noticed that the seat was loose. Underneath she found Mrs Peters' diary resting on a false bottom.

Restoring the seat to its rightful place, Millie sat on it and opened the diary. She went back to the weeks when her mistress had abandoned the habit of taking her maid when going around London. She read carefully, following the words with her forefinger. It was full of descriptions of the handsome young man who was a friend of her sister's and had declared he was wildly in love with her. She had never, Alice declared to her diary, felt anything like this before.

Suddenly a phrase leaped out at Millie: *If only I could be free of this terrible marriage.*

In the pages that followed there was more.

Millie felt as though a volcano was erupting in her stomach and she started to shake. Once again she saw the look of agony in Joshua Peters' staring eyes that morning.

Then Sarah came upstairs. 'The police are here, Millie. They're taking away the master, they think he's been poisoned.' The girl seemed torn between excitement and terror. 'They want to see us all in the kitchen.'

Poisoned! Millie picked up the diary. 'I'll see she gets what's coming to her,' she said to no one in particular since Sarah had gone already. She went downstairs and asked to see the inspector in charge in private.

★ ★ ★

With the arrest of Alice Peters, the Montagu Place household threatened to disintegrate. None of the staff could believe what was happening.

Millie spent most of her time in her room practising dressing in her mistress's clothes. For she had received an invitation, one she intended to accept. She wished, though, she wasn't waking every morning thinking she heard Sarah's scream again.

'It's a ship what's lost its pilot,' said Mrs Firestone. It was midday. Few of the daily routine tasks had been accomplished. As usual, though, everyone had gathered in the kitchen for dinner. The end

bits of a leg of ham had been served with boiled potatoes. They'd finished with a dried piece of cheddar cheese and oatcakes. Millie could
not make herself eat more than a mouthful or two. The volcano
inside her churned, a deadly mixture of anger laced with bitterness.

'Hardly up to your usual standard, Cook,' said Albert.

'You're unlikely to have to eat Mrs Firestone's cooking for
much longer,' Millie said spitefully.

He turned his unemotional fish eyes on her. 'Meaning?'

'Why, with no master to attend to and run errands for, you
won't have a place. That's all.' She reached into her sewing bag
and removed a crepe de chine bodice trimmed with Venetian
lace and turned her attention to repairing a minute tear.

'With no mistress to attend, you won't have a place either,'
Albert said smoothly.

'Don't know why you're bothering to mend that,' Sam the
young 'Odd Man' said quietly.

Millie, who had designs on the bodice and its matching skirt
for herself, said nothing.

Cook interrupted her pouring out of cups of tea and rapped
the table with a knife. 'Now, I won't hear this sort of talk in my
kitchen. Mrs Peters will be set free any day now. The very idea of
her doing away with the master is nonsense.'

'Only way she'll find freedom,' said Albert unemotionally, 'is
via the hangman's rope. There's a place in hell being prepared for
her now.'

'Oooh, you can't say that,' Sarah protested. 'Mrs Peters
couldn't … well, couldn't do what they said she did.'

Millie could bear it no longer. 'How do you know? She ran away,
didn't she? Left a husband who showered her with everything.'

'As you should know,' put in Albert, *sotto voce*. 'A jealous bitch,
that's what you are.'

Millie rounded on him. 'Yes, I know everything he gave her. All the
dresses and the jewels. I saw them, didn't I? Took care of them. And
then, when she realises the stupid mistake she's made, she comes back.'

'And a right blow that was to some,' muttered Albert again.

'We knows why she did,' put in Mrs Firestone. 'Because she's a
decent soul. Thought a father should bring up his child.'

'*His* child?' screamed Millie, throwing down her sewing. 'How
could he know that? He was a fool and he signed his own
death warrant.'

'Whoever did it,' put in Emily peaceably, 'did us all a favour. He was a nasty man.'

Albert rose. 'I can't listen to such vile things. I have errands to run. I'll be back for supper and shall expect better than the muck we've just had.'

'I does my best with what I has,' said Mrs Firestone. 'Larder's nearly empty, I'm not being given any more money and our credit's exhausted. I'm at my wit's end what to feed us on tonight.'

Through the turmoil of her anger, Millie heard a low gasp from the others. She found it as difficult as they obviously did to accept what she'd heard. Food in a household like this, even under the present circumstances, was taken for granted. Albert, though, appeared unmoved as he left the kitchen.

High up on the wall, the front doorbell jangled. Everyone looked at it for a moment without moving.

'Just as I've settled to my tea,' said Emily. She put the saucer on top of her cup.

'I'll go,' said Sarah. She rose, adjusting her cap.

A few minutes later she was back with Mrs Peters' aunt, Mrs Trenchard, a familiar figure, and an unknown gentleman.

The servants all rose to their feet.

'Sit, please,' said Mrs Trenchard. 'I have something to say.'

'I hope it is something that will replenish my larder,' Mrs Firestone muttered.

Millie hardly heard her, she was staring at the man who had accompanied her. Give him a moustache and brush his hair down across his forehead ...

'I know how concerned you all are for your mistress,' Mrs Trenchard was saying. 'And I am sure you will be as pleased as I am that Thomas Jackman, the renowned ex-Detective Inspector of Scotland Yard's Metropolitan Police, has agreed to investigate my brother-in-law's tragic demise.' She turned to the man standing at her side. 'Mr Jackman, will you please tell the staff how your investigation will be conducted.'

'I shall interview each of you in turn,' he said.

'I, of course, will be present,' said Mrs Trenchard.

Millie struggled to her feet. The man's accent was different but there was something about the voice that removed any doubt. 'That's no detective,' she screamed. 'That's Joe Banks.'

Chapter Thirteen

Thomas Jackman sat himself behind Joshua Peters' desk and arranged his notebook and a set of pencils on the green leather. He was not happy.

When Mrs Trenchard had announced that she would sit in on the interviews, he had murmured that that would not be necessary.

Then Millie Rudge had made her hysterical accusation and, Emily, the senior housemaid, had slapped her across the face. 'I'm sorry,' she'd said to Millie, rigid with shock. 'Only it had to be done.'

'Take her somewhere and calm her,' Mrs Trenchard had instructed.

It had not been Jackman's idea that Mrs Trenchard should introduce him to the household. He had imagined that Miss Fentiman would do that. On arrival at her home to announce that he would take on the investigation, though, Mrs Trenchard had been visiting and had taken charge.

Miss Fentiman had tried her best. 'Aunt, I really think I should accompany Mr Jackman to Montagu Place. You are far too busy.'

'Nonsense, Rachel. You are too young to have the authority that is needed for such action.'

And that had been that. Now Sarah, the younger of the two housemaids, had scuttled up the stairs ahead of him into the main part of the house, opened the study door, stood back as he entered, then scuttled away again, looking terrified. Mrs Trenchard was now sorting out the order in which the servants would be interviewed. That again was something Jackman had wanted to arrange.

Now he was forced to wait and see who she would bring in. Well, he would just have to make the best of it.

He sat in Joshua Peters' chair and took in the study's atmosphere. Normally an investigator who relied on evidence, he felt vibrating on the room's gloomy air the anger of the man who had died. Had it all been directed towards the wife he believed was betraying him? Or were there others who had suffered from his animosity?

And what about the wife? Was Alice Peters as innocent as her sister seemed to believe?

Thomas sat back and ran his hands over the green leather surface of the desk. It was an imposing piece of furniture: polished mahogany with a set of drawers each side and one in the middle. Nicely turned brass handles together with a keyhole were affixed to each. He opened the middle drawer. He would not have been surprised to find it empty, cleared by Detective Inspector Everard Drummond. Instead it held a manilla folder. Inside was a collection of yacht brochures. Which was something of a surprise; Jackman had not thought of Joshua Peters as a sailing type. There was a scribble on the top of one, something like: 'Meyer …' but the rest was impossible to read.

He started opening the pedestal sets of drawers. Most of them were empty. Thomas wondered if they had contained documents or letters that the police investigation had removed. The bottom drawers, deeper than the ones above, had thin lateral dividers, presumably for the purpose of aiding a logical storage of files and papers.

In the interest of speed, Jackman had used both hands to draw out matching sets of drawers, pushing them back into place once he had seen they were empty. They moved in and out of the desk quite easily. Except for the large bottom drawer on the left that seemed heavy and difficult to pull out.

Jackman tugged harder. Something was preventing it moving beyond a certain point. He knelt down to inspect what it was.

At that moment, the study door opened. Through the well of the desk he saw Mrs Trenchard's green linen skirt and the dark grey cotton skirt and white apron of one of the maids.

'Mr Jackman?' asked a puzzled Mrs Trenchard.

Cursing that he had allowed himself to be found in this position, he stood up.

The young maid gave a squawk of fright.

'Now, now, Sarah,' said Mrs Trenchard. 'Sit there, girl, in front of the desk. Mr Jackman, I will sit here, beside you.'

It was time to take control.

Jackman picked up the chair Mrs Trenchard intended sitting on and placed it in a corner on the other side of the room. 'From here you can keep a perfect eye on all the proceedings,' he said firmly. 'I find it is best in these circumstances if those being questioned have only one person in their line of sight.'

He held her gaze with his.

After a moment, she gave a graceful nod.

'Thank you, Madam. Now, miss, if you could please sit here, as suggested.'

She gave a nervous glance at Mrs Trenchard, now sitting in the corner, then perched herself on the edge of the chair.

Jackman sat again behind the desk, opened his notebook and picked up a pencil. He consulted the list of staff he'd made. Her age made it quite clear who she was.

'Now, you are Sarah Taylor, the under-housemaid, is that correct?'

She nodded.

'And you have been working here how long?'

She considered for a little, then said, 'One year, sir, and two months.'

He judged he'd given her enough time to feel a little settled and looked straight at her. Sarah Taylor was a slight girl with wispy hair, a cap that wasn't on straight and a soiled and creased apron. 'Now, you understand that I am here to see if I can discover how your master, Mr Peters, died?'

She still looked scared. 'Oh, sir, when you rose up like that, I thought you was he, come back to shout at me again.'

'Again?'

Sarah sat up a little straighter. 'I came in one time without knocking when I thought the room was empty ...' she paused.

Thomas smiled encouragingly at her.

'And he was on the floor, just as you was now, and rose up – just as you did – and shouted at me something terrible. Said I had to go without a reference.' She took a deep breath then seemed to gather confidence. 'Only the mistress came in and said what on earth was the matter? And when he said it was none of her business she said that housemaids was her business.' Sarah paused, seemingly lost in awe of how her mistress had faced up to her furious husband.

'And when he said I'd not knocked at the door before entering, the mistress said that was wrong and she'd speak to me but that it was not a hanging offence. Them's were the very words she used, sir:"Not a hanging offence."' Sarah burst into tears.'Oh, sir, they're not going to hang her, are they? Only Albert said they were.'

Mrs Trenchard rose. Jackman shook his head at her and after a moment she sat down again.

'That's why I'm here,' he said, making a note.'Am I right in thinking that you do not believe Mrs Peters poisoned her husband?'

Sarah found a handkerchief from somewhere and wiped her eyes. She twisted the linen in her hands and nodded vigorously. 'She couldn't, sir, not her!'

'Can you think why anybody would?'

'He was an awful man, sir.' She spoke with simple conviction.

'Awful because he shouted and threatened you with dismissal?'

She appeared to have forgotten about Mrs Trenchard.'He was always telling us we hadn't done things right. Everyone that is, except Albert. He'd say it in such a way – as though there was something really nasty inside him and he had to let it out. I left a brush in the drawing room hearth once and he threw it at me.'

'Very upsetting,'Thomas commented.'Did he threaten to dismiss you then as well?'

'No, sir.' The girl twisted the handkerchief again then gave Jackman an injured look.'He never thanked you, never thanked anyone. Mrs Peters always thanks you, whatever you've done.'

Jackman thought for a moment.'Tell me, Sarah, do you know if the drawers in this desk are usually kept locked?'

She looked scared again.'I wouldn't know, sir. I only passes the duster over the front of them. More than my life's worth to see if they'd open.'

'Of course, silly question.'

'Albert would know.'

'Albert?'

'The master's man, sir. He's called the valet but he does all sorts of things; runs errands, orders wine and spirits. He's always in here. Keeps the master's papers straight.'

'Sounds like more of a secretary than a valet.'

'He's called a valet.'

'And you say that Mr Peters didn't shout at him the way he did at everyone else?'

Sarah nodded, silent, her eyes wide.

'The only male in the kitchen when I arrived was a very young man, was that Albert?'

'Oh, no, sir. That's Sam, the Odd Man.'

'Odd Man?'

'Sam does all the odd things, you see. Bringing in coal and wood, keeping the kitchen stove stoked up, shining the shoes, running errands for Cook, that sort of thing.'

Jackman leaned back in his seat. 'Please, Sarah, take me through what happened the morning your master's body was found. It was you who discovered him, wasn't it?'

She gave a little, shuddering gasp. 'Yes, sir,' she whispered. 'I went into the drawing room with the coal bucket to lay the fire; now the nights are drawing in, it's lit most evenings. I didn't notice him at first and when I did it was, ooh, such a shock. I couldn't help screaming. And then Millie runs down and she's hysterical. Then Emily comes in and she wakes the mistress and sends Sam for the doctor. Not that there was any chance he was anything but dead.'

'Was Albert there?'

Sarah shook her head.

'Where was he? As valet to Mr Peters, would he not have discovered his master wasn't in his bed?'

'Dunno, sir. He came in later, after the doctor 'ad been an' all.'

'Were you there when he heard the news?'

Sarah nodded. 'We was all in the kitchen. All except Sam 'cos he'd been sent with a note from the mistress to 'er sister, Miss Fentiman. Cook was making us a cup of tea. There'd been such comings and goings and it was ten o'clock, when we usually had a cuppa, and Cook said we needed it. And she was right,' the maid added with quaint emphasis.

'So, there you were in the kitchen and Albert comes in? From the basement entrance?'

'Oh, yes, sir. We all uses that one. We're not allowed in or out of the front door.'

'And what happens then?'

Sarah looked puzzled. 'Nothing 'appens, sir.'

Jackman took a deep breath. He spoke slowly. 'I mean, who told Albert about Mr Peters?'

'Oh, that was Cook. Comes right out with it, she does. Did 'e know that the master was dead? she says.'

'And how did Albert react?'

Sarah looked struck by a sudden thought. 'It was as if 'e 'adn't 'eard. Just stood there while we all looks at 'im. Then 'e said "Dead?" and suddenly sits down. It was as if 'e couldn't see nothing. Not any of us; not the kitchen; nothing.'

'Do you like Albert, Sarah?'

She appeared to be completely as ease now. 'Like 'im? Well, sir, Albert's not really the sort you like. Very private 'e is. But I couldn't say I dislikes 'im. I mean, 'e's just there.'

'How long did Albert remain looking at nothing?'

'Not above a few moments. Then 'e says 'e wants to see Mr Peters. But Emily says 'e can't 'cos the doctor 'as locked the drawing room door and taken away the key. 'E said 'e had to report a … a sudden death I think 'e said.'

'So what did Albert do then?'

There was no hesitation about Sarah now. And Mrs Trenchard appeared to be riveted by what she was hearing. 'Gets up, says 'e's going to the study to sort out the master's papers and no one was to disturb 'im.'

Did he indeed! And where were those papers now?

'What did everyone else do?'

Sarah thought for a few moments. 'Millie was still being hysterical every ten minutes or so. I'd taken the mistress some breakfast in the morning room, but she didn't seem in any state to eat, not any state to do anything. She said the doctor had given her something to make her sleep but she wasn't going to take it, she needed to be able to sort out what had to be done. But she was in no state to do that to my way of thinking. Sam said he was going to make sure all the master's shoes were polished.' She thought for a moment. 'Don't know why, not as if he was going to wear them. And then Miss Fentiman arrives and she takes control.' Sarah sounded truly thankful that this had happened.

'What do you know about the box of cherry liqueur chocolates?'

'Me? I don't know nothing, sir.'

'Do you know when it arrived?'

'No sir.'

'Was it delivered by hand, or did it arrive by post?'

Sarah shook her head. Her composure had vanished and her voice wobbled. 'I don't know nothing, sir, as I said,' her voice rose to a wail and she burst into tears.

Mrs Trenchard rose. 'That is quite enough, Mr Jackman. Sarah, you can go back to the kitchen now. Tell Cook I said you should have another cup of tea.'

'Yes, mum.' Sarah gave a quick bob and scuttled out of the door.

Thomas rose and looked at Mrs Trenchard standing with her back straight as a board, and reckoned there was trouble ahead.

'I would like to question the senior housemaid now, Emily, I think her name is.'

'There will be no more questioning of the staff, Mr Jackman.'

'You'd prefer I waited until tomorrow, Mrs Trenchard?'

Her pale grey eyes acquired a gimlet quality. 'I mean, there will be no more questioning at all.'

'But …'

'First you send my niece's personal maid into hysterics, and then you reduce little Sarah to tears. I cannot allow this sad household to be treated so shamefully.'

Her voice was implacable.

'Mrs Trenchard, your niece, Miss Fentiman, has commissioned me to investigate how her brother-in-law met his death. In order to do this, I have to talk to everyone who was in this house at the time.'

'The police have done that. Miss Fentiman believes there are questions to be asked concerning Joshua Peters' life outside his home. That is where you should be investigating.'

And wasn't that what his immediate thought had been when he'd found how little Everard Drummond had looked into the business life of the murdered man?

'I have to be able to dismiss the members of the household from any involvement, Mrs Trenchard,' he said, trying for a tone of respect mingled with authority.

The door opened and Sarah reappeared. 'Please, mum, Cook says as how she must have words with you.'

There came a shout from the kitchen area, a long-drawn out 'Saraaaaaaaah'.

'Oh, mum, please come. Cook's in a right state.' She stood just inside the door, holding on to the handle, her face pleading.

Mrs Trenchard hesitated.

There came another yell from downstairs.

'All right, Sarah, I'll come and sort out whatever it is Cook needs.' She looked at Jackman. 'You will remain here until I return.

The moment she had swept out of the room, Jackman sat down with a sense of relief. For an instant he wished he was back in the police force with all its authority behind him.

Then he pulled again at the left-hand bottom drawer of the desk. Mrs Trenchard was unlikely to take long to sort out Cook. After that, he was next in line.

The drawer still stuck. He knelt down and gently manoeuvred it. Then slipped his hand over the back partition and found there was a catch. Pressing it down released the drawer. Jackman pulled it out to its fullest, revealing a hidden section.

The first thing he saw was a jar. He picked it up and looked at the fancy label: *Crème de Printemps*. He unscrewed the lid and revealed a gentle swirl of soft white cream. A sniff caught a delicate perfume that suggested a spring garden.

Thomas wondered if Joshua Peters used the secret compartment to hide presents he had bought for his wife. Or perhaps for another woman? He put the jar on the desk, examined the depths of the drawer and brought up a dirty-looking bundle of dark material. It was unexpectedly heavy and certainly didn't smell of a spring garden.

Unwrapping the bundle carefully, knowing from its feel what he would find, he revealed a Webley Mk1 revolver, almost identical to the one supplied to the police force. Thomas had never had to fire his in the line of duty but constant practise had made him familiar with the weapon. The barrel was empty. He looked again in the drawer but couldn't see any bullets or cleaning materials. Was Albert, the valet, responsible for looking after this as he did so many other matters in the Peters household?

Thomas heard the sound of Mrs Trenchard's voice, hastily rewrapped the gun and returned it to the drawer. The jar of cream, though, he put in his pocket.

Chapter Fourteen

Ursula's walk that morning to Mrs Bruton's was not as pleasant as usual. The good weather had broken and she pulled her jacket close around her against a nasty wind that spat rain.

'Time you got an umbrella,' said Mrs Evercreech as she entered the kitchen and removed her wet hat.

'And more practical headgear,' Ursula said, inspecting the damp straw. 'A beret, perhaps?' she suggested, a vision of Rachel in her large, floppy version floating before her. 'Is there a corner I can leave this to dry out?'

'Put it in the scullery, dear. Don't want to run the risk of cooking drips on it, do we? And better hang your jacket there too. Madam's got a visitor for lunch today.'

'One of her charitable ladies?' Ursula slipped out of her damp outer garment, wondering if by any chance it would be Mrs Trenchard. If it was, maybe she could provide news of Alice.

'It's her son!' said Enid unexpectedly.

'Her son?' It was the first Ursula had heard of any offspring of Mrs Bruton.

'Now, you know that's not right,' Mrs Evercreech said, beating her mixture. 'And get the tray ready for morning coffee, Enid. You know Madam likes it served as soon as Miss Grandison arrives.'

Cook placed her bowl to one side and reached for the coffee pot. 'Mr Bruton is Madam's stepson, visiting from Manchester.'

Ursula tidied her hair, feeling for where strands had escaped from the knot she kept it drawn back in at the nape of her neck, simple and neat, except the heavy hair constantly needed the replacement of pins. 'How nice for her,' she said neutrally.

Enid's long face grimaced. 'Madam's always in a right temper after he's been.'

'Don't you go speaking like that, you should know better, girl.' But the reprimand sounded almost automatic and Enid rolled her eyes at Ursula in a resigned way as she placed a silver tray on the kitchen table.

'Wish it was that count fellow. She couldn't have been nicer after he'd been yesterday. Gave me such a pretty blouse, hardly worn it was. Miss Huckle was in a right strop; reckon she'd had her eye on it for herself.'

'Stop your gossiping and sort out the cups.' Cook started cracking eggs and separating yolks from whites.

'A count?'

'Foreign he was. Ever so charming. Smiled at me as I handed him his hat.' Enid stood with a cup in either hand for a moment.

'Well it isn't him as is coming. So get on, do. I got the anchovy sauce to make for this spinach soufflé, and you better make sure everything upstairs is in apple-pie order.'

'Done that. More than my life's worth if there's a speck of dust when Mr Bruton is coming.' Enid placed the coffee cups gently on their saucers.

Ursula gave her a smile and nodded at Cook as she left the kitchen. She met Mrs Bruton coming down to the hall arrayed in a sober grey suit, her white silk blouse trimmed with a minute amount of lace, her only jewellery a pair of stud gold earrings. She looked distrait.

'Ah, Miss Grandison, I need you to sort through some business papers. Mr Bruton's son is to have luncheon with me today and will ask to see them.' She led the way into the back room where Ursula worked. It had a large, breakfront bookcase with glass doors above and commodious cupboards below. So far in her employment, Ursula had not been made acquainted with their contents. Mrs Bruton extracted a small key from a pocket in her skirt and opened the one nearest the window. Ursula could just see that various box files lay on two shelves.

'Ring the bell and ask Enid to serve our coffee in here.' Mrs Bruton took out files, inspecting contents, putting some back, then laying two on Ursula's desk. The spines identified one as *Trust Fund Portfolio* and the other as *Properties*.

Once the coffee had been served, she opened the first, swivelling it so it faced Ursula. 'I have to have meticulous order, Arthur will bear nothing less. My man of business sends in documents, notes of transactions, and I have been slipping them in; I cannot bring myself to do any sorting. But now that I have dear Miss Grandison, it is not necessary for me to do so, is it?'

She looked up with the nearest Ursula had seen to a look of entreaty.

Ursula took out all the documents, placed them on the desk and found herself giving a small pat of encouragement to Mrs Bruton's hand. 'It will not take long.'

Mrs Bruton sank into a chair and rested her head in her hand. 'I can trust you, can I not, Miss Grandison?'

Ursula assured her she was the soul of discretion. She rapidly sifted through the papers. Most of them concerned the buying and selling of stocks and bonds and only needed putting into date order. 'Would you wish me to pull out the assessments of the Trust's financial position and sort them into a separate pile?'

Mrs Bruton's expression brightened. 'That would be admirable. Then Arthur can see immediately that everything is being properly handled.'

Ursula soon had two piles of papers all neatly assembled in chronological order. 'Shall I return them to the box file, Mrs Bruton?'

'Oh, you are such a treasure, Miss Grandison; that would be perfect.'

'Shall I do the same with the other file?' Ursula found an index card she could use to separate the two piles of papers as she returned them to their home.

Mrs Bruton put her hand on the box marked 'Properties'. She seemed reluctant to have it opened. 'This is a little different, Miss Grandison. This is not part of the Trust Fund.'

Ursula tried to look interested but discreet.

Mrs Bruton started to speak, back tracked, started again, stumbled over several phrases, made more attempts. She seemed to have trouble in explaining how she had managed to acquire a portfolio of houses in a number of areas around London.

'Not in the most fashionable places, you understand? But where there is a market for reliable rentals. While I was in mourning for my dear Edward, I did not have much else to spend my income on.'

'It sounds an eminently sensible investment, Mrs Bruton. And now you have an income from the properties as well as from the Trust Fund.'

Mrs Bruton leant towards Ursula. 'The trouble, my dear Miss Grandison, is that Arthur may not consider the properties to be mine.'

'Why not?'

'Because they were bought with monies produced by the fund.'

'Were those monies not supposed to go to you, for spending how you thought best?'

Mrs Bruton fiddled with a cuff. 'It is something to do with the wording of the Trust. Something about "necessary expenditure". Arthur tried to explain once. It was just after Edward had passed over and I could not concentrate. Now, every time he sees me, he wants to know how the income is spent.'

'You haven't told him about the properties?'

Mrs Bruton shook her head. 'I tell myself it is none of his business. But now he considers it is time he looked at all the accounts. He is a Trustee, you see.'

Ursula thought for a moment. She felt in a difficult position. She had no knowledge of how these things worked in England. 'Do you have an attorney of your own, Mrs Bruton?'

'A lawyer you mean? Oh, Arthur would think it disloyal; he is a solicitor, you see.'

Ursula did see. 'I would think it sensible, Madam, for you to consult someone. You would not have to tell your stepson you were doing so, would you?'

Mrs Bruton's lips pursed and she sighed. 'Miss Grandison, what a support you are! And maybe, do you think, I might not have to show Arthur the property file?'

'Oh, I know so little about these matters,' Ursula said. 'But ...' she thought rapidly. 'But maybe if you showed him the Trust Portfolio and then waited to see if he asked for more details of your expenditure? There are all the household accounts he could be shown.'

'You have done such a splendid job sorting those out, Miss Grandison, and they are all quite clear. And my expenditure has risen considerably lately.'

'And maybe you could have some of your dressmaker's accounts to hand?'

'And explain that they are not complete? And, of course, that I spent a considerable time during my mourning period travelling on the continent?' Mrs Bruton appeared to have cheered up. 'And I will, of course, explain that it is not an unwarrantable extravagance to employ you, Miss Grandison. That you do not work for me full time, so to speak.' She broke off and seemed to consider the matter for a moment.

Ursula hoped that she was not going to say that she needed to cut down on her secretary's time. She was barely surviving on her current pay.

Instead, Mrs Bruton said, 'The count was here the other day. We shared a bottle of champagne and I congratulated him on the efficacy of the creams we were supplied with.'

Ursula agreed that her skin had certainly seemed much clearer and smoother since applying the treatments.

'He said that they are having such a success, so many recommendations, so many clients, that the administration of the accounts was sliding out of control. So I suggested, I hope you do not mind, Miss Grandison, that you might like to help on your free days with that side of things. You would, of course, be paid,' she added hastily. 'Now, do not say anything on that for the moment but perhaps you might consider it?' She looked hopeful.

'It was very kind of you to recommend me, Mrs Bruton. Did the count seem to think it might be a good idea?'

Her employer rose. 'He did indeed. I said that if you thought it might answer for you as well as for him, you would contact him. Now, I shall go and sit quietly and prepare my mind for dealing with my stepson. When I ring the bell, perhaps you will be kind enough to bring in the Trust Fund file? That will give me the opportunity to introduce you.'

Ursula watched Mrs Bruton leave the room. There were sides to her employer she had not guessed at.

Once she had sorted out the property file, her respect for the woman had risen. It represented a not inconsiderable sum of money, both in capital and income.

It was some time later that the buzzer sounded in the study.

Ursula picked up the Trust Fund file and went through to the drawing room.

Arthur Bruton did not think it necessary to rise when a secretary came into the room. He had a neat beard and moustache and a heavy nose. His eyes were dark brown but without warmth. A heavy gold watch chain stretched across a broad chest clad in a brown waistcoat beneath a brown suit. A black cravat was fastened with a diamond stick pin.

When Ursula was introduced, he merely gave a curt nod.

'I have been telling dear Arthur about my forays into charitable works, Miss Grandison.' Mrs Bruton fluttered her hands. 'He has advised me not to become involved with the campaign for women's suffrage.'

Mr Bruton's stolid face frowned, his thin mouth almost disappearing: 'We have the infuriating Mrs Pankhurst in Manchester making the lives of the Town Council miserable, insisting that women should be allowed to use the hall she has founded in memory of her husband.'

Mrs Bruton murmured something incomprehensible.

Ursula, thinking that this did not sound an unreasonable request, handed over the file saying, 'I believe you require this, sir.'

'Ah, yes. Let us see how my step-mama,' said in a voice that made little attempt to disguise dislike, 'has been guarding my inheritance.' He opened the file and Ursula felt waves of nervousness emanate from Mrs Bruton as she adjusted the set of her collar.

The cold brown eyes looked up at Ursula. 'You may go.'

Ursula gave a nod of acknowledgement and left the room.

'She is such a support to me,' she heard Mrs Bruton say, followed by Mr Bruton's toneless voice, saying, 'Is she. All Americans are impertinent and have to be kept in their place.'

Quietly seething, Ursula returned to the study. A little while later she was required to produce the household accounts.

Mrs Bruton's stepson left shortly after three o'clock. Two quick buzzes summoned Ursula to the drawing room.

Her employer had unbuttoned her jacket and sat in an exhausted slump, fanning her face with a woman's periodical. She waved Ursula to a chair.

'That man! Even dear Edward found him soulless. He told me once he admired Arthur's rectitude but could not love him. I think when Arthur's mama died, she took with her his ability to feel human kindness. How his poor wife could bring herself to marry such a frozen specimen of humanity, I cannot conceive.'

'Did he question you very closely, Madam?'

A gleam of satisfaction lit Mrs Bruton's face and she straightened her back. 'He grew tired of my flutterings, my inconsequentialities, accused me of a mind like a magpie's nest!'

Ursula was surprised the man could produce such an almost
poetic image.

'He has never forgiven his father for marrying me and post-
poning his inheritance.'

'The property portfolio is still on my desk.'

Mrs Bruton smiled delightedly. 'He is so contemptuous of me,
he assumed I was frittering away the Trust's income on fripperies,
as he called them. Now, ring the bell and let us have some tea.
I am glad you have brought your notebook, we must write some
letters about various of the properties.'

★ ★ ★

At the end of the day Ursula emerged from the basement steps to
find Rachel waiting for her.

'I need to be doing something,' the girl said abruptly. 'I can't
just sit around waiting for your Mr Jackman to produce results.'

Ursula gave her a small smile. She wanted to repudiate the
suggestion that Thomas Jackman was 'hers', but such a move
would be ridiculous. 'He has not been in contact with you, then?'

Rachel gave an angry shake of her head. 'And Aunt accused me of
hiring a mountebank and claimed he had upset the entire household.'

It sounded very unlike what Ursula knew of Jackman. 'You did
not go with him to the Peters' house?'

'I thought as Alice's sister it was my right but, no, I wasn't
allowed.' Frustration snapped in her voice. 'She should trust me
to know what to do, I'm not a juvenile.'

'I am sure Mr Jackman will be reporting to you.'

'I can't sit around waiting and the Movement needs action.'
Rachel tugged at a holder that hung from her shoulder and produced one of a large number of leaflets. 'I'm going to hand these
out and thought you might like to help.' Rachel sounded fired up.

The leaflet had a large headline: *Votes for Women*, and underneath a smaller one: *No Taxation Without Representation*.

'I'm surprised these weren't being handed around at
Mrs Bruton's tea party,' Ursula said as she quickly scanned the
trenchant phrases which put forward the case for women's suffrage.

'I've just had them printed. We need to be more militant. It's
what Mrs Pankhurst is saying. She's going to organise a proper
association in Manchester, the Women's Social and Political Union.

And she's going to get action going, militant action. Well, are you coming?'

Ursula had nothing better to do, no one to share her evenings with. She had tried to ignore the gap Alice had left when she returned to her husband but she couldn't help missing their times together.

'Where are we to hand out your leaflets?' she asked as they walked briskly towards the main road.

'Harrods. Good class of shoppers there; if they aren't aware of the cause, they should be. It's not far, just along Knightsbridge.'

Ursula was used to walking everywhere. She liked getting to know the various parts of London that could so dramatically change their identity, from the elegance of Knightsbridge and Mayfair to the busy bustle of Soho and Charing Cross, to the ancient charm of Fleet Street and the City of London. Everywhere the life of London pulsed around her: sober businessmen, fashionable women stepping out of carriages and cabs, not-so-fashionable women walking and using the public transport, street traders touting for business, urchins desperate for any task that would earn them a penny or two.

'Have you been able to visit your sister?' Ursula matched Rachel's brisk strides as they reached the main Knightsbridge road.

Rachel's look of concentration wavered. 'This morning. After I failed to convince Aunt I should take Mr Jackman to Montagu Place.' She came to a sudden stop, causing a muffin man to ring his bell as he almost knocked her down. She faced Ursula. 'Alice says she deserves to be in prison. That if she hadn't left Joshua, he would still be alive. How can she say that?'

'Does she say why she thinks that?' There could be one very obvious reason but Ursula couldn't bring herself to believe it.

Rachel shook her head and resumed walking. 'But I think she fears Daniel killed him.'

'Do you think that?'

Ursula expected a vigorous denial. Instead, Rachel gave a hopeless shrug. 'Someone must have – and I know it wasn't Alice.'

'But Daniel is your friend, don't you have some idea as to whether he could do such a dreadful act?'

For a few moments Rachel was silent as they made their way through busy shoppers. 'Daniel has Irish blood, he swears he will join with the militants over there, fight for their independence.

They stop at nothing, bombing, raids, whatever will advance the cause. Maybe he saw getting rid of Joshua Peters as clearing the way for Alice and he to live together?'

'And that's what you hope Mr Jackman will prove?'

Rachel's face tightened. 'I hate to think that Daniel could have been driven to such an act. But Alice has to be got out of prison.'

A moment or two later they reached Harrods, the elegant red-brick emporium stretching a whole block, its graceful windows marching down Knightsbridge. Ursula thought that compared with the New York stores their displays were not at all stylish, merely pedestrian arrangements of goods available inside.

There was an entrance to the store in a side road. 'We'll stand here, catch customers as they go in and out,' said Rachel, handing Ursula a batch of leaflets.

'Oh, no, you don't!' A smartly dressed doorman advanced on them. 'Move off or I'll have you for obstructing the pavement.'

'Then we'll stand in the road.' Rachel stepped off the sidewalk, and was nearly knocked down by a motor vehicle urgently sounding its horn. Leaflets fluttered through the air and littered the road. People shouted, either in warning or exasperation at such stupidity. The doorman caught her by the arm. 'Go on, get off with you or I'll summon the law.'

'I've done nothing illegal.'

'That's as maybe but you'll leave here now. Can't have innocent shoppers disturbed by your like. Or littering the highway.'

He was a big man and appeared to believe he was in the right.

'There must be a more suitable place for leaflet handing out,' Ursula suggested. No one seemed interested in the one she was offering.

'Now you got the right idea.' He loomed over them with his height, broad shoulders and expensive uniform.

'Rachel, we won't get anywhere by causing trouble.'

'I'm beginning to think it's the only way we can get anywhere.' But Rachel marched across the momentarily clear road. Ursula wondered if she'd even looked.

'Do you know where we're going now?' she asked as the girl retraced their steps towards Hyde Park Corner with its lethal traffic fighting its way round the complicated junction.

'I don't know why I didn't think of it before.' Rachel straightened the beret that had slipped to the side of her head.

'Think of where?' Ursula had to quicken her steps to keep up.
'Shepherd's Market.'

The market was just off Piccadilly, a jumble of narrow streets and small shops selling a vast variety of comestibles and other goods. Ursula looked at displays of fresh fruit and vegetables on open stalls. Away from the frantic traffic snarls of the main streets, she could almost imagine they were in a small market town.

Rachel immediately started handing out her leaflets. Some were taken automatically, Ursula hoped at least one or two would be read before being discarded, more were refused or immediately dropped in the road. 'Votes for Women,' she called out persuasively, moving over to the other side of the narrow road.

It seemed a hopeless activity until a couple of well-dressed women actually took one each and wished them well in the campaign. Maybe they were doing some good.

Then her attention was caught by a couple of men emerging from a quaint-looking public house. One, sporting a natty striped waistcoat, seemed to be pulling at the arm of a tall, distinguished gentleman in a top hat and suit of impeccable cut. With a jolt of surprise, Ursula recognised the count. As she watched, he freed his arm and, turning a glacial face on the other man, said a few words that seemed to her to have much the cutting effect of the Harrods doorman.

Rachel was suddenly at her side. 'That's Albert!' she exclaimed. 'What can he be doing here?'

Chapter Fifteen

Thomas Jackman was shown out of the front door by Mrs Trenchard.

'You will investigate the activities of Mr Peters outside his home.' Her tone allowed no argument. 'And you will report on your findings to me. You will not enter this house again without prior permission. Should you do so, your commission will be withdrawn. Do you understand?'

Thomas replaced his bowler and tipped it to her. 'Perfectly. I shall do my best, Madam.'

He walked quickly away from the house. Once out of sight, he stopped and considered his position. Mrs Trenchard had been more than angry, she had been frightened. From what he had seen of her, Jackman rated the woman as intelligent, certainly educated. Surely she must realise how important it was he eliminated the Peters' servants from his enquiry? Or had he, in his examination of the maid Sarah, come too close to uncovering something Mrs Trenchard would prefer was left alone?

He had to talk to Millie Rudge. The 'Joe Banks' business had to be cleared up. He felt in his pocket and brought out a realistic-looking moustache carefully packed in tissue paper. In a small envelope was a tube of glue such as was used by actors. Could she be persuaded that Joe, with his moustache and centre hair parting, was a different person from Thomas Jackman?

He scribbled a message on a page of his notebook, tore it out, then walked back to the house, took the stairs to the basement entrance and listened for a few moments. He could hear the cook shouting at someone. It was hardly likely to be Mrs Trenchard; either she was upstairs or had left. Thomas slipped his bowler to the back of his head and knocked on the door.

It was answered by young Sam. Thomas handed over the folded page, Millie's name on the front. 'Can you see Miss Rudge gets this?' With the note went a sixpence.

The boy's face lit up. 'You bet, mister.'

'I'll be waiting outside.'

'I'll tell 'er.'

As Thomas reached the pavement, he heard the front door open and quickly slipped down several steps. Sure enough, it was Mrs Trenchard who emerged and set off down the street without so much as a glance to right or left.

Thomas leant against the railings. The sun shone with a gentle warmth that warned summer's heat was giving way to autumnal chill. For the moment, though, the temperature was pleasant enough. While he waited, Thomas reviewed what he had gained from the one interview he'd been allowed to conduct. It was little enough but there were a couple of points that might guide his investigation. Then, as time went by, he wondered if Millie was going to ignore his note, make him suffer? He thought it more likely that her inquisitive nature would bring her to meet him. But she would no doubt need to give her appearance a certain amount of attention.

It was a good half hour before the girl eventually emerged. Then it was through the front door, her head held high, her long blonde hair worn in a complicated arrangement more suited to a lady than her maid, and wearing a pretty silk dress with a neat cape round her shoulders. She stood on the top step and looked around, her expression haughty.

Thomas stepped forward. 'Well, Miss Rudge, don't you look a picture!'

For a moment she preened, then gave him a look full of suspicion. 'Joe Banks, you've grown a moustache again. And combed your hair. What are you doing, pretending to be I don't know what?'

He offered her his arm. 'Shall we walk?'

'You needn't try to fool me. You got some explaining to do.'

'You're too bright for me to fool you.'

She placed her hand on his arm. He smiled at her, gave the hand a little pat. 'Shall we go to the park?'

He started walking. With a sniff and a little toss of her head, she kept pace with him.

For several minutes Thomas said nothing. At first he could sense her stealing little sideways looks at him, then tension began to rise in her. As they stood waiting to cross the main road, her elegantly shod foot tapped the pavement. They negotiated the busy traffic and Millie's breath quickened, like steam rising in a kettle. The moment they entered Regent's Park, she stopped. With her hands on her hips she faced him.

Thomas expected anger but her wide eyes looked full of hurt, and seemed as innocent and clear as a child's. For a moment guilt filled him. What right had he to deceive and manipulate this young woman? He took off his bowler hat and ruffled the centre parting of his hair. Dropping the cockney accent, he said, 'Millie, you're right, I haven't acted like a gentleman.'

Unexpectedly she laughed coarsely. 'You, a gentleman? Pull the other one, whoever you are.' She reached up and with a swift movement, pulled off his moustache. Triumph lit her expression. 'I knew it! It's time you came clean with me. Told me who you are and what you think you're doing.' With a look of challenge, she dropped the disguise on the ground, releasing the hairy accessory with a disdainful flick of her fingers.

Automatically Thomas picked it up, shoving it in his pocket, his upper lip smarting. A hand underneath her elbow, he steered her along a path through the park's generous sweeps of green grass and mature trees. Small birds pecked at the gravel round benches placed at the side of the path, no doubt seeking crumbs from sandwiches eaten in a Londoner's lunch hour.

'Do you think your mistress poisoned your master?'

She jerked her elbow away and swung round furiously on him, her eyes narrowing. 'Why should I answer your questions when you won't mine? Fine one you are.'

He was handling the situation badly. But how was he to know she could change her emotions as rapidly as a chameleon changed colour? Fun-loving, trusting Millie, with her innocent flirtatiousness had disappeared. It was as though the attractive sparkle of a calm sea had in a moment metamorphosed into a storm's dangerous power.

'Let's sit down and I'll tell you everything.' The birds scattered in a flurry of wings as he led her to one of the benches. Lunch hour long past, there was a choice of several free ones.

With a look full of suspicion, Millie sat, smoothing the silk of her sky-blue skirt. Jackson remembered Mrs Peters wearing the outfit to a meeting with young Daniel.

'As Mrs Trenchard told all the staff this morning, I'm a private investigator hired to look into the death of Mr Peters. Before he died, though, your master had previously charged me with following Mrs Peters; he was convinced she was having an affair.'

'So that's why you became Joe Banks; you thought I wouldn't know what you was up to.' Millie was triumphant, as though she had forced him to tell her the truth. 'You thought I'd tell you everything about my mistress.'

'From time to time it helped me to know where she was going,' he murmured.

Once again Millie underwent one of her rapid changes of mood. 'I didn't mind who I told,' she gave a little toss of her head. 'So you needn't think you was being so very clever. Mrs High and Mighty Peters; acted as though she was above us all. Didn't know how lucky she was.'

'Lucky?'

'Had a husband with money, didn't she? One who gave her everything she wanted. Jewels and clothes a princess wouldn't mind wearing.'

'Like that pretty dress you're wearing?'

Millie glanced down at the blue silk with a satisfied smile. 'Can't wear it where she is now, can she?'

'It does suit you,' he said, injecting a note of admiration. 'I always thought you were a girl with style. And I enjoyed our little outings, you've a way with you, young Millie.'

The satisfied smile deepened. 'Have to say I liked the champagne, it was something different, all those bubbles. And the music hall was fun, never been to one before. It was nice being taken.' The flirtatious look was back.

'So when Mrs Peters left her home without telling you where she was going or taking you with her, you didn't mind?'

Millie shrugged her shoulders and lifted her feet, glancing admiringly down at the smart little bootees.

'Didn't you worry that you'd lost your job ... or did you think she'd send for you?'

'Who's to say I wasn't offered a better position?' Millie said smugly.

'A better position?'

'One where I'd have my own maid … and be given jewellery.'

There was a long pause then Jackman said, 'So, just when you thought everything was going your way, Mrs Peters returns to her husband. Must have been a bit of a shock for you.'

'Shock?' With another of her rapid changes of mood, Millie sprang to her feet, snarling. 'The bitch!' She stood over Jackman, hands on hips, a virago. 'She hadn't wanted him but she crawls back expecting to take up as though she'd never left.'

'And he took her back,' Jackman said quietly, standing and looking down on her.

'I told him he was a fool, that no good would come of it.' She took a few unsteady steps away, turned and came back. 'I'd never have thought it of him. First he tells me to get back where I came from, how he'd deny everything if I tried to tell anyone. Says he's been given a second chance. What about me?' The words came out in a long wail. 'What second chance did I get?'

A passer-by looked interestedly at them. Millie paid no attention.

'Oh, she was so clever, so meek and mild. And he was taken in all along the line.'

'Taken in?'

She looked up at him scornfully. 'You don't think that baby is his? Popped up from a butcher's shambles have yer? And I thought you was an educated man. She needed respectability. Well, she wasn't going to get it with her fancy man, was she?'

'But Peters believed her?'

'Handle 'em right and a clever woman can get any man to believe anything.'

He had to admire her belief in her own cleverness.

'All she had to do was wait and take her chance.'

'Chance?'

'That she could have it all. Could have her baby, could have respectability, and could have all his money. *And* she could have her fancy man as well.'

'So you do think your mistress poisoned your master?'

'Well, what do you think, mister investigator? Why do you think I gave that diary to the police? Why should she get away with such a dreadful act?'

'You felt it was right to read her private diary?'

There was the slightest flush on her cheeks but she didn't say anything.

Jackman reached into his pocket and brought out the pot he had found at the back of Peters' desk. 'Know anything about this?'

'What is it?'

He offered it to her.

'Oh, that! It's,' she coloured a little. 'It's cream ... for the face. He gave me one. Said it would make me look even more beautiful.' For the first time her voice faltered and she blinked rapidly. 'Said he'd come across it in his business and made me take it. All I've got left to remember him by ... that and a little bracelet. Thought it was diamonds but the pawnshop said it was only paste, wouldn't advance me more than a few shillings on it,' she ended bitterly. 'Men, you can't trust them.' She looked up at him through her lashes. 'Don't suppose you'll be wanting to see me again, either.'

Jackman smothered another tinge of guilt. 'How did your master come across the face cream by way of his business? Thought that was arranging import and export.' He remembered the busy office, the desk piled with bills of lading, the docks outside ringing to the coarse shouts of dockers and sailors.

Millie looked sulky. She settled the set of her jacket a little more advantageously round her waist. 'Don't know nothing about that. You'd better ask Albert.'

Albert, the mysterious valet.

'Going to walk me back, are you?' Once again Millie was in flirtatious mode.

★ ★ ★

Jackman escorted the maid back to the Peters household and found himself bowing over her hand in a continental manner to say goodbye, watching as she ran prettily up the front steps to ring the bell, tossing her head as Sarah opened the door. Just how much of what she had said could he rely upon?

Jackman went back down to the basement entrance and asked Sam where he could find Albert.

'At the master's office more than like. Gets all the best jobs, he does.'

Jackman was certain Mrs Trenchard would not weigh out for a hansom cab to take him there. Traffic was its usual tangle and omnibus travel would be slow; the day was fair and he decided to opt for Shankses' pony. The walk through Holborn and Cheapside, and into the City brought back the days when he would patrol the streets as a humble bobby. Some fifteen years had passed since he'd become a detective but he reckoned that not much had changed. Checking who was amongst the crowds he had to negotiate, few matching his speed, was second nature to him and he reckoned he could identify a number of lowlife suspects without difficulty.

Suspicious characters increased as he approached Wapping, funnels and masts marking the docks and his destination. Small groups of idle and resentful dockers who'd lost out on a day's employment hung around, ready to cause trouble. Chinese faces became more and more prevalent, as did sailors with faces from around the world. Jackson had not been personally involved with patrolling the docks or the river but he was well aware of the opportunities for nefarious activities in the tangle of narrow streets, the network of gangs who controlled the illegal dealings that sidestepped officialdom, banned goods and import duties. Here sordid doss houses, brothels and opium dens created areas even the hardiest policeman hesitated to go.

Jackman skirted a brawling group of carters, their drays causing gridlock as horses dropped dirt while waiting for drivers to sort out just which conveyance could successfully claim a right of way.

A few moments later he arrived at the offices of Peters and Roberts, relieved that he had negotiated the various blocks of warehouses without hesitation. Here suited office administrators and uniformed officials bustled, carts rumbled over cobblestones, the odd carriage brought gentlefolk to claim passage or meet travellers. Here ships unloaded or took on freight, signed off sailors, found new crews, said goodbye or took on new passengers, and threw slops over the side. Gulls screeched overhead, swooping on any edible fragment. The docks had to be the noisiest of any part of London, and the busiest.

As Jackman approached the offices, Albert emerged from the shabby building. A few words from the detective sufficed to remind the valet of Jackman's investigation into Peters' death. At first suspicious and monosyllabic, Albert reluctantly allowed himself to be taken off to one of the many public houses in the vicinity.

Lunchtime being long past, the pub was half empty and Jackman had no trouble finding them a small table in a quiet corner.

Once seated with a pint of ale in front of him, the valet gradually relaxed as Jackman filled in his background, adding a few choice reminiscences of his time as an East End copper, all the while unobtrusively studying the person sitting opposite.

Albert was a small, neat man in a brown suit, the jacket worn over a bright yellow and caramel striped waistcoat. His features were as neat as his person: a narrow face with bright dark eyes, a pointed nose and chin, his skin badly pock-marked, thin lips revealing blackened teeth with several gaps. There was a stillness about him, a listening quality that to Jackman suggested someone who absorbed information and observations as efficiently as a sponge and forgot little.

'Not keeping you, am I?' Jackman asked. 'Only by rights I ought to get round to asking you about life in the Peters household. Justify my fee, as you might say.'

'You might, doubt I would,' Albert said, moving restlessly on his pew. 'You got what time it is? Only I got an appointment.'

Jackman got out his timepiece, careful to shield it from the sight of the mean-looking fellows who were their fellow drinkers.

'If you can supply the price of a cab back to town,' said Albert, 'I suppose I can spare fifteen minutes or so, specially if it means you can catch the bastard what poisoned Mr Peters.' He finished his ale in a pointed manner and Jackman quickly supplied both of them with fresh pints.

'First I ought to find out what your duties were. I've been told you were Mr Peters' valet?'

Albert shrugged. 'The master doesn't ... didn't set much store on how he was turned out. Main part of me job was running messages for him and making deliveries. Had me at it day in, day out, said he couldn't manage without me,' he added virtuously.

'What sort of deliveries?'

'Shipping schedules, papers, bits of official stuff. I never knows what it all is; just do what I'm told. Sometimes it's orders, what's arrived at the docks, if they isn't too large and needed special, like.'

'You mean imported goods?'

Albert's expression combined shiftiness with disquiet. 'Look, it weren't my business to know what was in the packages, I just collected and delivered. Anyway, you ain't got the right to question me like this. It's not got anything to do with the master's death.'

'That's for me to decide, not you. And I have every right to question all your dealings connected with Joshua Peters. For instance, you say you're a valet but it doesn't seem like you acted as one for your master.'

'Now, see here. Whatever I may have said about 'im not caring about 'is appearance, I knows just how to turn a fellow out right; how to tie a cravat, polish a boot or shoe, shave a neat chin, trim a beard.'

Jackman smiled reassuringly at him. 'So you would wake your master in the morning? Shave him and such like?'

Albert pulled at one of his ears nervously, the first indication the detective had seen the valet might lose his control. 'I didn't call him, I had to wait for his bell. 'E had a habit of waking early and studying papers and things before rising. Didn't want to be disturbed before he needed to dress and be shaved.'

'And on the morning he was found dead, what happened?'

The dark eyes were closed for a brief moment. 'I was waiting for his bell.' The narrow face looked pinched as though some strong emotion threatened to break out.

'Doing what?'

'Sorting the morning mail.'

'Takes you long, that?'

'A lot of business gets sent to the house.' The explanation appeared to have a steadying effect. 'If it's not marked "personal" I opens all the letters and arranges them as the master likes … liked, in different piles.'

'Sounds as though you were something of a secretary.'

A crafty smile stretched the thin lips. 'I'm a dab hand at reading and writing, me mother saw to that, she'd been a governess afore she, well, fell down on her luck, and Mr Peters liked the way I knows how to keep my mouth shut.'

Jackman said nothing and after a moment Albert added, 'Some of the stuff I do is confidential, like.'

Confidential, eh?

'Can you think of anyone who would want your master dead?'

For a brief moment something flared in the dark eyes and Jackman felt a moment of hope. Then the valet studied the nails of his right hand, his expression impossible to read.

'Dead?' he said. 'No, Mr Jackman, I can't. Unless,' he added with the air of a thought that had only just occurred. 'Maybe Mrs Peters. They had a right old ding dong the afternoon before.'

The detective tried to imagine the gentle and controlled Alice Peters having a 'ding dong' with her husband.

'Did you tell the police that?'

Albert appeared to think for a moment. 'Only just remembered it. Wasn't unusual for them to have a bit of a fight,' he added hastily.

'Is that so?'

Albert nodded. 'Hardly blissfully married they were.'

Jackman drew out the pot of cream once again from his pocket and watched Albert's face as he put it down on the table. 'What can you tell me about this?'

The valet grabbed it up, the first impulsive movement he'd made. 'Hey, how'd'yer get hold of this?'

Jackman firmly removed the jar from his grasp and returned it to his pocket. 'Part of the "confidential stuff" is it?'

The valet seemed to struggle for composure. 'Just one of the last things the master asked me to do; makes me realise he'll not be needing me to do anything more for him.' He rose. ''Ave to be off now. Like I said, I've an appointment. What about that cab fare you promised?'

Jackman handed over a generous sum and watched the valet slipping like an eel through a group of rowdy sailors.

Appointment, eh? Something to do with the firm of Peters and Roberts, or something to do with Albert?

Chapter Sixteen

Ursula was woken by rain beating on the window. She lay in bed and listened, wondering if there was an omnibus that could take her to Mayfair. It was to be her first morning working for Count Meyerhoff and Madame Rose and it would be unfortunate if she arrived with her skirts rain-darkened and shoes all wet; she had had no opportunity so far to acquire galoshes.

Ursula had called at the beauty clinic the day after she had seen the count coming out of the public house in Shepherd's Market. She'd felt nervous. Had he noticed her and Rachel passing out the women's suffrage leaflets? She had a definite feeling he would not like to be associated with such behaviour. If she'd been recognised, there would surely be no discussion of her secretarial skills and she could say goodbye to another source of badly needed income.

However, he had seemed pleased to see her and there was no mention of leaflet handing out. Instead, he'd told her she came highly recommended by Mrs Bruton and had taken her into an office-like back room dominated by a mahogany armoire more European in appearance than English.

'This is where,' he'd said, unlocking the doors, 'we keep all our accounts.' A torrent of papers fell to the floor.

'Fraulein Ferguson,' the count called sharply.

There appeared instantly the white-uniformed girl who had greeted Ursula and Mrs Bruton on their initial visit, her expression anxious.

'What does this mean?' He pointed to the cascade.

Miss Ferguson bent and tried to gather the papers. Her hands trembled and they fluttered and fell a second time.

'Why, Fraulein? Why?' A hand waved at loaded shelves that threatened to add to the chaos.

'You told me to use this cupboard for bills and receipts, Count Meyerhoff.'

'For organisation! This is a cabinet for orderly arrangement of accounts, not a place for, how would you call it, mayhem?'

The girl managed to scoop up an armful and attempted to thrust them back on to a shelf.

'No!' The count took a deep breath and said more quietly, 'You must see, Fraulein, that will not answer.'

Ursula bent to help the girl who now seemed near to tears.

'Fraulein Grandison, we talk before you assist, *hein?*'

She stepped back.

Miss Ferguson's eyes looked wildly for somewhere safe to offload her slipping sheaf. Ursula itched to help.

'Here, put them here.' The count indicated a spindly-legged side table, then watched trembling hands release their burden on to the polished surface. Soon the floor was clear.

'*Danke shön*, Fraulein. We do not need you further.'

The count closed the door behind the girl, shrugged his shoulders and smiled apologetically at Ursula. 'Fraulein Ferguson is laboratory assistant and receptionist, not secretary. You see how we need you, Fraulein Grandison?'

Ursula struggled not to feel daunted by what the armoire had revealed. What were all those papers? From the little she could see, there seemed to be more than simple bills. Official-looking documents, bills of lading, complicated invoices.

Tension was added to by an unfamiliar ringing. The count moved rapidly to the efficient-looking desk that stood opposite the armoire, picked up the earpiece of a telephone and barked a greeting. A subdued chirp answered him. He smiled broadly and waved Ursula out of the room.

She went into the corridor. Miss Ferguson came out of a back room and headed towards the main reception area, her eyes red. 'The man's a monster,' she hissed at Ursula.

Ursula was already doubting Mrs Bruton's oft repeated opinion that no man was more sympathetic or courteous than the handsome Count Meyerhoff. But he would not be the first difficult man she had managed to work alongside.

The office door opened and the count beckoned her back in.

'If this telephone should ring while you are here, please to answer, then fetch whoever is required. Or messages can be taken.' He smiled, showing a great deal of white teeth. 'I tell Madame Bruton she should install this instrument, it makes communication very easy.'

Ursula nodded. 'In New York it is used a great deal more than it seems to be in London.'

'This will change and quite soon I think. Now, we talk about accounts, yes?'

After half an hour or so, it had been agreed that she would come in two mornings a week to sort paperwork, send out bills to clients and receipts for payments made. She was also to begin the task of setting up a system for the *Maison Rose* accounts; Ursula made a mental note to acquire a guide to double-entry book-keeping.

'It is, of course, confidential work, Fraulein,' had been the count's last words to her before she left. 'Madame Bruton has assured me of your discretion in such matters.'

Listening to the rain as she lay in bed, Ursula shivered. Summer was definitely over. She wondered how quickly winter cold would arrive. It had been spring when she landed in England; she had not expected to stay beyond a few months, so had brought no warm clothes. At least working at *Maison Rose* might mean she could afford to buy a winter coat. Had she made a mistake in deciding to remain in England instead of returning to the States to rebuild her life there? There would not have been a job but at least she had friends, both in New York and San Francisco.

London, though, had beckoned her. The chance to discover one of the world's greatest cities was too seductive. She had never had difficulty making friends or finding employment, even if it was menial and badly paid. She hadn't considered either friends or a job would elude her in London and lo and behold she had been fortunate enough to be taken on by Mrs Bruton, even if it was only for two and a half days a week. And now there was this other opportunity.

Ursula had not, though, realised how difficult it would be to meet people. The other boarders at Mrs Maples' seemed determined to keep conversation to banalities and generalities.

Londoners were courteous but it seemed that if you had not been properly introduced, the possibility of a meaningful conversation, or even of passing a pleasant time of day, could not be contemplated. In America, apart from high society, people were much more open.

For a little while there had been the pleasure of Alice Peters' company and when the girl had returned to her husband, Ursula had missed her extremely. To think of her in prison was dreadful. There was the possibility, though, that Ursula's acquaintance with Rachel Fentiman could blossom into friendship. She lacked her sister's warmth and sympathetic manner but her lively mind and enterprise were refreshing.

A knock at the bedroom door announced that Meg had arrived with Ursula's morning cup of tea. Meg never had time for a proper chat but even a short conversation with her made Ursula feel better. After her morning at *Maison Rose*, she decided, she would treat herself to a visit to the Zoological Gardens at Regent's Park, that is, if the rain had cleared. And on Saturday she would find her way to the Tower of London and immerse herself in its history. No, Ursula wasn't going to give up on life in this capital city yet.

After breakfast, dressed in a mackintosh, equipped with a sturdy umbrella and with her skirt raised well above her boots, Ursula prepared herself to deal with the inclement weather. She opened the front door – and found Rachel Fentiman about to ring the bell.

'Oh, good, I've caught you.' The girl pushed past her into the narrow hall, shaking rain from her brolly. 'We can't talk on the doorstep and I need to beg for your help,' she added imperiously.

'I was just about to set off for work,' Ursula said, speaking with meaning.

Rachel opened the door into the boarders' living room, and drew Ursula in, holding her wrist in a tight grip. 'I can't get Alice to talk. No one can. The lawyer has given up. He says unless she explains what she wrote in her diary she will be tried and condemned … condemned to be …' her voice faltered and failed.

'Explains?' Ursula gently pulled her wrist free.

Rachel sat down, produced a handkerchief and blew her nose determinedly. 'The police believe because Alice wrote that Joshua deserved to die and she wanted to be free of her marriage, she must have killed him. They know of her … her relationship with Daniel. They believe that he is the father of the child she is carrying, not Joshua. She knew her husband loved cherry liqueur chocolates, and that he would reserve them entirely for his consumption, so there would be no danger of anyone else consuming one that had been poisoned.'

Ursula felt a chill creep through her. She thought of the scrap of paper upstairs. Even though it hardly made sense as it stood, producing it would surely incriminate Alice even further.

'Has Mr Jackman tried to talk to her?'

'He has been refused a Visitor's Permit.'

Had he indeed!

'What makes you think I would be allowed one?'

Rachel patted her handbag. 'I already have it made out in your name.'

Ursula found herself shocked that Rachel had taken her acceptance so for granted.

'How did you manage that?'

'I explained to Uncle Felix that you had become close to Alice while she was hiding from Joshua and so she might possibly speak to you.' Rachel paused and gave her a brief smile. 'You can be very persuasive, Ursula. So my uncle got in touch with some people of influence.' Her tone provided capital letters to 'People' and 'Influence'. 'A lifetime in the law has produced a network of contacts who regard him kindly. Come,' she rose. 'We should start now.'

'I cannot come with you this morning, Rachel. I am already late for my new job.'

'Are you not working for Mrs Bruton any more?'

'Certainly I am. This is an additional employment. One I badly need.'

'But, surely, whoever it is will understand?'

'It is you who must understand, Rachel. I have no income beyond what I earn and Mrs Bruton's stipend is only just enough to pay for my lodging here. I need a winter coat and … and other items. I cannot risk my new employers deciding I am unreliable and dispensing with my services. Surely if your sister will not speak to you or her lawyer, she will not to me?'

'But she must! She has told me how much she enjoyed your company while she lodged here. You are not family, you have no ties, she can be open with you in a way she maybe finds impossible with us.' Rachel's voice faltered.

It seemed she believed Ursula really could make a difference.

'I only have to work in the morning. Would it help if I went with you this afternoon?'

Rachel surveyed her with hostile eyes. 'I am not certain the Visitor's Permit will be acceptable in the afternoon.'

'Does it specify a certain time?'

'No, but I have always been in the mornings.'

Ursula began to lose patience. 'I am sincerely sorry, Rachel, but I cannot forgo my employment. I think it is doubtful I can help but I am willing to visit with your sister this afternoon.'

For a long moment Rachel looked stubbornly at her then she said wearily. 'Call on me as soon as you are free and we will go to the prison. I only hope we will be allowed to see Alice.'

★ ★ ★

Ursula arrived at *Maison Rose* out of breath, her heart hammering with nervousness over her reception there. She feared the count might deal as coldly with her as he had with poor Miss Ferguson.

It was Madame Rose who opened the door at her ring. 'Ah, Miss Grandison, I am so pleased to see you. Miss Ferguson has not appeared this morning, she has sent a note saying she is unwell, and I need to assess the state of my ingredients for the preparations. The count is out and I have clients coming. Please to put on a coat.'

This turned out to be one of the white cotton uniforms Miss Ferguson wore. Ursula drew it on, thankful Madame Rose had seemed not to notice the tardiness of her arrival.

She was led past the office and into a larger room laid out as some sort of laboratory. A long steel counter lined one side, above it were shelves holding a variety of glass apothecary-style jars containing different-looking ingredients. On the counter itself stood a sizeable pestle and mortar, a number of deep stainless steel bowls and implements for stirring, cutting and chopping. Below the counter were sets of baskets on wheels that held neatly arranged jars of various sizes. Ursula recognised them as the ones holding the creams she and Mrs Bruton had been given. On the wall opposite were more shelves on which were stacked cardboard boxes. Labels identified their contents as more jars. A large window flooded the room with light.

'We progress most satisfactorily with our business,' Madame Rose said. 'I have to compose supplies of my preparations for many clients. Every day more come.' She beckoned Ursula closer. 'Allow me to examine your complexion again.'

Ursula willingly advanced towards her. 'Both Mrs Bruton and I notice an improvement, Madame.'

The beautician nodded, 'Indeed, it is so. The skin, it is not so dry, particularly here and here,' she gently touched Ursula's cheeks and forehead. And the good Madame Bruton, she sends friends to me, which she would not do without satisfaction in my products. And other clients also do this. So it is necessary for many jars to be filled. Now, we will commence. I give you names of ingredients it is necessary we shall order and you write down, yes?'

'Of course, Madame. I have a notebook and pencil.' Ursula held these up.

'That is good. So, we commence.' Madame Rose reached up to tap the first glass jar. 'Beeswax.'

Ursula had no difficulty with writing this down but soon she was lost on the spelling of chemicals she had no knowledge of. Madame Rose then placed each jar on the stainless steel counter so Ursula could read the label and copy it down while Madame gave her the quantity that should be ordered.

As she named the contents of each jar, the beautician lovingly caressed it. Her absorption in the task was total. Ursula felt she was visualising the part each ingredient played in the various preparations she had created, how it nurtured or cleansed a woman's skin. She seemed to live for her mission – that of assisting her fellow females to realise their true beauty, while using products containing ingredients that rarely sounded as though they could help in such an enterprise. Petroleum jelly, for instance, was surely an unlikely aid to perfect skin. Yet, Ursula thought, she and Mrs Bruton had noticed a genuine improvement in their complexions after using Madame Rose's concoctions.

Did true beauty lie in looks? Madame Rose could not be called beautiful by normal standards; her skin was smooth and without imperfections, her eyes were clear, but her mouth was thin and her nose slightly hooked, her chin was too small and her cheekbones too prominent. Yet she had a sense of style that overrode such drawbacks. With her blonde hair arranged into a chignon secured with a carved jade comb and wearing pendant jade earrings, she had an aura that deceived you into classing her as dazzlingly attractive.

No, Ursula chided herself, writing down another ingredient, 'deceived' was the wrong word. Madame Rose practiced no deception, she was indeed attractive. Surely, though, it was her character as much as her complexion that made her so?

The last jar was tapped and as Ursula finished writing she looked over the list she had made. 'How often, Madame, do you need to order these ingredients?'

'How could I know more would be needed so soon? We must order larger quantities.' This was said with a note of satisfaction.

'Can you purchase them all in London?'

'Many I am accustomed to using come from the continent and beyond. In Vienna they are easy to obtain, the railway brings them. Here they have to come by boat and I am told delays are common. Many forms to fill! But the count is so good to organise all. We make good partners: I create and diagnose, he administrates.' She frowned anxiously. 'I hope Miss Ferguson is not too ill, she is also necessary to the business; she greets clients, assists with preparations, fills jars, maintains my laboratory.'

Ursula wondered if the count considered the girl as essential to *Maison Rose* as Madame seemed to.

'Shall I type this list out? With maybe two copies?'

'Type?'

'Surely you have a typewriter?' As she spoke, Ursula realised she had not seen one in the office.

Madame Rose looked puzzled.

'All your bills to clients, letters, you write them by hand?'

'But of course! Miss Ferguson writes a very clear hand, as do I and the count, though he only writes letters to his dear friends, inviting them to the salon.'

'If the count talks to Mrs Bruton, she will tell him how useful a typewriter is; there is no danger of misunderstanding numbers – dates, for instance, or amounts of ingredients or money. And names and addresses are clearly printed.' Madame Rose looked unconvinced. 'Carbon papers mean copies are made at the same time as the original. I could type out a list of the ingredients we have dealt with this morning with perhaps five or six copies, which could make the next order much easier to record.'

Ursula paused but the beautician seemed absorbed in checking the condition of more jars. 'And typing is so much quicker than handwriting.' At that Madame Rose looked up.

'You mean Miss Ferguson would not take so long to produce bills and letters of appointment?'

Ursula nodded. 'Exactly. Would you like me to talk to the count?'

'Did I hear my name?'

'Ah, Julius,' Madame Rose turned thankfully to her partner. 'Miss Grandison has idea, she will tell you. I go to meet client.' She made a dignified but rapid exit.

The count greeted Ursula briefly then demanded to know what was the idea that Madame had mentioned. Once again Ursula sensed how thin was his pleasant veneer.

'A typewriter?' He looked at her quizzically. 'What is the cost of such a machine?'

She told him the price of the one Mrs Bruton had bought.

The count waved a dismissive hand, 'Perhaps Miss Ferguson cannot use such a machine. First we need to discover that.'

Ursula remembered her battles with learning the keys and the time it had taken her to produce pristine results when she had first been faced with a typewriter in New York. Perhaps it would be better not to press the matter. She handed over the list of ingredients needed by Madame Rose. The count looked at it with a sigh.

'It will need to be copied neatly, Miss Grandison, if we are to rely on receiving the correct items in the correct quantities.'

Ursula took back the list without comment.

By the end of the morning she had carefully composed an order for Madame's requirements and made a start on sorting out the accounts stuffed so carelessly in the armoire. As she arranged the papers she had worked on in neat piles, the count entered.

'So, Miss Grandison, the work goes well, *hein*? And now you are finished for the morning, yes?'

She nodded. 'I shall come again as agreed on Tuesday morning. I hope there will be no need to disturb these?' She indicated the table with its carefully arranged sets of papers.

'I shall study your work, see what methods you are using, but on Tuesday all shall be as it is now. Tomorrow it is Saturday, do you work for my friend Mrs Bruton?'

'No, Count, not until Monday.'

He gave a little nod of dismissal and Ursula left, wondering if there was the possibility of working at *Maison Rose* on a Saturday morning or two. That would certainly help swell the winter coat fund. Just as she was about to close the front door, she remembered her umbrella and hurried back to collect it from the office. As she opened the door she heard the count speaking German to someone. Her schoolgirl knowledge of the language was enough for her to understand some of what he was saying, 'Not tomorrow. Tomorrow I go to Chat-ham ...' The last two words were pronounced carefully and sounded English but made little sense.

'I'm sorry to disturb you, Count,' Ursula said, a little flustered. 'I forgot my umbrella.'

'You do not have courtesy to knock on the door?' he said coldly, 'I am holding confidential telephone conversation.'

Ursula picked up her brolly from the corner of the office, apologised again and slipped out of the room.

Outside the rain seemed to have disappeared and a watery sun was shining through ragged clouds. Delighted at not having to use her umbrella, Ursula hurried off to Rachel Fentiman's. Her feelings on visiting Alice Peters in prison were mixed. She welcomed the possibility of seeing the girl; worries about her condition had plagued her ever since she had heard of her incarceration. But she could not visualise Alice opening up to her.

Chapter Seventeen

Thomas Jackman listened to the rain falling outside his front room window, feeling as depressed as the weather. He was trying to sort out all the details of the Peters case as he knew them so far. It was a frustrating business. It seemed that everywhere he turned he was being obstructed. He was not allowed to speak to Alice Peters in Holloway prison. He was not allowed to interview the staff of the Peters household. His old colleague, Inspector Drummond, refused to consider any evidence but the most obvious. To Jackman, Joshua Peters and his odd valet, Albert, had to have been involved in some mysterious, if not illegal, activity. But what?

For the first time since he'd left the police force, Thomas missed having colleagues to discuss a case with. He needed someone to bounce ideas around with, and preferably someone who understood the issues involved and someone used to the criminal mind. When he'd taken on the investigation, he had never imagined it would prove so difficult to solve. Every time he thought about Alice Peters locked in her cell, he knew despair. She was so lovely, so innocent, and in such danger.

Three days ago, when he had followed the valet, Albert, to Shepherd's Market, he'd thought that at last he was about to achieve a breakthrough in the case.

Everything about the man had suggested he was up to no good. His shiftiness at the docks, the way he had snatched the money Thomas had offered him, then hurried off. Following him, Thomas had been certain that the man would not be hiring a cab. And so it had proved. Without actually breaking into a run, the man was incredibly speedy on his feet. Thomas considered he himself was pretty fast but he found it difficult to keep up with the valet without betraying his presence. It did not seem, though, to have occurred to Albert that he might be being followed. Nor that he might spend money on some form of transport between the docks and Shepherd's Market, a distance of several miles.

Once the valet had disappeared into the public house, Thomas had taken a brief look inside and seen him accost some toff with a fine head of prematurely white hair. Though the way Albert was received did not appear to be warm – there was no grasping of hands, no smile of welcome – the curt nod the toff gave indicated that the valet had been expected. The saloon bar was small and Thomas saw no way of escaping notice if he entered. So he waited round a corner where he had a good view of the entrance. Eventually the toff had emerged with Albert almost hanging on his sleeve. Thomas watched as the valet had been brushed off with what must have been hard words, judging by the way he turned almost puce with anger, and the man had strode off in the direction of Berkeley Square.

Thomas decided to follow him; he already knew where Albert lived.

Merging unobtrusively into a group of people moving in the same direction, Thomas to his great surprise saw Rachel Fentiman and Ursula Grandison handing out some pamphlet or other from a hessian bag labelled 'Votes for Women'. Any other time he would have welcomed the chance of conversation but not now. Moving easily through the end-of-day crowds, he slipped out of the market into Curzon Street without attracting their attention.

The tall, aristocratic-looking man was an easy target to follow up the steps that led into stately Berkeley Square, its central green sward generously lined with trees. He crossed the square and walked up the short Hill Street, at the top turning left into Davies Street. As Thomas rounded the corner, he saw his quarry enter an imposing mansion. He allowed time for the front door to be properly closed, then walked past, giving an unobtrusive but comprehensive look at the brass plate that announced here was the *Maison Rose*.

Thomas continued walking towards Bond Street but felt for the jar of beauty cream in his trouser pocket. Its label had carried the words: *Maison Rose*. He stood still for a moment, then hurried back to Shepherd's Market. Ursula and Rachel might well have some information on such a product. But the home-going crowds had dissipated and there was no sign of the two girls.

Back home and stting at his desk, Thomas sighed, turned his notebook back to the page where he'd written down the details of that day and, once again, read through the notes he'd made, though his memory was excellent and he hardly needed to remind himself of the unanswered questions he'd identified.

He reached for the jar of cream he'd placed on his desk and turned it around in his hand automatically as he recalled his activities during the past three days. The interviews he'd wangled with Millie and Albert had brought no clues as to what that couple of sharpsters Joshua Peters and his valet had been up to. He would not, though, trust either of them to clean a baby's bottom without making off with the napkin. So he'd decided to look into the background of the Peters and Roberts import/export business. Whatever was going on, it was more than like something that had led to Peters' death. Thomas saw in his mind's eye the deep desk drawer, empty apart from a gun and that dratted jar.

He had spent two days looking into Peters and Roberts Ltd. Searches into Company House had required the disentangling of a cat's cradle of connected companies with no accounts lodged in recent years for any of them. Action was being taken against most and it looked as though the directors, both Joshua Peters, had he still been alive, and his partner Martin Roberts, were about to end up in court. 'About to be bottled, they are,' Thomas was told after he'd chatted up a clerk he'd once had dealings with while he was in the police force.

'You mean arrested?'

The man sucked his teeth. 'Well let's just say they're unlikely to remain in business.'

Chats with ex-colleagues in the dockland area identified a feeling that the operating company was deemed to be dodgy but nothing had occurred so far to bring them into real trouble, nor had anyone seemed able to explain exactly what 'dodgy' might mean. 'We're keeping an eye out,' was a phrase used more than once.

Abandoning this aspect of his investigation, Thomas had turned his attention to the *Maison Rose*. This enterprise seemed above board. He had made contact with a sergeant in the Saville Row police station whom he'd worked with in the past. 'Foreign gent has taken a lease on the first and second floors,' said George Parker. 'Lives on the second, as does his so-called partner, Madame Rose.'

'So-called?'

'They run some sort of beauty business on the first floor. She's a good-looking woman,' he added judiciously. 'If a bit too much on her dignity. They maintain separate apartments but, behind closed doors ...' he leered at Thomas.

'How come you know so much about them?'

'Just after they moved in, there was a right old fracas in Davies Street, outside their front door. Party of toffs, all drunk as lords, which in fact some of them proved to be,' he added with a cynical expression. 'One of them took exception to something another said, words led to fisticuffs and the noise was something else. They was all arrested. The foreign gentleman, now what was his name?' Sergeant Parker had scratched his ear, an action that Thomas remembered he'd habitually used to aid his memory. 'Count he was. Yes, Count Meyerhoff. Well, he'd been returning home and seen the start of the fight. He refused to be a witness, said he didn't want no trouble, but he did want to know how often that sort of thing took place. He said he'd thought it was a respectable neighbourhood.'

Thomas nodded. 'Always has been. Very far from the East End in every sense.'

'So I assured the count. Well, he wanted an inspection of his locks. Wanted to make sure he and his partner were safe in their beds.'

'In their beds?'

'Didn't actually use them words but it was obvious what he meant.'

Trust George Parker to see innuendo in the most common-place of situations!

'No other trouble in the area?'

The sergeant shook his head and finished off the pint of ale Thomas had bought him in the police station's local. 'It gets regularly patrolled, as you'd expect, being as 'ow we don't want no trouble there. And the *Maison Rose* property don't seem to attract any suspicious night life, know what I mean?' He winked meaningfully at Thomas. 'Daytime they get a very good class of custom calling there.'

Thomas had returned home little wiser. But he was unable to rule the *Maison Rose* out of the investigation until he discovered what business Albert had had with the foreign count. Frustrated, he'd written up his notes then had shut his notebook with a decisive air and gone next door to the *Bottle and Glass*.

The pub was seething with drinkers. Exchanging greetings, Thomas worked his way through to the bar, where he was surprised and bothered to find Betty Marks serving alongside Schooner. Perspiration ran down the sides of her face as she pulled on the ale handle, sharply told one customer he must wait his turn and rejected the invitation of another to come outside. Then she saw Thomas and her face lit up. 'Hey, stranger, where you been, then?' The foaming beer was handed over, money received, and she automatically wiped down the surface of the bar as she smiled a welcome.

'Didn't know you were barmaid as well as cook,' he said awkwardly, aware that she was the main reason he hadn't frequented the *Bottle and Glass* the last few weeks.

She flicked him a saucy look. 'Mavis is off sick and Schooner hauled me in from the kitchen, said drink was more important than food. What can I get you?'

'Pint of the usual, thanks, Betty.'

'You take it over there,' she indicated a little table in the far corner of the bar. 'It'll soon quieten and we can talk. Eaten, have you? There's a mighty tasty pie in the back; cut you a slice in a twinkling. And you know you like my pickled onions.'

Schooner gave him a welcoming nod and Thomas knew he was caught. He was also hungry.

Little Patty, the girl who worked at whatever was needed doing, brought over a plate of generously cut pork pie, a small dish of pickled onions and a doorstop slice of bread.

'Got you in the kitchen today, have they?' Thomas gave her a smile.

She placed the food carefully before him, tongue peeking from her mouth as she concentrated on making sure nothing fell to the floor. She was very thin, her shoulder bones almost cutting through the worn cotton of her dress, its original pattern long since lost through wear and washing. Say this for Schooner, he made sure his staff were clean, no easy feat in this area of London.

'I'se cook today,' she said proudly, large eyes anxious. 'Missus Marks, she tells me to watch the stew and spoon it out for customers. I'se not to let pot boil. Keep it simmering; that's the trick she says.'

'You'll soon be taking over.'

'You want stew, Mister Jackman?'

'This is fine, Patty.'

She gave him a wide grin and disappeared back to the kitchen.

Thomas looked around to see if there was someone whose eye he could catch who would take the other chair at the little table. But that night's clientele studiously ignored him. He might no longer be a member of the law but there were many who would rather not lay themselves open to his attention. Then a rough-looking fellow approached him in a sideways movement.

'Eli Martock, isn't it?'

'Get you a pint?' the man offered, hovering, obviously anxious to have words with him.

'Thanks, but I'm fine.' Thomas waved a hand at his more than half-full glass. 'Take a seat.' He nudged the opposite chair away from the table with his foot.

'Don't mind if I do.'

Eli Martock placed his tankard on the table and sat down heavily. He wore battered and none-too-clean canvas workmen's trousers and jacket. Having made the move, he looked down at his hands and seemed unable to state why he'd approached the ex-policeman.

'Carter for Jim Stevens, ain't you?' said Thomas in an effort to move the conversation along. 'Remember talking to you when Jim had stock go astray.' Stevens was a wholesale ironmonger. It had been a simple case, one of the first Thomas had investigated after he'd left the police force; Stevens hadn't wanted the authorities involved and Schooner had told him to have a word with Jackman. It hadn't been difficult to establish that one of the other carters had been quietly slipping the odd item of this and that to a mate along his delivery route, reckoning they wouldn't be missed.

Eli nodded, opened his mouth, then closed it again.

Thomas ate a piece of pie and waited for the other man to find his voice.

'Dunno as 'ow you'd want to help.'

'Won't know if you don't tell me what it is.'

A bit of heavy breathing before Eli looked at him, his weathered face creased with anxiety. 'You ain't a copper any longer, is you?'

Thomas shook his head.

'It's just, if I tells you sommat, you don't 'ave to report it, does you?' Eli looked around them, no doubt checking who was in earshot. But the little table was quite private.

Hands held up, Thomas said, 'I can be as silent as any grave.'

'It's just that Mr Stevens fired Walker, you know? 'Im what 'ad been doin' that stealin', you know?'

Thomas nodded. 'He was lucky not to end up in prison, as he would have done if he'd been charged.'

''E doesn't think 'e's lucky, an' … an' 'e reckons 'tis all my fault.'

Thomas put down his knife and fork, conscious they had arrived at the nub of the matter. 'Threatening you, is he?'

'Says 'e'll tell the boss as 'ow I was in on it, too.'

'And were you?'

A vigorous shake of the head. 'Only the cart wot I drive 'ad a right tear-away driver crash into it the other day and while the mess got sorted some varmint scarpered off with several boxes of goods. I told the boss as 'ow it weren't my fault, I'd 'ad me work cut out dealin' with the 'orses, right state they was in, and there'd been witnesses, like. So 'e said as it were all right, though 'e's dockin' me pay until what was lost is covered, said I should 'ave bin able to guard everything better.' The hands with their huge knuckles worked together. 'Only Walker, 'e 'eard all about it and says unless I pays 'im, 'e'll tell the boss as 'ow I was in on 'is scam. An' then it'll be me for the 'igh jump. An' me and the missus, well, there's a littl'un on the way … an' if I lose me job, well, I won't get a reference; Stevens didn't give Walker one.'

'And that's why he's asking you for money?'

Eli nodded miserably. 'Reckon so. Can't get no job without one.'

'What makes you think Mr Stevens will believe him rather than you?'

Feet were shuffled unhappily. 'Long time ago, there were an incident. An' boss gave me another chance but said anything else an' that would be it.'

Thomas remembered Jim Stevens very well. A fair but tough man. He hadn't wanted to prosecute Walker, said it would only give rise to a host of claims against him for goods that hadn't disappeared at all, but he'd never be able to prove it because his paperwork wasn't bang up to rights. Walker had been told the evidence was against him and he was to go without that essential piece of paper every working man or woman required, the reference that stated their abilities and their honesty.

'Have you given Walker any money?'

''E said It was only the once, to tide 'im over like. But …'

'He's come back for more.' Thomas sighed. 'You should never have given him anything. He thinks he's got you now.'

'Reckon that's it. I'm that worried. And then, when I saw you tonight, well, I thought as 'ow you might …'

'Might what?'

Eli put his hands beneath his armpits and looked more miserable than ever. 'Dunno, really. Only, that time it was you wot caught Walker, and I thought, maybe …'

Thomas took a good look at him. Early twenties, strong in arm, weak in head. With a missus in an interesting condition and disaster staring him in the face. By the time Thomas had finished his investigation into the missing goods, he'd been certain Walker was the only carter involved in the scam. The man was an unpleasant type, quick to see where any advantage might lie.

'You know what you should do, don't you, mate?'

Eli looked at him helplessly.

'Go to your boss and tell him everything. Then there's nothing left for Walker to threaten you with.'

Consternation filled Eli's face. 'But suppose as 'ow the boss gives me me marching orders.'

'Stevens is a fair man. More like he'd report Walker for extortion.'

It took a little longer but eventually Eli Martock nodded his big head with its untidy thatch of dark hair. 'I'll do that, Mr Jackman. Right after tomorrow's rounds.'

Thomas made a mental note to call on Jim Stevens first thing the next morning. No need for Eli to know anything about it but best to make sure Stevens understood just what a rat he'd been employing with Walker. He watched the carter walk out of the pub, his shoulders held back.

Nobody else joined him and he'd finished the pie by the time the drinkers had thinned out and Betty came over to his table, pushing back damp curls, a little sparkle in her eyes.

'Supper all right, then, Tom?' She settled down into the other chair with a little sigh of tiredness.

'Excellent, Betty. Best I've had in a long time. And you seem to be training young Patty in the ways of cooking.'

She gave him a smug smile. 'Cook a decent meal and you'll find a job or a husband, maybe both,' she added coyly, looking up at him through her thick dark lashes.

Once again Thomas was conscious he was passing up an offer most men in his situation would feel grateful for. Unable to think of anything safe to say, he finished the last piece of pie.'

Betty waved over Patty, now clearing dirty glasses left by departed drinkers. 'Take Mr Jackman's plate and bring him that last piece of apple pie I told you to save. You have still got it?' she added sharply as the girl hesitated.

Patty nodded. 'But Mr Marks said he wanted it.'

'Then he must have it,' Thomas said quickly, happy to go without one of his favourite dishes if it meant he could escape back home.

'I'll make another tomorrow; he can have some then,' said Betty dismissively.

So Thomas had to remain a captive. Betty asked if the meeting that had interrupted her visit with the oyster stew had gone well. Soon he found himself telling her a little of the Peters case. No names were mentioned, of course, nor any detail that might reveal identities. He concentrated on generalities. 'And tomorrow I must try and get hold of another of the servants and see if there is anything they can reveal of what has been going on.'

'You should talk to the cook.' Betty had followed everything he'd said with keen attention.

'Really?'

'Kitchen is the heart of the house. If someone isn't home for meals, or is off their food, the cook knows. If there are valued visitors, cook knows. If money is short, cook knows.'

Thomas looked at her with new eyes. He had not thought she was capable of such perception, and immediately felt guilty. He should have known she was not lacking intelligence and what she said was only common sense.

★ ★ ★

Now, listening to the rain as he finished going through his notes, Thomas reckoned Betty was right. It was time he turned his attention back to the Peters household and the cook was an obvious target.

He closed the notebook and took himself off to Jim Stevens in High Holborn. It hadn't taken long to put the wholesale iron-monger in the picture regarding Eli Martock.

'Daft bugger,' Jim Stevens said. 'If only I could get my hands on Walker. I was wrong not to prosecute him and I don't mind saying so. I'll put out the word that if he tries anything on Eli, I'll have his guts for garters.'

Thomas left the ironmongery confident that Eli's problem was more or less solved. The rain looked as though it was clearing and the ironmonger's depot wasn't a million miles from Montagu Place.

Hoping Mrs Trenchard had not decided on calling on the Peters' house that morning, he knocked on the basement door. Young Sam opened up. The production of a sixpenny piece ensured his willing co-operation.

'I need to speak to Cook, but not in the house. Best would be to run into her outside. What are her shopping habits?'

Sam picked his nose and stared at him.

'I mean, will she go shopping for food today?'

'Hasn't been for several days,' he said gloomily. His hair needed washing, his collarless shirt bore various stains and there was a decided lack of polish on his shoes. Joshua Peters would have had a fit if he could see the youngest member of his staff so neglecting his appearance.

Suddenly Sam's expression lightened. 'We're to have a proper meal today. I heard Cook tell Mrs Trenchard yesterday it were a disgrace there weren't no money for food. Credit's all used up, she said. We've been living on the store-cupboard for weeks and now its empty. But this morning she told us we could look forward to dinnertime.' He looked expectantly at Thomas.

'So you think Mrs Trenchard has given her some money and that Cook will need to do some shopping before she can produce a proper meal for you all?'

Sam nodded vigorously. 'Last few days we've been starving. Never thought I'd be serving in a gentleman's house what couldn't afford to feed its staff.'

'When do you think Cook will be going out?'

'Dunno. But she went upstairs 'bout five minutes ago.'

'Thanks, Sam.' Thomas thought of something else. 'Millie around?' he asked in an offhand manner.

'Nah! Went off early this morning, dressed in one of Mrs Peters'
best gowns and with her hair done all la-di-dah. She thinks now
she doesn't have to look after her mistress, she can come and go
as she pleases. If you ask me, she's a disgrace.'

'And you don't know where?'

'Found a fancy man, must 'ave.'

Thomas wished fervently that that would turn out to be true.
'Better go back in, Sam,' he said. 'I'll wait around the corner and
see if Cook comes out. Now not a word about this to anyone.'
He slipped Sam another sixpenny piece.

With amazing speed it vanished into an invisible pocket.

Thomas had already reconnoitred the local shops. Unless the
Peters' cook was adventurous, there was everything she needed
by way of fresh produce within a ten-minute walk. He took himself off to hang around the butcher's that seemed to offer good
quality at a reasonable price. It wasn't long before a lanky female
in a serviceable jacket and remarkably plain hat and carrying a
basket came along. He folded the newspaper he had pretended
to peruse and shoved it behind a crate conveniently sitting on
the pavement.

'Mrs Firestone, isn't it?' he asked courteously, falling in beside her.
'What a piece of luck meeting you.'

'Well, Mr Jackman as I live and breathe. And what, pray, do you
do here?'

He looked at her. The dour features were unsurprised, the eyes
disillusioned. 'Why, waiting for you, Mrs Firestone. I hoped you
would welcome a strong arm to carry your basket.'

'And in return?' She stood with feet seemingly anchored to the
pavement proclaiming her unwillingness to co-operate with him.

'Mrs Firestone, Cook, you were there when Mrs Trenchard
announced to all the staff that I was investigating the death of
Mr Peters …'

'I know that she has forbidden you the house.'

'Has she told you all never to speak to me?'

'Forbidding you the house cannot mean anything else.'

'Did Mrs Trenchard tell you why I was forbidden the house?'

'Not my place to ask.'

'I think Mrs Trenchard believes I might uncover something
unpleasant about one or more of the inhabitants. She thinks I should
concentrate on contacts Mr Peters had outside his household.'

'So why aren't you doing that?' But a little of her belligerence had leaked away.

'Why don't we proceed with your shopping.' Thomas took her basket and she made no move to object. 'Might you, perhaps, be visiting the butcher?' He indicated the shop a few doors away.

She looked down at the ground. 'Not there.'

Thomas looked around but there wasn't another. 'Then where?'

The cook squared her shoulders and set off down a side street, Thomas following with the basket.

A number of streets later, they entered another butcher's.

A large joint of topside was requested and shown for inspection.

'Too fresh! I'll not be your customer if that's the sort of meat you try to pass off on them.'

The butcher seemed unmoved by this remark. He went into the rear of his shop and returned with what seemed to Thomas an almost identical piece of meat, except it looked darker than the first. It was held up for scrutiny.

'That's better. I'll take it and start an account.'

The butcher was a man of mature years with a sour expression. He shook his head. 'You may know your meat, missis, but I knows customers. It's cash or nothing until I knows where I am. I'll take the address details, then we'll be able to deliver should it be needed.'

An address was spelled out; not the correct one. Mrs Firestone's back seemed to dare him to comment. Thomas said nothing but took the wrapped packet of beef together with one of suet that had also been requested. He placed both in the basket, watched cash handed over, a gracious farewell given the butcher, and followed the cook outside.

She said nothing but went in the direction of a greengrocer's, where vegetables were purchased, then a grocer's for eggs, a small packet of sugar and an equally small one of currants. In each case cash was handed over.

Outside the grocer's the cook gave a sigh that sounded one of relief. 'Beef is a little extravagant but we deserves it and it will last the week being as it will be served with Yorkshire pudding. Milkman is still delivering milk; well, he's my sister's husband's nephew so he needs to keep in. Then roast tatties and carrots, and they're new season's, followed by dead baby's leg.' She gave him a challenging look.

'Steamed currant roll is one of my favourites, Mrs Firestone; and I suspect it will be served with custard?'

She nodded. 'Bird's, none of that fancy cream unglaze.'

Thomas felt his tummy rumble. 'Wonderful! I am only sorry I cannot be invited to join you all. Tell me, what was your performance with the butcher all about?'

She checked the items in the basket and seemed reluctant to speak. Thomas waited. Finally she gave him a straightforward look. 'Look, if I'd gorn to my usual butcher, the one you was waiting outside, and he'd had a sniff of cash, which he would as he wouldn't have served me without, our account being so adrift, and I don't mind telling you that me housekeeping money's been short a long time. When the master asked me to do special buffets for his friends during the time the mistress was away, I told him I had to have extra cash, which he give me. Made it help with feeding the staff as well. Now, if our regular butcher had got a sniff of cash, I'd've been forced to hand over all the money Mrs Trenchard give me to put against the Peters' account. Which would have left nothing for nothing else.'

'I understand. But a false address?'

Now her look was distinctly shifty. 'You never knows how pally these tradespeople are. I may have to go back there next week. Who knows how long this state of affairs is to last.'

Thomas had been given the opening he'd been waiting for. 'It's to sort things out that I've been hired. Mrs Firestone, do you believe that Mrs Peters murdered her husband?'

Her face flushed and she clasped her hands in their brown cotton gloves tightly together. 'Think that little angel would do any such thing? What do you take me for?'

There was no doubting her sincerity.

'Do you suspect anyone else in the house?'

'Indeed not! We're a respectable household.'

'I'm sure you are. My visits to Mr Peters suggested nothing else. But I wanted to hear it from you. I am sure as cook you must have your finger on the pulse of everything that goes on there.'

Mrs Firestone looked gratified but started to walk back the way they'd come. 'That's as maybe but as cook, as you say, I declare it's time dinner was started.'

The basket was heavy but Thomas was happy to bear it. 'How about Albert? Would he have had reason to want Mr Peters out of the way?'

A loud snort. 'Albert? Far as 'e was concerned, the sun shone out of Mr P's trousers, if you'll forgive the phrase. Not that he isn't a sneaky sort. None of us trusts Albert.'

'He seems to have been involved in Mr Peter's business life. If, for instance, he had decided to, as you might say, freelance, and Mr Peters suspected as much, and challenged him, maybe even warned him that he was thinking of calling in the police, might Albert not then want to remove him from this life?'

Mrs Firestone stopped dead and turned to look at Thomas. 'My, what a mind you've got, Mr Jackman.' She appeared to give the matter some thought. 'Do you think that accounts for why he has upped and left?'

Thomas stared at her. 'Left? Albert has left Montagu Place?'

'Took 'is case and one that looked mighty like the one Mr Peters used to carry 'is papers in. Sarah remarked on it.'

'Sarah?'

'Albert came in this morning as we was finishing breakfast. Dumped the two bags on the floor, drank his tea and ate his toast. Then said he knew he wasn't favourite with any of us and that we wouldn't be sorry to see the back of 'im but not as pleased as he was to see the back of us. Then he picked up his bags and left. We was all gobsmacked. All right, there wasn't no job for him with Mr Peters gone but Mrs Trenchard has promised us all our wages – whatever 'appens, she said.' Mrs Firestone's voice trailed away as though she did not put full faith in those words.

'And Sarah commented on the briefcase Albert was carrying?'

'It was after 'e'd gone up the basement stairs, whistling like there was no tomorrow. "Why, that looked like the one Mr Peters always carried," she said.'

Thomas thought about the empty drawers in the study desk. 'Did it look as though it had a lot of papers in it?'

'Don't know about that. I wouldn't know if it had anything in it. But as I said, that Albert's a shifty sort. None of us trusts him far as we can see him – and that's too far.'

'Where has he gone?'

'Now there's a thing!'E wouldn't say. I reckons 'e didn't know. Said if anything came for him, to forward it to the master's company, he'd be in touch with them. And that, he said, included the wages he was owed.'

Thomas wondered how closely the valet was, or had been, involved with the import/export company.

'What about Millie, Mrs Peters' maid?' Thomas shifted the basket from one hand to the other as they made their way back to Montagu Place.

'That too heavy for you?'

He shook his head. 'Not at all, but I'll say you must be strong, Mrs Firestone.'

'All cooks is. We 'ave to be, 'eaving heavy pots around, wielding choppers and such.'

'Do you trust Millie?'

The cook sighed. 'There's another you never knows where you are with. Sweet as anything when she first comes. On her dignity, of course. Well, a lady's maid always thinks she's above the rest of us staff.'

'Why should that be, Mrs Firestone?'

''Cause she's in such close contact with the mistress. Knows everything that goes on, she does.'

Fleetingly Thomas wondered whether Betty knew anything about the position a lady's maid held in the household.

'And did she tell you about Mrs Peters' friendship with Daniel Rourke?'

Mrs Firestone shook her head. 'Nor she did! And I wouldn't have believed it if she had. Another sneaky one, Millie is. Though when she went for the master after Mrs Peters left, well, you could have knocked me over with a basting spoon.'

'She did, did she?'

Mrs Firestone made a face as they crossed Marylebone High Street. 'Sweet as sugar, she was; couldn't do enough for him. Those evenings what I told you about when the master had his friends round, well, it was Millie what acted as hostess. Course I didn't see what went on above stairs but Emily reported to me.' Mrs Firestone stopped. She hesitated for a moment then said in almost a whisper, 'She saw Millie slip into his bedroom! And she was dressed in a gown belonging to the mistress. Well, I didn't know what to think.' Though it was obvious that she did. 'Of course, when the mistress returned, all that stopped. After Mr Peters died and the mistress had been arrested, Sarah wanted to know if we should tell Mrs Trenchard what had been going on.'

'And you said?'

The cook sniffed. 'Spreading gossip like that isn't any part of our jobs. Ten to one, she wouldn't believe us, and if she did, what could she do? The master's dead. Nothing can harm him now. Millie's a silly girl what will get her comeuppance sooner or later. If she's fired now, what will Mrs Peters do when she comes 'ome? Better she should find out about her in her own good time.'

'I don't suppose Albert was too happy with Millie making up to Mr Peters?'

Mrs Firestone sniffed derisively. 'I'll say not. Thought the master and all his affairs was his, if you ask me. Look, is there anything else you want of me or can I get back to my kitchen? They'll all be wanting their lunch.'

Thomas saw that they had reached Montagu Street. He handed over the basket and doffed his hat. 'Thank you for your courtesy, Mrs Firestone.'

She gave him a sharp look. 'If anything I've said is of help to Mrs Peters, I'm right glad. The idea she could have anything to do with the master's death is …' She huffed and puffed, trying to find words for her outrage. 'Well, any who thinks that should be in a lunatic asylum. We shall 'ave to rely on you, Mr Jackman, 'cause that policeman ain't no good, and you can tell him I said so. Mrs Peters in prison!' She carried her basket down the basement stairs, her straight back expressing how ridiculous it was.

Thomas watched her go for a moment, then walked rapidly away, anxious not to be found in the vicinity should Mrs Trenchard suddenly appear. He thought that he now had a very clear idea of matters in the Peters household. It was time to move the focus of his investigation.

Chapter Eighteen

Rachel welcomed Ursula's arrival with a sigh of relief.

'Thank heavens you're here! Let's set off.' She crammed a hat on her head, put on a jacket then hustled them both out of the door. The sun had come out and there was no hint now of rain.

'Where is the prison?' Ursula asked as they started hurrying in the direction of Victoria station.

'Holloway is north of Islington,' Rachel said, leaving Ursula no wiser. Her present knowledge of London was minimal. She regarded its vast sprawl as an ongoing project for which considerable time was needed. For the moment she was only concerned with how long it would take to reach Alice and the impossibility of the task she was expected to perform.

The noise of the traffic, the blaring horns and cries of drivers as they tried to negotiate the crowded streets, together with a struggle not to be separated from Rachel, made conversation difficult.

As they approached Victoria station, Rachel shouted at her, 'Have you travelled underground before?'

The underground railway! Ursula was aware of its existence but had not had occasion yet to travel by its means. Tunnels had always seemed thrilling to her. To burrow through land like a mole, to be like the Romans and force a direct way through whatever obstructions nature placed in your path, made man seem mighty. Below the streets there could be none of the congestion she saw all around them, the only traffic there travelled on well-ordered lines.

Not quite so well-ordered were the crowds of travellers Ursula found herself jostled by as they made their way below ground to a beautifully brick-lined tunnel.

'We shall not have long to wait,' Rachel said. 'The trains are frequent. The line goes round in a great circle, one can travel in either direction and it is much the fastest way of getting across town. It will only take us some twenty minutes to reach Islington.'

It might be the fastest way to travel, but the steam of the train's engine made the air sulphurous. Ursula spent the journey trying to tell herself the atmosphere was nothing compared with the indignities Alice was having to suffer. It was a relief to rise above ground once again.

Outside the Islington station, Rachel found a hansom and gave their direction. The cab offered privacy and the chance of conversation. As they drove off, Rachel turned to her and said very quickly, as though she didn't want to think too hard about what she had to say, 'Ursula, it is good of you to come to visit Alice. I never asked if you are reluctant to enter a prison. Many would feel it beneath their dignity.'

Ursula laughed. 'I am not a stranger to prisons.'

'You aren't?'

'I lived for a time in silver fields in California, and then ran a boarding house in San Francisco that made the one I live in now seem a palace. The company I mixed with then often found themselves locked up, for all sorts of offences. Usually, though, for days rather than weeks or years.' She might have added that she once had been arrested herself but the blackest period of her life was not one to be talked about. Here, in civilised London, she was able to put that time behind her.

Rachel looked thoroughly taken aback.

'So, you see, I don't mind at all visiting your sister. My reluctance this morning was purely because of having to go to my new job.'

'I hope you will forgive me for my behaviour then. I had no right to expect you to be prepared to come with me without notice.'

Ursula was touched. Rachel seemed a very proud person and to apologise in such a generous manner must have cost her dear.

'I was sorry not to be able to respond as you wanted. To have your sister in such a dreadful situation and not be able to help must be terrible.'

Rachel's lips tightened and she looked away. After a moment she said, 'Ursula, do you really have no income apart from what you earn?'

'Indeed not,' Ursula said cheerfully. 'But I am used to earning my living and looking out for myself.' For a fleeting moment she wondered how Rachel would survive in a mining camp or running a seedy bed and breakfast establishment in San Francisco with its down and outs, Chinese quarter, property profiteers and women of easy virtue. It made the area where Thomas Jackman lived that had so upset Rachel seem a haven for civilised living.

After a little pause Rachel said, 'What ... what did you and Alice talk about during the time she stayed at your lodgings?'

Ursula thought back. 'She was very interested in my travels. Although Mr Peters frequently went abroad, it was on business and she did not accompany him. She said she longed to see Paris and Vienna, to climb the Alps, sail on Lake Lucerne. She told me she loved to hear Daniel talk about his travels. Apparently he had spent much time in Europe. She said he brought the places he'd visited alive for her.' Ursula remembered the way Alice's eyes had glowed with an inner intensity when she talked of how Daniel had wanted the two of them to make a home in either France or Italy.

Rachel seemed surprised. 'I hadn't realised she was so anxious to travel. Or that she wished to leave England. I am several years younger and since her marriage Alice has not always been open with me. She said there were things she as a married woman could not discuss with someone unmarried. I can't think why. Surely marriage is not such a mystery!'

Ursula said nothing.

'Did she not talk about Joshua, Mr Peters, and why she had run away?'

'Your sister seemed to me a very private person, one who kept her innermost feelings to herself.'

'That is Alice. She has never been very communicative. So what else did you talk about?'

'It was mainly what you might call safe subjects; for instance we discussed books we had enjoyed. She recommended I read the works of Mrs Gaskell and I suggested she should try the American writers such as Mark Twain and Edith Wharton. We both said we loved Mr Dickens and Mr Trollope. And she was very interested to hear about life in America. Perhaps she wondered if she and Daniel could live there rather than in Europe.'

Rachel sighed heavily. 'It must have taken so much courage to leave that dreadful man. My aunt was devastated with the shame of her action. Did you, Ursula, feel that she would indeed be happy with Daniel?'

'Oh, yes! She seemed desperately in love. And I think that parting from him broke her heart.'

Rachel was silent.

'Tell me,' said Ursula, 'were you able to discover what Albert was doing with Count Meyerhoff in that public house? Have you talked to Mr Jackman and discovered why he was there as well? Was he, as it seemed, following Albert?'

Alice gave a contemptuous snort. 'Neither Albert nor Mr Jackman has been available. When I went round to the Peters' household only Cook was there. The servants seem to think they have been given a holiday! My aunt has spoken to them about the necessity for keeping everything in proper order ready for Alice's return. I do feel Mr Jackman should call on me with details of how his investigation is doing. I wonder,' she said angrily, 'whether we were right to employ him.'

'I believe him to be very reliable,' Ursula tried to sound reassuring. 'I am sure he will let you know as soon as he has something to report.'

Inwardly, she wondered what Thomas Jackman had been up to in following Albert, if that indeed was what he had been doing. Did she really know enough about the ex-policeman to be completely convinced he was to be trusted? Then there was Count Meyerhoff. It seemed so unlikely that Joshua Peters or his valet had any business with him. That morning, beginning to sort out the *Maison Rose* accounts, Ursula had looked for a mention of a Mr or Mrs Joshua Peters, thinking that perhaps Alice had visited *Maison Rose* as a client. So far, the name of Peters had not appeared.

The cab came to a stop. They alighted and Ursula had her first, astonished sight of Holloway prison. 'But it looks just like a castle from a fairy tale!' she exclaimed, taking in the towers, the battlements, the fanciful lines and elaborate stonework.

Rachel turned from paying off the cab and gave a snort of derision. 'Some fairy tale! Heaven only knows what the authorities were thinking of to choose such a design, for it has always been a prison. Originally both male and female inmates were housed there but this year it was converted to hold all females. At least that has worked to Alice's advantage.'

There was nothing fairy tale about Holloway's grim interior. Dark corridors led to a series of wings that reached back in several directions; the prison was much larger than had seemed possible from its frontage. There must be room for many, many cells. A depressing smell of boiled cabbage and unwashed bodies hung about the reception hall. The walls were whitewashed but, though there was no discernable dirt, nothing appeared clean. Odd cries and the sound of clumping feet echoed down the stone corridors giving an impression of constant activity. A girl in an arrow-decorated prison uniform worked at scrubbing the floor on her knees. She didn't glance at the visitors.

The two girls were directed to an office, where a thorough search was made of the change of clothes Rachel had brought for her sister; as a remand prisoner, Alice did not have to wear the official uniform.

Rachel handed over Ursula's Visitor's Permit. It was scrutinised by a wardress whose expression suggested she doubted it would be in order. She then fixed Ursula with a basilisk stare, laid the permit on her desk and watched while another wardress conducted a quick but comprehensive search of Ursula's person. Finally she gave a nod.

'You are not allowed any contact with the detainee. You must not touch her hand nor any part of her. You must not ask about details of any prisoner she may have come into contact with or their treatment. You understand?'

'Yes, ma'am,' Ursula said hurriedly. 'I will abide by all your regulations.'

'You, Miss Fentiman, will remain here.'

By now Ursula wondered whether there wasn't a danger she could end up in one of the cells herself. She followed another wardress to a small room that held a plain table and two chairs.

'Sit, Miss Grandison.'

She did so and waited on her own for several long minutes before Alice was brought in by the stern-faced wardress.

Ursula rose and the officer held out a warning hand, enforcing the space between the two girls.

Alice's appearance shocked Ursula. She had lost weight. Her dark dress hung on her small frame, it was so loose it took a second look to discern that she was with child. Her face was very pale, her hair greasy and pulled back without any attempt at style. Her eyes, though, lit up when she saw Ursula and she smiled.

'How kind of you to visit me,' she said in a low voice. 'I cannot imagine what has brought you.'

The wardress took up a position by the door, her face expressionless.

Ursula wanted so much to enfold the girl in her arms, to offer comfort and reassurance. She had to force herself to make no movement but could not stop herself saying impulsively, 'How can you bear it here?'

Alice's gaze flicked towards the wardress, who was frowning.

Ursula sat down and tried to look innocent.

'It is not so bad,' the girl said steadily, sitting at the other side of the table. 'Rachel has visited and so have my uncle and my lawyer.'

Ursula drew a deep breath. 'Alice, Rachel is very anxious about you. We all are. We understand you will not explain, will not comment in any way on the writings in your diary.'

For a moment something flashed deep in Alice's eyes, then she looked away.

Ursula waited.

Finally, in the same low voice, the girl said, 'I wrote what I wrote. I cannot deny it. I have told my sister so.'

Without thinking, Ursula extended her hand across the table.

'Contact with Peters is not allowed,' the wardress said sharply.

Ursula flushed and withdrew her hand. 'But why, Alice? We cannot believe you meant those words, that you really wished Mr Peters could leave this life.'

Alice gave her a straight look. 'It was wrong of me to write in that way. I have offended against the preachings of the Church. But I did not send Joshua poisoned chocolates.' It was a solemn declaration.

Could Ursula believe her? Here, faced with such a dogged spirit in these surroundings where despair seemed to leach from every wall, she felt that maybe she could. She knew she wanted to.

'We understand that you wrote you had reason for believing that your husband was a wicked man and did not deserve to live. Can't you tell us why?'

Alice closed her eyes and said nothing.

'I believe before your husband died, you met with Mr Jackman. At that time he had been hired by Mr Peters to follow you. Have you heard that he is now investigating your husband's murder and trying to discover who did send those chocolates so that you can be released?'

The faintest of nods.

'Can't you help him? Can't you tell us what it is you know about Mr Peters? It must be more than that he mistreated you.'

Silence.

'Surely you understand what danger you are in?'

A long pause, then Alice placed a hand over her thickened waist. 'I know that whatever happens, my child will be safely delivered.'

Ursula cried out in frustration. 'Do you want your child to be born in this place?'

The girl flinched. 'You don't understand. I am innocent but I cannot have my child growing up to despise its father.'

'And what will he or she think of a mother hanged for murder?' Ursula felt she had to shock Alice into revealing what it was she thought she knew.

Again Alice closed her eyes. 'I cannot believe any jury will convict an innocent woman.'

'Your sister has been trained in law and believes that they could.'

A shudder ran through Alice's frail frame. 'I must believe otherwise.'

'Please forgive me for asking this but I think it could be important. Alice, you were obviously very unhappy with your husband. If he had not died, were you planning to take your child and leave him a second time?'

The girl did not seem upset by the question. 'I should have remained with him. It was my duty; a child should be with both its parents. Nor could I have brought myself to abandon him or her. If I left their father, I would not be allowed to take his child with me.'

The situation seemed so extraordinary, Ursula was left bereft for words.

'Miss Grandison, Ursula, I miss our discussions on books. Can you perhaps see that I am sent some volume that will allow me to forget this place while I turn its pages? I believe it is permitted.'

'Of course I will. But Alice, Mr Jackman needs your help to uncover why Mr Peters died. Please, you must tell him what you know.'

Alice gave Ursula such a sweet smile, it almost broke her heart. 'Our time will soon be up. Please, tell me how Mrs Maple is and Meg and Mrs Crumble. And I would love to hear how your employment with Mrs Bruton proceeds.'

Ursula tried to think of some approach that would break through Alice's determination and could find none. So she related a few details of life at the boarding house and Wilton Crescent.

'And I have another job now. I am to attempt to sort out a tangle of accounts at the *Maison Rose* beauty clinic. Tell me, have you visited there?'

Before Alice could respond, the wardress announced that Miss Grandison's visit was at an end and it was time for Peters to return to her cell.

'Thank you for coming,' Alice said, just as though it had been a social visit. 'Please give my love to my sister. She is not to worry: I am fine. And I wish Mr Jackman well in his search for whoever it was that sent those chocolates.'

Alice Peters was taken away.

Then Ursula was returned to the office where Rachel waited. To the hopeful look the girl gave her she had to shake her head. 'Your sister will only say that she did not send the poisoned chocolates.'

Rachel closed her eyes for a moment but said nothing until they had found a cab to take them to the underground station. Once settled she turned to Ursula. 'Alice said nothing at all about why she wrote those words in her diary about Joshua not deserving to live?'

'She says she cannot have her child believing its father was an unworthy person.'

Rachel cried out, 'Oh Alice, Alice!'

'She said that if her husband had not died, she would have remained with him, that a child should have both its parents and she could not have brought herself to abandon him or her.'

Rachel put a hand over her eyes. 'How like Alice.'

'I can understand wishing your child to have its father but if she believed her husband was such a dreadful man, could she not

have taken it and gone to Daniel? Would he not have been a sur-
rogate father and given the child a happier start in life?'

Rachel shuddered. 'Do you not realise that she would not
have been allowed to do that?'

'What do you mean?'

'It is illegal for a mother to remove her children from the care
of their father.'

Ursula was appalled.

'But surely a mother has every right to nurture and care for
her child, especially if the father abuses her.'

'The law does not agree. No matter how foul the father, how
badly he treats the mother, he has sole rights to any offspring.'

'That is dreadful!'

'Now you can see what we are fighting for in our campaign
for the female vote.'

It wasn't votes for women that were concerning Ursula. If the
situation was really as Rachel had outlined, it could well be
suggested that Alice had a cast-iron motive for removing her
husband from her life once and for all.

'Do you really think that Alice could be found guilty of
murder?'

Rachel looked out of the window and said nothing. Ursula
wondered if she had begun to believe Alice might actually be
guilty. Rachel might not know everything about her sister's marriage but she surely knew enough about its dreadful aspects and
how ensnared Alice felt herself to be.

The cab arrived at the underground. Rachel got out and paid
for their fare.

Once back at Victoria station, Ursula said goodbye and went
to find a bookshop.

Chapter Nineteen

As part of his commission for Joshua Peters, Thomas had looked into Daniel Rokeby's background. By dint of a session at the local library and visits to several literary magazines, Thomas had amassed a considerable amount of information on him. The poet's presence had been noted at several society gatherings; he had had two romantic stories published in magazines provided for the entertainment of women with little to occupy their time. And in several publications he found poems by him.

Thomas did not consider himself an intellectual in any way. He'd rather read accounts of petty crime than poetry lauding a woman's looks or the joy in a blackbird's song. Daniel's verses to 'Night', which spoke of a 'hushing wind' and 'the owl's ghostly wings' and 'quivering planets shining through the black garb of night' left him unmoved. But one of the poems contained a credit after the author's name noting he was a member of a poetic society.

After his encounter with Mrs Firestone, Thomas made his way to the public house in Bloomsbury where he had followed Daniel for the first time.

It was approaching lunchtime and both bars were busy but there was no sign of Mr Rokeby. On his way out, though, Thomas caught sight of notice fixed in the entrance. The poetry society Daniel Rokeby belonged to was holding a lunchtime meeting there that day in an upstairs room. For a small fee, members of the public were invited to hear some of the poets read their most recent work.

Even as he read the message, two men passed him heading for the stairs. Thomas followed, thinking he should have gone home and changed his suit for a loose jacket and linen trousers. A cravat would have also been a good idea, as would swapping his trilby for a panama.

At the door a young woman with a straw hat on long, fair hair sat with a metal moneybox and a sheet of paper on which she noted the names of, presumably, those who were not members of the poetry society. Thomas felt in his pocket for the entrance fee, handed it over and was given a beaming smile. 'May I take your name and address, sir? This is so we can inform you of other events of our society.'

'Michael Prescott, 2 Cheyne Walk,' Thomas said urbanely.

She wrote, and the box chinked as she added his coins. 'Please, take a seat,' the girl said, waving her hand at the room. 'Our poets will soon be here.'

The audience was not many. The two young men Thomas had followed upstairs sat on the far side of the group of chairs, very close to a dais on which the poets no doubt were to stand as they read. Three seats at the front were occupied by a couple of smartly dressed middle-aged women accompanied by a young girl who looked as though she could be sister to the one manning the door. Another slightly older but just as smartly dressed woman sat on her own. For a dreadful moment Thomas thought that it was Mrs Trenchard. He did not imagine she could be a follower of modern poetry but she might have heard that the young man her niece had left her husband for was to perform and come out of interest. Then he realised that, under the severe hat, the women's hair was brown not iron grey.

Minutes passed. Then more minutes. A few more people entered without paying, obviously members of the society. Thomas looked around but there was no one who looked like a poet.

The two women with the young girl grew restless. 'If nothing happens in five minutes, I think we should leave,' said one.

'No, Mama, we must stay; I'm sure Rupert will be here soon,' said the girl.

At last four young men entered carrying sheets of paper and glasses of beer. Long haired, wearing velveteen jackets and linen trousers, Thomas thought they looked exactly how he imagined poets should. And he was relieved to see that Daniel Rokeby was one of them.

The leader, short and chunky with a sparse beard the colour and appearance of hay, bounced up on to the dais and beamed at the scanty audience. 'How very good it is to see you all here today. I am Boris Humphrey, Chairman of the Society. It is our very good fortune this lunchtime to have to read to us three of society's leading poets ...'

Thomas stopped listening. He was watching Daniel Rokeby. The other two poets were nervously shuffling their feet and sorting through their papers. When it came to moving up on to the dais, they stumbled and apologised awkwardly. Daniel, though, stood quietly, as though in complete command of himself, or in a trance.

He was the last poet to read his work. The other two, whose names Thomas did not bother to register, read three or four shortish works. All were bad and were read badly. At least, Thomas considered that works comparing a girl's eyes with twinkling stars, or her hair with silken waterfalls, could not qualify for good poetry. Nor did a comparison between a beating heart and a racing horse, particularly when the heart had been spurred into action by the sight of yet another girl. It seemed all that the poets could be concerned with was the effect on them of pretty girls. Their delivery was histrionic and did their works no favours. By the stillness of the girl sitting with the two middle-aged women, and the fervour of her applause after the second poet finished, Thomas deduced that she had provided the inspiration for his work, particularly as he flushed deep crimson as he caught her gaze while bowing to the audience.

Then it was Daniel's turn.

He stepped up on to the dais with a dreamy air, looked straight at the audience and said, 'These are poems I wrote recently while staying in the Lake District. They are in a new style for me.'

Well, at least there seemed a good chance they would not be concerned with comparing Alice's eyes to sparkling diamonds or the Milky Way.

The verses were simple, and as far as Thomas was concerned, all the better for it. Sheep and rocks and lonely farmers were more in his line, as was the image of a steamboat seen from above, sailing across a wide lake with the grace of a bird flying through an empty sky. The verses were read almost in a monotone and received only a spattering of applause.

Daniel, however, bowed and in a low voice thanked those who had come. As he straightened, he looked in Thomas's direction and his eyes widened. The detective rose and came up to him. 'I enjoyed that,' he said. 'Went to the Lake District myself once; I could recognise the pictures you created.'

Daniel looked modestly pleased.

'Can we talk, or do you need to meet up with anyone?'

There was the slightest of hesitations then, Daniel said, 'I'd be delighted to converse with you.'

'A drink downstairs, perhaps?'

'By all means.'

Daniel took his farewell of the stocky chairman and thanked him for the opportunity to read his verse.

'Sorry there weren't more people here, I'd expected a larger audience but it probably isn't a good time of the year. Winter's better. We'll do another one in a couple of months' time, say early November.'

The girl who had been taking the money went up, looking coquettish. For a moment Thomas was reminded of Millie. 'Daniel, are you not to lunch with us? Boris said all the poets were invited.'

'Now, Esther, I never said they were all coming.'

'Boris has been very kind but Mr Jackman needs to talk to me.'

The girl's face fell. She was sweet looking and Thomas didn't think he'd have been as curt with her as Daniel had.

Downstairs, to enter the saloon bar they had first to exit on to the pavement. Standing in the road were two women handing out leaflets from a hessian bag bearing the slogan *Votes for Women*. Not many passers-by were taking the offered leaflet.

Daniel made an exclamation of disgust as he followed Jackman into the pub. Thomas got them two pints of the landlord's special and they took their glasses out into a small courtyard. The day was warm and the courtyard, with two wooden benches and a dilapidated iron table, was more private than the bar.

Thomas looked at the young man speculatively. 'You don't approve of giving women the vote?'

'They wouldn't know what to do with it. Women are made for creating a home, not interfering with politics.'

'Yet women serve on some councils now, and decide on matters pertaining to their lives.'

Daniel looked down at the foam of his beer. 'Can you see Alice Peters running a campaign for, I don't know, testing fallen women for sexual diseases?'

Thomas was shaken. 'Is that the sort of thing that's being talked about?'

'Oh, yes! Talk to Rachel, she'll fill you in on all the shameful ideas these women have.'

'I thought she was a friend of yours.'

'Oh, she is. Rachel's sterling, top of the pole, if only she didn't have these ridiculous ideas in her head.' Daniel put his glass down, removed a cigarette case from inside his jacket and offered it to Thomas. Both men lit up. The cigarettes were Turkish and strong. Thomas resisted an urge to cough and studied Daniel. He might look like a cartoon version of a poet, with his velvet jacket, tasselled beret and linen trousers, but the verse he'd presented had been, in Thomas's estimation, a cut above that of the other fellows. Someone who could compare sods of earth to the creation of a potato showed more sense than poets usually managed. Yet his radical objection to the Votes for Women campaign struck an odd note. Surely one expected a poet to be liberal, at any rate with a small 'l'? And the night he had come with Rachel Fentiman and Ursula Grandison to his house to enlist his help, Daniel had been obstructionist and a downright boor.

'Have you been in communication with Mrs Peters?'

Daniel flushed. 'I am not a relative and the Trenchards look down on my relationship with Alice.'

'Was Mrs Peters in touch with you after her husband died?'

Daniel kicked moodily at a stone on the courtyard. 'There was hardly time before that sod of a policeman arrested her.'

Thomas did not agree with the use of such language to describe members of His Majesty's Police Force but it matched so exactly with his own opinion of Inspector Drummond that he let it go.

'It must have been a shock when Mrs Peters decided to leave her husband and fly to your protection.'

Daniel looked at him suspiciously. 'I don't like your use of the word "protection", it seems to refer to a different sort of woman altogether.'

Thomas made a graceful gesture, 'I apologise. Yet,' he mused aloud, 'would I be wrong in suggesting that Mrs Peters was indeed in need of protection from her husband?'

'No, by God, absolutely right!' The words were almost shouted. 'He was a fiend of the first order.'

'Because of the way he treated his wife?'

'Of course.'

'No other reason?'

'What do you mean?'

'I wondered if Mrs Peters had ever suggested to you that her husband was involved in illegal activities.'

'What sort of "illegal activities"?'

Thomas shrugged his shoulders. 'I was hoping it was something you might be able to give me a hint about.'

'You mean, something Alice, Mrs Peters, had told me about her husband?'

Thomas nodded and waited.

Daniel dropped his cigarette stub, ground it out with his foot, lit another one and offered the case again to Thomas, without success.

'You're a dashed careful sort of cove, aren't you?'

Thomas contemplated the glowing end of the man's cigarette and said nothing.

'Look, I reckon Alice, Mrs Peters, would want me to be square with you. She might, in fact, I suppose, already have said something when she was arrested. Though if she did, I can't work out why she was hauled off to gaol like that.'

'Yet you didn't say anything at that meeting when you came to my place.'

Daniel shifted his feet uncomfortably. 'Thing is, she made me promise I wouldn't. But that was before …'

'Before what?'

'Before it looked as though the police were happy to accept the evidence of her diary as sufficient proof she … she dosed that rotter with prussic acid.'

'Now you think she would want you to be "square with me"?' Thomas felt exasperated. This young man didn't seem able to put two thoughts together logically. He was reverting to his first impression of Daniel Rokeby. When he had been following Alice Peters, he had been unable to understand what she found attractive in him. All right, he was tall and handsome. He seemed to be fathoms deep in love with her; he would stroke her cheek, take her hand, buy her a rose, hold animated conversations, but was that enough for such a lovely girl?

Thomas had finally come to the conclusion that life with Joshua Peters was so difficult and unpleasant, it made spending time with Daniel Rokeby like being offered a glass of clear spring water after having to drink the muddied remains at the bottom of a well.

'So, what did Mrs Peters tell you about her husband?'

Daniel drank deep of his beer then lit another cigarette.

Thomas waited.

'It was nothing definite,' he said at last.

Thomas gave an inward sigh. He had been mad to think anything concrete would come of this conversation.

'There must have been something that suggested … what? Illegal activities? Abuse of some sort?'

'Good heavens, no!' Daniel seemed truly shocked.

'Perhaps if you told me what, exactly, Mrs Peters said about her husband?'

'Of course, you are quite right. So, let's see now.' For a long moment Daniel seemed lost in thought. 'What she said was,' he broke off then said, 'I hope I get it right.'

Thomas gave a long sigh.

'She said that if she had known what sort of man Joshua Peters was before they became engaged, she would never have promised to marry him.'

'And what sort of man was he?'

'I asked her that and she said she couldn't tell me, it was too dreadful. But she promised that if ever she decided to leave him and he made trouble, she would act.'

'How?'

'She didn't say, only that it would mean we could be free to live our lives together.'

'Why do you think that means she didn't poison her husband?'

'You can't think that is what she did!'

'The evidence is beginning to mount against her.'

'What evidence?'

'Her diary and now what she said to you.' Thomas felt he was being brutal but Daniel's lack of understanding made him feel he was hewing at a coal face that refused to yield usable fuel.

'But she must have meant something else!'

'What?'

'Well, that she would tell Peters she knew something about him that was to his detriment.'

'We come back to the same question. What did she know?'

Daniel was merely holding the cigarette he'd lighted.

'Surely you have to see that that evidence against Joshua Peters is the only thing that could save Mrs Peters from the hangman's rope?'

Daniel stared at him aghast. 'You can't mean that.'

'I'm afraid I do. Apparently the evidence given in the diary is damning. Mrs Peters wrote that she hated her husband and wished he could vanish from the earth. I have witnessed his treatment of her and it was not pleasant. I can well understand that she would want him removed from her life. Now you tell me that if she left him and he made trouble, she would act. We know she did leave him and we know that she returned to him because, she says, she was with child by him. Now the only way she could give that child a respectable life and fund its upkeep and education was if her husband died. Or,' Thomas deliberately paused. 'Or, if she decided that maybe life with him was not so insupportable after all.'

'Don't say that! I can't believe it!' Daniel walked agitatedly around the little courtyard.

'Did you believe it when she told you she was returning to him?'

'No!' Another agitated walk. He stopped and turned to face Thomas. 'I truly believed that once she'd returned she'd find she couldn't after all stand life with him. I waited for her to contact me. I hung around outside the house and gave notes to Millie to give to her. Even when days stretched into weeks, I still believed it was only a matter of time.'

'And when you heard Joshua Peters had been poisoned, you didn't suspect for one moment that Alice Peters might have been responsible?'

'No! No! No!' Daniel sank on to one of the benches and put his head in his hands. 'It was the last thing I could think.'

'And even after he had died, she didn't tell you why she so despised and hated him?'

He shook his head. 'She only ever said what I have told you. Why can't you believe that?'

'It seems I have to.' Thomas felt extreme frustration. Here he was so near to the heart of the mystery and, like an eel, it slipped away from him.

'You should speak to Rachel, she might know. After all, she worked for him.'

Jackman looked at him in consternation. 'Rachel Fentiman worked for Joshua Peters?'

'Not for long. It was after she came down from Manchester.'

★ ★ ★

Daniel left the public house with every appearance of having realised, at last, just how perilous was Alice Peters' situation.

For Thomas the question was, could he believe Daniel's fervent conviction that she was incapable of poisoning her husband?

He had hoped that Daniel would manage to produce some sort of lead that he could follow. Instead all he was left with was the upsetting news that Albert had disappeared from Montagu Place. He decided to set out immediately for the docks again. He was unlikely to be lucky enough to run into the valet but at least he could ascertain if Albert had informed Peters' company of his new address.

And he must talk to Rachel Fentiman.

Chapter Twenty

Two days after visiting Alice, Ursula walked into chaos at Wilton Crescent. Paint-splashed drugget lined the hall and stairs. Dungareed workmen carried canvas tool holdalls up to the first floor. Already, hammering could be heard from the bathroom. As Ursula emerged from the basement, Mrs Bruton was drawing on a pair of grey kid gloves; two leather cases had been placed by the front door and her maid, Huckle, stood solidly beside them, while Enid watched the road through the front door's glass side panel.

'Ah, Miss Grandison. Thank you, my dear, for being so punctual. Dick is fetching me a hansom and I'm expecting it to arrive any minute. I cannot stand the mess and the noise here a moment longer. I am removing to Brown's Hotel. Call on me there tomorrow morning at eleven o'clock. You will need to bring my post so I can go through it.' Mrs Bruton checked her appearance in the mirror above the hall side table, adjusted two of the curls that artfully emerged from below the brim of a wide felt hat festooned with feathers, and gave a little nod of satisfaction.

'Cab's here, Madam.' Enid opened the door and Huckle and she each carried out a suitcase.

'There are a few letters with notes on them that I've put on your desk, Miss Grandison. Please be good enough to deal with them. Then you can perhaps go through the cupboards and see if they need tidying. Here are the keys.' Mrs Bruton handed over a small, inlaid wooden box that rattled as Ursula took it. 'And, Miss Grandison, please to keep an eye on the workmen.'

Mrs Bruton picked up a slim leather enveloped-shaped hand-bag that matched her grey suit, tucked it under her arm and followed Enid and the second suitcase out to the cab.

One of the workmen came down the stairs. Ursula caught his attention. 'How long before you finish the work you are undertaking for Mrs Bruton?'

'Better ask the guv, miss. He's the one what knows.'

'Is he here?'

'No, miss, not now.'

'When your boss arrives, please ask him to let me know the timetable for these works.' Ursula went off to the room she thought of as her office, found the letters, looked at them, then decided to investigate what was going on upstairs.

It had been a little while ago that Mrs Bruton had mentioned that her bathroom needed bringing up to date.

'I was shown such a handsome bath when I visited a friend a little time ago. And the room was lined with marble; Cleopatra would have felt so at home there. I asked for the details of all the suppliers.'

Orders had been placed, Ursula's opinion sought over the choice of taps, tiles and floor covering. The fittings were to be exactly the same as the ones Mrs Bruton's friend had had installed.

A thunderous noise came down the stairs as Ursula climbed up to the first floor. It sounded as though a major work of demolition was taking place. As she approached the bathroom, dust filled the air. Coughing, she stood in the open doorway. Two sturdy men wielded heavy hammers; huge pieces of the existing porcelain bath already lay on the floor and total destruction was well on the way.

'This door surely should be kept shut,' Ursula said firmly, retreating and closing it as she left.

Back in her office, sneezing from the dust and envying Mrs Bruton's ability to remove herself from chaos, the letters were attended to. Enid, complaining about the dust, brought her the usual mid-morning coffee together with the latest delivery of mail.

'It'll take I don't know what to get rid of it when those dratted men have finished. Any idea how long it's going to take, miss?'

'I've asked the foreman to tell me the timetable, Enid. If I'm not here when he comes, please ask him to return early tomorrow morning, will you?'

'Yes, miss.' The girl sounded doubtful.

'Tell him Mrs Bruton has requested his presence.'

'But she won't be here.'

'He won't know that, Enid.' Ursula gave her an encouraging smile.

There was little to engage her in the letters that had been brought in. Ursula set them in a small pile ready for her to pick up with the early morning mail the next day to take over to Brown's Hotel, making a mental note that she would have to call in at the library on her way home to see if they had a gazetteer that would reveal the location of Mrs Bruton's new habitation. Then she opened the little wooden box that she'd been entrusted with and found the key for the first of the cupboards that ran beneath the built-in shelves along one side of the room. It contained the files that held all the details of Mrs Bruton's properties.

Ursula placed these on the floor. It seemed to her that how she had organised them the day that Mrs Bruton's stepson had visited, was not necessarily the best method.

Soon she was immersed in her task, until the chiming of the clock on the mantelpiece warned that it was lunchtime and Mrs Evercreech would be expecting her downstairs. Ursula looked at the papers on the floor. With workmen upstairs it would be reprehensible to leave them on view. Carefully she placed them back in the cupboard and locked it again.

There was a knock at the door and a flustered-looking Enid entered.

'Oh, miss, Mr Bruton has called. He wants to see the mistress.'

'Have you explained that she is not at home?'

'Yes, miss, and now he wants to come in here.'

'Here?'

'He says he needs to consult some of the mistress's records. I don't think Mrs Bruton would like that, miss, do you?'

Wanted to see his stepmother's accounts again, did he? Ursula looked at the maid's worried face. 'I will see him. Have you put him in the drawing room?'

'Yes, miss. Thank you, miss.' Enid almost gasped her relief.

Arthur Bruton was standing by the mantelpiece, drumming his fingers on one of his heavy thighs as he waited. He came forward as she entered.

'Ah, Miss … ?'

'Ursula Grandison, Mr Bruton.' She held out her hand.

'Ah, yes, of course.' His small eyes narrowed and he ignored the hand. 'Well, Miss Grandison, I understand my step-mama is not at home.'

'No, sir. Can I take a message?'

'I wish to consult again the account books I was shown the other day when I lunched here. You can bring them to me.'

At their brief previous meeting, Ursula had already decided that Mr Bruton was a man used to getting his own way but the peremptory nature of his request took her by surprise.

'I'm sorry, sir, that is not possible.'

'Not possible? What do you mean?'

Ursula considered telling him that the cupboards were locked and Mrs Bruton had the key, then decided not to. Why should she lie?

'Mrs Bruton trusts me with her confidential papers. Without her consent, I cannot make them available to others.'

'But I was here the other day. She asked you to bring them for my perusal.'

'Yes, sir,' Ursula said steadily. 'But she was present then. She is not here now.'

The cold brown eyes narrowed. Then the thin lips widened into a semblance of a smile. 'I can see that my stepmother chose wisely when she hired you, Miss Grandison. You see,' his tone lightened, became conciliatory, 'I am about to return to Manchester. There is a small matter I need to check, it is in Mrs Bruton's interest, I assure you. So if you could lead me to the books, I will be able to check it and leave. It is a considerable nuisance my stepmother is not here herself.'

If anything, the man's change of attitude increased Ursula's distrust of him. She was certain Mrs Bruton would not want him anywhere near her accounts while she was absent. And she herself considered the man capable of walking off with them should she be foolish enough to give him the opportunity. Had he, she wondered suddenly, known that his stepmother was not at home and considered it would be easy to get her nonentity of a secretary to show him the books? She remembered his overheard comment, 'Americans need keeping in their place.'

She stiffened her shoulders. 'I am sorry, sir, I cannot abuse Mrs Bruton's trust in me.'

His lips drew back in a snarl. 'This is insufferable behaviour. I suppose you imagine being a foreigner gives you licence. You have no licence. You are insolent.'

'And you, sir, are a bully.'

For a moment he was taken aback.

Before he could recover, Ursula said smoothly, 'As soon as I see her, I will let Mrs Bruton know that you were here this morning and require another look at her accounts.' She held his gaze with hers and watched his face redden. Then she moved to the side of the fireplace and rang the bell.

Enid must have been in the hall for she appeared immediately.

'Mr Bruton is leaving, Enid. Please show him out.'

'I shall be sure to tell my stepmother of your behaviour.' His face almost puce, his voice low and threatening, Arthur Bruton stalked out of the drawing room.

Ursula heard the front door close and sank into a chair.

'Oh, miss, you were so brave!' Enid came into the room. 'If looks could kill, I reckon you would have had it.'

'Nonsense, he was like a small boy denied a treat, nothing dangerous about him at all. And definitely not a gentleman.'

★ ★ ★

At lunch with Cook and Enid, Ursula heard just how difficult Arthur Bruton could be. 'Looks at the food as though he's paying for it, and it's cost too much,' said Enid. Ursula wondered exactly what the man had wanted. Just a look at the accounts without Mrs Bruton fluttering beside him, she decided was most likely.

Arthur Bruton vanished from her thoughts, though, as she returned to her office and the property details. As she studied the address of each, Ursula realised how little she knew about London. 'East London' and 'West London' were all very well, but exactly how much area was covered and exactly where was a road called 'Clerkenwell'? After a little, she took a piece of paper and started writing down the various addresses. It would be a good exercise for her to discover exactly where each was. She could offer the suggestion to Mrs Bruton and propose that she checked on the condition of each property. One road, though, she did recognise. It was where Thomas Jackman lived. Checking on the date of purchase, it looked as though it was one of the first houses that Mrs Bruton had acquired.

Ursula gathered together the various files and stacked them in the cupboard. She would need to tell Mrs Bruton what she had done. Would her employer approve? It seemed unlikely there would be any objection, Mrs Bruton always seemed to welcome any suggestion Ursula produced for organising her records. 'You must think me such a noddle-head,' she had said once.

One of the properties was in Islington, which made Ursula think of Alice Peters. How, she wondered, was Jackman proceeding with his investigation? It was vital that he discovered evidence that would free her from that prison and the threat of the hangman's noose.

In the way that thoughts sometimes presage events, Ursula found a letter waiting for her at her lodgings and recognised Jackman's handwriting. The postmark was for a place called Leeds, not a town Ursula was familiar with. What could have taken him there? She tore the envelope open and scanned the letter. It was quite short:

> Dear Miss Grandison,
>
> An old case has called me away to the north. It should not take long to complete the enquiries I have to carry out but until then, I cannot continue to pursue the Peters case. I wonder if I can call upon your good offices. Daniel Rokeby has told me that Rachel Fentiman once worked for Joshua Peters. He could not tell me more than that. It would be very useful to learn what she can tell of his business practices. Could I ask that you broach the matter with her? The more we know about the man, the more leads we will have to follow in the matter of his murder.
>
> I am, Miss Grandison, your humble servant,
>
> Thomas Jackman

Ursula was shocked. She read the letter twice. Then tucked it in a pocket and set off.

Martha showed Ursula into Rachel's living room. 'She's packing, I'll fetch her.'

Rachel appeared with a skirt over her arm looking harassed. 'Did I hear the bell?' Her expression lightened as she saw her visitor. 'Ursula, how good to see you.' She held out the skirt to Martha. 'Be a love and finish my packing, will you? You'll do it so much better than I. But first, please, some tea for Miss Grandison and myself?'

The maid gave a small snort, took the garment and disappeared.

'Take a seat.' Rachel flung herself into a chair, stretched out legs and arms and gave a big sigh. 'Mrs Pankhurst has summoned me to Manchester. She wants to discuss where the Movement is going.'

'The Movement for Women's Suffrage?' Ursula sat opposite Rachel and took off her gloves, smoothing them on her lap, wondering what the best way was to bring up the reason for her presence.

Rachel gave a big grin. 'Is there another Movement? I think we are about to get militant.'

'Militant?'

'The Movement has been working for decades on the lines that if we are persuasive enough, point out the logic of our arguments, our parliamentary representatives will pass a bill that will give women the vote. As they nearly have on a couple of occasions.'

'What happened to prevent it?'

'Politics! And they will continue to prevent it until we make them realise there is no alternative.'

'And Mrs Pankhurst has ideas as to how that can be achieved?'

Rachel nodded vigorously. 'We're going to get right up the noses of those who consider themselves our lords and masters. Chaining ourselves to the railings outside the Houses of Parliament is one suggestion. Bricks through windows is another. Disruption of normal life in all kinds of ways. Until the powers that be realise they have to give us the vote.'

'Is there no alternative? Has terrorism ever won through?'

'It's action, don't you see, Ursula? Oh, how I have longed for action!' Rachel leaned forward, her expression alive. 'Something more than handing out leaflets. This is a war! And it's a fight we must win. To think that we women in this modern age can travel underground, can speak across miles by telephone, can capture images with a camera, and yet have no power to control our lives! It is not to be borne.'

Ursula saw once again the girl who had leaped up on to the table at the menagerie. Then she had felt an instant comradeship with her. Now, though, she was doubtful if the path it seemed the Movement was going to follow was one that she could endorse. Then she remembered why she had come.

'Rachel, have you heard anything from Alice?'

The excitement drained away from Rachel. She shook her head.

Ursula took out the letter from her pocket. 'Mr Jackman has had to go north on other business but he has heard that you worked for your brother-in-law at one time and he's anxious you tell me as much as you can about that time.'

All expression left Rachel's face. It was as though a shutter had come down. 'It was a long time ago,' she said curtly.

'Why didn't you mention it before?'

The girl sprang up and walked across the room and then back again. 'Why should I? It had nothing to do with Joshua's death.'

'You cannot tell that.'

'Has your Mr Jackman told you to interrogate me?'

'Not interrogate! Merely to ask what information you can give on Mr Peters and his activities.'

Rachel stood poised as though she might suddenly take flight.

'Surely you can see there could be a detail that might be the saving of Alice?'

'You know how to cut to the quick!'

Ursula said nothing.

'Well, then, I'll tell you about my few months working for Mr Joshua Peters. But not in here. Let's go out, walk by the Embankment.'

'Here's your tea, dear.' Martha set a tray down. 'Will you pour?'

'I'm sorry, Martha. You'll have to drink it yourself. Miss Grandison and I are going out.'

Rachel laid a hand on her maid's shoulder, gave a quick peck to her lined cheek and led the way on to the street.

A few minutes later they were walking beside the Thames. The tide was out and birds were feasting on worms that popped up from the mud. It was early September, but the day was warm and the air pleasant. Rachel wore a long, fitted cardigan, belted round the waist, and walked with her gloveless hands sunk into the front pockets. Ursula, wearing her old linen jacket, envied the ease of the knitted garment.

For a little they walked in silence towards the ornate Albert Bridge. Office workers occasionally passed the girls, hurrying home to their evening meals.

'If it might help Alice, I suppose I have to tell you about that time,' Rachel said at last. She turned up on to the bridge, laid her arms along the parapet, and looked down at the water. Ursula stood by her side, trying to discern her expression, she could tell little from her tone of voice.

'I had just finished my degree. As far as I was concerned, I was a fully qualified lawyer but unable to practice because I was the wrong gender.' The bitterness was palpable. 'Alice had married

Joshua, bullied into it by our father. However, she did seem reasonably contented. I think she enjoyed running a household. And then she discovered she was with child. Once I had come down from Manchester, I visited her often. Joshua was usually at his office but occasionally I would dine with them and after a time I was willing to believe that I had misjudged him and perhaps the marriage would be successful.'

For a while Rachel studied the swiftly flowing water, racing out to the far distant sea, and said nothing. Ursula waited.

'I was getting more and more depressed. My degree seemed to be for nothing. Then one Sunday when we were all, my parents as well as myself, eating at the Peters', Joshua suggested that I work for him. "I need someone who understands contract law," he said. "We are expanding; lawyers' fees are high, you are unable to charge what a properly practicing solicitor would so it would benefit us both. What do you think?" He sat there at the head of the table, exuding bonhommie.

'Part of me wanted to throw my glass of wine in his face; how dare he offer me fees less than an equally well-qualified man would receive, but part of me was thrilled – yes, that is the word – thrilled to be offered a job, any job. And I had the idea that perhaps it would lead somewhere.' Ursula heard the derision in Rachel's voice and saw her hands, resting on the parapet, clench. A passenger boat passed beneath the bridge, hooting hoarsely. A child looked up as it emerged and waved at the two girls. Ursula found herself waving back. Rachel didn't seem to notice.

'So how was it, working for your brother-in-law?'

For the first time Rachel turned to look at Ursula. 'I quickly lost the good opinion I'd been forming of him. Joshua Peters was a mean, scheming, cut-everything-to-the-margin operator.'

'What in California we'd call a son of a bitch, if you'll forgive the phrase.'

Rachel laughed scornfully. 'Fits exactly.'

Ursula paused for a moment, then said, 'Did he operate illegally?'

Another scornful laugh. 'He was far too clever for that. He'd milk every last legal detail out of me, then find a way round that met the law but would protect him while exposing the client to outrageous charges.'

'How long did you work for him?'

'No more than a few months. It took that long to realise exactly what he was doing; no, making me do! I was the one checking the contracts. When I complained that what he was doing was not fair, he'd ask if it was illegal. Because, if it was, then that was my fault. When I had to say that in my opinion the contracts were legal, then he said that as far as the client was concerned, it was *caveat emptor*. If they couldn't go to the expense of a bright lawyer, then it wasn't his fault. Ursula, these were small firms he was presenting with the contracts. Firms trusting the Peters' company to arrange their shipping on a fair basis.'

'What wasn't fair about it?'

'I didn't work with him long enough to see if my fears were realised but I could see that if anything went wrong: ships sinking, theft or damage of goods, loss of sales through delays, and a host of other possibilities, well, it wasn't going to be the Peters' company that suffered; the small print would see to that.'

'So you left.'

Rachel nodded and went back to studying the river.

'What did you tell your sister?'

A shrug of the shoulders. 'That the matters Joshua wanted me to work on were too complicated; I didn't have enough experience, I said.' Rachel's bleak expression softened. 'Dear Alice, she accepted everything I told her; all her thoughts were on the coming happy event. And it was happy. Both she and Joshua were ecstatic about little Harry. We all were. Until it all ended so tragically.'

'You didn't think that you should tell Mr Jackman all this?'

'How could it help him?'

Ursula found it difficult to believe that such an intelligent girl couldn't see what seemed blindingly obvious to her. 'Don't you think it possible that a client who lost possibly large sums of money through signing one of these clever contracts and unable to obtain restitution through the law might not want to extract vengeance another way?'

Rachel stared at her. 'You mean, kill him?'

Ursula nodded.

Rachel put her head in her hands. 'Oh, my God,' she said. 'What an idiot I've been. I only saw the manipulation of the law, and then I tried to forget what I'd been party to. I never, ever considered it could lead to Joshua's death!'

Chapter Twenty-One

Ursula picked up Mrs Bruton's mail from Wilton Crescent, then walked to Brown's Hotel in Mayfair. She had consulted the gazetteer in the public library to discover its location. Why, she wondered, had she not been surprised to find that it was in the next-door road to *Maison Rose*? After she arrived, she was equally unsurprised to find Count Meyerhoff in the sitting room of Mrs Bruton's well-appointed suite taking coffee with her employer.

He rose on Ursula's entry. 'Ah, Miss Grandison. My dear Mrs Bruton, you will have matters to attend to, I shall take my leave with many thanks for the delicious coffee. If I may, I will call on you at 12.30 and take you to lunch at Claridge's. I hope that by then you will have been able to consider my proposal.' He took Mrs Bruton's hand, bent over it graciously, then straightened, gave a small nod to Ursula and left.

'Good morning,' said Ursula, trying not to let her curiosity over the exact nature of the relationship between her two employers show. She was, though, very interested. Was Mrs Bruton seriously contemplating giving up her independence for marriage, however charming the count was? But perhaps it was a liaison she was considering. Was she a woman who missed the physical closeness that could be offered by a member of the opposite sex? For a fleeting moment Ursula remembered when she had had the comfort of a man she believed loved her.

Mrs Bruton, a small, self-satisfied smile on her lips, fluttered the hand the count had bent over. 'What do you have for me this morning?'

'As you requested, I have brought the mail.' Ursula handed over a little stack of envelopes. 'There are some personal letters and one from your property agent, which I opened. He suggests some renovations are necessary at the Earl's Court property.' She retrieved a notebook and pencil from her bag and waited.

Mrs Bruton flipped through the personally addressed envelopes and laid them down without interest. She read the agent's letter, her expression inscrutable. 'I think, Miss Grandison, you had better inspect the property and assess the truth of what he claims,' she said at last.

'You would like me to do that today?'

Mrs Bruton gave a slight adjustment to the set of her lace jabot, then smoothed down her cream linen skirt. 'It would be best. There is little else for you to do at the moment for I can make no arrangements for entertaining at Wilton Crescent until the builders have finished my bathroom. You will draw up a report on the situation. Bring it here tomorrow morning.'

'It is one of my days for working at *Maison Rose*, Mrs Bruton.'

A hand selected one of the unopened envelopes. 'So it is! Well, it would not be difficult for you to deposit the report at reception for me on your way there. You can use the hotel door that leads into Davies Street, it will take but a moment.'

'Of course.' Ursula returned notepad and pencil to her capacious bag. 'I hope you enjoy your lunch with the count,' she added smoothly, pulling on her gloves.

'Ah, the dear count.' Mrs Bruton hesitated, then waved her towards a chair. 'Perhaps you will sit down for a moment.'

★ ★ ★

Ursula left Brown's Hotel some thirty minutes later and, after obtaining directions from the hall porter, proceeded to walk to the agent's offices in the Cromwell Road.

'Hmm, Mrs Bruton and the house in Nevern Square,' said the agent, a small, sallow man with a rushed way of speaking and a large, spotted handkerchief with which he kept wiping his brow. It appeared to be a nervous gesture, as the day was not particularly warm. 'The last tenants left a few days ago.' He looked up from a desk covered with papers and files. 'You work for Mrs Bruton, I understand?'

Ursula nodded.

'I inspected the house and, really, such people should be ashamed of themselves. Respectable, I made sure of that, but, well, all the paintwork is in a terrible state. Can't imagine how they reduced it … well, no use speculating I suppose. It was, of course, let unfurnished, and departing pictures have left the walls marked, that's no fault of theirs, I suppose. But the damage to the plaster! Young boys in the household – could have been playing darts, or worse. Rents in the area are right down. Know Mrs Bruton bought the lease at a bargain but even so. Want to suggest she turns it into a boarding or apartment house, or does it up before trying to let at a decent sum. Could be difficult. Getting you to make a report, is she? You'll need the key; it's here somewhere.'

He rattled around the contents of a couple of drawers, inspected the labels of a couple of keys then handed one over. 'Bring it back when you've completed your inspection. Not an easy decision Mrs Bruton's got but she's got a sharp head on her for a woman.' Another wipe of his forehead with the spotted handkerchief. 'Anything else you need to know – Miss Grandson, was it?'

Ursula gently corrected her name, took the key and left. She decided to leave any consideration of what might be done with the property until after her inspection, and instead turned her mind to the matter Mrs Bruton had discussed with her before she'd left her hotel suite. Her employer had wanted her advice and it was not easy for Ursula to know what to say.

'The count has paid me the compliment of asking if I would like to invest in *Maison Rose*,' Mrs Bruton had told her. 'He says that the business is expanding most successfully; Madame Rose's preparations are being used by some very distinguished women of society, and there are now possibilities for just one or two investors to take shares in the company. He …' Mrs Bruton coloured just a little and fiddled with her gold bracelet, 'he considers me a woman of discernment and says he has approached me first, ahead of other of his friends. The thing is, Miss Grandison, I wonder how safe an investment *Maison Rose* would be. You are working there, you must know something of the business and I would value your opinion.'

Ursula felt caught between her two employers. Her loyalty was owed to each.

'The count is quite right,' she said slowly. 'The business is expanding. Madame Rose's clientele appear very happy with her products and also happy to recommend them to their friends and acquaintances. But I have little knowledge of its financial background. Do you not have a man of affairs who could look at the company for you?'

Mrs Bruton looked at her intently, her light eyes very steady. 'Thank you,' she said at last. 'Please ring for my maid.'

Ursula wanted to apologise for her lack of information; she didn't want to think she had said anything that could have been of help but words slipped uneasily around in her mind and silence seemed the best option. She rose. 'I will visit your agent and then your property. You shall have a report tomorrow morning,' she said and left.

Nevern Square was attractive, a central garden surrounded by iron railings (the householders paid two pounds a year for its maintenance, the agent had told her), the houses built of contrasting yellow and red bricks, quite different from the stucco façades of the London terraces Ursula had grown used to seeing.

The house was exactly as the agent had described. Ursula returned to Wilton Crescent, composed a report and delivered it to Brown's Hotel the next morning on her way to *Maison Rose*.

She had now been working there for several weeks. Mrs Bruton's request for information the previous day had been unsettling as Ursula had begun to be uneasy about the finances of the beauty company. At first there had been a great many cheques to enter and take to the bank, and there seemed a healthy balance to cope with the payment of a sizeable number of bills. The bills covered not only the direct costs of the beauty business but also household matters and even what to Ursula's eyes appeared to be personal expenses. She had, however, been instructed to enter all in the company's accounts.

Having brought the paperwork up to date, it seemed to Ursula that, though a satisfying number of accounts were being sent to clients, very few payments were being made. That day she found awaiting her details for a number of accounts to be sent out but no cheques to be entered. There was, though, a brand new typewriter sitting on the desk, together with an invoice for its cost.

Ursula found Miss Ferguson and asked if the count was available.

'I don't know where he is, Miss Grandison.'

'You may address your query to me.' Madame Rose had come up behind them. 'Be quick, please; Lady Constance is due for her second consultation. You have the creams ready, Miss Ferguson?'

'I am in the process of assembling them, Madame.' Miss Ferguson disappeared.

Madame remained, an eyebrow raised imperiously.

'It will wait,' Ursula said.

'No, you have query; I will answer.'

Ursula took a deep breath. 'Is it usual that clients do not settle their accounts?'

Madame Rose gave her a sharp glance. 'We do not question our client's standing. They will pay.'

'Yes, Madame, but when?'

'Boh! I do not concern myself with such details.'

The count joined them. 'Perhaps you should. I would like to see the accounts,' he said to Ursula, holding out his hand for the books she held. 'Madame,' he said curtly as his partner moved to leave the room. 'You should see these.'

Ursula explained her double-entry system. 'As you can see, at present outgoings exceed income by some degree.'

'But the accounts sent to clients, they add up to large amounts. And yet you complain!' Madame sounded exasperated.

'Miss Grandison is right,' the count said curtly. 'We must think about sending, what would you call it? A second request for payment?'

'A statement, I think, requesting settlement of the invoice,' Ursula said.

'I will not have my clients insulted in such a way!' Madame Rose was indignant.

'It would only be sent if four weeks have elapsed since the despatch of the invoice, Madame.'

'Count, tell Miss Grandison, she goes too far. My clients are high society. This would be, what is the word? Dunning? They must not be dunned like common folk.'

'Rose, they owe you … they owe us, money.'

Madame Rose glared at him.

Ursula hurriedly picked up the account books and went back to her office.

Later the count came in. 'You are not using the machine I ordered. Does it not please you?'

'It is excellent, exactly the one I suggested, Count. Only, I wondered if …'

'If perhaps *Maison Rose* cannot afford such articles?'

She nodded.

'Such decisions are mine.'

Ursula said nothing.

'You will send out the proposed statements four weeks after invoices, *hein*?' He hesitated for a moment. Then, 'These matters, they are confidential, no?'

'Of course, Count Meyerhoff. I do not discuss my employer's business with anyone.'

'That is good, your employers are fortunate to have your services.' He lingered for another moment then left.

★ ★ ★

Walking home across the park, Ursula, for the first time since she had started work in London, felt out of sympathy with both her employers but she knew she had to be grateful for the work. She had been able to afford a winter coat. It hung now in her room, dark brown in good quality wool and a style that seemed to flatter her tall figure. A couple of leaves floated down from one of the trees in the park; the slight crispness in the air was attractive. She looked forward to the leaves turning colour. Ursula remembered with nostalgia the wonderful October richness of the New England trees.

With an effort she dismissed any wayward thoughts of dissatisfaction with her life. Instead she thought about poor Alice Peters, awaiting trial for her life, and wondered whether Thomas Jackman had received the letter she had written him after her meeting with Rachel Fentiman.

It had seemed at first difficult and then impossible to give an intelligent account of her conversation with Rachel. In the end she wrote that she had learned details that would interest him in his investigation into Joshua Peters' death and would he please contact her as soon as he could. His note had given no address in the north, so she had sent it to his home.

That was a week ago. Ursula wondered how long it would be until he returned.

As she entered Mrs Maples' boarding house, Meg met her.
'Mr Jackman's here, miss. Come to visit you. He's with the mistress,
she says to go to her parlour.' Her eyes were wide with interest.

Ursula gave a quick knock at the door of Mrs Maples' sanc-
tum and entered.

'Ah, Miss Grandison, here you are! Mr Jackman has been all
impatience waiting for your return.' The landlady gave a sly
smile as the investigator leaped to his feet with a look of relief.
To Ursula's astonishment, he was wearing a policeman's uniform.

'I understand you are working with him on a case,' Mrs Maple
continued. A tray of tea had been supplied though Thomas
Jackman had left his cup untouched. 'No doubt with matters to
discuss.' Another sly smile. 'There won't be anyone in the boarders' lounge at the moment, if you need a confidential chat, you
must take him there.'

'Mrs Maple, you have been, as always, the most delightful of
companions. I thank you for your hospitality.' Thomas Jackman
bowed quickly over her hand and she simpered at him.

Another time Ursula would have been entranced to see this
side of her normally practical and down-to-earth landlady but
now the sight of the investigator in such an unfamiliar outfit and
with every appearance of barely controlled impatience made her
realise this was not in any sense a social visit.

The moment they were out of Mrs Maples' parlour, Jackman
took hold of Ursula's arm. 'Miss Grandison, I have come for your
help. Do you have another engagement this evening?'

She turned to face him. 'Are you back in the police force?'

He shook his head and ran a finger round a jacket collar that
looked uncommonly tight. 'Dug it out. Thought it would do but
it seems to have shrunk a bit.'

'What has happened? Is it something concerned with Alice
Peters?'

'Yes, something has happened. Whether it's concerning
Mrs Peters or not, I cannot say. Forgive me for asking, but do you
have something dark you could wear?'

Ursula looked down at her tan jacket and cream cambric skirt.
'Mr Jackman, Thomas, you need to explain.'

He drew a watch from a pocket. 'I'll explain as we go. But
I ask again, can you change? I have no time for manners, Ursula.
I would not ask if it was not important. Black would be best.'

'Wait here, I'll be as quick as I can.'

'And bring a coat or cloak with you,' he called after her.

Ursula went swiftly up the stairs. She knew the investigator well enough to know he was exceedingly worried. Why and where he wanted her to go with him was obviously going to remain a mystery until she had changed. At least the mourning garments she had had to wear during her last days at Mountstanton should serve his purpose. Changed into her black outfit, she looked at her new coat. It was not cold enough for wear now but he had asked her to bring one. She folded it over her arm and left the room.

As she returned downstairs, he studied her simple but well-made jacket, blouse and skirt and her black straw boater.

'Will I do?' she asked.

He gave her a quick nod. 'Excellent. I thank you. I have a hansom cab waiting outside.' He opened the front door.

As soon as they were in motion, Ursula turned to her companion.

'Now, Thomas, please tell me what this is all about.'

He sat for a moment, uncharacteristically hesitant, then drew a piece of paper from a pocket. 'I have just returned from Leeds. I found your letter waiting for me and also this ...' He offered the paper to Ursula.

'Dear Joe,' she read and looked at him enquiringly. He was tapping his fingers irritably on the side of the cab as traffic slowed their progress. She looked again at the piece of paper. It was written in a childish hand, the letters carefully formed.

> Dear Joe,
> For old times sake, help me. I thought I was going to be in heaven instead I am in hell. If you don't rescue me, I am finished. Flat 4, Albemarle Mansions, Marylebone Road. Come as soon as you can,
> Your Millie.

'Millie?'

'She's Alice Peters' maid.' Thomas looked at the tangle of traffic that had brought them to a full stop outside Victoria station. 'When Joshua Peters first hired me to follow his wife, I, well, I have to admit I used her to find out Mrs Peters' movements.' His voice was tight, embarrassed. 'She knew me then as

Joe Banks. When I turned up with Mrs Trenchard to interview the staff after Peters' death, Millie nearly ruined my standing by blurting out that I could not be Thomas Jackman. Took some explaining, I can tell you.'

'But she knew where to write to you?'

He nodded. 'Last time I saw her, I gave her my card; told her to get in touch if she ever needed my assistance. Before I was called away north, she seemed to have left the Peters' house. Sam, the boy who runs all the errands, said he thought she had a fancy man.'

'Did you think that likely?'

He fiddled with his policeman's helmet. 'She's a bit of a flighty thing. Flighty but ambitious. Wants to get somewhere in the world.'

'And you reckon she's been seduced into some sort of situation she can't handle?'

He looked grateful for her understanding. 'That's about the size of it.'

Ursula looked again at the letter. 'There's no date. Do you know when she wrote it?"

'Postmark was the day before yesterday. So I hope we'll be in time.'

'In time?' The hansom jerked forward and picked up speed. 'And why are you wearing a policeman's uniform. Are you going to arrest someone?'

'Could be the easiest way out.'

Ursula's mind was spinning. She was no stranger to girls who found themselves exploited by ruthless men. Hadn't she fallen foul of one such herself? Had poor Millie been promised marriage? Had she thought she was gaining respectability and a secure future?

'What do you want me to do, Thomas?'

He smiled. 'That's the girl, knew I could count on you. No need for you to say anything after we arrive, just take your cue from me.'

'You don't really know what you're going to find.' It was not a question.

'Had to deal with any number of situations when I was a bobby. Reckon it won't be anything I haven't dealt with before.'

'None of them attractive situations?'

'Not as far as Millie is concerned.'

'Are you armed?' It seemed unlikely, there was hardly room for the man inside the uniform, let alone a gun.

'I'm hoping it's not that sort of affair. Millie is not the kind of girl to go for the rough stuff.'

Was that a guarantee of anything? Ursula wanted to ask more questions but the cab had stopped.

''Ere yer are, officer, Albemarle Mansions.'

'Thank you, cabbie. Please wait while we carry out Her Majesty's business.'

'I'll do that, officer.'

Thomas helped her down. The apartment building appeared to be a solid, respectable place in a dark red brick. Many of the white windowsills bore window boxes with brightly coloured geraniums. Net curtains guarded privacy.

Thomas slipped a hand under Ursula's elbow and ushered her towards the entrance. Inside, cream paint was in need of a new coat and a spiky green plant, looking sad and unloved, was the only decoration in the silent foyer. 'Now, remember, whatever we find, you leave things to me.'

Ursula's heart was thumping. The investigator's gravity, his uncertainty about what could be facing them, was unsettling. Unconsciously levity took over. 'Right you are, officer.'

'Look, whatever we find, it's going to be serious. I have no right to involve you but I need female assistance and I know you are resourceful and courageous.'

Ursula was touched. 'Thomas, I'm sorry, it was nerves.'

'You with nerves? Never!'

She gave him a brief smile and together they climbed stairs sporting a worn carpet. On the first floor landing were two doors. More cream paint needed new coats but the brass number plates bearing a '1' and a '2' were well polished.

As they approached the second floor, sounds of someone screeching reached them. Thomas gave Ursula a brief look and adjusted his uniform jacket. The screeching came from flat No. 4. As Thomas raised his hand to knock, the screeching changed to an agonised crying. He rapped hard.

'Open up in the name of the law!'

Chapter Twenty-Two

Through the door, Ursula heard a hard slap and a male voice shouting, 'Damn you.'

The crying stopped abruptly and in the sudden silence, Thomas rapped again and repeated his command.

'Make yourself scarce, Bee,' said the same voice. 'Guy, open the door before it's beaten down.'

The lock was turned and the door opened a crack. Ursula could just see an eye surveying them from inside. Thomas pushed hard and entered, and she followed him.

A tiny hall led through an arch into a living room dominated by gold-framed mirrors and couches upholstered in scarlet velvet. A baroque side table was laden with a cold collation. Beside it stood a wine cellar containing several bottles of champagne.

Awaiting them stood a large, well-dressed man, his grey silk cravat hanging open over a half-buttoned shirt. The man who had opened the door scrambled over to the other side of the room, drawing a checked jacket over a bare chest. Crushing herself against a tallboy, a young woman tried to draw a negligee around her flimsy underwear, but not before Ursula had noticed a nasty bruise on her upper arm. A red mark on her cheek betrayed where the slap had landed. Large eyes were full of tears and blonde hair hung undressed in tangles.

'And what may you be doing disturbing innocent citizens in private premises, may I ask?' The tall man's voice was both insolent and confident.

Ursula saw the girl fix her gaze on Thomas. Her eyes widened and she raised a trembling hand to her mouth. A memory of Thomas saying how Millie had blurted out his assumed name at the Peters' house came to Ursula. She marched over to the girl, gave her a stern look and said, 'If you know what's good for you, you'll keep your mouth closed, miss.'

'I have information that prostitution is operating on these premises,' Thomas said with official solemnity.

Ursula heard another girl give a little gasp. She was cowering in the corner of a couch. Dressed in a bustier with a tiny tulle skirt barely covering her buttocks, Ursula saw with amazement that black silk stockings sported a sequined and embroidered silver snake that curved round her legs, a hooded head decorating each foot.

'Bee, I told you to make yourself scarce,' the tall man hissed at her.

'Too late, sir. I've seen all I need,' said Thomas. He marched over to the first girl. 'Millie Dowd, I arrest you under subsection thirteen of the Criminal Law Amendment Act of 1885 for running a house of ill repute.' With difficulty he extracted a pair of handcuffs from his trouser pocket and reached for the girl's hands.

'Sir,' said Ursula quickly. 'Miss Dowd needs to clothe herself.'

'She seems to have been happy enough to appear like that in front of these gentlemen. Give her the coat.'

So that was why he'd wanted her to bring it! With great reluctance, Ursula held it out. After a moment, the girl slipped her arms into the sleeves. It was too big for her but the collar stood up framing her face in an attractive way.

'Now look here …' the tall man started.

'You cannot arrest Millie, I mean Miss Dowd,' the smaller man blurted. The girl with the extraordinary stockings was snivelling.

The tall man held up his cigar in a supercilious manner. 'As I was saying, before my friend here interrupted …'

'Oh, I say, Hector!'

'No, you do not say, Guy. I am trying to inform this useless hunk of humanity who imagines he has some authority over us, who I am.' He turned back to Thomas. 'You are addressing Sir Hector Rutland; the Chief Constable is a good friend of mine and he would be appalled to hear what you are attempting to put over on us this evening.'

Thomas squared his shoulders, took hold of Millie's wrists and fastened the cuffs on them. He handled her roughly and Ursula noticed he did not look at the girl.

The man called Guy tried again. 'You can't go behaving like this. Miss Dowd has done nothing against the law.'

'It is against the law for two women to occupy the same premises with the aim of selling their favours. It becomes a brothel,' said Thomas severely.

'But …' squawked Bee, raising a tear-stained face.

'Millie Dowd,' Thomas overrode her. 'Transport awaits. You will be taken to Marylebone Police Station, where you will be held until tomorrow's court sits. You can then persuade your case before the magistrate.'

'Hector, do something,' said Guy.

'Do you intend to arrest us all?' said Sir Hector. 'I warn you I shall be sending a note to the Chief Constable first thing in the morning.'

'By all means, sir,' said Thomas. 'But it will not be necessary to arrest anyone other than Millie Dowd, since we understand she is the main occupant of the property.'

'It's outrageous,' squawked Guy. 'Do something, Hector,' he repeated.

But the tall man leant against the mantelpiece and drew on his cigar. 'I don't think there's anything to be done at this time,' he drawled. 'You must fulfil your duty, officer.'

'Thank you, sir. Come on, miss. You keep hold of her left arm, Miss Culpepper, and I'll take the right. Quick march.'

'Don't think this is the end of the matter,' Sir Hector said. 'I'll be posting bail tomorrow morning and applying to the Chief Constable for your dismissal from the force.' He moved across, slipped a finger under the girl's chin and forced her to look him in the face. 'Millie, you will be back here tomorrow, no doubt a wiser girl.' The voice was silkily sinister and the girl closed her eyes and whimpered.

'Quick march,' repeated Thomas stolidly.

As they left, Sir Hector was heard to say: 'The bitch needed a lesson and now she's getting it. I was tiring of her protestations.'

The door closed behind them and Millie's whimpering turned to sobbing. Forcing her down the stairs, Ursula and Thomas got her out of the building and into the waiting cab.

★ ★ ★

The three of them were squeezed tightly together. Millie's sobbing gave way to a series of shivers as the cabbie called down, 'Same destination as what you told me, orficer?'

'You have it, cabbie,' said Thomas. He released the top buttons of his uniform and gave a sigh of relief. 'Thank God for that. I'd have expired if I had to spend another minute stuffed into this jacket. He squirmed for room as he tried to access a pocket. 'Now, then, Millie, hold out your hands.' She stared at him without moving. It was as though she thought he intended to produce a truncheon and whack her one.

Ursula lifted the handcuffed wrists and held them out to Thomas. He applied the key. 'There you are. Now you're a free woman again.'

Millie gave a hiccup. 'You mean, I'm not arrested?'

'Of course not. Didn't you send me a letter asking to be rescued from your new life?' His voice was softer now.

Ursula felt a long shiver run through the girl. 'And you're not a policeman?'

'You know I'm not, Millie. I told you, I left the force and these days I'm a private investigator.'

'And not above pretending to be someone what you ain't!' From somewhere Millie had found a spark of spirit. She turned to Ursula. 'And I suppose you don't work in a prison?'

'She's an old friend who kindly agreed to help with your rescue.'

'An old friend of his?' Millie tipped her head towards Thomas. 'Then I don't suppose you're any better than you should be.'

'You should wash your mouth out,' Thomas said quietly.

Millie tried to shrink back and tears welled up.

'I've led an up and down sort of life,' Ursula said cheerfully. 'You'll learn that, however bad things seem at the time, there can always be a better day around the corner. Look at this evening: you were despairing of getting away from those awful men and, all of sudden, there's Thomas whisking you off in a hansom, with Hector and Guy, whoever they may be, unable to lift a finger.'

'They'll be after me, I know they will.' Millie sounded genuinely afraid. 'Where are you taking me?'

'You'll see,' said Thomas.

'It had better be somewhere safe.' Away from Albemarle Mansions, she had perked up amazingly.

'It's somewhere those pillocks who had you will never think of looking in a lifetime of evil living. What were you thinking of, Millie, setting up store with them?'

'Sir Hector made it all sound so great. He said I was the most beautiful girl he'd ever met.'

'Friend of Joshua Peters, was he?'

She nodded. 'After the mistress ran away, Mr Peters would ask men friends round of an evening. He'd tell Mrs Firestone to lay out a cold buffet then say the staff needn't be on duty any more. Except he'd ask me to serve drinks and talk prettily to his friends, like as if I was his hostess.' Pride was in her voice.

'And you wore your mistress's gowns?' suggested Thomas.

'Well, I had to look nice, didn't I? And she'd left them behind, like she didn't want them anymore.' She looked down at her negligee, peeking out from Ursula's coat. 'I took them with me. Now, I suppose I've lost them.' She was silent for a moment. 'Anyway, him and me was getting close. He said I knew how to make a man feel good.' There was a touch of pride in her voice.

'And after Mr Peters died,' Thomas said. 'His friend Sir Hector Rutland suggested he would supply you with somewhere to live so you could make him feel good whenever he wanted, did he?'

'Don't you come the high and mighty with me, Joe Banks, Thomas Jackman, or whatever you call yourself.' Millie sounded aggrieved. 'A girl has to look out for herself. Mr Rutland said it was a crime beauty such as mine shouldn't have the proper setting and that he'd provide me with every luxury.'

'And you understood that that meant becoming his mistress?' asked Ursula.

'I suppose you've never done anything like that! That's because you haven't got the looks for it.'

Ursula couldn't help being amused at this. 'When did it all go wrong?'

'Two days after I arrived,' Millie wailed.

'Up until then it had been all sweetness and light, had it?' asked Thomas.

'He treated me as though I was special. Said I made him happier than any woman ever had!'

A cart cut across their path, the cabbie hauled on the reins, the horse neighed loudly and almost reared. Ursula grabbed at the side of the cab to avoid ending on the floor. The cabbie swore at the cart's driver, who returned some equally salty words. The incident slowly sorted itself out. 'Sorry folks,' said the cabbie. 'Weren't my fault.'

As they resumed the journey, Thomas said resignedly, 'You better tell us what happened.'

'He only brought in Guy, what he said I had to make as happy as I'd made him. Well,' Millie drew herself up with a quaint dignity. 'I said if he thought I was that sort of girl, he could think again.' Suddenly she lost her poise once more. 'So then he hit me on my arm ... and my ribs and ... and said he knew exactly what sort of girl I was and if I knew what was good for me, I'd do as I was told.' Tears poured down her cheeks. 'And ... and after that it was awful. I was locked in and they came and demanded what they said was their right. And that Bee girl told me I had no choice and she'd learned to make the most of it. Do what they wanted, she said, and I'd get what I wanted. What I wanted was to get away from there!' she ended on a long wail.

Ursula was thankful that the noise from the road made it unlikely their cabbie could hear anything.

'So that's when you wrote to me?' said Thomas.

Millie nodded. 'Well, you'd given me that card and said you was an investigator and that if I needed help at any time to let you know. Only you didn't come!' Another wail. 'And I hated what I was asked to do. Bee didn't seem to mind what went on. Only I did.' She slumped back, seemingly exhausted.

Ursula had to feel sorry for the girl. She'd been incredibly foolish and had received bitter coin.

'What's to become of me?' Millie whispered despairingly.

At that moment the cab came to a halt and Thomas climbed down. 'We're here,' he said and held out his hand first to Millie and then to Ursula. She shook out her skirts, looked around and realised that the scene confronting her was familiar. She had seen that carved screen with its amazing animals before, had heard that lazy leonine roar and the bright monkey chatter, and had smelled the earthy animal odours. Then from somewhere she heard the roll of a drum and a crowd gasping in excitement. To the left of the menagerie was a large tent.

'It's a circus!' breathed Millie.

Thomas paid off the cabbie and took Millie's arm. 'Come with me, ladies.'

The ground was rough; Millie cried out several times as she stumbled in her slippers and even Ursula, wearing sensible shoes, had difficulty keeping her balance. Another roar came from inside the tent.

Once round the back of the circus, Ursula saw a collection of caravans arranged in a circle around a large fire. It made her think of wagon trains drawn up for the night. Were they ready to repel Indians?

Dusk was drawing in; the soft light blurred the outlines of the buildings beyond the fire, they could be anywhere but in the middle of a bustling city.

Thomas approached the largest of the caravans, climbed the little flight of steps and knocked on the door. 'Jackman, Ma,' he called.

An oil lamp hung by the door illuminated the scene as a huge woman dressed in a flowing crimson dress patterned with paisley, a turban round her head, emerged from the caravan. 'Ah, Thomas, Thomas,' she cried and drew him into a warm embrace. Almost he vanished from sight. 'Thank you, Ma,' he said, emerging again.

Ma gave him an indulgent look, then surveyed the two women. 'And you bring me someone in need, yes?'

Thomas leaped down the steps and brought the girl forward. 'This is Millie, Ma.'

The woman came down and took hold of her hands. Millie stood nervously as though she feared also being drawn into that vast bosom. From the menagerie came the muffled roar of a lion and she started to tremble, shrinking into the warmth of Ursula's coat.

Ma cupped her hand round Millie's chin and nodded approvingly. 'Ah, sweet girl. And another one you bring, yes?' she added, looking at Ursula, her dark eyes bright with curiosity.

'I'm happy to meet you but I'm not in trouble,' said Ursula.

Ma climbed back up the steps into the caravan. 'Come in, my dears. Hungry, are you?'

Ursula realised that she had had nothing to eat since a roll at lunchtime and that she was indeed in need of food. For the first time she noticed that a slim tin chimney came through the caravan's roof; smoke emerged from it and the smell of some sort of stew made her mouth water.

Millie seemed reluctant to enter. She looked at Thomas and reached for his hand. 'What will happen?'

'We shall eat. And you will be safe.'

She gave him a wobbly smile then allowed him to lead her up the steps.

Inside the caravan was all the splendour of the East, with spangled cushions, Turkish carpets and hangings, and beautifully polished brass ornaments arranged with style on a series of shelves. In one corner a gently glowing stove bore a steaming pot. Ma moved over to it and started spooning deliciously smelling meat and vegetables into individual pottery bowls decorated with gaily painted motifs.

'Ma, you're magic,' said Thomas.

'Sit, sit,' ordered Ma, indicating benches lining the caravan, all furnished with soft cushions. A long table ran in front of one of the benches. Ma placed three well-filled bowls on this and provided three spoons. A dark loaf of bread was cut and heavy-looking slices placed beside the bowls. Then she extracted a firkin from beneath one of the benches and poured ale into three tankards. 'You must enjoy,' she said and Ursula tried to place her slight accent; probably Eastern European, she decided.

The stew was subtly spiced and the bread tasted of rye. 'This is delicious,' said Ursula gratefully. 'You are a wonderful cook.'

'I like food,' said Ma. 'Food is elixir of life, no?' She settled herself beside the stove, opposite her guests, and regarded with approval the speed with which the bowls were emptied.

From outside came the sound of loud applause. 'Ah,' said Ma. 'Circus, it is over. Soon comes Pa.'

More applause.

'Show must have gone well this evening,' said Thomas.

'Pa has ideas for new show. When we go to winter grounds, we work on them. You must come, see.'

'You can be sure of that, Ma.'

'Hey, hey!' came a booming voice and the caravan door opened. In came a moustachioed man that Ursula recognised as the lion-tamer from her first visit to the menagerie. But this time he was dressed in a tail coat over an elaborately embroidered waistcoat and bright red cummerbund. He took off his top hat and threw it on to a bench. 'Thomas, my Thomas! You came!'

Thomas rose. 'We are very grateful, Pa, for your and Ma's hospitality.'

'My boy, you are welcome. And this,' he turned to Millie. 'This is the pretty lady who will stay with us.'

Millie shot an alarmed glance at the investigator. Ursula could see her thinking that a cooking pan had given way to fire.

Pa gave a deep, rumbling laugh. 'No need to look like that, my dear. Thomas tells us you are in deep water and need a safe docking. We offer you one here.' He patted her cheek. 'You will be very safe with us.'

Millie gave a panic-stricken look around the caravan.

Ma gave her a warm smile. 'Pa and I, we sleep in back,' she indicated a door at the rear and Ursula realised that this travelling home had another room. 'You are happy to sleep here?' She indicated the bench. 'We have feather bed for you; very comfortable.'

Millie looked doubtful.

Thomas placed a hand on her shoulder. 'You have my word that you will be completely safe. No one will abuse you or treat you with anything but courtesy.'

Millie's gaze switched between Ma and her ringmaster husband. 'I have no money,' she stammered.

Pa drew himself up till his head almost touched the roof of the caravan. 'You insult us!' he boomed out.

Millie shrank back and suddenly looked exhausted. 'I ... I'm sorry, sir. I ... I'm not used to being treated so well. Please, I'm very happy to be here.' Then she straightened her shoulders. 'I do not like to be beholden, you see.' She looked at Ma. 'Perhaps I can help you in some way?' She picked up one of the cushions and gently stroked its embroidery. 'These are so lovely. I cannot do such elaborate work but I am good with the needle otherwise.'

Ma threw out her hands in a gesture of delight. 'You can sew? That is wonderful, is it not, Pa?'

'It is indeed. You see,' he turned back to Millie. 'With the circus there are always costumes that need repair. It is hard work for Ma to keep up.'

'I can help,' Millie said eagerly.

'Now you are tired. We are all tired,' Ma said. 'We arrange for night-time, yes? And Thomas and the so nice other lady will go home. And perhaps come again tomorrow to see friend safe and well?'

'An excellent idea,' said Thomas. He took hold of one of Millie's hands and held it in his. 'You must sleep well and not worry about Hector Rutland. You are safe here and I will be back tomorrow. I will collect your clothes from the Peters' house. Don't worry, I won't tell them where you are.'

Ursula looked longingly at her precious coat. Millie had wrapped her arms around herself, hugging the coat, as though it was part of the safety that had so suddenly been given to her. It was impossible to ask for it back tonight. Perhaps Thomas could do that tomorrow. She stifled a yawn and wondered how long it would take to walk back to her lodgings.

★ ★ ★

Thomas guided Ursula away from the circle of caravans. People were flooding out of the circus, happy, chatting, calling out to others. In the background the monkeys were chattering.

Soon they were once more in the heart of London, traffic all around them. Further down the street was a stand for hansom cabs. Horses stood, one leg bent, heads hanging low, half asleep.

'Are you tired?' Thomas asked Ursula.

'Not at all,' she said brightly. 'Though I might take an omnibus from here. If there is one that goes towards Victoria.'

'We should talk about the meeting with Miss Fentiman that you mentioned in your letter.'

'We should.' Ursula yawned. She really was very tired.

'Hey – Jackman, isn't it?' yelled a voice.

A cabbie was fitting a nosebag on his horse. 'Where you bin, mate?'

'Alf, my friend!' Thomas went over to him. 'I should ask where've you been? Or perhaps I shouldn't.'

'Around, mate, around. And in and out, don't yer know?'

'Petty larceny, was it? Yet again?'

'Ah, yer know 'ow it is, mate.' The cabbie was a big chap in a flowing caped coat. 'Come in and chew the cud for a while.' He indicated a rectangular wooden shelter, light spilling out of an open door. 'Bring yer lady friend.'

'Do you mind?' Thomas asked Ursula. She shook her head. Cabbie Alf looked interesting, his face a mass of wrinkles as though he was continually smiling, his nose a smashed cauliflower.

They entered the little shelter; there was a fire burning in an enclosed stove with a coffee pot sitting on top. A plain wooden table was surrounded with half a dozen mismatched chairs. A collection of mugs sat huddled on a small shelf.

Two cabbies already sitting at the table looked up as they entered. 'Me old policeman mate, Tom Jackman,' said Alf with a broad grin. 'Ain't seen 'im in an age.'

'Hey, cabbie!' A loud cry from outside. A well-dressed gent pushed his face round the door. 'Need transport, don't yer know.'

One of the cabbies rose hastily. 'My turn.'

'Need two, we do.'

Both cabbies vanished outside.

Alf picked up the coffee pot and waved it at Thomas and Ursula.

'Won't say no,' said Thomas but Ursula shook her head. If the coffee was anything like that continually available in California, it would be over-brewed and disgustingly strong.

In a couple of minutes they were seated at the table, Thomas and Alf supplied with mugs.

'So, tell us how you got banged up,' said Thomas.

It was a cheery tale of golden opportunities that turned out to be lead-bottomed. 'So here I am, back on the cabbie run, thanks to me old dad, who never gives up on me.'

Thomas seemed about to say something but another customer yelled for a cab and Alf disappeared. 'Make yourselves at 'ome, I'll be back shortly, and it's starting to rain,' he called as he left.

Thomas leaned back in his chair. 'Might as well accept his invitation, where better to have that conversation on Miss Fentiman?'

Ursula had no desire to get wet. So she told Thomas all about Rachel Fentiman's job with her brother-in-law.

'He sounds as though he was an out-and-out bastard,' she finished.

He tutted. 'Never be taken for a lady with that sort of language.'

For a moment Ursula was taken aback, then she saw his eyes twinkling and laughed. 'I'll never get over living in a mining camp. But,' she said, hastening on. 'As I told Rachel, if Joshua Peters was giving his customers such a raw deal, wouldn't it be possible one of them decided to take his revenge?'

Jackman looked thoughtful. 'That all fits in with what I've heard in the docks. It seems as though Peters' cheating ways have been catching up with him; the firm appears to be on the verge of going bust.

'So there could be more than one angry client who suffered a raw enough deal to make him take his revenge on Joshua Peters.'

Chapter Twenty-Three

The next three days were busy ones for Ursula. On her way to *Maison Rose* on the Wednesday, she had to deliver the morning's mail to Brown's Hotel, where Mrs Bruton was still staying.

After leaving the letters with the concierge, she used the Davies Street exit of the hotel. As she stopped to draw on her gloves, Ursula saw the front door of *Maison Rose* open and a man propelled roughly out of the building. He stumbled down the steps and collapsed at the bottom.

The man collected himself, dusted down his trousers and picked up his bowler hat, then he raised his fist and shook it at the closed front door. As he did so, Ursula recognised his striking yellow and caramel striped waistcoat. She had last seen it in Shepherd's Market, with its wearer importuning Count Meyerhoff. Rachel had recognised him as Albert, Joshua Peters' valet. It hadn't been possible to see who had ejected him from *Maison Rose* but the odds were on the count. What was going on?

The valet staggered a few steps in the direction of Bond Street, then leant against the entrance to another building, took off his hat and produced a handkerchief to wipe his face. He was still recovering as Ursula made her way into *Maison Rose*.

No one else seemed to be around. She went to her office and settled down to send out what seemed a goodly number of accounts to new clients.

Five minutes later the count entered. His mouth was a thin line and a tiny tic pulsated at the corner of his left eye, always a certain sign that something was amiss.

'Statements must be sent to all clients who have invoices that have remained unpaid for more than a month,' he announced without greeting her. 'They must be sent today.'

'Today?' The outstanding invoices were arranged in alphabetical order by client, not by date. It would take time to identify which needed a statement sent.

'You question my instructions, Miss Grandison? It is as well you remember who gives them.' The count's usual charm had vanished; underneath the continental suavity there lurked a bully.

'It was only that Madame Rose has dealt with an impressive number of clients this week and many new invoices need to be issued. But, of course, I will start immediately on identifying the ones that need statements.'

'Count!'

Madame Rose appeared in the doorway, her face stormy. 'My laboratory, if you please.'

The count hesitated for a moment. 'I shall return later to check progress, Miss Grandison,' he said smoothly and followed Madame.

It seemed the laboratory door had not been shut properly because the sound of angry voices easily percolated through to Ursula's office. Madame Rose and the count were speaking German and perhaps assumed they could not be understood by anyone within hearing distance. There had been no reason for Ursula to inform them she had studied the language in Paris. Her command of it was not as good as her French, but it was enough to be able to understand the gist of their argument.

Madame was afraid that sending out statements would alienate her clients. When the count insisted that it was only good business practice, she became irate and accused him of wanting to dominate. 'You Germans, you want to rule the world,' she flung at him. Ursula, having tried and failed to shut out their voices, expected the count to retaliate that he was Austrian, not German; there had been an Austrian girl in their Parisian school who had spent some time explaining that to call an Austrian a German was tantamount to insulting them. However, the count retorted that Madame Rose should remember who controlled the money side of their business.

To this, apparently, Madame had no answer. Ursula saw her pass the glass door to her office in an angry flash of white coat, head held high.

Ursula buried hers in the invoice file and added another unpaid bill to the growing pile of those needing statements.

A moment later the Count entered wearing a tight smile. 'You progress, Miss Grandison?'

She nodded.

'You will, please, send out all necessary reminders this evening; together with new invoices.' he added crisply.

Despite sending out for a sandwich and working through the lunchtime period, Ursula had to remain some hour and a half beyond her usual departure time.

★ ★ ★

The following day Ursula had a meeting with Mrs Bruton at Brown's Hotel. Adjusting the curtains of the sitting-room window of her employer's suite to Mrs Bruton's satisfaction, Ursula cast a glance across at the *Maison Rose* building and wondered fleetingly how matters were progressing there.

'Now, dear, these builders' estimates for Nevern Square that you have been collecting,' Mrs Bruton waved the little bundle of papers she had been studying. 'I am not happy with these prices. Today I wish you to visit each of them and obtain lower ones. I am sure you can persuade them their charges are far too high. And they must give quotations, I don't want to be told at the end of the job that they were out in their estimates. This one, for instance,' she picked out one, 'it is quite outrageous.'

Ursula took the bunch back. She was unsurprised by the request. 'I was once told by a New York entrepreneur that estimates are very often inflated to allow for a reduction when clients complain.'

'Such a help to have someone working for me who is so efficient and knowledgeable,' Mrs Bruton purred. 'Now, could you be kind enough on your way out to order coffee to be sent up? And please deliver a report on your activities by the end of the day.'

It had taken all that time to visit each of the builders and argue with them. She had then to prepare and deliver the report her employer had ordered. Late again for the evening meal at

Mrs Maple's, Ursula was disappointed to find that Thomas Jackman had not fulfilled his promise to keep her up to date with his investigation, nor retrieved her new winter coat. Ursula tried to tell herself she was uncharitable to care so much for a mere item of clothing when Millie seemed in such dire straits, but the fact that she had worked so hard and guarded her expenditure so carefully in order to acquire the garment meant she could not take its loss lightly.

Ursula reminded herself that her situation was nothing compared with that of Alice Peters, suffering in prison, facing trial for murder and the hangman's rope if she was found guilty – a prospect that was beginning to seem more and more likely.

Taking a plate of the food that had been kept for her, she retired to her room. During her rounds of the builders, Ursula had managed to fit in a visit to the circulating library she had become a member of to see if there was a novel available that might lift her spirits.

'You are in luck, Miss Grandison,' the librarian had said. 'This has only recently been published and it has been excellently received.' The title seemed promising and Ursula slipped the book into her bag with the builders' estimates.

The book did indeed prove compelling and she soon found herself caught up in an exciting story. By the time she went to sleep, she had read half and looked forward to finishing it the following evening.

Friday was one of her *Maison Rose* half days. When she arrived, Hilda Ferguson, Madame Rose's assistant, was rearranging the jars of products displayed in the salon's vitrines.

'Madame and the count have gone to visit someone in the country,' she said excitedly. 'Madame told me he's very rich and they hope he will invest money in the business. She took a bag full of products for him.'

Ursula was amused to see how excited the girl seemed. Usually she was a shadow attending on Madame. Now, chubby cheeks pink, forget-me-not blue eyes alive, small hands moving rapidly as she sorted out the rows of jars, she seemed transformed.

'Last night Madame made up two new batches of cream,' Hilda said as she closed the glass doors. 'She said you are to help me fill the jars.'

'No invoices to send out?'

'Yes, we had a full day of clients yesterday, but Madame said filling the jars shouldn't take all the morning.'

Ursula left her jacket in her office. On the desk was a pile of invoice details and bills that needed cheques made out. She was not sorry to leave the deskwork and join Hilda in the laboratory.

A chrome forcing machine had been set up and Hilda had already filled several jars. She showed Ursula how to place a special seal on them and add a lid, then she wound the machine's handle to fill another jar with creamy mixture.

'What about a label?'

'We'll do that when all the jars have been filled. We're starting with *Crème de la Printemps*, then we'll do *Crème de la Rose*. Madame told me that was the first preparation she created.' Hilda passed a filled jar to Ursula for its seal and lid and placed an empty one underneath the machine's nozzle. 'I shall be glad when this week is over, Count Meyerhoff has been so rude! I was surprised Madame allowed it. He would not have dared to speak to her like that if she was a man; a man would knock him down!'

'What did the count say?'

Another filled jar was passed to Ursula. 'Madame had lost a button on her white coat and he said she looked like a gypsy. He complained that her hair was untidy and went on and on about how important it was to give the right impression to their clients. I left the room, of course, but I could hear him shouting even though I'd closed the laboratory door. Then at last Madame said something that sounded really angry but she was speaking German so I don't know what it was, and after that he went out.'

'Was this yesterday?' Ursula remembered the argument between Madame and the count she had overheard on the Wednesday.

Hilda nodded. The jars were being filled quickly now and Ursula had to work at keeping up with her part of the process.

'I hope they set off in a better mood this morning,' she said after a little.

'The count wasn't saying much but Madame was wearing a wonderful pink silk jacket and skirt, and a small hat to match, ever so smart. Such a change to see her without that white coat.'

Ursula made room for more jars by pushing the finished ones to one side.

'For the last two days the count has found fault with everything.' Hilda's hands moved automatically, continuing the filling process.

'He complained that the shelves were untidy, just because one jar was out of place. He made me so upset I dropped it and it broke and he told me if it happened again I would have to leave.' The girl brushed a piece of hair out of her eyes. She looked very upset. 'I was so pleased when I got this job. My grandmother used to live in Devon, but she came to live with us in Tottenham when I was eleven; her legs wouldn't work no more, not as legs. She had a book that had been handed down from her mother with all these receipts for using herbs and plants for medication, and for keeping the skin soft and clear, and she taught me all about them. I was so interested and started to make some. Only simple ones but my mother said she thought they helped clear her skin of spots.'

Ursula lined up more finished jars. 'Are you going to make your own creams, like Madame?'

'She mixes them in secret, doesn't want anyone to know their receipt. But at least I know what sort of ingredients she has to choose from. And I'm going to night school to learn more about science,' Hilda gave a charming little giggle. 'There's only one other girl in the class and she says she joined because it's a fine place to meet young men.' She grew serious again. 'And I'm doing a business course as well. I want to be able to start up on my own one of these days, like Madame. I don't want to go into service or become a shop girl.'

Ursula was impressed with the girl's ambition. It was the first time she had had the opportunity to have a proper conversation with her.

'How long will it take before you can start your own business?'

Hilda shrugged, 'Several years, I think. Maybe once I have created some products I am pleased with, I can start in a small way with friends and hope that they will tell other friends.' She looked round the immaculate laboratory with its well-stocked shelves and large jars full of ingredients. 'A place like this would cost a great deal to set up. I am not like Madame, I do not know men like Count Meyerhoff who have money and rich friends who will invest in someone like me. What do you think, Ursula? You are American where it seems fortunes can be made overnight, am I foolish to think I can create my own business here?'

Ursula looked at this girl who could conceal ambitious plans beneath a subservient attitude while quietly learning the secrets of running a beauty salon. 'People who make fortunes never question whether they can or not, they just get on and do it. I think you have exactly the right attitude, Hilda. Stick to your plans and you will get there.'

'Oh, I will.'

'Tell me, Hilda, do many English girls want to become independent like you?'

'There's quite a few want to be a bit more adventurous than people expect. Another girl at the college was telling me the other day that she's joining the Women's Suffrage Movement. And I'm going to as well. We women should have the vote; why do men think it's only they who decide who is to govern us and how?'

'I'll introduce you to my friend Rachel Fentiman, she's involved with the Movement. She thinks they should be more militant.'

Hilda stopped filling jars for a moment. 'Militant? What does that mean? Surely not something to do with the army?'

'I don't know but it will definitely be something aggressive. Rachel mentioned chaining herself to some railings outside Parliament, oh, and breaking windows.'

'What will that achieve?'

'She says it will be in the newspapers so that more people will know about the Movement and the government will realise how serious women are about getting the vote.'

'I think that sounds a great idea!'

'You don't think it could alienate people?'

'Where has being nice and polite got us?' In charge of the shiny chrome machine, the girl looked positively militant herself.

★ ★ ★

That evening Ursula finished reading the book that had so enthralled her. Gradually, as she read, she found herself piecing together fragments of the conversation between the count and Madame Rose that she had overheard the previous Wednesday together with other oddments from her time with the *Maison Rose*. The picture they began to create was a worrying one and she continued to read with a growing sense that she should talk to someone in a better position to judge whether it could be important.

Chapter Twenty-Four

It was well after midnight when Ursula turned the final page of the novel but her mind was too active for her to fall asleep at once. She tossed and turned, finally drifting off just before dawn and woke late on Saturday morning. It mattered little as she did not need to be at either Mrs Bruton's or the *Maison Rose*.

Conscious she had already wasted time that could have been spent exploring, or having a walk in one of London's many parks, Ursula had a hasty breakfast and hurried out of the front door. A nasty wind that hit her as she turned into the main road carried a reminder that autumn was here and winter approached.

The faint idea of a contemplative walk in Green Park vanished. Ursula turned her attention towards checking the destination of omnibuses. A friendly conductor told her which number she needed and some little time later she was at the junction of Tottenham Court Road and Oxford Street.

A steady stream of visitors was heading for the menagerie. Once again the carved screen fascinated Ursula as she passed it on her way to the encampment beyond.

The circus area was a scene of happy activity with large pails of water and feedstuff being carried to the menagerie, jugglers working at spinning plates on sticks, acrobats practising handstands and using a spring board to jump on to one another's shoulders in complicated tiers of performers. Ursula, forgetting for a moment why she was there, stood watching all the activity.

'Ah, lovely lady from other night!' Ma suddenly appeared, her colourful robe replaced by a plain canvas skirt and loose tunic, her turban exchanged for a cotton scarf printed in a colourful pattern, wiry curls of dark hair escaping from it.

'Good morning! I thought I'd come and see how Millie had settled in,' Ursula said. 'I hope I am not intruding.'

Ma beamed at her. 'Millie fine. She sewing in my caravan. Go, talk!'

Ursula turned towards the splendid travelling van that was Ma and Pa's home and saw that Millie was in fact sitting on the top step, bent over a lapful of red material, wielding a needle and thread. She caught sight of Ursula and waved.

What a change had occurred! The distraught and depressed girl in her diaphanous lingerie had vanished. From somewhere Millie had acquired a neat cotton skirt and bodice and a large knitted shawl. The greatest change, though, was her wide and confident smile.

'I'm Ursula Grandison, we met the other night,' said Ursula, uncertain whether the girl would remember her.

'Oh, miss, it was the best thing ever, Mr Jackman and you bringing me here!'

'You like it, then?'

'I'm sharing with one of the circus riders, Ilaria, that's her over there,' she pointed at a girl riding bareback, her legs either side of a sturdy piebald pony. Then, demonstrating complete control, she moved from a sitting to a standing position, her slippered feet seemingly secure on the broad back, her arms held gracefully out.

'You watch,' said Millie.

To Ursula's astonishment, without fuss, the girl performed a somersault, making a perfect landing without the horse having changed its pace. A moment later she slid down again to a sitting position and patted the piebald's neck in thanks.

'She's being doing that over and over,' said Millie. 'Amazing, i'n't it?'

Ursula agreed.

'She doesn't seem to mind me sharing. Her English i'n't good but she can understand me and I can work out what she's saying. This is one of her costumes.' She shook out the red velvet and held it up. It didn't look as though it would cover much of the girl's body.

'It has a tear and she needs a new fringe.' Millie picked up a length of cream trimming, and showed where it would go. She grinned, 'It's not going to cover up much of her legs, is it? And to think I was afraid of showing too much in that negligée! D'you want to come up? Ma says I can make a cup of tea when I like.'

Inside the caravan, Millie put the kettle on the stove, took down a teapot and a tin painted with a country scene. 'Isn't this a wonderful place to live?' she said, dipping a spoon into the tea caddy.

Ursula looked at her in amazement. The other night this girl had been desperate. She had been rescued from a scandalous situation to find herself without a position, clothes, or shelter. And now she seemed to have all three.

'You look quite at home.'

The kettle came to the boil and Millie made the tea. Bone china mugs were produced. 'Do you take milk?' she asked.

The girl showed all the aplomb of a society hostess. Ursula sat on one of the cushioned mahogany cupboards that formed part of the caravan's furnishings, took her tea, and accepted a dash of milk. What an extraordinary number of twists of fortune this girl had lived through during the last few weeks. Her mistress disappearing, her master making her act as his hostess in the house in which she had been a lady's maid, discovering that master dead, then accepting an invitation to be set up as a 'lady of the night', only to find that she was expected to perform a role little different from that of a common prostitute. Perhaps, after all that had passed, finding herself set down in a circus and menagerie, and sharing a caravan with a bareback rider was not so strange after all.

'I'm glad you've found some suitable clothes,' Ursula said, thinking that they fitted the girl very well. Maybe she had used her sewing skills to alter them.

'Ma produced a skirt and blouse from one of the other girls and then I went to Montagu Place and got my own ones.' Millie giggled as she leant against the doorframe with her own mug of tea. 'That old witch, Mrs Firestone, had the cheek to tell me I needn't think of having my place back. I told her it was the last thing I'd want.'

'You don't wish to see if you could return to your position when Mrs Peters comes out … that is to say, when she is able to return home?'

Millie gave a toss of her neatly coiffed head. 'She won't be coming back. Not after she murdered the master.'

'You really think she killed him?'

'"Course she did. Wanted to have her child and her fancy man, didn't she? Gave the old man a packet of lies of how she'd never been unfaithful to him and he was the father – and the silly old fool swallowed it all.' She managed to talk and drink her tea at the same time. 'I told him when she disappeared how it was with her. All sly and treacherous. Couldn't be content with having a comfortable home with a husband what provided her with everything a woman could want.'

Ursula remembered the tragic figure she'd seen in prison, her dignity and her staunch reliance that justice would see that she was released.

'That Inspector Drummond, he saw through her at once,' Millie added. 'Reckon he was pretty impressed with what I had to tell him about her goings-on.' She drank the last of her tea, rose, refreshed the teapot and offered Ursula a refill.

Ursula handed over her mug, fascinated by Millie's tale.

'I told Mrs Firestone I was well suited and she'd better be looking for a new position herself. Then I packed up my old clothes and left. Oh, yes, and I told Emily she'd better find another position and all.'

Ursula watched the way Millie wielded the strainer as she poured tea into the mug and gracefully passed it back to her and had a sudden vision of her dressed in Alice's gowns dispensing alcohol and refreshments to Joshua Peters' guests.

'Do you expect to remain here?'

Another little toss of the head. 'Who's to say? Ma and Pa have told me I can stay as long as I want. They say they've needed someone to deal with the costume side of things for some time.'

'But what about when winter comes? Don't they stop touring then?' Ursula remembered Ma mentioning the working out of new routines in winter quarters.

Millie shrugged her shoulders. 'Could be they need a whole set of different outfits and what better time to make them? But maybe I'll set myself up as a dressmaker, a costumier,' she brought the word out with pride. 'Reckon there's any amount of things I could do. Learned a lot over the last few months I have. I thought becoming a lady's maid was the best thing ever; now I reckon there's other things. Things that would mean I could do more what I want rather than be at the beck and call of someone else. Know what I mean?'

Oh, yes, she knew exactly what Millie meant. If the girl hadn't been so accusing of Alice, Ursula could admire the resourcefulness she seemed to have discovered.

'Am I intruding?' said a voice and there was Thomas Jackman coming up the steps leading into the caravan.

'Well, look who's here!' said Millie cheekily. 'Been wondering when you'd turn up.'

'There was other business that called for my attention.' Thomas removed his bowler hat and entered. There was something about his wiry body and clean-shaven appearance that made the well-ordered living space seem impossibly crowded, yet they'd all managed well enough the other night, sitting and eating at the moveable table while Ma bustled about.

'Cup o' tea?' Millie continued to fulfil her role as hostess.

'Millie, you're a lifesaver. Nice and strong and plenty of milk.' Thomas placed his hat on a convenient hook and neatly tucked himself down on the seat. 'Good to see you, Miss Grandison.' He gave her a nod of acknowledgement.

'Ursula, please,' she murmured, admiring his neat appearance and the aplomb with which he had taken control of the situation.

'So, what you been up to, then?' Millie handed over his tea and sat beside him, closer than was strictly necessary. Thomas rearranged the set of his tweed jacket; manufacturing a little distance between their thighs.

'This and that, you know,' he said, raising his mug in a salute. 'Now, tell me, are you happy here?'

Millie gave him a brilliant smile. 'Oh, yes, Joe … whoops, must learn to call you Tom, mustn't I?'

There was a little pause.

'And I got lots of work,' Millie indicated the bundle of red velvet. 'Ma says she's ever so lucky to have me.'

'Excellent,' he murmured and surveyed her thoughtfully. 'Changed your manner of dressing, I see.'

She gave him a provocative look. 'Not got the goods on display, you mean? Doesn't mean they aren't a draw anyway.'

Almost as if prompted, a lithe figure ran up the steps. Short dark hair was brushed back from a mobile face with a snub nose and sparkling eyes. Dressed in rough trousers and tunic, he carried what looked like a clown's outfit over his arm. 'Miss Millie, Ma says you repair tear, no?' His accent sounded Eastern European, his smile was pure charm.

'Of course, Rinaldo.' She held out a hand for the costume, then sorted out the damage: a long rent down the baggy trousers of the all-in-one garment. 'Rough in the ring was it last night?' she asked sympathetically.

'That Marko! 'E think clever make me fall – not as arranged, so I not expect.'

'You'll have to sort him out. Cup of tea?'

Rinaldo looked as though he would like to say 'yes' but he glanced at Ursula and Thomas. 'No, my turn fix more feed for animals. Later I come for costume and then have tea, yes?'

'Any time,' Millie smiled warmly at him and carefully folded up the costume. 'I'll have this mended in an hour or so.'

Rinaldo blew her a kiss and neatly tripped down the steps.

'See what you mean,' said Thomas. 'Glad you've come to a safe landing here. But where did you get the clothes?'

'Millie went back to Montagu Place and reclaimed her stuff,' said Ursula. 'I think it says a lot for the Peters household that it was there waiting for her. They might well have given the clothes to the poor box, if that's what it's called over here.'

'They weren't theirs to give, they was mine! I'd have had something to say if that had happened, I can tell you.'

'Albert there?'

'Oh, Albert! He's taken himself off. Moment Joshua … that is, the master, died, he knew there wasn't anything there for him. He'd tried to get it off with me when I arrived.' She gave Thomas a meaning look. 'Told him where he could keep his hands and his suggestions. Said I wasn't that sort of girl. And we all knew he was that close to the master.' She held up two crossed fingers. 'Always running to him with tales against the rest of us. Wanted to be top dog, he did.'

'So after Mr Peters died, he, as you might say, abandoned ship?'

'Well, he went. That's all I know.' Millie equipped herself with needle and thread and picked up the clown's costume with an air of closing the conversation.

'Where could he have gone to? That's what I'd like to know.'

'And why, may I ask?'

'Matter of this investigation into your master's murder.'

'Oh, that!' Millie looked sulky. 'Isn't that all wrapped up? What with Mrs Peters arrested and all?'

'All wrapped up? That what you think, is it?' Thomas cocked his head on one side and held her gaze till she bit her lip, bent her head and started mending the rent.

'Well, Millie, there are threads to be followed, ends to be tied. And that's why I'd like a little chat with Albert.' He paused for a moment, then continued in a meaningful voice, 'He's got some questions to answer.'

Milllie brightened. 'Oh, has he!' She rested her needle and thought for a long moment.

Thomas said nothing and Ursula sat quietly and finished her tea. She didn't know where this conversation was going but she was very grateful the investigator had turned up. He was the perfect person to discuss her problem with.

'Albert did once say,' Millie said slowly, 'as 'ow he was looking forward to living as a gent. Mind you, that was when he was trying it on with me; thought he had to make an impression and said as 'ow he wasn't far off acquiring such residential accommodation as would suit someone moving up in the world. And he knew where that was. Well, Mr Peters wasn't going to stand for that and I told him so.'

'And he said?' Thomas asked negligently.

'Only that he and Mr Peters could continue in partnership with him living in better style and someone else running the errands. Partnership! He was living in some sort of dream world!'

'Sounds like it. Did he tell you where this accommodation "suitable for someone coming up in the world" was, by any chance?'

Millie gave him a sharp look. 'Maybe; not sure I remember, though.'

'With this investigation, I get expenses. There could be something in it for you if your memory managed to conjure up an address that turned out right.'

''Ow much?'

'I'm sure I can be generous, once I know the information isn't worthless.'

Millie's eyes narrowed and she continued stitching.

Thomas waited.

'It were somewhere country-like,' she said slowly.

'You mean, not in London? I can't believe that.'

'No, in London but sounding country.'

'You mean such as Kentish Town? Doesn't sound likely, too far out for a high flier like Albert.'

'Like that but not that.' Millie closed her eyes and concentrated. Finally: 'Dorset, that's what he said.' She opened her eyes and smiled happily at Thomas. 'Dorset Square; I'm sure that's what he said.'

'Hm; Marylebone that is. Might well have apartments that could suit. Sounds as though it could be right.'

'Right? 'Course it's right. Worth a lot, that'll be.'

'And it's Albert Pond, ain't it?'

She nodded, her expression delighted and challenging.

'Well, that's grand.' Thomas set his tea mug down and rose. 'Now it's just a matter of that nice coat Miss Grandison lent you on Tuesday night. Or have you returned it to her already?'

'I'm sure Millie was about to do so when you arrived,' murmured Ursula.

For the most fleeting of moments Millie's expression was sulky again, then she caught Thomas's look and smiled brightly. 'I'll get it right now, Miss Grandison. Hold this,' she dumped the clown costume on to Ursula's lap and tripped down the caravan steps.

Thomas looked after her thoughtfully. 'Never quite know where you are with Millie,' he said.

'Are you intending to visit Dorset Square now?' Ursula asked.

He nodded.

'Would you mind if I went with you? There's something I need to discuss and you are the perfect person. It might even be relevant to your investigation.'

'I would be highly honoured, Miss ... Ursula. Can I ask what it's about?'

'I need to be able to explain certain matters; perhaps after we have left here?'

'Of course.'

When Millie returned, she was carrying the coat. 'I must thank you very much, Miss Grandison, for lending it to me.' She handed it over with a longing look. 'It's new, isn't it?'

'Yes, I bought it the other day. Now that winter's coming, I realised I need something warm.' Ursula placed it over her arm and couldn't help caressing its soft Melton wool.

'We'll get out your hair, young Millie. But you can tell Pa that I'll be back soon to see how things are.'

Ursula handed back the clown costume and was conscious of Millie's look of frustration as she and Thomas Jackman left the caravan.

'Hey, what about the money you promised me? For remembering where Albert wanted to live?'

He looked back, 'After I know you haven't been pulling a fast one on me.'

She stamped a foot in frustration.

'You can trust me, Millie. If Albert's there, you'll get your money.'

With a swirl of skirt she disappeared back into the caravan.

Chapter Twenty-Five

Thomas helped Ursula into her coat then led her away from the circus site into the busy main road.

'I've just read a most interesting book,' Ursula said as he started to guide her through the traffic.

'Wait until we are safely on the other side.' He pulled her back as an errand boy on a heavily laden bicycle appeared from behind an omnibus. 'Whoa!' he added, taking a firm grip on her arm as an automobile came from the other direction, overtaking a cart drawn by a wayward horse.

'What a dangerous business,' gasped Ursula as they gained the safety of the other pavement.

'I think Tottenham Court Road has to be one of the worst for traffic. Now that more and more automobiles are beginning to appear, we pedestrians take our lives in our hands.'

'There isn't nearly as much automotive traffic as in New York. Even the French are ahead of the English.'

'When you think that we pioneered steam transport and railways run all over England, I suppose it is odd. But I am sure it won't be long before we realise that the advantages of automobiles outweigh the disadvantages. Now, what was it you wanted to tell me? It can't be just that you have read a book, however interesting!'

He liked hearing Ursula laugh, it had a companiable sound.

'I don't suppose you read much fiction.'

'No time.' But it wasn't lack of time, more an instinctive dislike of storytelling. Perhaps it was because he had had to listen to so many fanciful tales from those he tried to bring to justice.

'I can understand that, but this novel got me thinking. I was first attracted by the title, *The Riddle of the Sands*. But it wasn't the tale of mystery I expected. It's about two young men sailing along the North Sea coast and discovering a German plan to invade England. There's a spy involved who has researched an English naval dockyard called Chatham.'

He was amused by the way Ursula split the name into two: 'Chat' and 'ham'. He said, '"Chattum".'

She smiled and repeated his pronunciation.

'So, sounds as though it could be exciting but what has this book to do with anything?'

'Am I wrong in thinking England fears Germany is planning an invasion? Or that there is a feeling that German spies could be checking out your naval preparedness?'

'It's something our newspapers certainly concern themselves with.' Thomas guided her through a tangle of small streets and lanes. 'Do you have a spy in mind?'

She said nothing for a little as they negotiated badly maintained cobblestones. He glanced at her shoes, worried they weren't up to what he was putting her through, but they seemed sturdy enough.

'It's the count,' she said as they gained a better surface.

'Count?'

'Have I told you that I have another job; that as well as working for Mrs Bruton, I am a sort of bookkeeper for the *Maison Rose*?'

Thomas heard the name with a jolt. He was suddenly conscious that, since he'd returned from his visit up north, he'd done nothing about the jar he'd found in Joshua Peters' desk. '*Maison Rose*? Surely that sounds like the sort of establishment that ...' Thomas trailed off, feeling it didn't sound amusing said out loud.

Ursula seemed unembarrassed, he had forgotten how straightforward she was. 'Mrs Bruton thought the name sounded as though it was a fashion house but it turned out to be a beauty clinic. Madame Rose is an Egyptian, she has scientifically studied women's facial skin and prepares creams and lotions to help them look beautiful. She has given me some and I really do believe that my skin shows an improvement.'

She stopped walking and turned towards him as if she wanted him to judge for himself.

Thomas was having none of it. 'If a woman asks me to comment on her looks, I can never get it right; I'm either accused of flattery or she gets upset because I haven't complimented her enough. So, Ursula, I'll take your word that you consider your more than passable good looks have been improved.'

Another laugh that sounded completely genuine. Most women in Thomas's experience would have either pretended not to understand him, or taken offence. 'And you say you don't know how to compliment a woman! Thomas, you are a fraud!'

He felt a surge of delight that they appeared at last to have recaptured the easy friendship that had built up while they were working in partnership earlier that year.

'You're suggesting that a count could be a spy? Should I know who you mean?' Even as he asked, Thomas remembered the name.

'I don't why you should. Count Meyerhoff is Madame Rose's partner. I was helping Rachel distribute her women's suffrage literature late one afternoon, in an area very near to *Maison Rose*, I think it is called Shepherd's Market, and I saw the count come out of a public house followed by a shortish man who pulled at his coat sleeve in a most unwelcome way. As soon as she saw him, Rachel said it was Albert, who worked for Joshua Peters, her brother-in-law, and she couldn't imagine what he was doing there.'

He nodded. 'I remember, I was there too.'

'You were? I didn't see you.'

'I didn't intend anyone should. I'd followed Albert from the docks, after we'd had a short, very unhelpful, conversation. So the gentleman he seemed so anxious to chat to was your count?'

Ursula moved a little away from him. 'Not a description I would accept.'

'You don't like him,' Thomas said decisively. 'He looked every inch the gentleman to me, yet perhaps a little too suave for my taste.'

Ursula flashed him a smile. 'I'm glad you said that. Count Meyerhoff has great charm but it is only a veneer. Underneath he is a bully and, well, dangerous.'

Thomas was taken aback at the word. He viewed Ursula Grandison as practical; she approached problems and people from a logical point of view. Now she was betraying signs of what he would refer to as a feminine instinct, that judged from sentiment rather than relying on evidence.

'What makes you think this Count Meyerhoff could be a spy?'

Ursula sighed. 'If I hadn't read that book, I have to confess the idea would never have occurred to me. I may not like the count but it seems to be he who is behind Madame Rose's success with her beauty salon.'

Thomas began to be irritated. 'Ursula, let me be the judge of your evidence, whatever it is.'

She glanced at him with the glint of a smile. 'I'm being horribly feminine, aren't I? And I'm sure you're wanting to tell me to report as straightforwardly as one of your policemen. Well, I overheard the Count and Madame Rose having an argument. They were talking, almost shouting, in German. No doubt they thought no one would understand them but it was one of the languages I studied at my French school. They were arguing about the count's right to dictate everything to do with the salon and I heard Madame say to him, "You Germans want to rule the world".'

'That's hardly branding him a spy!'

'No, listen. Mrs Bruton met the count in Austria and spoke of him as a native. I expected the count to retort that he was Austrian, not German. It may be the language that is spoken there but it is not their nationality; they have their own Emperor and the Austrian-Hapsburg empire is huge. Austrians consider Germany little more than an extension of Prussia and to be called German an insult.'

'So you now assume that he is German and has ambitions to take over the world?'

'I don't blame you for not taking me seriously, but there is more. A little time ago, I overheard him speaking on the telephone, saying he was to visit "Chat-ham", using just that pronunciation, then he suddenly shut the door as though he didn't want anyone to hear what he was saying. Well, it didn't mean anything to me then and I'd forgotten all about it until I read this book and realised that it is a naval dockyard. And before you say anything else, the final little piece of evidence that made me wonder was that yesterday morning as I was approaching *Maison Rose*, I saw that valet, Albert, being booted out of the front door. It was slammed shut after him; then when I entered the salon, I found the count in a foul mood.'

'And you remembered Albert getting the brush-off in Shepherd's Market and thought he'd come back for more?'

'Exactly. At first I couldn't think what connection there could be between him and the count. Then I remembered that Joshua Peters was involved in shipping and that *Maison Rose* received consignments of ingredients for Madame's creams and lotions by ship.'

'So maybe Albert was arranging to deliver a new consignment,' Thomas said slowly. He was by no means sold on the idea of Count Meyerhoff as a spy but that he could be up to some nefarious activity that Albert knew about seemed highly likely. And there was something about the name, Meyerhoff, that tugged at a memory he couldn't for the moment identify.

'But why should that upset the count? No, it seems to me that Albert must know something about him, probably because Peters did. I remember Alice saying that before she was married, her husband had spent some years in Egypt, that's where he started to make his fortune, through trading. And Madame Rose is Egyptian.'

It still didn't add up to the count being a spy.

Thomas thought through what he had heard. Ursula was right about the threat of Germany's naval ambitions. And there was the matter of England's North Sea fleet, or, rather, lack of one. Thomas had a well-versed contact employed in drafting legislation in the House of Commons. Over a drink one day, the contact had complained that it seemed essential to build up England's naval defences against a belligerent Germany but that there was not any current policy to do so. However, it was a long stretch from there to branding a Germanic count, whatever his exact nationality, a spy merely because he wished to visit Chatham; it could hardly be counted a tourist attraction but he might well have a friend there. Thomas reckoned that if reading novels meant otherwise sensible minds such as Ursula's could be persuaded to latch on to unsustainable theories, then he was right not to read them himself.

'We need to talk to Albert,' he said, unconsciously quickening his footsteps.

He saw Ursula biting her lip as though aware of the fragile nature of her theory but she kept up with his pace without comment.

Thomas had plodded these streets as a uniformed constable and he was able to guide them unerringly through a maze of small streets. Then he saw a hansom cab disgorging its fare and hailed it. 'I think we are justified in more rapid transport,' he said, assisting Ursula inside. 'Dorset Square,' he instructed the driver.

'What number, guv?'

'Anywhere in the square, cabbie.'

The cab was put in motion.

Ursula said, 'So you think there is something in my theory after all, Thomas?'

'I think the sooner we track down Albert, the sooner we may be able to find out exactly what his business with your count is.'

The Saturday morning traffic was busy but it didn't take them too long to reach the pleasant square that was no more than a couple of streets away from Marylebone station. Nor was it far from Montagu Place, though that was in a slightly smarter area. Had Albert reconnoitred to find somewhere in the vicinity of where he was working that he felt could give him an upward step in the world while also being somewhere he could afford?

On arrival in Dorset Square, Thomas helped Ursula down from the cab then paid off the driver and made a note of the amount in a small notebook he carried. 'Important to keep expenses straight,' he murmured.

Ursula appeared not to hear him, she was studying the houses that lined the square. She pointed across from where they were standing. 'They look as though they could be apartments,' she said.

Together they approached. Sure enough, the first building Ursula had picked out had the sort of double door favoured by up-market apartment houses.

'It looks too smart for a rat like Albert, however on the make he is,' said Ursula.

'We'll check it out though.'

'What did you say Albert's other name was?'

'Pond, Albert Pond. I obtained all the full names of the Peters' servants at the start of my investigation.' He led the way inside. A small porter's lodge was on the left of the hallway, occupied by an elderly man in a sober uniform reading a newspaper. Immediately he noted the newcomers, the paper was put down.

'Ex-army, I would take a bet on it,' Thomas whispered, then, 'I wonder if you can help us, we have come to visit a Mr Pond, I believe he is resident here?'

'Mr Pond, sir? No, sir, no one of that name here.' The porter had the air of a man who knew whereof he spoke.

'We must have the number wrong,' Thomas said apologetically. He took Ursula's arm and exited the building, conscious of the porter's gaze as they went.

The next building produced the same response.

The third one they looked at had a locked front door with a panel of bells beside it together with a list of names. 'Look,' said Ursula excitedly. Sure enough, at the top, in a copperplate hand there the name was: A. Pond.

Thomas pressed the bell and they waited.

'If he has rooms on the top floor, it will take time to descend,' said Ursula.

After several more minutes Thomas pressed the bell again. It was impossible to tell if it was in working order or not.

Still no one came. 'If Albert's not in, I'd like to gain access to his apartment,' said Thomas. 'We could surely find some clue as to what he's up to.'

'The bell at the bottom says Caretaker,' Ursula pointed out and pressed it.

A door in the basement opened and a voice shouted up: 'What you want, then?'

She was a middle-aged woman dressed in a soiled apron over a faded cotton dress, her hair roughly gathered into a mob cap, her face worn and set in depressed lines.

Thomas watched as, unprompted, Ursula dropped down the basement steps. 'We've come to visit a friend, Albert Pond,' she said, 'but he doesn't seem to be home. Would you know his whereabouts? Or is it that his bell doesn't work?'

The woman hesitated for a moment then shrugged and said, 'Wouldn't know. Though he'd be sharp enough to tell me if it wasn't.'

'Then would you be aware if he has gone out?'

'It's not my place to keep tabs on the residents.'

'I expect, though, said Ursula, 'that they rely on you in all sorts of ways, doing their cleaning and such? Mr Pond was expecting us and it's not like him not to be there when he says he will be.' She smiled at the woman. 'Perhaps you would be good enough to tell us your name?'

The woman unbent slightly. 'Ivy Duggan, Madam, and I does his cleaning on a Tuesday, and take up any deliveries and such like.'

Thomas joined Ursula, a hand in his trouser pocket jingling some coin. 'Then, Mrs Duggan, I expect that you'll have a key to his apartment.'

'I might have,' the caretaker said slowly, flicking a glance at the pocket with its coins.

'It's just that Miss Grandison and I have become worried about our friend. It really is very unlike Mr Pond not to be on the doorstep looking out for us, let alone not answering his bell. At the time we made this arrangement, he did mention that he was worried about a return of his old trouble – heart you know. I wonder, would you be willing to take us to his apartment and check that he hasn't collapsed?' He withdrew his hand, a sovereign held between thumb and forefinger. 'Such assistance would deserve recognition,' he added tellingly.

The caretaker's gaze latched on to the sovereign. Her hands twitched, then she snatched it out of Thomas's hand. 'Stan,' she shouted back through her open door. 'Stan, I'm going upstairs, you're to mind the place.'

A shrunken man, older than the woman, with watery eyes and trembling hands, mean clothing hanging on his frame, appeared behind Mrs Duggan, who immediately spirited the sovereign away into a pocket. 'Upstairs, you say? Where's me tea?'

'I'll not be long. These people need to check on Mr Pond.'

Sam shuffled back into the apartment. The caretaker took a couple of keys from a board by the door, 'Well, you'd better come up,' she said and pushed past them up the steps.

Thomas and Ursula followed her as she opened the front door to the house, then led the way up to the third floor. Thomas noted the poor decorative condition of the hall and stairs, which sported a wide band of white paint in place of carpet. The higher up they went, the narrower the stairs and more dilapidated the doors that gave off each landing. On the mezzanine floors as they climbed Thomas noted first a lavatory, then a bathroom. At the very top, where the ceiling sloped attic-like, the caretaker stopped in front of a door and banged on it. 'Mr Pond, folks to see yer,' she shouted.

There was no response.

Thomas said nothing, nor did Ursula. The three of them were uncomfortably crowded on to the small landing. In the silence the sound of a train entering or exiting Marylebone station could be heard.

'He could 'ave gorn out,' said Mrs Duggan slowly.

'If he's not there, we'll leave; you can lock up and Mr Pond will be no more the wiser,' Thomas said soothingly, he was damned if he was going to ante up more money, a sovereign was more than enough, perhaps more than had been wise. He'd think of some way to be left in the apartment once they were inside.

With a quick sigh, the caretaker inserted the key and opened the door. As they stepped into a small living room, a stale scent compounded of dirty clothes, unwashed body odour and unaired rooms greeted them.

If Albert reckoned moving into Dorset Square meant he'd gone up in the world, it could only be because of the number of stairs he had to climb to reach his accommodation. Maybe the lower floors offered apartments with more style. Here a rapid glance revealed a threadbare carpet, dirty walls that were ignorant of any pictures, a few unassuming items of furniture, a small fireplace with an aged wing chair before it, and on the floor, face down, with his head resting on the fender, Albert Pond.

Ursula gasped. Thomas held out a hand to her but she swallowed hard and straightened her back. 'I'm fine,' she said quietly.

'Gawd save us!' The caretaker brought a hand to her mouth. 'Yer was right! 'Is 'eart must've given out. 'Ere, I got to sit down.'

She swayed and Thomas moved the armchair a little distance from the body and helped her sit.

'Would you like some water?' Ursula asked.

Mrs Duggan shook her head. 'Nah, but 'e keeps brandy in that cupboard …'

Ursula opened the doors of a wooden cabinet and revealed a few items of crockery, a couple of glasses and a half-empty bottle of fine cognac. 'Well,' she said, 'Albert Pond is not going to need it,' poured some out and gave it to the caretaker, who downed the drink in one, coughed slightly, wiped her mouth with her sleeve and gave the empty glass back to Ursula. 'Better 'ave one yerself,' Mrs Duggan said.

Ursula looked across at Thomas but he shook his head and she returned the bottle to the cupboard.

Thomas bent and carefully turned the body over. One look at the contorted face and the way the hands clutched at the throat convinced him that heart attack was not the most likely diagnosis.

'When did you last see Mr Pond?' Thomas asked.

She looked vacantly at him until he repeated the question. 'I dunno.'

'Think, woman,' he said urgently, then caught himself; they'd not get anywhere by upsetting her. 'A doctor may well order a post-mortem examination to establish exactly how he died. It may even be possible that the police need to be informed.'

'Police!' Mrs Duggan looked stricken.

'They could well ask you the same question, so you might as well establish the answer now,' he said slowly and calmly.

She took a deep breath and considered his words. Then, 'It would be Tuesday, that was the day I did 'is rooms.'

Looking round, Thomas thought that 'doing the rooms' couldn't take very long. ''E was going out as I came up. 'E was in an 'urry, said 'e'd left me money on the table and ran down the stairs. Didn't seem no difficulty with 'is 'eart then.' She carefully avoided looking at the body.

'And you haven't seen him since?'

'Not until I opened that door.'

'Did you see him return that day?'

She shook her head.

'Or see anyone visit him between then and now?'

Another shake of the head. 'But I doesn't 'ave the time to winder gaze.'

'Do you clean rooms for anyone else in the building?' Ursula asked.

'I looks after most of them. And they got more furniture and stuff in them than 'ere.' She shot a glance at the sparse furnishings. 'Respectable, they are, them that stays 'ere. What they're going to say about this, I don't know.'

'So you would be in and out of the apartments, up and down the stairs?' Thomas said.

A nod.

'Which would mean that, without window gazing, you might well see a visitor paying a call?'

'That's as may be, but I didn't see anyone that didn't 'ave any right to be 'ere. Nor anyone to see Mr Pond.'

'We shall need a doctor to examine him,' Thomas said. 'Please send for one, Mrs Duggan.'

'Me? I ain't got no one to send. Stan's no use and I can't leave the building.' She looked at him almost pleadingly.

Thomas sighed and brought out another sovereign. 'If I write a note, I'm sure you can persuade Stan to go, or you can leave him looking after the building and go yourself.' He held up the coin.

The woman looked greedily at it and finally gave a little nod. 'Suppose I could.'

Thomas took out his notebook, extracted a page, wrote a quick request and handed it to Mrs Duggan together with the money.

'Could take me a little time. Stan'll not understand.'

'The dead can wait and Miss Grandison and I will keep him company. You'll need us as witnesses.'

'Witnesses?'

'That you didn't do him in.'

''Ere, what you suggesting?'

'Nothing, Mrs Duggan; I'm suggesting nothing. But you need us to declare that you opened that door in all innocence and were as horrified at what you saw as we were.' Thomas looked at Ursula.

'You have had a very nasty shock,' she said in a calm voice. 'We all have. But I'm sure you can understand that Mr Jackman is giving you very good advice. When the doctor calls, he can examine Mr Pond's body, and we can state exactly what has happened this morning. Then you should have nothing to worry about as far as police are concerned.'

Mrs Duggan looked from her to Thomas and back again. 'Well, yer seems to know yer fingers from yer toes, which is more than wot I can at the moment.' She levered herself out of the chair and plucked coin and note out of Thomas's hand. 'I'll get Stan to go along to Dr Morrison's, 'e knows where it is, been there often enough.' She cast another glance at the body on the floor; her face seemed to have grown older since they'd entered the apartment. ''E wasn't a bad old sod, which is more than I can say for everyone in this building; stuck-up lot some o' them.' She sniffed hard and left.

'Sure you don't want a drop of that brandy yourself?' Thomas said to Ursula as the door closed behind Mrs Duggan.

'Thank you, no. One of the benefits of living in a California mining camp is that you are no stranger to unexpected death and I prefer to keep a clear head.' She gave a quick look at the body. 'Is your verdict a heart attack?'

Thomas was profoundly grateful for the hardening effects of rough living, the last thing he needed at this moment was an hysterical woman, or one prone to swooning. He undid Albert's waistcoat, tie and shirt and pushed the material back to reveal his chest. 'No, it looks more like a case of cyanide poisoning to me, the same cause of death as Joshua Peters.'

'But wasn't he killed with prussic acid?'

'Another name for cyanide.'

Chapter Twenty-Six

Ursula forced herself to look at Albert Pond's body. 'What tells you he was killed with prussic acid, or cyanide?'

'I can't be certain but look at those livid spots and discolourations; they are more likely to be caused by cyanide than a heart attack.'

Ursula looked at Albert's mottled chest and thought about the awful result of swallowing poison. She drew a sudden breath. 'Could it have been in the brandy? Mrs Duggan drank some!'

Jackman unstoppered the bottle and smelled the contents. 'No trace of almonds and I think if she had ingested any cyanide, she would have collapsed. It's not quite instantaneous but doesn't take long to take effect.'

'What a relief! But if not the brandy, what? There doesn't seem anything here to eat.'

'The killer could have removed the means when he left,' said Jackman.

Ursula tried not to show how shocked she felt. The dead body, with its twisted limbs and contorted features, looked horrible. Had Joshua Peters looked like that when he'd been found? No matter how unpleasant or even evil both men were, it was a terrible end.

She went into the other room and returned with a bedcover which she spread over Albert's body. 'I can't help remembering the way he was ejected from *Maison Rose* the other day,' she said. 'How he stood on the pavement and shook his fist at the closed door. He was a very angry man.'

'We should try and find something that will tell us why he was there,' said Thomas. He opened the doors to the little cupboard, and placed the pieces of crockery and glass on the top beside the brandy bottle. Then he knelt and ran his hands over the interior.

Ursula went back into the bedroom. Sun shining through a dormer window that matched one in the other room revealed that Albert had not yet managed to surround himself with the trappings of a genteel lifestyle. There was a night cabinet beside the bed but the china pot it should house was beneath the iron bedstead. Ursula wrinkled her nose at the odour of its contents. She opened the cabinet's door but found only empty space inside. Nor was anything in the drawer. She checked that nothing had been fixed to its underside.

In a corner was a basin supplying water. A cupboard to one side held shaving equipment, a small bar of soap and a bottle of pills. A pharmacy label announced that they were aspirin. Ursula picked up the thin rug that lay on the boarded floor but could see nothing that required closer attention. She stripped the bed and examined the pillow, establishing that it contained nothing more than a meagre supply of feathers. The horsehair mattress had a stained ticking cover that looked undisturbed. Only bare springs were underneath.

She dropped the mattress back into place and went over to the dormer window. Instead of a bird's eye view of Dorset Square, she saw Albert's furious figure shaking his fist at the *Maison Rose*'s front door. Why had he been there? Was her theory that Count Meyerhoff was a German spy any more than the result of reading an ultra-persuasive work of fiction? When she had been outlining her theory to Jackman, it had sounded thin, a romantic girl's fantasy. She was not, though, normally the sort of person who got carried away by novels. And, whatever Mrs Bruton's opinion, Ursula felt there was something slippery about the count. Her father, at one time a top financier, had a saying about men he didn't trust: 'I wouldn't leave a kitten in his care.' Ursula had laughed when he used it but found that it became a rule of thumb for her when dealing with men.

A pigeon swooped down on to the narrow windowsill and sat cooing. Ursula hardly noticed. What, exactly, was Count Meyerhoff's motive for being involved in *Maison Rose*? Purely financial? So far the income didn't cover the expenses. Did he really believe the clinic and Madame's preparations were going to make a great deal of money? How much had outside patrons invested? Ursula had seen no capital sums deposited in the company bank account. And what was the relationship between the Count and Madame? Hilda Ferguson, the assistant who worked closely with the beautician, didn't like Count Meyerhoff, that had become clear during the session she and Ursula had spent filling the beauty preparation jars. Her loyalties and affiliation were to Madame, for whom she seemed to have a passionate regard.

Ursula sighed and gave the bedroom a final survey. Then, satisfied no possible hiding place had been left unexplored, she picked up the bottle of aspirin and went back to the other room.

The investigator was standing beside the fireplace and Albert's shrouded body was now lying a little way away from the fender.

'Look here,' Thomas said.

A short floorboard by the side of the grate had been raised to reveal a space large enough to hold a box of some sort, or perhaps an attaché case.

'Nothing there now,' he said. 'But I would lay a monkey that it has held someone's secrets.' He replaced the board. 'The doctor may well be here any time now, the place should not seem to have been searched.'

Ursula hurriedly replaced the items he had taken out of the cupboard. 'Do we give him the same story as Mrs Duggan?'

Thomas checked the replacement of the floorboard then gave a satisfied nod. Nothing suggested now that it might have been raised. 'Exactly the same. Albert Pond was a friend. He had invited us to see his new accommodation, after which we were to repair to some local hostelry for a drink and something to eat. We are very shocked by the discovery of our friend's body. And, yes, we can say that he had been worried about the state of his heart.'

'Let the doctor diagnose a suspicious reason for his death, rather than suggest it?'

Thomas nodded. 'That would be much the best. He will have to inform the authorities in any case.'

Ursula pushed her hands deep into the pockets of her new coat. 'I've just thought – if it can be proved that Albert has been poisoned by the same way as Joshua Peters, wouldn't that mean Alice could be released from prison?'

Thomas looked doubtful.

'Surely the same person must have committed both murders?'

'You and I might believe that, but whether Dandy Drummond will be as easy to convince is questionable.'

'"*Might* believe that"?' Ursula looked at him and her eyes narrowed. 'You believe she's guilty, don't you? And yet you accepted a commission to prove her innocent!' Ursula could not bring herself to consider for a moment that the girl was capable of killing her husband. Yet, nagging at the back of her mind was the bit of paper that the maid, Meg, had rescued from the fire. Why hadn't she shown it to Thomas, and why did she feel so guilty about that? Because it was difficult to read into the fragmented words Alice had written anything that wasn't incriminating, that was why.

'Look, I said I would investigate the circumstances of Joshua Peters' death. I approached the matter as I would if I'd still been in the force and officially on the case. I had no idea whether Alice was guilty or not; in fact, I still haven't.'

'Because you went away!' Ursula hadn't forgiven him for disappearing from London.

Thomas sighed. 'That was most unfortunate but there was little I could do. It was connected with a previous case and I couldn't refuse. I'd expected it wouldn't take more than a day or so. Once back I gave my full attention to the matter of Peters' death.'

Ursula found that she believed him and that, yes, she would leave a kitten in Thomas's care.

'The more I looked into things, the more it became apparent that Peters and his servant, that is Albert, were up to something.'

'You mean blackmail?' When Thomas didn't immediately respond she said, 'Surely that's the most obvious conclusion. You said that the business is in trouble. Rachel told me that Felix Trenchard, the man who is trying to sort out the legal situation, has said there's no money for the upkeep of the house and that it's heavily mortgaged. It will have to be sold. Joshua Peters must have been desperate for money.'

'So Alice Peters will have nothing?' This seemed to be news to Thomas.

'She apparently has a small income left to her by her mother; Rachel has the same. What I'm getting at is that Alice is not a rich widow.'

'She may have believed that she would be. And with or without money, she is now free to marry the man she is in love with, who may or may not be the father of the child she is carrying.'

'I believe her when she says her husband is the father and that she did not kill him.' Ursula spoke steadily but she felt so frustrated she could scream. She had not thought that Thomas Jackman could be so obtuse. 'And now, if Albert has been poisoned, surely it has to be by the same person who despatched Joshua Peters. Alice is in prison, ergo she could not have done this.'

'But how about her sister?' Thomas asked quietly.

Ursula stared at him.

'You yourself have told me that she believes in women turning militant to achieve their aims. Isn't she prepared to break the law to persuade the government to give women the vote?'

'Chucking a brick through someone's window is not the same as killing someone! And she brought you in to prove Alice innocent.'

Thomas shrugged. 'Maybe she thought she was. Maybe Albert showed her evidence that her sister did poison her husband. Evidence that she was desperate to get hold of. If she didn't have money to pay Albert off, killing him and seizing the evidence would solve the whole situation.'

Ursula's mind felt like a rat caught in a maze. He made it all sound horribly plausible. Yet could Rachel or Alice actually be a killer? Once again she thought about that bit of half-burned paper.

'But what about the count and *Maison Rose*?'

'Blackmailers usually attack more than one victim. Your theory that Count Meyerhoff is a spy for the Kaiser could have foundation. Or maybe there is something fishy about the beauty clinic. I am convinced Albert removed papers and maybe other items from his master's desk. There was that pot of *Maison Rose* cream I found there. Maybe he missed that or thought it wasn't important. If we could find what he did take, we'd know a great deal more.'

Ursula cast a look around the room. 'If they were here to find, we would have discovered them, surely.'

'I fear they will have vanished with his killer and have probably been destroyed.'

'Leaving us with nothing,' Ursula said helplessly.

'We can try and find a witness.'

'You mean someone might have seen Albert's visitor?'

There came a knock at the door and Mrs Duggan entered without waiting for permission.

'I've brought doctor. It's not our usual. He tells me he's sitting in. Well, here is Mr Pond, sir, as I told you. Ah, covered him up, have you? Quite right.'

'Thank you, Mrs Duggan. You have been very helpful. We'll say goodbye when everything has been taken care of.' Thomas took firm hold of her upper arm and guided her out on to the landing.

The doctor had entered in haste, then had seen the body beneath the coverlet. 'Doctor Barton,' he said. 'This is the heart victim, I take it?'

'It seemed the decent thing to do,' Ursula murmured. 'We were sure he had breathed his last.' She forced herself to remove the bedcover.

The physician was very tall, thin and probably in his early thirties. 'Hmm,' he said. 'Medical professionals, are you?' His tone managed to sound non-judgemental.

'As an ex-police inspector, I have some training in the assessment of comatose individuals,' Thomas said, closing the door behind Mrs Duggan. 'Thomas Jackman, and this is Miss Grandison,' he added.

'Ex-policeman?' said Doctor Barton, giving each of them a keen look. He placed his medical bag on the table, removed a well-worn three-quarter-length grey overcoat, slightly hitched his shabby trousers and knelt beside the body. Ursula could see a hole in the sole of one of his well-polished shoes.

She received an impression of easy competence as Dr Barton checked for a pulse, lifted up the eyelids, then inspected his bony chest.

He looked up. 'I take it this man was not lying on his back when you entered the room?'

'No,' said Thomas. 'He was on his front with his head on the fender.'

'Why did you move him?'

'To see if he was alive and in need of assistance.'

'And you found …?'

'That he was dead.'

'And you sent for me because …?'

'A death certificate will need signing.'

Dr Barton sighed as though disappointed in the answer but not surprised. 'Help me remove his jacket and shirt, will you – Jackman, was it?'

Thomas nodded.

As the two men stripped the upper garments off the body, Ursula saw that the livid stains she'd noted on Albert's chest were all over his skin. And there was a dark patch of what looked like bruising running down his front into the lower part of his body. She hoped that the trousers would not have to be removed as well.

Instead the doctor rose, looked down at the dead man and sighed again. 'The note that you sent – via Mr Duggan? – mentioned a friend suffering a heart attack, not that the man was dead. Yet this man died some time ago.' His tone suggested that he was only commenting on the situation; there was no sense of outrage.

'You can tell that?' asked Ursula curiously. Somehow the removal of Albert's brown jacket and striped waistcoat had robbed him of his identity. She could look at the body now without thinking about the man.

'How long has he been dead?' asked Thomas.

Another sigh from Dr Barton. 'Ex-inspector of police, I think you said. So you will understand why I find difficulty in accepting this story of a friend with heart trouble. Who, if Mrs Duggan is to be believed, had invited you over?' He glanced around the room. 'Sociable fellow, was he? Hadn't been here long, said Mrs Duggan, so I suppose you are about to tell me he wanted to show off his new home?' He waited politely for one of them to say something.

Ursula decided it was better she said nothing.

'You're a bright lad,' said Thomas with the air of handing over some sort of award. 'I dare say you may have been called in by some of my former colleagues from time to time.'

The doctor nodded. 'I've had dealings with several officers. At the moment I have no practice of my own, I act as a locum for general practitioners who go on holiday or have other reason for not being able to fulfil their duties to their patients. Several of these practices are in areas less salubrious than Marylebone. Areas where it is difficult to make a living,' he added, giving the bare walls of Albert's room another cursory glance.

'Your account for today's visit will be settled, you have my word on that,' Thomas said.

Dr Barton gave a slight nod in acknowledgement. 'It is not, perhaps, my business why you are here. And I suggest that you do not need me to tell you that this man,' he gave a slight wave of his hand towards Albert's body, 'did not die of a heart attack.'

He seemed very sure of himself, this Dr Barton, thought Ursula. But if he was having to deal with a vast variety of patients he had little opportunity to get to know, perhaps he had to be.

Thomas went over to Albert's cupboard. 'It's good to meet a doc who knows his way around. We'll tell you the full story but, first, since Mr Pond will not be needing this quite respectable bottle of cognac, can I offer you a glass?'

The doctor consulted a watch then returned it to his waistcoat pocket. 'I seem to have time in hand. Why not?' He received a charged glass. Thomas sent an enquiring glance at Ursula.

She gave him a smile and shook her head then sat down on one of the upright chairs.

'Please,' said Thomas, 'can you start by giving me some idea of when Albert Pond died and what you think was the cause of death.'

Dr Barton carefully sniffed his glass then drank some of the brandy thoughtfully, looking at Thomas as though he needed to assess how far he could trust him. Then, still holding his brandy, he went and stood over the body, produced a thermometer, stuck it in one of Albert's ears, then manipulated his arms and finally checked the thermometer reading. 'First, time of death. Probably yesterday afternoon. I would say that rigor mortis has only just passed. The way the blood has settled down the front of his body,' he waved towards the dark bruising Ursula had already noticed. 'That tells me he fell face forward, not on his back, and was undisturbed until you moved him.' He crouched down beside the body and used his brandy glass to indicate the livid spots. 'Those look to me like cyanide poisoning. I shall have to report my conclusions to the authorities. I am unable to sign a death certificate as an autopsy will be required to ascertain cause of death. However, I shall be very surprised if tests prove anything other than death by cyanide.' He rose, brushed off the knees of his trousers, finished his brandy and looked at both of them. 'Do you have any idea who it could have been administered by?'

Thomas shook his head. 'I'm afraid not.' He gave a small cough. 'Would you have any idea how it was administered?'

'I assume it was ingested; that is the usual method with poisoners.'

'We haven't found any food, nor medicines, apart from some aspirin tablets,' said Ursula, indicating the bottle she'd brought through from the bedroom and placed on the windowsill. 'Could the poison have been in something he ate outside this place?'

Dr Barton shook his head. 'A lethal dose of cyanide will take effect within minutes. If he was poisoned elsewhere, he would not have been able to climb the stairs or let himself in before collapsing.'

'So the poisoner must have taken any evidence away with himself,' murmured Thomas.

'Himself or herself – don't they say poison is the weapon of the female of the species?' said Dr Barton.

'Not necessarily,' said Thomas thoughtfully. 'I have known cases where it has been used by men.'

'So,' Dr Barton seated himself in the armchair and stretched out his long legs. 'Perhaps you will now be good enough to fill me in on why you are both here in what do not seem to be the sort of surroundings you would normally be found. Well, Mr Jackman perhaps, but Miss Grandison appears used to better things.'

'You'd be surprised,' Ursula said with a chuckle.

Dr Barton raised an eyebrow but waited for one of them to provide the promised explanation for their presence.

Thomas recharged both the doctor's and his glasses, set the bottle back on the cabinet, then took the free chair. 'I'm now a private investigator and I was commissioned to look into the death of one Joshua Peters. He died of cyanide poisoning in a box of cherry liqueur chocolates that had been sent him through the post. This man,' he waved towards Albert's body, 'was his servant.' In even tones Thomas outlined the bare details of what had been discovered so far. He left out any mention of Millie but explained that Alice Peters was in prison charged with the murder of her husband.

'So you think,' said Dr Barton when he had finished, 'that both master and servant have been murdered by someone they had been blackmailing; is that about the size of it?'

Thomas nodded.

'Well, I can see why you are here, Mr Jackman. However, you haven't explained the presence of Miss Grandison.'

Without looking at him, Ursula knew that Thomas was at a loss.

'I'm Mr Jackman's assistant,' she said.

Chapter Twenty-Seven

'Assistant, eh?' Dr Barton's left eyebrow rose. 'I didn't realise investigation could be women's work.'

'Women have valuable skills,' said Thomas negligently. 'As a case we worked on together six months ago proved. Miss Grandison is an excellent assistant.'

'Well,' the doctor rose. 'Mr Pond may not need my services but others do. I shall go directly to the police station to report a suspicious death and arrange for the coroner to be informed.'

Thomas handed him a card. 'Send me an account and I will see that you are paid.' He paused for a moment then added, 'I would appreciate knowing the findings of the autopsy. Whether cyanide poisoning was confirmed.'

'It will be.' The doctor picked up his case and held out his hand to Ursula, who rose and took it. 'Goodbye, Miss Grandison. I wish you and Mr Jackman luck with your investigation.' He felt in his breast pocket and brought out a card of his own and offered it to Thomas. 'Perhaps you will let me know the result?'

'Of course.'

'No need to see me out.' The doctor closed the door behind him.

Ursula remained standing and looked at Thomas. 'I couldn't think of any other reason for my being here.'

He grinned. 'Well, as I said, we worked together before – I don't see why we can't again, do you?'

She felt relief.

'After our good doctor has informed the police, my old friend Inspector Drummond will almost certainly be round here. If we are to stay ahead of things, the other inhabitants of this apartment house need to be questioned now.'

A surge of excitement filled Ursula. 'And you want me to help?'

'That way we will take half the time. These rooms seem to be the only ones on this floor. I'll take the next floor down and you the one below that.'

'What shall we say?'

'Let us stick to the story we gave Mrs Duggan: we came to visit our friend, Albert Pond, and it appears he has been poisoned.' He paused for a moment. 'We could also say that there are important papers missing. Papers that were the reason for our visit.'

'And, quite naturally, we want to know if Albert had someone call on him yesterday?'

'Exactly.' He looked at her, 'Not nervous, are you? I remember you handling matters in Somerset extremely well.'

Ursula remembered how unthinkingly she had taken up the case of the nurserymaid whose body she had discovered, and how deeply she had become embroiled in the investigation that had gradually gathered pace; the terrible shocks and the heartache that had followed. At least this case would not involve her so deeply. And just maybe questioning some neighbours might give Thomas Jackman a lead that would enable him to clear Alice of the murder charge.

'Let's to it,' she said, putting on her gloves. Jackman gave a last look around the room as he held open the door for her, then closed it behind them. Their steps echoed on the uncarpeted stairs.

On the next landing Thomas gave Ursula a nod and knocked at the door that bore the number 6. She continued down to the floor below, suddenly conscious that up these same stairs had come a murderer. Or had there been more than one? Had Albert recognised his killer? If they were blackmail victims, though, surely he would have not have let them in, even if they had come to make a payment? But would he have been foolish enough to let someone he was blackmailing know where to find him?

Ursula reached the first floor landing and flat No. 4. The door had recently been painted, the brass figure in its centre was brightly polished, as was a knocker, and a neat label announced that it was the residence of Mrs Digby Walters. Ursula took a deep breath, called upon her creative powers, took a handkerchief from her bag and knocked on the door. Nothing happened; she banged the knocker again, a little harder this time.

After a moment the door was opened by a small woman dressed in a slightly faded dress of some printed material and holding an item of embroidery; delicate sprays of flowers decorated a piece of organza. 'Yes?' said the woman. 'Do I know you?' Bright eyes behind pince-nez looked curiously at Ursula.

'I'm afraid not, Mrs Walters.' Ursula clutched her handkerchief. 'I have just come from Mr Pond's apartment on the top floor,' she dabbed at her eyes.

'What did you say?' Mrs Walters leaned forward a little. 'Can you speak up?'

Ursula repeated what she had said in a louder voice.

'Mr Pond, did I catch the name correctly? Didn't he move in a few weeks ago? I haven't met him but I know Mrs Duggan cleans for him, and is grateful for the business.'

Ursula nodded.

'And what does Mr Pond have to do with me?' Mrs Walters asked brightly.

'It's terrible!' Another dab with the handkerchief. 'We came to visit him this morning and … oh, Mrs Walters, he has passed away.'

'Oh, my dear, I am so sorry. How very upsetting for you and your husband.'

Ursula did not correct her.

'But I fail to see how that sad occurrence has anything to do with me. Did he have a heart attack?' Mrs Walters lowered her voice as though she might be in church.

Ursula gave a little gulp. 'I fear that our friend's demise was not natural. It would appear that, oh, it is too dreadful but the doctor we called in says he has been poisoned!'

The woman fell back a step. 'Poisoned!' Then leaned forward and brought her voice back to a hush, 'Arsenic?'

'The doctor thinks cyanide. The thing of it is, Mrs Walters, certain papers that we were to sign and take away have disappeared. We wondered, do you know if Albert, Mr Pond, had a visitor yesterday? Did you hear him take somebody upstairs?'

'Oh, no, dear. I never know what transpires in this building. I am too busy,' she held up the embroidery. 'It was something of a hobby until my dear husband passed on. Now I am not ashamed to use my skills to increase my pensioner's pittance. People commission me; I am known for the delicacy of my work.' She offered the piece of organza for Ursula to admire. 'This will be a nightdress case. And being a little hard of hearing, elephants could pass by my door and I'd not know.' She blinked, her expression troubled. 'But I am truly sorry to hear of such a dreadful event taking place here.' She glanced around nervously.

Ursula sighed deeply. 'I am sorry to have troubled you, Mrs Walters. But I am sure you have no need to worry; I fear Mr Pond must have suffered from a personal vendetta.'

'Vendetta!' Mrs Walters looked even more disturbed.

'As I said, it would have been personal. Please do not allow yourself to be worried for your safety; I am sure no one else in this building is at risk.' Ursula glanced behind her at the door across the landing. 'I wonder, could you tell me who lives opposite you? They may have been aware of a visitor to Mr Pond.'

'Ah, that is Mr Barnes. Such a nice man, if a trifle eccentric. I hope he may be able to enlighten you; his eyesight is weak but he has lived here forever and can tell you details of every occupant since the year dot. Well, if I can't help you any more, dear, I must return to my work. I can only do it in the daylight, you see.'

Ursula thanked the woman and turned to flat No. 3.

While she was waiting for Mr Barnes to answer her knock, Thomas came down from the upper floor. 'Any luck?' he murmured as he passed her.

She shook her head and he continued to the ground floor as the door of No. 3 was opened, first a crack and then a little further and someone, surely it had to be Mr Barnes, peered at Ursula. He was a gaunt figure of medium height wearing an ancient suit that hung as a sad testament to weight loss, and he sported a pair of spectacles with lenses that resembled nothing so much as bottle ends. Just as Ursula was about to break into the same approach as she had used for Mrs Walters, the cadaverous face broke into an excited smile. 'Why, it's the angel come down.' His voice quavered with emotion.

What was it Mrs Walters had said? That her neighbour had bad eyesight and was a little eccentric?

Mr Barnes reached for her hand. 'And you're visiting me today! Come in, come in!' He opened the door wide and, with surprising strength, pulled Ursula into his flat, closing the door behind her. 'There, now I've got you. Come, sit you down.' Now he pulled her into a living area furnished with two ancient arm-chairs sporting anti-macassars on the backs. A fire burned in the grate and a small kettle sat on an iron hob that jutted over the coals. Beside one of the chairs was a low, round table. On it stood a cage and inside the cage was a mouse. Ursula gave a little gasp of surprise.

'Seen him, have you?' said Mr Barnes happily. 'My little friend, Mousie?' He let go of her hand, felt for the latch of the cage door, opened it and took out his pet. It sat on his hand, upright, whisk-ers twitching, and waved two tiny paws. 'Want a little cheese, do you, Mousie?' On the table was a plate with small, roughly cut bits of a hard cheese. 'Would you like to give him a piece?'

Feeding a tame mouse was a new experience for Ursula. She picked up a fragment and held it out. Tiny dark eyes inspected the offering, then the slim snout delicately took it in its sharp little teeth. Mr Barnes gently put his pet back in its cage. It put the cheese down, inspected it, then started to eat in dainty, darting movements.

'Mr Barnes ...' she started.

'Sit, sit,' he urged her.

Since he clearly wasn't going to pay any attention to what she was saying unless she did, Ursula settled herself on the edge of one of the chairs. With a little sigh of satisfaction, he sat in the other and, speaking slowly and clearly, she launched into her story.

'Pond, Albert Pond,' Mr Barnes said in his high-pitched, squeaky voice. 'Up in the top flat, you say? Let me see, Mrs Duggan told me about him, how he'd taken it over from that actor chappie, been there for years; what was he called now? Jenkins, yes, that was it, Henry Jenkins. Never saw him act. Think he only ever had small parts. Bit of a ne'er do well, I'm afraid, with ideas above his station. Always behind with his rent; our good Mrs Duggan complained a lot about him. Went to live with his sister in Folkestone a couple of months ago. Now, what was it you asked me?'

'Did you, Mr Barnes, see Albert Pond with any visitor yester-day? Or did you hear or see anyone passing up the stairs who didn't live here?'

He looked sad. 'I never see anyone.' Then his expression brightened. 'Except my angel.'

'Angel?'

'You're the angel,' He leaned forward and took both her hands, peering into her face. 'Saw you.'

Ursula remembered how she'd heard a door close as she followed Thomas and Mrs Duggan up the stairs to Albert's apartment. Had Mr Barnes been peering out after them?

'I've been waiting for my angel to come for so many years.' His face wrinkled into sadness. 'Why has it been so long?'

'My name is Ursula Grandison,' she said gently, rising. 'I am afraid we have never met before today.'

'But yesterday you were on the stairs: you are my angel on the stairs.'

Ursula felt a flutter of excitement, but how was she to trust anything Mr Barnes said? 'I wasn't here yesterday.'

His face fell, then brightened again, 'Maybe it was the day before; how should I know, every day is like every other.'

'You couldn't have seen me, Mr Barnes. But did you perhaps see someone who looked like me? Going up the stairs? When was it? In the morning or the afternoon?'

He shook his head. 'I saw my angel. I see my angel. Listen, the kettle is boiling.' Indeed it was singing a thin whistle. 'We shall have some tea. You shall share my pot of tea.' He felt along the top of a sideboard and ladled tea from a tin caddy into a pewter teapot.

'I am afraid my husband is waiting for me,' Ursula said firmly. She felt sorry for him, he was obviously very lonely. 'I shall try and visit you and Mr Mousie another day but now I must say goodbye.'

Chapter Twenty-Eight

Thomas waited for Ursula at the foot of the stairs, mulling over the results of his questioning of the inhabitants of the Dorset Square house.

'Any luck?' she asked as she reached the last step. He could not gauge from her expression whether she had had any more success than he had.

He shook his head, put on his bowler hat, tilting it slightly, opened the front door and offered her his arm down the steps and on to the pavement. He looked up at the sky. Dark clouds had invaded the blue and rain was in the air.

'Do you have anything to report?'

'I'm not sure,' Ursula said slowly.

'Well, that's better than a flat "no". I don't know about you but I'm hungry. Let's say goodbye to Mrs Duggan and then find somewhere we can have a bite to eat and talk over what we've learned. After all we've gone through in the last few hours, I think we deserve some refreshment.'

The caretaker had not yet recovered from the shock of finding Albert and it took a little time to extract themselves from her desire to relive the awful moment, hear exactly what the doctor had said and to lament the dreadful prospect of a visit from the police.

'What it will do to our reputation, I do not know. And such a lovely man as Mr Pond was, such an improvement on Mr Jenkins, who never wanted to avail himself of my services. Lord, how I had to scrub that place after he left!'

'Tell me, Mrs Duggan,' said Ursula, just as it seemed they could take their leave. 'What do you think of Mr Barnes?'

She bridled. 'What should I think of someone who keeps a nasty little mouse in a cage? Though what he thinks it is might be anything; seeing as how he can't hardly see to tie his shoelaces.'

'Thank you, Mrs Duggan,' said Thomas hastily. 'You have been most helpful this morning. Come, Miss Grandison, we must not take up more of Mrs Duggan's time.'

'No, indeed,' said Ursula. She gave the caretaker a swift smile and started up the basement steps to the pavement.

'I know a nice little eatery in Marylebone Lane,' he said, guiding her in the right direction. 'It looks as though it is going to rain. If we get a move on, we might get there before the deluge, then we can talk comfortably.'

★ ★ ★

It was a close-run thing but Thomas found the *Plate of Beef* just as the first drops of rain started. He pushed open the door and they entered.

A small, smiling man with several chins and a long white apron immediately approached. 'Mr Jackman, long time no see!'

'Billy, good to be here again. I'm glad business has brought me in this direction. Let me introduce Miss Grandison, she is assisting me in some enquiries.'

'I'm honoured, Madam. May I take your coat? I've a nice little table at the back where you won't be troubled.'

'What a wonderful place,' Ursula said, looking around the small but lively eatery. It was halfway through the afternoon but there were a number of customers attacking the hearty food the *Plate of Beef* served up. 'I can imagine Mr Dickens using it in one of his great books.'

Billy looked delighted. 'My dear old dad started this place and he said that the great Charles Dickens did indeed eat here.' Billy led the way to the back and a small table for two. He held out a chair for Ursula and magicked a white tablecloth over the bare pine. 'There's a couple of servings of steak and kidney pudding left, if that would please you?'

'Wonderful! Ursula, are you acquainted with one of England's great culinary delights?'

'No, but I would like to be.' She smiled up at the proprietor.

'And a couple of pints of your best ale,' said Thomas. He watched Ursula take in her surroundings. 'It's very plain here, but the food is excellent and Billy and I go back a long way. I helped him and his dad over a minor difficulty with beer tax while I was a constable on the beat.'

'I love it!' Ursula's eyes sparkled and Thomas realised he had forgotten how large they were and such a clear grey. They turned her from a pleasant looking but far from beautiful woman into something out of the ordinary. 'It's just what I imagined ye olde England would be like. Look at those leaded windows, the panes are the old type of glass. And I would imagine that the customers are all locals. Manet should paint them.'

Thomas looked at the customers, mainly men, who sat finishing their meals. 'I don't know who Manet is, does he specialise in capturing ordinary people instead of the rich and powerful?'

'I saw several of his paintings in Paris, they were usually of the French bourgeoisie, the middle classes. He has a way of getting under the skin of the people he paints and presenting them without pretension. Now,' Ursula took off her gloves and placed them at the side of the table. 'Did you learn anything from the residents you spoke to?'

Before he could start, two tankards of ale arrived. Thomas watched Ursula try hers and he smiled as she said, 'This is wonderful and just what I needed; it's been an extraordinary morning.'

'Hasn't it!' Thomas drank deeply and began to feel himself relaxing. He had endured harder mornings of work but few that had offered such a variety of experiences. That minx Millie and the circus; the walk across to Marylebone with Ursula relating her wild theory of the Count Meyerhoff as spy – not that it was without the bounds of possibility but, no evidence! – and then finding that blighter Albert dead – and of cyanide poisoning! For Thomas that fact both simplified and complicated the Joshua Peters case. Simplified it because if the same killer had disposed of both man and servant, then the possibility of mistakes on his part had multiplied and made identification more likely. Complicated because all the indications pointed to blackmail as the motive for the murders. But for blackmail to be effective required there to be proof behind a threat of exposure and proof in this case was missing. Again, no evidence, just theory. Yet everything pointed to blackmail. Apart, that is, from Alice Peters wishing to dispose of an inconvenient husband.

'Not much luck with those neighbours I managed to speak to,' he said, putting down a half-empty tankard with a sigh of satisfaction. 'I had high hopes of numbers five and six. They are nearest to the attic apartment and therefore the most likely to have noticed anyone visiting there. However, there was no answer to number five. Number six is the home of Miss Hart, a woman of indeterminate years who seemed on the point of collapse when I told her what had happened to Pond. I had to assist her to a chair and find a glass of water.'

'Oh dear, had she become friends with him?'

'After apologising for being the bearer of bad news, I managed to get out of her that she had had a couple of brief conversations with Pond and thought him,' Thomas brought out his notebook and flipped to the page he wanted. 'Thought him, "Someone who needed the love of a good woman".'

'And believed that she could be that good woman?'

'I identified her as the sort who reads sentimental stories in women's magazines and lives in a world of her own imaginings.'

'Daniel Rokeby writes stories for magazines,' said Ursula, smiling. 'Not that I think that is anything to do with the matter we're discussing. And you think Miss Hart – was that the name? – that Miss Hart could have built a fantasy of bringing love into the life of Albert Pond on the basis of a couple of brief conversations with him? Well, I have known women like that. In fact there is at least one living at Mrs Maples'. But was Miss Hart aware of a visitor to the attic flat yesterday?'

'She said she wasn't there. She is employed as a clerk in an insurance company.' Thomas referred to his notebook again. 'Leaves every day except Sunday at half past eight and gets back at around six; half past one on Saturday. She'd only just returned when I knocked.'

Ursula looked thoughtfully at her tankard of ale. 'All these lonely women. There are several where I am living. They work at boring jobs for little pay. When I suggested we might visit a theatre together or go out for a meal, at a place like this, for instance,' she glanced at the other tables. 'Well, they were shocked and said that without a male escort it just would not be possible. Not for a single woman.'

She paused for a moment. 'Would having the vote make them more free? More able to take advantage of life? Or is it a mind-set? I don't think Rachel Fentiman, for instance, feels like that. With or without the vote, she makes the most of life. However, let's return to Dorset Square. How about the ground floor?'

'Not much luck there, either. At number two, I spoke to a young wife who told me, very proudly, that her husband worked in the City of London but would be home shortly, did I want to wait? Asked about possible visitors the previous day, she explained that she had spent it visiting her mother in Putney.'

'A dutiful daughter and loving wife, I expect she is already doing charitable works of some sort or another while waiting to become a mother.'

Ursula's arms were folded in front of her on the table, her attention concentrated on his report. Thomas found himself grateful for her interest and intelligent responses. He realised again how much he missed working with his fellow officers on the police force.

'So, how about number two?' she asked.

Thomas glanced again at his notebook. 'A retired couple, Mr and Mrs Blanchard. Well dressed, pleased with life and very jolly – until they heard my news. He said it was "bally awful" and that he didn't know what the neighbourhood was coming to. She said she hadn't liked Mr Pond at all. Whereupon Mr Blanchard turned on her, saying she'd never spoken to the feller beyond a "good morning" and he thought Pond had been "all right". Then she told him he'd ever had any ability to judge his fellow men.

'When I could get a word in, I asked about visitors the previ-ous day. Mrs Blanchard had been out for tea with a group of women friends; Mr Blanchard called them, "the harridans from hell". At that she said I should take no notice of him, he was only upset at being left on his own. And he told me he'd spent the afternoon reading and snoozing., then added that he may have heard Mrs Duggan go upstairs at one stage but that was all. When I asked how he knew it was the caretaker, he said it sounded like her footstep. Mrs Blanchard claimed he wouldn't know the dif-ference between a giant and a fairy going upstairs. I couldn't get any estimation of what time he heard those footsteps.' Thomas closed his notebook with a little sigh. 'What about you?'

At that moment their steak and kidney puddings arrived. 'Better sample this first,' Thomas said, setting to with enthusiasm.

'It's wonderful!' Ursula exclaimed after a couple of mouthfuls. 'Such a flavour, and the suet crust is so light. We get very reasonable food at Mrs Maples' but this is in a different league.'

Thomas felt a sense of triumph, as much as if he had cooked the food himself. He let her eat half of her serving then asked again if she'd heard anything useful.

She frowned a little then told him of a deaf widow and what sounded like a very odd old man.

'What did you say? He saw an angel?'

Ursula chuckled. 'Oh, dear, I don't think I've made much sense. I'll try again. Mr Barnes is very old, very eccentric and almost blind. He seems to have very little idea of time and I don't think he knows one day from another. When he opened the door to me, he looked utterly delighted and called me his angel. Then he claimed to have seen his angel going upstairs the prevous day, or it could have been the day before.' She fiddled with her cutlery for a moment, then said, 'He wanted me to have a cup of tea with him, I think he is very lonely.' She glanced across at Thomas. 'I'm afraid I told him my husband was waiting; I do apologise for taking your name in vain like that.'

To Thomas's delight, he saw a little colour rise in her cheeks, almost a blush.

'I am honoured,' he said gravely.

'I had to tell you in case we needed to go back and talk to him again.'

Thomas's attention sharpened. 'You think he might really have seen a female going upstairs?'

Ursula carefully finished the last scrap of steak and kidney pudding and put her knife and fork neatly together. 'So many Americans leave their cutlery all adrift on their plates, I think it is very sloppy. And if the food isn't quite finished, the waiting staff do not know whether to take the plate or not. That was truly delicious.' She applied her napkin to her lips, then looked at Thomas. 'Do I believe he saw someone going upstairs? I honestly do not know. If he did, maybe it was Mrs Duggan.'

Thomas smiled at the idea of the caretaker as angel. 'But Mr Barnes would have seen her time after time; no possibility he could mistake her for anyone else, with or without wings.'

He thought a little. 'Suppose, just for a moment, that Barnes did see an unknown woman climbing the stairs.'

'Who went to the attic, called on Albert and somehow fed him cyanide?'

He nodded. 'And suppose it was the same person, or someone in league with them, who sent Peters a box of poisoned liqueur chocolates?'

'It couldn't have been Alice,' said Ursula quickly. 'She's in prison.'

'But her sister isn't. I know you don't think either girl could be involved,' he said quickly as he saw Ursula about to protest. 'But let's just think of candidates, ignoring any attachment we might have to them.'

'You think I'm as sentimental as Miss Hart!' Ursula said with a quick laugh but Thomas recognised that she wasn't really amused.

'Ursula Grandison, I would never, never call, or even think, you sentimental! But you will have to admit that you think of those sisters as friends and we never like to think of those we have given our friendship to as capable of any crime, let alone murder. But if you are an investigator, you have to look at the evidence and nothing but the evidence.'

She slowly nodded her head. 'I understand what you are saying. OK, then,' she suddenly sounded very American. 'So let's look at all the women who might, just possibly, have had cause to wish Albert Pond removed from life.'

'Ah here comes Billy to see if we want anything else. They have excellent apple pie here.'

'Everything all right, folks?' said Billy.

'I'd love a cup of coffee,' said Ursula quickly.

After Billy had taken an order for two coffees, Thomas said, 'So, let's see.'

'You've already mentioned Rachel, but how about Millie?' Thomas recognised a hint of challenge in Ursula's voice.

'Ah, you want me to tell you I don't believe she could have done it. I shall certainly consider the possibility that Millie fed Joshua Peters and Albert Pond cyanide. Let's look at the three important questions that have to be asked in connection with any suspect for a crime: motive, means and opportunity.'

'Millie certainly had motive: revenge for the way Joshua Peters had treated her. She also had opportunity. Means? How easy is it to get hold of cyanide?'

'Quite easy. Potassium cyanide and sodium cyanide have a host of uses, pesticides being one. Any good chemist could provide you with the means to kill your rats; you'd have to sign the poison register but the name you give need not be your own, or the address anywhere near where you live – and, of course, you would approach a chemist some distance from your residence.'

Ursula looked fascinated and appalled at the same time. 'So, we have to include Millie in our list of suspects,' she said. 'Do you think Albert could have been blackmailing her, that he had some evidence she had sent those poisoned chocolates?'

Thomas opened his notebook, took out a pencil and wrote down the name of Rachel Fentiman. 'It is certainly possible. Though if she did poison him, why give us his address?'

'She said she didn't know the number,' Ursula reminded him. 'She could have thought giving you Dorset Square was being helpful and removing suspicion from her and that we wouldn't be able to locate the right building.'

Thomas wrote Millie's name down under Rachel's then tapped the notebook with his pencil. 'Any other female candidates?' He suddenly remembered his search through Joshua Peters' desk drawer. 'What about your Madame Rose? Maybe it wasn't your count who was the target, maybe it was his business partner. Peters had a jar of *Maison Rose* beauty cream in his desk drawer. Could he have discovered that there was something injurious in the creams they were peddling?'

'Good heavens! What an idea!' Ursula ran a hand over her face. 'I've been rubbing *Maison Rose* preparations into my skin every day. And, as I told you, I truly believe they have done some good.'

Thomas couldn't see that there was any difference in the way she looked now from before. However, 'Do they import ingredients for the beauty preparations?'

Ursula nodded. 'An order was placed only the other day.'

'Hmm. Something to be looked into. Are the accounts being fiddled? Or could they be making use of details extracted from their clients. Didn't you tell me a great many society ladies patronise the clinic?'

Ursula nodded. 'I suppose that's possible, but I think it more likely the count was the blackmail target. After all, if he is ruined, so is she.'

'So she might have decided to protect them both?'

'I suppose it's possible. She's certainly a powerful personality,' Ursula said thoughtfully. 'And her training must have given her a scientific background, so she probably knows about cyanide.'

'Do you know if she had the opportunity? Sending chocolates through the post is easy enough to do; visiting Albert more difficult.'

'It would be quite easy for me to find out what she was doing yesterday.'

'Good.' Thomas added Madame Rose's name to his little list. 'That's three possibilities.'

'But mightn't it be someone we know nothing about?'

Thomas threw his little pencil on the table in a moment of frustration. 'Somewhere there has to be a stash of evidence the two of them had gathered for their blackmail attempts. Peters's firm was going bust; no doubt because he had cheated so many of his customers. He needed another source of income. Albert was the perfect partner. Resourceful, able to carry out a wide range of duties, as criminally minded as his master. He would have known exactly where the evidence was kept and removed it as soon as he could after Peters died. And, yes, there could well be female targets we know nothing about who took matters into their own hands.'

Billy brought a pot of coffee and placed it on the table together with cups, milk and sugar.

'Madam would like to pour?'

'Certainly,' said Ursula, picking up the pot.

'I shall try and talk to Drummond and see where he's going with Pond's death. Mrs Duggan will have told him we were visiting Pond, he won't waste much time getting in touch. But I don't have any confidence he will be looking at the wider picture.'

'At least he knows it can't have been Alice.' Ursula handed Thomas a cup of coffee.

He helped himself to three spoonfuls of sugar and stirred the liquid thoughtfully. 'No, even he can't see her escaping from Holloway, doing the deed, and then returning to prison without being missed. But he will undoubtedly consider the sister.' He looked at Ursula. 'Next step is to see what Miss Rachel was up to yesterday. Are you up to taking that on?'

'With you or on my own?'

'I think you'll get more out of her if I'm not there. I'll see if I can have another word with the Peters' cook. I want to see if Peters left an address book.'

'So, I get another chance at being an investigator,' said Ursula.

'Do you mind?'

'I always like a challenge. However, I shall find it difficult to suspect Rachel.'

'Just find out where she was yesterday,' said Thomas.

'And, of course,' said Ursula, 'after all our consideration of the women who could be administering cyanide, is there any reason why it should not, after all, have been a man? Didn't you admit to Doctor Barnes that you have known male poisoners?'

Thomas added two spoons of sugar to his cup of coffee.

'We mustn't lose sight of that possibility,' he said, stirring slowly. 'There is also the faintest of chances that Peters put evidence in a safe at Montagu Place. I shall go there and ask Mrs Firestone if she can open it. If I tell her about Pond's death, she could be co-operative. There could even be a notebook containing names and addresses. With both of them dead, paper evidence is our only remaining chance to find out who their victims were.'

Chapter Twenty-Nine

'Do you have the time?' Ursula asked.

Jackman retrieved a hunter watch from his waistcoat pocket. 'Any particular reason you want to know?' he said, clicking its gold cover.

'All you English seem to stop around four o'clock for, what do Mrs Crumble and Meg call it? A cuppa? That would be the best time for a chat.'

'You should be able to time it just right.'

Jackman called for the bill and Ursula's coat.

Outside they could see an omnibus coming. 'That'll take you to Victoria station,' he said.

Ursula broke into a run. There were other passengers waiting and she was able to jump on to the back platform just as the vehicle started to move. Jackman stuffed money into her pocket. 'For expenses', he called. 'Remember, you're my assistant now!'

Sitting down, she found the silver coins added up to ten shillings. It seemed a ridiculously large sum. She decided she would, like the investigator, keep meticulous note of any sums she spent in pursuit of this investigation.

Settled on the vehicle next to a thin lady who snuffled and muttered to herself, Ursula tried to work out how she was going to approach her task. It seemed inevitable that the rescue of Millie would have to be at least touched upon. How else was she to account for her and Thomas knowing where Albert Pond was living? But she would not tell Rachel where the girl was. Thomas had been adamant about that.

'The fewer people know where she is, the less possibility that Sir Hector Rutland will find out,' he'd said.

'Do you really think he would kidnap her or injure her in some way?'

'He gives the impression of being a powerful man and powerful men do not like being crossed. If he finds out where Millie is, he will take some action. It could mean unfortunate consequences for the circus and the menagerie.'

Ursula could believe him. She could not forget the angry eyes of Millie's seducer; the contemptuous way he had spoken. This was a man of status and easy authority, one used to having his own way. She had grown up with men like that, knew how they behaved: expecting and getting their own way and instituting an easy vengeance when they didn't. A cold shudder ran through her.

'I'm getting out here,' the woman next to her suddenly said and rose from the bench.

The omnibus proceeded in stops and starts, making its way towards the Thames. The random nature of so many of the areas of London fascinated Ursula. New York, after a similar start at the tip of Manhattan Island, was now growing in a workmanlike grid pattern, avenues running north to south, streets east to west, from the sea to the Hudson River, apart from the odd maverick like Broadway. Nothing so planned and regular about London. There were squares, crescents and streets of every size, connected one to another by roads that seemed to dart in any direction. Even the main highways that contained shops and offices didn't seem to conform to any particular pattern.

Ursula forced her mind back to the matter in hand: she had taken on the task of finding out what Rachel's movements had been the previous day. She wondered how the girl would react to hearing about Albert Pond's death. She would have known him well; with her sister in prison, it was important she was put in possession of all the facts surrounding his demise as soon as possible.

Martha opened the door, her expression mulish. It lightened a trifle when she saw Ursula. 'Oh, it's you,' she said. 'You'd better come in.' Ursula wondered what had upset her.

In front of a cosy fire in her large and untidy living room, Rachel was sitting next to a young man on the sofa, and appeared to be deep in conversation. 'You know I'd do anything for you,' he was saying with an odd emphasis as Martha announced Ursula.

'Miss Grandison,' she said loudly.

Rachel turned abruptly, as if to deny she was at home, then rose and smiled in what seemed genuine welcome.

'Ursula, how nice to see you! Come in. Do you remember John Pitney? This is Ursula Grandison, John.' The young man was already on his feet. 'Perhaps you remember me persuading you to drive Alice and her to their lodgings a little time ago? Martha, do you think you could bring us some fresh tea? And please take Miss Grandison's coat.'

Martha disappeared with it, muttering something that sounded like, 'infernal machine'. Ursula wondered if tea would be forthcoming and, if so, how long it would take. What had upset her? Was it the presence of the young man?

She had no trouble recognising Rachel's friend. 'Of course I remember you, Lord John,' she said, offering him her hand. 'I very much admired your automobile and the way you were so kind to Alice and myself that day.'

He shook her hand warmly, smiling with a straightforward but somewhat awkward charm that distinguished him from many of the well-born young men Ursula had met since arriving in England; unlike them, he didn't seem to believe that acceptance was his right.

'Come and sit down,' said Rachel

Ursula took a chair; the young man hovered for a moment.

'Perhaps,' he said, 'it is time I left.'

'No, John,' Rachel said quickly. Then, more smoothly, 'You haven't anything you must get back to, have you?'

'Not at all.' He sounded relieved.

Rachel waved at a chair. The two of them settled again on the sofa, Rachel slipping her hand down and finding John's.

'Now, Ursula, what brings you here? Not that I am anything but delighted to see you.'

'I'm sorry to turn up without warning but there's something I think you need to know.'

Instantly, the girl released John's hand. 'Is it something to do with Alice?'

'In a way.' Ursula gave a quick account of how she and Thomas found the body of the valet.

'Pond? Dead?' said Rachel, incredulous. 'How?' Then, almost immediately, 'Are you saying he died the same way as Joshua did?'

'Mr Jackman isn't sure, but the doctor who came to certify the body said that he appears to have been poisoned by cyanide,' Ursula said carefully.

John Pitney closed his eyes for a brief moment. 'Not a pleasant death.'

Ursula looked at him. 'You are acquainted with cyanide poisoning?'

'I wouldn't say acquainted,' he said carefully.

'But you know how the poison behaves?' Ursula pressed politely.

He shifted a little uncomfortably on the sofa. 'A friend of mine is a doctor. He told me a little of the effect of various poisons one day.' He rose and prowled round the room.

Rachel broke in abruptly. 'It sounds dreadful. Where did you say Pond was living?'

'It's an apartment house not far from Marylebone station. I understand it is quite near to Montagu Place.'

'I suppose Mr Jackman discovered the address. You say you found him this morning; do you know when he died?'

Ursula was grateful not to have to explain Millie's involvement. 'Difficult to say for certain but the doctor thought probably yesterday afternoon.' Ursula paused for a moment, then added, 'Nobody seems to have seen anything. Mr Jackman has spoken to most of the other inhabitants there but nearly all were out during the daytime.' She played with her gloves. 'No doubt, Rachel, you were handing out some of your leaflets for women's suffrage?' Then she held her breath.

'Me?' It was almost a squeak. 'Good heavens, I ... I don't think so.'

'Don't you remember, Rachel? You were with me all afternoon,' John said urgently.

'Of course! It must be the shock of hearing what happened to poor Pond. How could I forget our time together?' Rachel gave a half-hearted laugh and they exchanged a long look.

Ursula was immediately convinced that Rachel and John had not spent yesterday afternoon together and also that they were closely involved with each other. She had seen passion in the glances John had been giving Rachel, and there was something different about the girl. It was as though, like an onion, a layer had been peeled away, leaving her more vulnerable. In other circumstances, she would have been delighted for her. This young man seemed attractive and extremely suitable. Rachel was perhaps the more intelligent of the couple – but that need not necessarily be an impediment.

'I'm being stupid!' said Rachel suddenly. 'Surely if Pond has died from cyanide poisoning, it must be by the same person responsible for Joshua's death. And that means they will have to release Alice! Why didn't you say so?'

'Mr Jackman is going to talk to Inspector Drummond and see if he will be organising her release.'

Rachel frowned. 'Surely there cannot be any question about it?'

'There's a possibility that the inspector may take the position that two persons could have been involved.'

'You mean he may still think that Alice sent those chocolates to Joshua and that someone else killed Pond?'

Ursula nodded.

'That's ridiculous! It was ridiculous to think that Alice had been responsible for sending the bonbons in the first place, even more so to imagine that someone else could have poisoned Pond!'

'What do you know about the valet? '

Rachel shrugged. 'A thoroughly unpleasant piece of work.'

'What makes you say that?'

Rachel screwed up her face, as though scenting rats. 'He was always eavesdropping; turn round, and there he was, with a smirk on his face as though he'd caught you in the middle of doing something disgusting. I couldn't stand him but Joshua seemed to think he could do no wrong. Alice hated him and he always acted as though he was laughing at her.'

'I say,' said John from the other end of the room. 'That's going it a bit, isn't it?'

'You didn't know him.'

John opened his mouth, closed it again, then said. 'I think I'm glad I didn't.'

'Do you think he and your brother-in-law were up to anything?'

'Oh, undoubtedly. He was always running errands for him. When I was working for Joshua, Pond would be there, popping in and out of his office, whispering to him. Then the two of them would go outside and stand on the wharf smoking cheroots and discussing who knew what.' Rachel ran her fingers through her hair, unrestricted today by plaits, ribbons or comb, in a gesture of frustration. 'I asked him once what he and Pond were up to.'

'What did he say?'

'Told me to mind my own business if I wanted to go on working for him. It wasn't long after that I left.' A shudder ran through her.

'Did you discuss it with your sister?'

'Not really. She just said that she was surprised I'd stayed as long as I had.'

'You shouldn't have worked for him at all,' said John.

'Hush; I've told you how it was,' Rachel said. He coloured and put his hands in his trouser pockets.

Ursula looked from one to the other of them for a moment then asked Rachel, 'How surprised were you that Alice returned to her husband?'

'I couldn't believe it!' Rachel broke off and tears gathered in her eyes. It was the first time Ursula had seen the girl become emotional rather than fired up. 'Not only did I think she at last had got free of him but since … well …' she hesitated and Ursula saw a bright red flush suffuse her face. Then she rose, went across to John, took his hand and looked up into his face. He smiled down at her, his eyes full of love and put his arm around her shoulders.

She turned back to Ursula. 'After I learned what love was really all about, I realised what she had found with Daniel. If I'd been in her place, I could not have returned to Joshua.' She spoke with a simple conviction that to Ursula seemed more telling than a passionate outburst. 'She had more courage than I.'

'Yet you say you are prepared to break the law, fling bricks through politicians' windows and do other aggressive acts for women's suffrage. That must take considerable courage.'

'But that's very different! That would be for something I believe in. I'm prepared to do anything for our Movement.'

Ursula looked at the girl, now full of passion in the same way as she had been at the menagerie. Yes, Rachel was prepared to do anything for a cause she believed in.

'And your sister felt her husband had the right to be a father to his child?'

Rachel made a disgusted sound, gently disentangled herself from John's arm and came towards Ursula. 'His right! Oh, yes, the law would have seen to that. Poor Alice. If she hadn't returned to Joshua, her only hope to be mother to her child would have been to leave the country with Daniel. I suggested she did that even if she knew he wasn't the father. But Alice has such a strong sense of duty. She said the child was Joshua's and he had been robbed of two other children.'

'Two? I knew there was one that died, but are you saying there was another?'

Rachel nodded. 'Joshua was married before. His first wife died in childbirth and the child with her. He told Alice that after they were wed.'

'How sad. Perhaps that was why he was such an unpleasant man.'

Rachel sat beside Ursula and took her hands. 'If Pond's death doesn't mean that Alice is going to be freed, it's imperative that Mr Jackman discovers something that will get her released. She's losing more and more weight and I fear for the child she is carrying.'

'He is pursuing every avenue. That is why he wanted to talk to the valet this morning. He thinks Joshua Peters has been black-mailing people and that Albert Pond was his accomplice.' Ursula decided not to mention Count Meyerhoff or *Maison Rose*. 'He was going to try and offer the man a deal, warn him it was almost certainly one of their victims who murdered Mr Peters and that he could suffer the same fate if the killer wasn't identified.' She looked from Rachel to John. 'And it would seem that this is what happened. We looked for the documents they must have had in their possession – but there was nothing. We think the killer removed them. I came here to tell you about Pond's death and Mr Jackman was going to go to your sister's house to see if there was a safe that could hold some of the evidence.'

'There is one,' said Rachel. 'Alice and I tried to open it after Joshua died but we couldn't find the key. Then she was put in prison and I forgot all about it.' She rose in a burst of energy. 'Why don't we go round there and try again?'

At that moment the door opened and Martha announced, 'Inspector Drummond!'

In came a tall man wearing a sharply cut dark suit. He removed a curly-brimmed bowler to reveal startlingly yellow hair. Behind him came a uniformed constable. The inspector halted in the middle of the room like a general about to address his troops.

'Ladies, gentleman,' he said with a curt nod of the head. 'Miss Fentiman, I'm arresting you for the murder of Albert Pond.'

Chapter Thirty

For a moment the three of them could have been waxworks in Madame Tussaud's famous museum.

Ursula rose. 'I think you must be making a mistake,' she said.

Drummond hardly glanced at her. 'You would be?'

'Ursula Grandison, a friend of Miss Fentiman's.'

She received a piercing look. 'Ah, according to Doctor Barton, my old colleague's new assistant,' he said, his upper lip curling in a pronounced sneer. 'I cannot imagine you will have anything to say I need to hear.'

John Pitney took a step forward. 'Miss Grandison was about to say that Miss Fentiman spent all yesterday afternoon with myself. We were discussing her sister's plight,' he added.

'And you are?'

'Lord John Pitney,' said Rachel, moving to his side. 'Younger son of the Duke of Walberton.'

Inspector Drummond blinked. He looked from the young man to the girl. 'Is there anyone who can confirm Miss Fentiman's movements, my lord?' He spat the title out.

'I think my word is good enough.'

Ursula would not have believed that the gentle-seeming John Pitney could sound so haughty. In the background, the uniformed constable shifted from one foot to the other.

Once again the door opened and Martha showed in another visitor. 'Mr Jackman,' she announced in a resigned tone.

Ursula felt profound relief.

'The proverbial bad penny; I should have known you would show up.'

'Indeed, Charlie,' Thomas said smoothly. He nodded to Ursula and Rachel and held his hand out to John Pitney, who shook it. 'Thomas Jackman, sir. Miss Fentiman commissioned me to investigate the death of Joshua Peters.'

'And are causing a great deal of trouble to the official police,' said Inspector Drummond.

'Really?' Thomas raised an eyebrow. 'The impression is that very little investigating is being done by "the official police".'

'You need to watch yourself, Tommy, or you'll be in my clink. Which is where Rachel Fentiman is going. Constable ...'

'Just a minute, Inspector,' Thomas broke in. 'Do I understand Miss Fentiman is under arrest?'

'That is so. For the murder of one Albert Pond,' Drummond said.

'You have evidence of that?' Thomas challenged him.

For a moment it looked as though the inspector was not going to say anything more. Thomas regarded him steadily.

After a minute's silent battle between the two of them, Drummond checked the condition of his fingernails and said, 'We have a witness.'

'A witness? To murder?' Thomas could not have sounded more surprised.

'Fentiman was seen entering the deceased's lodging. Around the time the doctor declared the poison would have been administered.'

'This is a lie!' Rachel shouted. 'I don't even know where Pond lives – lived.'

John Pitney caught hold of her hand. 'Of course it's a lie and we'll prove it.'

'You have a description that fits?' Thomas asked Drummond.

The inspector nodded.

'If you are arresting Miss Fentiman, may we assume that you will be releasing her sister from prison?'

'Why should you assume that, Tommy?' A negligent, almost throwaway comment.

'You surely don't think there are two poisoners in action here?'

'When they are sisters, why not?' Drummond sounded matter-of-fact.

'How dare you suggest Mrs Peters and I would administer cyanide?' Rachel was almost incandescent with rage. 'To start with, we wouldn't even know where it could be obtained.'

'Never been involved with rat poison?'

'No, inspector, I have not had to sully my hands with any such activity. Nor have either my sister or I had any reason to remove my brother-in-law or his valet from this life.' She pulled her hand away from John's, ignored his beseeching glance, and stood alone.

'I would question that.'

For a moment Rachel was disconcerted. 'What possible reason could there be?'

'Freedom.' Drummond threw the word at her almost insolently.

'Freedom? From what?' The girl was magnificently disdainful.

'From the shackles of a marriage that no longer suited, a husband who had been thrown over for another man; and you from the demands of a blackmailer.'

Rachel had lost her rage; now she confronted the inspector with a coolness that, given her situation, Ursula found extraordinary.

'My sister returned willingly to the father of the child she is carrying.'

'A father who would have complete power over that child. Either your sister or you decided he needed to be removed. Since then the man Pond has been blackmailing you.' Drummond sounded very certain.

'Indeed?' Rachel's voice was contemptuous. 'And what would he be blackmailing me about?'

'The fact that you were an accessory to murder.'

'That is ridiculous. I had nothing to do with my brother-in-law's death. And Pond was not blackmailing me. '

'I disagree.'

Ursula glanced at Thomas and saw that for the briefest of moments he looked startled. Was he revising his opinion on Rachel's possible guilt?

'Constable, cuff her.'

The uniformed policeman advanced, holding out a pair of cufflinks.

'You are making a great mistake,' John Pitney said with simple authority. 'I shall be contacting your Chief Constable regarding your treatment of Miss Fentiman; we are affianced.' It was said quietly but proudly.

'But …' Rachel started, then was silenced by a look from him. For the first time since Ursula had met her, the girl seemed at a loss.

'Take her away.' Inspector Drummond waved an imperious hand.

'Come with me, miss,' the policeman said, fastening one half of the cufflinks to her right wrist and the other to his left one.

Rachel looked panic-stricken but drew herself up. 'You will soon realise that you are making the second serious mistake of your career. Neither my sister nor I is a murderer.'

'I advise you to go quietly.' The inspector put on his bowler hat and turned to Rachel's fiancé. 'Don't think you can scare me with talk of grand relations.' His eyes narrowed. 'Drummond can and Drummond does; that's what I'm known for. No one catches more villains.' With that he swept out, followed by the constable with Rachel.

The moment the door closed behind him, Martha rushed in. 'What's happened? Where's that man taking her? Oh, not Miss Rachel as well!' Her eyes were full of tears and her hands scrunched up the apron she was wearing. 'What would Mr and Mrs Fentiman have said!'

Ursula put her arm round Martha's shoulders and gently sat her down on the sofa. 'I'm sure there's been a dreadful mistake. But Mr Jackman is going to try and sort it out.' She looked up at Thomas.

'Can you help, sir?' John Pitney asked.

'I came here from Montagu Place. I'd hoped to be able to search for Mr Peters' address book but the cook, who seems to be in charge at the moment, would not let me in. Mrs Trenchard's orders. I was looking for Miss Fentiman to provide me with a letter of authority. As it is …' he shrugged his shoulders helplessly.

'We were about to go there with her,' Ursula said. 'Apparently there is a safe and we were to look for the key.'

'We'll go to Mrs Trenchard,' said Martha with sudden resolution. 'I'll tell her what's happened and she'll give you your authority.' She spoke as though there could be no doubt. Ursula, having seen the elderly maid with Mrs Trenchard, could not doubt it either.

'I will go and cable my father,' said John Pitney. 'He will know whom to contact to get Rachel released.'

Chapter Thirty-One

They found a hansom cab and Ursula, Martha and Jackman squeezed in.

'The last time I saw Mrs Trenchard,' Jackman said after he'd given their direction and the cabbie managed to get his horse into motion, 'she banned me from ever entering the Peters' house again. Is there a chance she will have forgotten or forgiven?'

Martha harrumphed, 'Mrs Trenchard doesn't forget and she doesn't often forgive. But she'll be that beside herself to hear of Miss Rachel's arrest, I reckon she'll be grateful for any help.'

Ursula looked at the indomitable figure sitting between her and the investigator, cotton-gloved hands clasped tightly together. Here was someone who gave her loyalty wholeheartedly to the family she had served for so long. What was it Rachel had said? Martha had been her mother's personal maid.

'You must have known Miss Rachel since she was small,' Ursula said to her.

'Since she was born. And a right fighter she was from the start. Nanny had such a time with her. "Miss Imperious" she called her.' Martha gave a tight smile. 'It wasn't for herself she wanted anything, though. Miss Alice was the older but from the moment Miss Rachel could haul herself upright and stagger around clutching on to the furniture, she was her sister's protector.'

Ursula could sense Jackman listening intently. She wanted to say that Rachel being Alice's protector didn't mean she would murder for her. 'Did you say you weren't at home yesterday afternoon, Martha? I'm sorry,' she added. 'I don't know your surname.'

'I'm Battle, Miss. But Mrs Fentiman said she couldn't have me called that so I've always been Martha. And, yes, I wasn't there yesterday. Mrs Trenchard had garments to sort out for one of her charities.' She looked down at her gloved hands. 'Supposed to be clean them clothes were but if that's what's called clean, I'm a dustman.' Her nose wrinkled. 'Wanted a hanging in the fresh air but Mrs Trenchard said there wasn't a point. Better to sort and get them over to the Reverend who'd know who needed them, that's what we had to do.'

'So you don't know where Miss Rachel was yesterday afternoon?' Jackman said, his tone carefully neutral.

'That young man says she was with him!' Martha gave a snort. 'Well, if Lord John says that, that's what we have to accept.'

'You don't sound as though you approve of him,' Ursula slipped in.

Another snort. 'Someone who tinkers about with machinery all day! A salesman! I don't care if he does call himself a lord; I wouldn't trust him further than that auto thing he drives can go.'

Ursula quashed the temptation to say that would mean a long way. 'I think we're here,' she exclaimed as the cab drew up outside a solid-looking semi-detached house in a road that had every appearance of respectability and comfortable living.

Jackman reached up the fare through the little door in the cab's roof then helped out his fellow passengers.

'You'd best let me do the talking,' said Martha. She advanced up well-whitened steps and banged the gleaming knocker hard. 'We need to see Mrs Trenchard, Polly,' she said to the neat maid who opened the door.

'She's not receiving,' Polly said, not looking impressed with the trio on her doorstep.

Martha shouldered her way in. 'You should know better than that, my girl. Tell the mistress I'm here and it's important.'

The maid's face set in a sulky expression.

'Look lively,' said Martha.

'It's that the master isn't well,' Polly said in a voice that mixed triumph with resentment.

A door opened and Mrs Trenchard appeared, 'Who was it, Polly?' She sounded exhausted.

'Miss Battle, Madam. Says it's important.'

Mrs Trenchard's face was pale and drawn. 'Why, Martha, what brings you here?' Then she saw her other visitors. 'Mr Jackman!' She did not sound welcoming. 'And Miss Grandison.' Still disapproving. Then her expression changed, became almost hopeful. 'Is it something to do with Alice, that is, Mrs Peters? Is she being released?'

Martha's control vanished. 'Oh, ma'am, it's Miss Rachel. She's been arrested!'

Mrs Trenchard's hand went to her throat. 'No!' She staggered for a moment and Ursula slipped a hand underneath an elbow.

'Let's sit you down.' She led the woman back into the drawing room and settled her into a comfortable chair.

'A glass of water, Polly,' said Martha sharply.

Mrs Trenchard put a hand to her forehead. 'I knew Rachel would take matters too far. All that talk of militancy. Emmeline Pankhurst will have a lot to answer for; I will never forgive her for leading my niece so badly astray.'

'I'm afraid Rachel's arrest has nothing to do with the fight for women's suffrage,' Ursula assured her.

'She is being charged with the murder of Albert Pond,' said Jackman quietly.

Mrs Trenchard looked at him, her expression blank. 'Albert Pond? Joshua's valet?'

Jackman nodded. 'His body was found this morning. He was almost certainly poisoned in the same fashion as Mr Peters.'

'And my poor Rachel is being accused of causing his death?'

'I am afraid so.'

Mrs Trenchard looked wildly around the room, her fingers digging into the padded arms of her chair. 'Oh, it's dreadful, too dreadful. But will Alice now be set free? I cannot allow that Rachel could have been responsible for so terrible an act but at least the accusation should release her sister.'

'I am afraid not. Inspector Drummond is convinced that Mrs Peters poisoned her husband and Miss Fentiman copied her in killing the valet.'

'But why?'

'My investigation into the death of Mr Peters has led me to believe that he and Pond have been blackmailing various persons.'

Mrs Trenchard stared at him. 'Blackmail! Surely not!'

Polly entered with a glass of water; Martha insisted on taking and handing it to Mrs Trenchard.

Jackman watched in silence as she drank a little, then said, 'Miss Grandison is assisting me in my investigation and we are here because there is a possibility Joshua Peters has left some evidence that could prove this assertion in a safe at his home. We would like to visit Montagu Place and see if we can open it. In order to do so, we require authority. Miss Fentiman was about to accompany us there when Inspector Drummond arrested her.'

'And now you would like me to go with you instead?'

Jackman nodded.

'I am afraid that will not be possible. Mr Trenchard is not at all well and I have sent for the doctor. When you arrived, I thought it might be him.'

'Madam, if you wrote a letter,' said Martha, 'and I went with the lady and gentleman, then I think Mrs Firestone would be willing to allow us access.'

Mrs Trenchard closed her eyes. After a long moment she looked up at Ursula. 'I cannot bring myself to believe such a dreadful thing. Oh, that my sister had never allowed that benighted match between Joshua Peters and poor, dear Alice. Martha, give me your arm as far as my desk and I will write a note to Mrs Firestone.'

Some five minutes later, an envelope was handed over. 'One thing: Martha, you are to remain with Miss Grandison and Mr Jackman at all times. You will report to me tomorrow on exactly what has transpired. You understand?'

Before Martha could respond, the doorbell rang. 'Ah,' said Mrs Trenchard. 'That will be the doctor. At last!'

Instead, in rushed Daniel Rokeby, Polly just managing to snatch his broad-brimmed hat from his head. 'Sorry, Madam,' she blurted, 'I couldn't stop him.'

'Where is Rachel? She's not at home and nor is Martha. I'm so worried about Alice.' The words poured out of him. Then he realised that Mrs Trenchard was not alone. He stood for a moment, taking in the scene he'd disturbed, his long hair tousled, brown cord trousers badly worn, dark red velvet jacket creased and with the corner of one of the pockets torn, cream silk cravat crumpled. 'Oh my God, something's happened, hasn't it? Tell me where Rachel is.'

Mrs Trenchard reached a beseeching hand towards Jackman. 'You're the investigator,' she said in a low voice. 'Please tell Mr Rokeby.'

As Jackman gave brief details, Daniel dipped his head and thrust his hands into his trouser pockets. When the investigator had finished, he looked at him. 'I'll come with you to Montagu Place. I came here because Alice has sent me a letter and it reads as though she has realised she has little hope of liberty. We must do something.'

'Do you have the letter with you?' asked Mrs Trenchard.

Reluctantly he produced a piece of paper and handed it to her.

Mrs Trenchard read it carefully, then closed her eyes and allowed it to drop on her desk as she rested her face on her hand. 'It would seem that Alice anticipates the worst. At least she is safe until her child is born.'

Ursula felt frozen by this development. 'When I was with her in Holloway,' she said, 'Alice seemed to believe that because she was innocent, justice meant that eventually she would be freed.'

'Justice! Justice! When has justice ever done the right thing?' Daniel ran a hand desperately through his hair, leaving it even more dishevelled. 'We have to find whoever it is who has done these foul deeds. Jackman, you said you would discover the perpetrator.'

'We are hoping this visit to Montagu Place will yield some vital evidence.'

Mrs Trenchard folded Alice's letter and returned it to Daniel. 'Yes, Mr Rokeby, go there with the others. The more witnesses the better.'

Ursula caught sight of Jackman's face. Like her, he obviously felt the addition of the poet to their party was more likely to be a hindrance than a help but there was nothing that could be done. She said goodbye and led the way out of the drawing room with an indelible picture of Mrs Trenchard's white and agonised face in her mind. Surely there had to be some evidence that would at the very least identify other suspects for the deaths of Joshua Peters and Albert Pond? The Fentiman sisters must not have to stand trial for murder.

★ ★ ★

A four-wheeler cab was found without much delay. Throughout the mercifully short journey, Daniel bombarded Jackman with questions: How was his investigation going; what was the evidence against Rachel; how had Pond's whereabouts been discovered; why couldn't Jackman make Inspector Drummond see that neither sister was responsible for murder? Ursula leaned her head against the seat back and tried to ignore the throbbing that was threatening to turn into a serious headache.

All the time she fought to keep her mind clear, Ursula felt a terrible fear that this expedition to investigate Joshua Peters' safe was not going to produce any evidence that could persuade Drummond to release the sisters. She was certain that all Rachel's protestations of innocence would be useless. Until she and Jackman could identify at least one blackmail victim who had sufficient to lose from exposure to make murder the only option, Rachel and Alice seemed doomed. The uncertain motion of the cab racked up the headache to the point where it seemed hammers were beating at the inside of her skull.

At Montagu Place, Daniel immediately jumped out, ran up to the front door and banged the knocker. There was a long delay before it was finally opened. Emily's eyes widened as she took in the group. Martha explained matters and they were all taken down to the kitchen where she and Mrs Firestone, apparently the only two members of staff left in the house, were eating supper.

At any other time, Ursula would have found the aroma of macaroni cheese appetising. Now it induced nausea and she quietly left the kitchen and waited on the hall stairs for Mrs Trenchard's letter of authority to be produced. The quiet was blissful and she began to hope that the hammering in her head would soon go away.

Instead, stray thoughts intruded. Why had Daniel insisted on coming with them? Had he perhaps already known about Albert Pond's death? But how? Ursula felt a tingle along the nape of her neck, a sure sign something was asking her to concentrate. Had Millie, she wondered, been in touch with Daniel? Told him where Pond was living? After all, Millie had been Alice and Daniel's go-between; she would know him quite well. Was he afraid there would be something in the safe that could incriminate him?

'Are you all right?' asked Jackman quietly. She had not been aware of his approach. She nodded. 'It is only a slight headache.' Then she summoned a smile, 'I would not like you to lose your assistant as soon as she started her duties.'

Martha and Daniel joined them, together with Emily. 'I'll show you Mr Peters' bedroom. That's where his safe is.' She led the way upstairs.

Joshua Peters' bedroom was dark. Emily switched on the electric light then drew back heavy brown velvet curtains trimmed with gold fringing to reveal a window overlooking the rear of the house.

It was a very masculine room, with red and black striped wall paper, a mahogany tallboy, a large bed with carved walnut head and foot boards, and a heavy quilted bedcover in a dark red paisley pattern. On one side of the bed stood a night cabinet very similar to the one in Albert Pond's rooms. A carpet with swirls of dark caramel on a darker brown covered the floor.

Opposite the bed was a fireplace with a nicely blackened grate, slate hearth and Delft tiling. To one side stood a heavy wardrobe, on the other was a free-standing cheval mirror, with behind it a large oil painting of a stag at bay.

Emily moved the mirror and fiddled with the frame of the painting, then swung one side of it away from the wall. Jackman gave a sigh of relief as they saw a large, iron safe. 'Quite a simple lock, no codes required, just a key.' He ran his fingers over it. 'I wouldn't reckon much, though, to the possibility of cracking it open without one.'

'As I said downstairs, sir,' said Emily, ' we haven't been able to find a key.'

'Right, team,' said Jackman. 'Any ideas as to a devilish clever hiding place?'

Daniel lifted the bedcover, swung himself under the bed and ran his hands over the exposed springs. Martha tried to move the headboard to check behind it – and failed. Ursula started to take out drawers from the tallboy, searching their contents, checking underneath each drawer, then piling them up on the floor. Martha came to help. Emily stood by the door, watching the activities with a slightly scornful look on her face. 'We've done all that,' she said.

Jackman checked underneath the window sill and behind the curtains, then cleared out the contents of the wardrobe and the long drawer at its bottom. 'Rokeby, you check the underside and back of this piece. I'm going downstairs to the study. The desk has at least one hiding place.' He left the room.

Ursula carried on checking the tallboy's multitude of drawers.

'Never seen a chap have so many socks,' Martha said. 'Or with such natty clocks.' She held up a dark grey pair with an ivory silk pattern down the side. 'Hardly worn,' she added.

They reached the last of the drawers without result. Daniel had finished his searches and replaced the contents of the wardrobe.

'Not a sign of a key.' He stood back and surveyed the room. 'It can't be here, we've searched everywhere.' He sounded thoroughly frustrated. 'Yet it has to be somewhere. You, girl, has the entire house been searched?'

'Her name is Emily,' said Ursula frostily. 'You'll have to forgive him,' she said to the maid. 'It's been a long and trying day.'

'That's all right, miss. The master hardly ever called me by name.'

Daniel struck his forehead. 'To think I've displayed manners as bad as that brute! Emily, I present my deepest apologies.'

For the first time since they'd arrived, she smiled. 'Thank you, sir. And, yes, we have all checked every inch of this place. We even looked in the garden.'

Ursula put the drawer from the top of the tallboy back in place, listening to the slight 'clunk' as it moved smoothly in and met the wooden back.

Martha slotted in the next drawer.

'Just a minute,' said Ursula. 'Let me check something.'

She started to correct the haphazard way she had piled the drawers on top of each other, lining them up carefully, matching their outlines. In the middle of her task Jackman returned with a depressed shake of the head. 'Yes!' she suddenly breathed. 'Look …' She pointed to the drawer in the middle of the first pile. 'Don't you see, it's slightly shorter than the others.'

'But it hasn't got a key stuck to it,' said Daniel, running a hand over the back.

'No,' said Ursula, reaching into the space it had occupied in the chest. 'But, look what I've found!' She withdrew her arm.

'Oh, my heavens,' said Emily, both hands at her mouth.

'Well done, assistant investigator,' said Jackman, taking the heavy iron key. 'Now let's see if it's the one we need.'

They all watched as he fitted it into the lock, turned it – and opened the safe's door.

Daniel, Martha and Emily crowded round to see what was revealed and Ursula blessed the fact that she was tall enough to see over the heads of the two servants.

An iron shelf split the interior of the safe into two. The top half looked empty; in the bottom rested a collection of jewellery cases.

Jackman lifted out several. 'Martha, will you please put these on the bed. Emily, please check their contents and see if you can identify any missing items.'

Gradually, nearly a dozen open cases were assembled. Joshua Peters had good taste in jewellery, Ursula thought as she looked at necklaces, bracelets, earrings and brooches set with diamonds, emeralds and amythests, plus a lovely double string of pearls with matching drop earrings. Emily reverently touched the contents of each case. 'I wasn't the mistress's maid but I saw her dressed for evening occasions often enough and I recognise them all.'

'Anything missing?'

Slowly she surveyed the glittering collection. 'One thing,' she said finally. 'A gold chain and locket.'

'That was her mother's,' said Martha. 'She wore it almost all the time, unless she was dressed up for a function. It would have gone to prison with her.'

'There's a small fortune there,' said Daniel in astonishment. 'If I'd known, I'd have told her to bring as many as she could when she came to join me. Selling them would have meant a great start to our life together and I reckon she earned them, the way that brute treated her.'

'But she was leaving him,' said Ursula quietly. 'I can understand her reluctance to take any.' She remembered Alice describing the functions Peters had insisted they attended together. 'I felt I was a doll, dressed up and hung with jewels to demonstrate how successful Joshua was,' she'd said.

'He probably made sure she didn't know where the key was kept,' said Jackman.

'Anything else in the safe?' asked Ursula. 'Papers? Notebook with addresses?'

Jackman stood back, revealing the empty spaces above and below the shelf. 'That seems to be it, I'm afraid.'

'So Pond cleared out the evidence,' said Ursula with a frustrated sigh. She wondered why he hadn't taken at least some of the jewellery as well, but maybe he thought he'd be branded a thief and sent to jail.

Jackman knelt down in front of the safe and ran a hand round the inside, reaching into the back and then round the sides and front. 'Just a minute, there's something here.'

The safe had a frame at the front that the door fitted into. Working carefully, Jackman detached a slim envelope that had somehow been forced against it at the top, out of sight.

It was unsealed. As the others watched, fascinated, Jackman took out a sheet of paper and rapidly scanned it.

'It appears to be a love letter addressed to "My Darling Pistachio", and signed "Your loving Almond".'

'Couple of nuts,' murmured Daniel.

Jackman handed the piece of paper to Martha. 'Is that Miss Fentiman's writing?'

She took one look and shook her head. 'Nor is it Mrs Peters',' she said.

Daniel snatched it out of her hand, immediately denied knowing the handwriting but started to read the letter anyway. He raised an eyebrow. 'I say, maybe written by a nut but it's pretty fruity.' He handed it to Ursula. She gave it a brief glance then gave it back to Jackman.

He returned the piece of paper to the envelope. 'We'll need to subject it to a closer scrutiny than is possible here.' It was slipped into an inside pocket. 'Now, Emily and Martha, please close up the jewellery cases. We need to return them to the safe and I think the key should be given to Mrs Trenchard.'

Ursula watched the return of the cases to the safe, her mind in a daze. All she could think about was gratitude that Jackman had not asked if she recognised the writing.

Chapter Thirty-Two

Back at Mrs Maple's boarding house, Jackman helped Ursula descend from the cab.

After demanding that the investigator clear Alice and Rachel's names, Daniel had stalked off. Jackman had sighed and found a cab. It had taken them first to the Trenchard residence, where he handed over the safe key, then to St George's Square, where Martha was dropped. She had said she'd be very happy to find her own way home, but neither Jackman nor Ursula would hear of such a thing. As Martha opened the front door, Ursula thought that she seemed older and frailer than when they had first met. With both the sisters she had known all their lives now in prison accused of murder, it was no wonder.

The headache that had been growing ever since that afternoon made Ursula long, above everything, for her bed. Now, however, she realised that Jackman was insisting that they discuss the day's events.

'Wouldn't it be better to leave it until tomorrow? I'm quite worn out,' she said, drawing a hand across her forehead.

'I'm sure you've managed to cope under worse conditions,' he said, giving the cabbie a salute of farewell. 'If I didn't think it was important, I wouldn't insist.'

It was easier to accept the situation than continue to protest. Ursula led the way in.

The boarders' lounge was occupied but Meg said it would be quite all right to use the dining room to talk. 'So long as you don't mess with the breakfast laying,' she added. 'Can I bring you some coffee?'

Ursula looked at Jackman, who said, 'I'd kill for a pot of tea. And a sandwich if you had such a thing; we haven't had anything to eat since midday.'

'You poor things! You go in there and I'll bring you something that'll keep you going.' Meg disappeared down to the kitchen.

Ursula removed her coat and hung it over the back of one of the chairs then sat and fingered the material. 'It's hard to believe it was only this morning that I retrieved this from Millie,' she sighed.

'It's the first time I've seen you less than one hundred percent,' Jackman said, sitting opposite her.

'Have you forgotten what we went through in Liverpool?' she smiled faintly.

'You have a point. That Mountstanton business was taxing.' He crossed his legs, unbuttoned his jacket, and put his thumbs in the armholes of his waistcoat and returned her smile. 'Regretting taking on the position of investigative assistant once again?'

She tried to rally. 'Of course not. I just wish we were making more progress. Were you as surprised as I was to see Daniel Rokeby turning up like that?'

'You think there was more to his appearance than a letter from Mrs Peters?'

She shrugged. 'Do you think Millie could have been in touch with him? They must know each other quite well.'

He sat up a little straighter and ran a hand over his chin; Ursula heard the faint rasp of new-grown stubble. 'Hmm! You think our friend Albert Pond could have been blackmailing him and that he took action? Any suggestions as to what the blackmailing could have been about?'

Too tired to think, Ursula shook her head. 'Nothing, other than, perhaps, the death of Joshua Peters?'

'Don't think I haven't given consideration to that possibility. There is, though, absolutely no evidence whatsoever. I conducted a thorough investigation into him after Peters first hired me and could find nothing to blacken his name apart from his being a second rate poet and scratching a living with the odd article.'

'Which isn't a crime.'

'Quite.'

Ursula saw Jackman slightly narrow his eyes and knew without any doubt that he was about to bring up the matter of the letter found in the Peters' safe.

The dining room door opened and Meg manoeuvred a tray on to the table. There was a pot of tea, milk and sugar and a plate with several rough-cut sandwiches. 'Supper today was salt beef, with enough left over for these,' said Meg, unloading plates, cups and saucers and napkins. 'I'll collect them things after you've finished, no need to bring them down to the kitchen, washing up's all been done for tonight.' Then she was gone.

'What a treat,' said Jackman, lifting the brown teapot. 'Shall I pour?'

'Please.'

'Now, get yourself outside that and you'll feel miles better.' He handed over the nicely large cup and saucer then offered sugar. Ursula refused but he helped himself to two large spoonfuls, carefully stirring it in.

The tea was refreshing but Ursula found that she didn't really feel up to consuming the thick sandwiches; however Jackman soon demolished his portion.

'Right,' he said, dusting off his fingers with the napkin. 'Now, are you going to tell me who wrote that letter? The one Rokeby called "fruity"? And don't try to tell me you don't know because it won't wash.'

Ursula wished she had done a better job of concealing her reaction. But Jackman knew her too well. She forced herself to remember what she had gathered from the letter.

'Thomas, did you think it contained anything that a black-mailer could use to extract money?'

He took out the envelope and re-read the love letter.

'Ah! Well, it depends on whether it is adulterous or not.'

'You mean, if the writer isn't married and the letter was sent to another unmarried person, then it could be considered innocent?'

'And that's what you believe? That it is innocent?'

'Under those circumstances, yes.'

'And you are not going to tell me who writer and recipient are?'

'I have particular reasons for not doing so,' Ursula said slowly.

'I can see that. But, surely, you can understand that because it was found in a blackmailer's safe, it almost certainly is not innocent.'

Ursula found it difficult to counter his logic or to meet his gaze. Instead she rose. 'Please, wait here, I'll be back in a moment,' she said and hurried upstairs to her room. Here she took out her copy of the fragment of paper Meg had rescued from Alice's fire.

Re-entering the dining room, she found Jackman had refilled both their cups. She handed over the scrap of paper and explained its history. 'I should have given it to you sooner,' she said.

'And what stopped you, may I ask?'

'I think you can probably see why not.'

'Read it to me, I can't make any sense of it myself.'

Ursula cleared her throat and took back the piece of paper.

'you, my darling, I have worked it

'Daniel, I can do it, I know I can. It

'readful, but then we can be free for

'He will be gone.'

She looked at Jackman. 'As I explained, Meg found the original half burned in Alice's grate and wanted to keep as a memento of someone she had grown fond of. Alice was very kind to her. After I'd copied the wording down, I tore off a piece from the left-hand side of the paper so what was left more or less matched the singed bit. I think the right hand side hadn't been touched by the fire. If it's an ordinary piece of letter writing paper, not much of it can be missing.'

'You didn't show it to me because you thought it was evidence that Alice was at the very least thinking of murdering her husband,' he said flatly.

She nodded, feeling as disloyal to him as she had earlier over withholding the identity of the letter writer. But she had other loyalties.

He reached for the piece of paper again and sat scrutinising it. Ursula waited, surprised he hadn't immediately taken it as proof of Alice's guilt. But she should have known that that wasn't the way Jackman operated.

After a few minutes he looked up. 'Surely a woman of your intelligence could see that there is another way to interpret this?' He waved the scrap, then caught himself. 'But of course when you first read this the possibility of blackmail had not been raised.'

Ursula stared at him, then understood. 'You mean, Alice might have discovered what her husband was up to and was trying to bring herself to tell the police about his activities with the idea that they would lock him away and she and Daniel could live happily together.'

'See, you can do it!'

Ursula hardly heard this; her mind, becoming clearer by the minute, was racing on. 'But then she discovered there was a child on the way and felt she could not deprive it of its rightful father, or the father his right to bring up his child.' She shuddered. 'Alice had more courage than I would have in the same situation.'

Jackman remained looking thoughtfully at the scrap of paper. 'The question remains, why hasn't she revealed to the police what she knew about the blackmail activities of her husband? Before that rat Pond could remove all the evidence? Drummond would then have had a range of possible suspects to Peters' murder to be investigated.'

'She couldn't, can't, endure the thought of her child knowing its father was a criminal.'

'Instead it will have a mother hanged for the murder of its father! Hardly a worthwhile bargain.'

'She has been convinced an innocent woman will not be convicted. I tried to warn her that it was all too possible but I couldn't get through to her. Perhaps the possibility is beginning to hit home at last. Thomas, I'm sorry, but I really cannot think straight any more. Could we continue this discussion tomorrow? I have no other plans.'

'Of course.' He rose, doing up his jacket. 'Have some rest. I have a few ideas I can follow up. Suppose we say four o'clock? For a cup of tea?' He smiled and tapped the now empty teapot.

Ursula saw him out, then took the tray downstairs. Meg was sitting by the stove with the cat on her knee.

'Don't get up.' Ursula put her burden on the kitchen table. 'I just wanted to say thank you very much for the tea and the sandwiches. It was just what we needed.' She was thankful Jackman had managed to eat her portion of salt beef as well as his own.

'Oh, Miss Grandison, Mrs Maple wanted to see you when you came in. I didn't like to tell you before, what with you being with Mr Jackman. Hope I didn't do wrong.'

Ursula stifled an inward groan; wasn't she ever going to be allowed to go to bed?

'That's fine, Meg. I'll go and see her now.'

Mrs Maple was in her parlour working on her accounts. She greeted Ursula and said, 'A letter was delivered for you this afternoon. It was marked URGENT so I thought I'd better give it to you myself.' She reached over to the back of her desk, found an envelope and handed it over.

Upstairs in her room, Ursula opened and read the note. It was not good news. Mrs Bruton wanted to move back into her home but her maid had had an accident and broken her arm. Huckle was to stay at her sister's until she could be useful again. So would Ursula come round to Brown's Hotel immediately to pack up her things and arrange the move back to Wilton Crescent.

Ursula flopped down on her bed. Her loyalties were being stretched in all directions!

Chapter Thirty-Three

'I have been so upset,' said Mrs Bruton. 'I wanted you to come yesterday afternoon.'

'I'm very sorry,' said Ursula, taking off her gloves. 'I was elsewhere. I didn't get your message until yesterday evening.'

Mrs Bruton sighed deeply. She was sitting in a chintz-covered chair in her hotel suite. On a little table beside her was a glass; it looked as though it contained whisky. Drinking spirits at ten o'clock in the morning was not something Ursula had seen her do before. The chair had its back to the window, meaning it was difficult for her to see her employer's face but she seemed to be distressed. Ursula found another chair, brought it up to Mrs Bruton's, sat down and took hold of one of her hands.

'Now, tell me everything. How did Huckle break her arm?'

'It was so silly!' Mrs Bruton's voice grew a little stronger and she sounded annoyed. 'She had Friday off. She wanted to see her sister. I wanted to do some shopping. When I got back, there was a message from the sister that Huckle had fallen getting out of the underground railway carriage, overcome by fumes apparently. She's broken her arm; it has been put in a plaster cast and the sister says she won't be able to use it for weeks!'

Ursula stroked her employer's hand soothingly. 'How very annoying. But perhaps Enid can act as your maid until Huckle returns. She is a very efficient girl and will enjoy looking after you.'

'She won't be able to deal with buttons or dress my hair or wash and iron my clothes the way Huckle does. I didn't even trust her to do my packing, not the way that you will do it, dear Miss Grandison.' Mrs Bruton turned away sounding sulky.

Ursula saw that her dark chestnut hair hung girlishly down her back. She wore pearl earrings and two long strands of pearls over a chiffon and lace blouse with cashmere skirt, both in cream. 'You have managed to dress yourself beautifully.'

'I'm not completely helpless!'

'Of course you are not. I have always admired the manner in which you have ordered your life since Mr Bruton's demise. Shall I help you with your hair before I start your packing?' Ursula began to rise, only to have Mrs Bruton grab hold of her arm and force her to remain seated.

'Huckle's accident is not the worst of it!'

'Please, tell me what else has upset you.'

Mrs Bruton rested an elbow on an arm of her chair and buried her face in her hand. 'Oh, I wish I could. It is too awful!'

'Why don't I order some coffee while you compose yourself? Whatever it is, you will feel better if you share it with me.' She rose and pressed the service bell.

Waiting for the coffee to arrive, Ursula sat and stroked Mrs Bruton's hand soothingly. 'I am sure you are going to be pleased with your bathroom. New York always prides itself on being in the forefront of household fixtures and fittings but I haven't seen anything to beat your new arrangement. Venus herself would be proud to bathe in such luxury.'

Mrs Bruton jerked her hand away. There seemed to be something of the spoilt child about her this morning.

Ursula sat back and waited. After a moment she realised something was different about the arrangement of the furniture in the room. Then she saw that the chair Mrs Bruton was sitting in had been pulled away from the window. Previously, Ursula had been amused to think that her employer might be keeping an eye on *Maison Rose*, just across the road from the hotel and almost opposite Mrs Bruton's sitting room and bedroom windows. Now, though, she seemed literally to have turned her back on the place.

Ursula sat down again and leaned forward. 'Is the reason you are upset something to do with *Maison Rose*?'

'How did you know? Is there something you have been keeping from me?' The woman's voice was high pitched, accusing. Ursula had never seen her in anything approaching this state.

There was a knock on the door and the coffee arrived. Ursula asked for it to be placed on a convenient table and said that she would attend to it.

After the waiter had left the room, she brought a cup of coffee over for Mrs Bruton. 'I recently saw a letter Madame Rose had written. It was, I suppose it should be called, a love letter. Nicknames were used but I assumed it was intended for Count Meyerhoff. I know you have become very close to the count. Have you discovered that they are in a relationship? Is that why you are upset?'

Mrs Bruton ignored the coffee, gave an hysterical laugh and threw up her hands. 'In love with the count? In love with the count? If that was all!'

Ursula set the cup down and sat again. 'Please, tell me exactly what has happened.'

It took time but eventually Ursula got the story out of her.

The previous morning Mrs Bruton had woken early. 'I don't know why but I couldn't sleep. I'd been tossing and turning all night.'

'I expect you were worrying about Huckle and her broken arm,' said Ursula gently.

Mrs Bruton ignored her. 'Eventually I got up and pulled back my bedroom curtains.' She paused and drew her hand across her eyes for a moment. Ursula offered her the cup of coffee again. 'Through the net curtains I could see directly across the street into a room on the second floor of *Maison Rose*; the floor where the Count and Madame have their apartments. There are no net curtains on those windows.'

The cup of coffee was put down and after a little pause Mrs Bruton took a deep breath, closed her eyes and said: 'It was very early. No one was about. The sun was just rising, with no hint of the rain to come.' She opened her eyes, looking directly at Ursula. 'As I was about to return to my bed, I saw a woman in a nightgown come to the window, just as I had. I recognised her. It was Miss Ferguson!' Mrs Bruton clutched her throat. 'I thought for one terrible moment that I was looking at Count Meyerhoff's room and … and …'

'They were having an affair?' Ursula offered.

Mrs Bruton sank back. 'It was much worse than that. As I looked, I saw Madame Rose come to the window and slip

her arms around and embrace her. Her hands caressed her ....
her ... then Miss Ferguson turned in her arms, so languidly,' she
made it sound an insult. 'And they kissed. Such passion ...'

More silence. Finally, 'I staggered back to my bed and collapsed,
trembling with shock and ... and disgust!' She sounded hysterical again. Suddenly she rose and walked shakily about the room.
'I shall never be able to set foot in that place again. I don't even
know if I can face dear Count Meyerhoff. Thank heavens I didn't
agree to invest money in *Maison Rose*. Now I can't wait to leave
this place. If you had been able to come,' she said reproachfully,
'I would have done so yesterday.'

'I can quite understand how upset you must be,' said Ursula
carefully. 'Such a nasty shock. But you must not allow it to upset
you. There is no need ever to enter *Maison Rose* again.' Ursula
rose. 'Have you asked for your cases to be brought to your room?
Then I'll start packing your things. Why don't you come with
me and we'll fix your hair. Then you can sit and enjoy some
more coffee. We'll soon have you home.'

She took Mrs Bruton through to the bedroom and sat her
down in front of the dressing table. But instead of being allowed
to act as lady's maid, Ursula found herself watching while
Mrs Bruton gave her loose hair a quick brush then twirled
its length into a rope before coiling it on top of her head and
securing it with a selection of combs. The whole process was
conducted with easy efficiency. How much of Mrs Bruton's
need for a well-trained maid arose from a belief her position as a
wealthy – and attractive – widow demanded it?

'I suppose that will do,' Mrs Bruton said, patting her hair.
'Thank you, dear, I feel easier about things now.' She returned to
her sitting room.

Suitcases had indeed been placed ready for packing and on
the bed were two large hatboxes. In the cases were sheets of
tissue paper, neatly folded and ready for the careful packing of
clothes. Ursula opened the commodious wardrobes and started
to remove and fold garments, her movements almost automatic
as she considered the implications of Mrs Bruton's tale.

Ursula had immediately recognised that it was Madame
Rose's handwriting on the letter Jackman had found in the
Peters' safe. It had never occurred to her that it could have been
meant for anyone but Count Meyerhoff. She had refused to tell

Jackman whose handwriting she had recognised because she was
convinced that the letter could not form the basis of a blackmail
attempt. Both parties were mature and unmarried. How could
anyone object to a liaison?

A lesbian relationship, however, was an entirely different
matter. Could Mrs Bruton have misunderstood what she saw?
Highly unlikely. Ursula remembered her conversation with Miss
Ferguson while they filled jars with beauty products. How full
of admiration for Madame Rose the girl had been. Yes, Ursula
thought, it was a small step from her attitude then to sexual
worship.

She herself had come across similar relationships both in Paris
and San Francisco. So long as they did not harm other people,
she saw nothing wrong in them. But Mrs Bruton's reaction had
been damning.

Ursula remembered how when Madame Rose had assessed
her skin, she had used her hands to indicate various areas such as
beneath the eyes, had traced the line of her cheekbones. It was a
highly personal service the beautician offered and were it to be
generally known that she found sexual satisfaction with members of her own sex, the business would undoubtedly collapse.
The financial loss would be great and the count's reputation
would suffer along with Madame Rose's.

Busy inserting tissue paper between the folds of Mrs Bruton's
clothes and neatly packing silks, linens, cashmere, chiffon and
other costly materials, all beautifully made up into the costumes
her employer wore with such style, Ursula remembered her
sight of Albert Pond being ejected from *Maison Rose*. Had that
been the occasion he had found the letter? Surely it could not
have been left around for anyone to read and steal? Or had Pond
returned one night and broken into *Maison Rose* and found the
love note? Perhaps while looking for evidence with which to
blackmail the count? Ursula remembered her belief that Count
Meyerhoff was a spy. Had he found proof of that as well?

Had Madame Rose realised that the letter had been stolen?
She could hardly ask if anyone had seen it.

The letter was undated, it could have been stolen before
Ursula had seen Pond leaving *Maison Rose*. Even, perhaps, before
Peters had been killed. Ursula knew she had to discuss the whole
matter with Jackman when he came round to Mrs Maple's for

tea that afternoon. And she would apologise for not revealing the name of the writer of the letter.

Ursula opened the hatboxes and started to pack the large amount of headgear that Mrs Bruton had seemed to require for her stay in Brown's Hotel.

The hats were as beautifully designed and constructed as the garments and as varied. There were wide ones sporting artificial flowers, others decorated with feathers, some with veils, others without. There was one that looked like an officer's shako, another that was almost a pill box. There was one that looked like a cream pancake. Ursula held it and wondered if it would be the perfect choice for wear with Mrs Bruton's current outfit.

'Thank you, dear. A job beautifully done,' said Mrs Bruton, reappearing. 'No, not that one.' She neatly removed it from Ursula's hand, and picked out a much larger hat with a sweeping brim in a shade of café-au-lait, then poised it carefully on top of her head, using two long hat pins to secure it into place, making a fetching frame for her face. Then she put on the long, cashmere jacket with striking mother-of-pearl buttons that matched her skirt. It all formed a very stylish outfit.

Ursula looked around to check that she had packed all Mrs Bruton's possessions. 'Does that clock belong to you or the hotel?' Ursula pointed to a small one sitting on the bedside table.

'That is mine. My goodness, look at the time, midday already. Now, I am feeling much better, we will not mention again the matter which I told you about this morning. But I feel in need of a diversion. Why don't we have luncheon here and then visit the menagerie I have heard so much about. I would love to see the animals.'

Ursula was taken aback. That would mean it was unlikely she could keep her appointment with Jackman. But Mrs Bruton was her employer and she needed to keep her job. Also there was no doubt the woman had been very upset earlier. Ursula remembered the times she had been asked to accompany her on various enjoyable expeditions when she had been treated generously.

'Why don't you go to the dining room while I speak to the concierge and arrange for your luggage to be sent to Wilton Crescent.'

Mrs Bruton immediately looked happier.

The concierge was very helpful. 'We hope Mrs Bruton has enjoyed herself at Brown's Hotel, we are sorry to see her leave.'

Ursula assured him Mrs Bruton had been very satisfied with her visit and while he made the arrangements for the luggage, she took the opportunity to write a note on the hotel paper. It required a little thought. Once finished, she addressed it and asked the concierge if the postal system would manage to deliver it before three o'clock.

It appeared the late morning post had just been collected. So Ursula arranged for delivery by a messenger. She had just enough left over from the money Jackman had given her to cover the cost.

'I wondered what was taking you so long,' Mrs Bruton said, appearing at her side. 'Is there any difficulty with the luggage?'

'No, all is arranged.'

'And I have asked for a table. Come along.'

As they sat down, Ursula caught sight of a familiar-looking piece of headgear. 'Why, surely that is Mrs Trenchard,' she said as the waiter unfolded her napkin and spread it on her lap. 'I remember that hat from your tea party. I wondered how many birds had donated their feathers for its decoration. I'm glad to see her here, it must mean that her husband has recovered.'

Mrs Bruton looked round. At the same moment the woman turned and Ursula saw it was someone quite different.

'Fancy mistaking her in that way,' said Ursula in a light tone. 'I must learn to look at faces before making an identification. But it was a remarkable hat, and a remarkable afternoon,' she added.

But Mrs Bruton was securing the attention of a waiter and asking for a jug of water on their table. 'You always have to ask for anything that is free,' she said to Ursula as he hurried to carry out her command.

'In America glasses of water are served even before an order is taken.'

'I think I should like to visit there,' Mrs Bruton said. 'It seems a most interesting place.' Then she grew serious. 'I am afraid, Ursula, I shall have to ask you to give up your work at *Maison Rose*.'

Though she had been half expecting some such request, it still came as a shock. But her first loyalty must be to Mrs Bruton.

'Of course,' she said lightly but even as she said it, she wondered how easy it would be to find another part-time job.

Chapter Thirty-Four

The door of the police station slammed shut behind her and Rachel was left standing on Marylebone Lane. After the dark of her overnight cell, the brightness of the day was blinding. All around was mid-morning bustle but all she was conscious of was the prison smell that had soaked through to her central core, an odour of rank bodies, neglected dirt, and a despair compounded of ignorance, aggression and hate. She felt she was now marked as clearly as if she had a sign round her neck as 'criminal', a 'jail bird'.

John placed his arm around her shoulders and held her tightly. 'Let's get you home, dearest. My motor is just down here.' He guided her away from the police station.

Anger boiled in her. An anger so intense she was incapable of words.

She pushed away John's arm as he tried to help her into the passenger seat and sat, her face as set as a stone buddha's as he swung the starting handle. The vehicle backfired with a jerk and Rachel grabbed at the side door. It was the only movement she made until they pulled up outside her building. Then she jumped down and was inside before the engine was switched off.

Martha rushed to her. 'Oh, my precious!' she cried. 'They have let you go.'

Rachel pushed past her outstretched arms and screamed, 'A bath, I need a bath. I must have a bath.' She discarded clothes as she went through to her bedroom, Martha picking them up after her. John, without his goggles, driving coat and helmet, sat uneasily in the living room, his expression worried.

Half an hour later Rachel emerged wearing a dressing gown tied tightly around her waist, and rubbing wet hair with a clean towel. She stopped as she saw John.

'I shall never forgive you,' she said, her voice tight with anger.

'What for? For asking my father to help get you out of prison?' He tried to draw her into his arms.

She pulled back. 'Just because he's a duke! All he has to do is snap his fingers and that vile inspector decides I should be freed. How many dukes are there in England?'

'What does it matter?'

'Thirty! That's all. And how much of England do they own?'

'I don't know.'

'I expect a goodly slice of London is your father's as well as acres of land elsewhere. He has power. I have none. None! I should never have been arrested. Where was the evidence?' She struggled to keep her voice from breaking.

'That is what my father told the Commissioner of Police. He said it was a miscarriage of justice that had to be corrected.'

She ignored this. 'I achieved my law degree with honours. But I am not allowed to practice. Why? Because I'm a woman. Your father has done nothing but be born in the right cradle and yet what he says goes.'

'Dearest, I know how frustrating it is for you …'

'How dare you call it frustrating!' Rachel threw away the towel, her half-dried hair falling about her shoulders. 'Women have spent decades battling for the vote. Without it we will never have equality.' She wrapped her arms around her body and paced up and down the room, an angry energy coming off her like electricity. 'The Liberals were supposed to support our cause; now Mrs Pankhurst says they are terrified that if we get the vote, it'll mean men's wages will be forced down! As if we would not want to earn, job for job, the same as they do. Can you believe such twisted thinking?' She caught hold of thick strands of her hair and pulled at them as though they could be torn from her head.

'Mrs Pankhurst says that our suffrage battle isn't getting us anywhere and it is time for deeds, not words. Without equality, without an equal moral code for men and women, half the human race – that's we women – will be fair game for men to continue treating viciously. So now it is time for us to turn ourselves into an army, use intimidation and violence, force Parliament to recognise our rights.' She flung out her arms, her voice triumphant.

John stared as though seeing her for the first time.

Rachel dropped into a chair. 'Oh God, John, I'm just so tired and so angry I don't know what I'm saying.'

'Sounds to me as though you aren't having any difficulty.' He sounded halfway between admiration and despair.

'I'm amazed your father didn't refuse to have anything to do with rescuing me from that brute of an inspector. Didn't he tell you to have nothing to do with a criminal such as I? That he couldn't sully his name with such a sordid matter?'

He dropped down beside her and caught up her hand. 'I told him I love you. That you are the most wonderful girl in the world.'

She looked into his eyes, their gaze fastened passionately on hers, and for the first time felt guilty. He was such an innocent. What did he understand about what drove her? What had he actually told his father, that so-powerful duke? Surely she had to be grateful to be freed from that vile cell? She couldn't bear to think of Alice, suffering weeks and months in such conditions.

What did her own freedom mean? Was she now bound to John? Or should she make him understand they could not have a future together?

Martha entered. 'Mail has come, late again; that postman needs a rocket put under him. Just the one letter.'

Rachel took it, didn't recognise the writing and slipped it into her pocket. 'Martha, why haven't you got your coat and hat on? It's time you left for your Sunday visit to your sister.'

'With you only just out of that prison? I must prepare a luncheon for you both. Sister can wait.'

'Nonsense, John and I can find something to eat without your help. Off you go now.' Rachel rose and planted a kiss on her maid's cheek. 'I'm fine.'

Martha gave her a searching look, then capitulated. 'I'll be back around six o'clock. And what would your dear mother say to see you entertaining a young man in your dressing gown? You're not even affianced.'

'Oh, I think we are, Martha,' said John. 'At least, I hope we are.' He looked across at Rachel. 'I told my father that you were to be my wife.'

Irritation fought with a rising passion in Rachel. 'Now go along, I can get dressed without your help,' she said to Martha. 'I'll see you this evening.'

As the door closed behind her maid, Rachel turned to John. 'Let's forget about the future,' she said, her voice now warm, intimate. 'Instead of me getting dressed, how about you undressing?'

A little while later she turned to him in bed. 'How could Alice return to that brute, Joshua, after finding love with Daniel? I could never have done that.'

He smiled into her eyes and drew his hand through the shining hair spread over the pillow. 'Then you do love me!'

She smiled back but laid a finger on his lips, 'How could I not? Now, I'm hungry, let's see what food's about.'

She slipped out of bed and drew her dressing gown on again, then took out the envelope that had arrived that morning and opened it.

'How strange; it's from Millie, Alice's maid. It doesn't seem to make any sense.' She handed the letter to him.

'Dear Miss Fentiman,' he read out loud. 'I am with the menagerie circus, I have no choice. But you could give me choice. I know things. You need to see me. Millie.' He gave Rachel back the piece of paper. 'It's a schoolgirl's hand, look how carefully she forms her letters.'

'I'm looking at what she's saying. Does it sound like blackmail to you? "I know things"?'

'What could she know?' he asked.

Rachel didn't answer; she was too busy dressing.

★ ★ ★

An hour or so later, Rachel and John were at the menagerie and asking for Millie. They were sent to the area behind the circus tent, where there were a number of travelling wagons.

Millie saw them approaching and waved. She was sitting on the steps of one of the caravans, wearing some sort of uniform; Rachel had noticed other circus and menagerie staff dressed in brown tunics and trousers or skirts, all trimmed with flashes of red.

Rachel looked at her sister's ex-maid searchingly as the girl came towards them. Did she know something?

'You got my note,' said Millie.

She seemed taller than Rachel remembered and carried herself with a new confidence.

'What are you doing here?' asked Rachel bluntly. She'd never particularly liked Millie; thought she was untrustworthy and sly. But Alice said she was loyal and was very fond of her. 'What do you want?'

Beside her Rachel could feel John looking around, interested in everything that was going on. There was a great deal of activity. Men, dressed in workmanlike gear, were carrying items of equipment about; all seemed to be heading for the big, round tent that stood to one side of the menagerie.

'Is Mrs Peters out of prison yet?'

The question struck Rachel almost like a physical blow. She herself was free but her poor sister was still incarcerated in Holloway gaol.

'I am afraid she isn't.' Rachel dragged Millie's note out of her pocket and held it out. 'What do you mean, you "know things"? And why do I need to see you?'

Millie's confidence immediately wavered. She looked down at the ground and kicked at a small pebble. 'I dunno, really.' Then she looked up at Rachel and seemed to gather courage. 'I've learned things here. I've made all sorts of costumes; Ma says I've a real gift for design.'

'Ma?'

'She and Pa run this whole show. Thomas Jackman brought me here; he saved me from an awful fate worse than death,' she said with dramatic emphasis.

'I don't know what you are talking about, Millie. I would like you to get to the point.'

John put his hand on Rachel's shoulder. 'The thing is, Millie, Miss Fentiman found it difficult to understand what it is you want from her. She even felt ...'

Rachel shook herself free. 'The thing is, Millie, the stories I hear about what went on between you and Joshua Peters after my sister left him make me reluctant to give you any help, if that is what you want.'

Millie coloured but looked straight at Rachel. 'I could say he left me no choice. And, yes, that's what happened. I had no choice.'

'We women have to fight for our choices.' Rachel looked around at the busy scene again. She had no desire to know what had happened to Millie, she only wanted to get to the bottom of the girl's note. Was it, she wondered for the first time, that poor education had meant Millie hadn't been able to find the right words? 'You seem to have found something of a home here.'

'It's all ending. Soon they'll be packing up and on their way to winter quarters in the north.'

'So you want me to give you a job.'

Millie kicked at another pebble. 'It's not just that I can be a very good lady's maid – Mrs Peters will say I gave every satisfaction – I can design and sew costumes now.'

'Circus costumes!'

'But I can make your sort of clothes, I have the skills.' Millie clutched at the other girl's sleeve.

Rachel felt an instant repulsion followed almost immediately by guilt. What was it that she herself was fighting for? What was the battle that lay behind every action she had taken since she had left Manchester University and particularly in the last few months? 'We women,' she had said to Millie only a few minutes ago, admitting her into the sisterhood.

She straightened up. 'You must join the fight for women's suffrage. Once we have that, doors will open, we will have equality with men. Then you will have any number of choices laid before you.'

Millie looked astonished. 'Women's what?'

'Suffrage. The vote! It will empower us.' Rachel yanked out a notebook and pencil from her bag. 'You say the circus is going up north. I will give you Emmeline Pankhurst's address in Manchester. She will find you a job and you can make uniforms for all us suffrage fighters. I will write and tell her you will be getting in touch. She will inspire you, Millie. She inspires all women.' She tore the page out of the notebook and handed it over.

Millie looked at it suspiciously.

At that moment two uniformed attendants rushed by saying, 'Come on, time to get the show under way. You're on Aisle C today, Millie.'

The piece of paper was scrunched into a pocket. 'Got to go now. But, thanks, Miss Fentiman. And you'll let me know when Mrs Peters comes out of prison? She'll need a maid.'

Then she was gone.

Rachel went over to where John was inspecting an item of machinery. 'It's a generator,' he said, wiping oil off his hand with a handkerchief. 'Haven't seen one like this for years. I suppose they can't afford anything more up to date.'

Rachel slipped her hand through his arm. 'Come on, we're finished here.'

'Did you get what you wanted out of the girl?'

Rachel thought for a moment. 'I'm not sure there was anything to get. But I may have enlisted a new worker for Emmeline's Women's Army.'

Chapter Thirty-Five

Brown's doorman whistled up a hansom cab for Mrs Bruton and Ursula.

'You see,' said Mrs Bruton, placing hand on Ursula's knee as they pulled away from the hotel's main door, 'I could not, really could not, bear anyone around me who was in contact with, with …' her voice trailed away for a moment or two; then she seemed to recover herself. 'I realise, my dear Ursula, that the loss of the additional pay you have been earning at *Maison Rose* may cause you embarrassment …'

Ursula could not prevent herself shifting a little in the confined space.

'… I shall be happy,' Mrs Bruton continued smoothly, 'to see if I can find amongst my acquaintances someone who requires the services of a person so highly qualified as yourself. And perhaps,' she gave a short, judicious pause before adding, 'perhaps I myself may be able to raise your wages a modicum. My stepson is due to visit again shortly, I shall ask him if my finances could stand the additional outlay.'

'That would be very good of you,' murmured Ursula, wondering a little at Mrs Bruton's sudden wish to discuss her financial situation with the stepson she had previously shown herself to dislike, even to be slightly afraid of. 'And I can apply to the employment agencies I contacted on my arrival in London; they may well have details of a part-time post for which I could be suitable. After all, I think *Maison Rose* will give me a good reference.'

Or would the count feel he was within his rights to withhold such a document since she would be giving him so little notice?

'But let us forget such matters for this afternoon,' Mrs Bruton went on. 'I hope you enjoyed your lunch?' she added pleasantly. Then, taking Ursula's agreement for granted, said, 'I have been wishing to visit the menagerie for some little time. Being able to see all those fierce animals at such close quarters, what a thrill!' She gave a little shiver.

The brightness of the morning had given way to an overcast, chilly afternoon. Ursula appreciated the warmth of her coat and wondered whether visiting the menagerie would mean that they would see Millie. Now there was someone whose financial position was much worse than hers.

For once traffic was not slowing their progress and sooner than Ursula would have thought possible, the cab had reached their destination. She climbed down, then offered her hand to aid Mrs Bruton's descent. The flash of a suede bootee suggested that her employer had not perhaps considered what the conditions underfoot might be like.

Ursula once again found herself transfixed by the sight of the mighty carved screen.

'Oh, my,' said Mrs Bruton, similarly overawed by the variety of wild animals it carried. There came the roar of several lions and the breeze suddenly brought a strong whiff of the beasts themselves.

'There is a marvellously dressed lion-tamer who gives performances from time to time,' said Ursula.

Mrs Bruton looked expectant. 'Will we see him with the lions this afternoon? That would be wonderful.'

'Would you like me to get the tickets?' It was a small service Ursula had performed when she had been out with Mrs Bruton. She had grown used to her employer producing a well-filled purse from whichever handbag she carried that day. The one she had chosen to accompany her cashmere outfit was of a matching blonde suede and large enough to hold several bulging purses.

Mrs Bruton smiled. 'I think I would enjoy performing that small task myself this afternoon,' she said. 'Look, there is a man selling sweeties. Do go and buy us some.' She took out her purse and gave Ursula a sixpenny piece. The morning's upsetting event when Madame Rose's true nature was revealed seemed to have been forgotten. Once again Mrs Bruton was her quietly assertive self.

Ursula went over to the sweet seller and joined a small queue. Soon she was supplied with a paper cone stuffed with striped, mint-flavoured humbugs.

There were not nearly as many people queuing up for the menagerie as there had been at Ursula's first visit. She couldn't help remembering Jackman and her reaction to the realisation that he was actually involved in following a couple: how cross she had been; she had seen Jackman as using her as camouflage for his main purpose.

That afternoon, though, had been the first time she had seen Alice and Rachel. How tremendous Rachel had been in saving Alice from being photographed with Daniel, leaping on to the little table and addressing the crowd with her message of freedom for the animals and for women, and what a delight it had been to find her on Mrs Bruton's doorstep for the tea party.

At that precise moment, Ursula saw disappearing round the corner of the menagerie the back view of a girl that looked exactly like Rachel, wearing a beret on long dark hair. Except it could not be her because Rachel had been arrested by Inspector Drummond and was now in prison – as was Alice.

The afternoon seemed to darken further. So much had happened since that first visit and somewhere there was a murderer handing out doses of cyanide poisoning. Ursula shivered. For an instant she wished Jackman was with her.

She joined Mrs Bruton, who had reached the top of the ticket office queue and asked whether there would be a show in the menagerie that afternoon.

'I'm sorry, Madam, not today. But Arturo the Magnificent is just about to perform in the Big Top. Would you like to buy tickets for that?'

'Shall we see the other animals there?'

'Bareback riding and jugglers and trapeze artists will all be on display. And you could buy a combined ticket that would admit you to the menagerie after the circus performance.'

'Why, that would be perfect,' said Mrs Bruton, handing over money. 'There,' she said to Ursula, slipping a hand into her secretary's arm. 'We should be beautifully entertained. I have long wanted to see a show with lions.'

As they entered the big tent, the bareback rider Ursula had seen practising when she'd visited Millie was riding round the ring, standing on the broad back of her grey pony, the light coat shining like a polished pearl, the girl's bright red and gold leotard jewel-like.

An attendant indicated a pair of seats half way up the ramp but Mrs Bruton headed for the top rows, all empty, and took two at one end, from where they had a clear view of the ring. As they settled themselves, the rider performed a series of somersaults as her horse continued to circle the ring.

Loud applause greeted the girl as she slipped on to her mount and waved; a final circuit of the ring and she rode out of the arena.

Two clowns chased each other around the ring. A rattle of metal heralded the erection of a run between the menagerie and the circus arena. It looked as though the next act would be the lions.

Mrs Bruton sat very erect, clutching her handbag and looking a little awkward. 'Shall I look after that for you?' Ursula asked.

'Why, no, thank you, I am quite happy.' She gave a little sneeze. 'I hope I am not coming down with a cold.' She opened the bag, took out a handkerchief and delicately applied it to her nose. 'We have an excellent view from here, have we not?'

Indeed they could see right across the ring and there, standing in an entrance dressed in the same uniform as the other attendants, was Millie. She was directing some late-comers to seats. Ursula opened the cone of humbugs, offered one to Mrs Bruton and took one herself. They sat contentedly sucking on the sweets.

From the direction of the menagerie came the growl of a lion.

Working rapidly in the centre of the ring while the clowns kept the audience entertained, circus workers finished erecting a metal cage and into it strode Arturo the Magnificent, his outfit every bit as colourful and stylish as when Ursula had first seen him. He cracked his whip and along the caged runway loped the first lion, his large head bearing a wonderful mane of thick hair. Another crack of the whip and the lion leaped on to a circular stand decorated with streaks of jagged red. In came another one, his hair not quite so exuberant. The whip cracked and he, too, mounted a stand. A lioness followed, sleeker and younger-looking. A third crack of the whip and she mounted the last of the stands.

Arturo circled the beautifully balanced trio, raised his whip with a flourish and the three lions lifted their front legs, waving their paws to maintain their balance. For a moment there was silence. Ursula was mesmerised.

Suddenly the lions turned their heads, as though seeking something beyond the cage. As applause broke out, the first lion jumped down and stalked round. Arturo cracked his whip, ordering him back, but now the other two followed. The applause died down and the audience held its collective breath as the trainer tried to shoo his animals back into place, cracking the whip so it zinged right beside each without touching them.

In the silence all could hear the lions growling fiercely, then they advanced on the trainer. He backed towards the metal frame of the cage.

Ursula, appalled at the tragedy that seemed about to happen, glanced at Mrs Bruton, and saw her snatch something from her mouth, secreting it in her hand.

It wasn't a humbug. Ursula gasped and tried to wrench it from Mrs Bruton. 'That's your dog's whistle! It's you who've upset the lions. Why?'

Mrs Bruton said nothing, her mouth a hard line. She pushed at Ursula's shoulder. With the unexpectedness of the move, she found herself thrown down along the bench.

Astonished, she tried to right herself. Then she saw Mrs Bruton open her large handbag and remove a wicked-looking syringe. Horror surged through Ursula.

It was no use calling for help. The audience was screaming as the lions advanced on their trainer, their growls increasing in volume and aggression. Attendants were shouting; Arturo was cracking his whip. And the smell of fear pervaded everywhere.

Mrs Bruton lunged forward but her jacket caught on a protruding nail and for a moment it held her back. Ursula rolled off the bench and landed on her back along the slats supporting the seating. Mrs Bruton pulled away from the nail, ripping her jacket, and lunged forward again, aiming the syringe at the base of Ursula's throat.

This was how Arthur Pond had died, Ursula knew it without any doubt. Somehow she managed to jerk up her own handbag as a shield and caught the syringe needle in its stout leather.

Mrs Bruton gave a determined grunt, pulled the needle clear and drew back her arm for another assault.

Ursula kicked out, trying to thrust the woman away, but the confining material of her skirt destroyed the power of her legs. Her situation seemed hopeless. There was the bitter taste of fear in her mouth, and her mind was paralysed. A picture of Albert Pond's contorted face and body flashed before her. With a despairing effort she managed to roll herself down to the next level of the seating.

From the menagerie squawks of parakeets and excited monkey shrieks joined with the lions' roars. Mrs Bruton produced a series of rapid grunts that could hardly be heard above the general clamour and managed to crawl down to the bench immediately above Ursula. Another attempt to inject the syringe into any part of her victim that she could reach was being launched.

Recklessly, with both hands, Ursula grabbed Mrs Bruton's wrist and tried to force her to drop the lethal weapon. Then cried out as the woman bent her head and bit her wrist, drawing blood.

The teeth were sharp, the pain was intense but Ursula held on, pulling herself up from the slats, amazed at Mrs Bruton's strength. She dared not let go of the woman's wrist and at any moment that needle could connect with some part of her body and inject the deadly cyanide into her bloodstream.

Mrs Bruton's free hand fumbled for her handbag. If she managed to hit Ursula's head then the battle would be over.

'Oh, no, you don't!' said a male voice and the woman suddenly slumped down, unconscious.

Ursula couldn't understand that death was no longer poised above her. Her hands had to be prised away from her assailant's wrist. Then she started shaking.

'It seems I was just in time,' said Jackman cheerily. He picked up the cyanide-loaded syringe with great care and returned it to Mrs Bruton's handbag then felt for her pulse. 'She'll live,' he said after a moment. Then he turned his attention to Ursula. 'Are you all right?'

She looked up at him, still trying to take in the way he'd appeared from nowhere. 'I'm … I'm fine …' she stuttered, wrapping her arms around herself, trying to realise that the danger was over and she was safe. Jackman slid down beside her and gently bent her head on to her knees.

'Deep breaths,' he said calmly and massaged her shoulders.

Gradually the shakes subsided.

Shouts from the circus ring rose along with loud cracks of the whip. Arturo the Magnificent had brought his lions back under control. They were prowling the cage but seemed more puzzled than aggressive. More cracks of the whip and shouts returned them to their stands.

Ursula sat up straight and looked gratefully at Jackman. 'Where did you spring from?'

He glanced at Mrs Bruton's recumbent body. 'Don't have to worry about her for a bit,' he said, then turned to Ursula again, his eyes assessing her condition. 'You sent me a note this morning that said the two of you were to come here this afternoon so I wasn't to call on you at Mrs Maple's until this evening. I decided to meet you here instead.'

Ursula rubbed at her forehead, still unable to believe she was alive. She looked at the comatose Mrs Bruton. 'What did you hit her with?'

He reached into his jacket and brought out an efficient-looking revolver. 'Lucky I thought to bring it.'

Jackson was not a person who allowed luck to play an important part in his dealings with life. Ursula thought back to the note she had sent. 'Certain things have occurred that suggest I might have identified Albert Pond's killer,' she had written. But she had never suspected Mrs Bruton's reason for suggesting a visit to the menagerie and she had never been so glad to see anyone in her life than Jackman that afternoon.

'Should we call the police?'

'Oh, I think so. If the struggle I interrupted means what I think, that syringe contains cyanide.'

Ursula shuddered. 'She killed Albert and Mr Peters. If we tell Inspector Drummond that, he has to release Alice.'

'I presume you know why they were blackmailing your employer?'

'I have a theory.'

Chapter Thirty-Six

It was easy enough, thought Ursula, to say she had a theory but would it convince Jackman? She watched him use strong arms to pull the unconscious Mrs Bruton up from the slats and arrange her body in a sitting position.

They were high above the rest of the audience. Attention had been so fixed on what was happening in the lion cage with Arturo the Magnificent, even those people sitting directly across the ring from herself and Mrs Bruton did not seem to have noticed their struggle. Instead, everyone's eyes were on the battle Arturo was having to bring his lions back under control.

Jackman gave a series of small slaps to Mrs Bruton's face. Her head lolled backwards and sideways. He lifted one of her eyelids and checked her pupils.

'Will she be OK?' Ursula asked. The woman had tried to kill her but she did not want Jackman to have taken her life. She was glad the woman's eyes were closed; the look of hate Mrs Bruton had given her as she tried to insert her syringe into Ursula's flesh had been shocking.

'She's just out for the count. Help me take her outside, then we can send for the police.' He picked up the handbag that contained the syringe.

With one of Mrs Bruton's arms across each of their shoulders, Ursula and Jackman manhandled her unconscious body down the steps and out of the circus tent, her head lolling from side to side, their progress noted by no more than a few of the audience. Ursula caught a 'Disgraceful, she's drunk,' comment as they went.

Outside, Jackman steered them round the circus tent towards the encampment area. One of the menagerie workers came up and asked if they needed a hand.

'I've got this woman under arrest,' said Jackman. 'She tried to kill Miss Grandison.' He indicated Ursula. 'Had to knock her out.'

The worker, a small man with a droopy moustache and lank black hair, dressed in brown dungarees with a large white and red checked handkerchief round his neck, whistled. 'You don't say! I better get Ma.' He ran off towards the caravan site.

Jackman and Ursula dragged Mrs Bruton in the same direction. Then Ma appeared and took control.

'Those lions! They was gone crazy! You know why?'

'I think she used a dog whistle,' said Ursula. 'That's what it looked like and I know she has one. It's in her handbag.'

'Along with the syringe she tried to kill Miss Grandison with.' Jackman tucked the bag more securely beneath his arm.'

Ma stood with her hands on her hips. 'What we do with 'er, eh?'

Mrs Bruton, showing no signs of regaining consciousness, was still suspended between Jackman and Ursula.

'Over other side is empty van,' said Ma. 'You take her there, yes? Willie help.'

'Sure,' said the droopy moustached worker.

'Better if he went for the police,' said Jackman. 'You all right?' he asked Ursula, still helping to support the unconscious woman.

She nodded but her legs didn't feel as though they could keep her upright much longer. Shock was beginning to turn her muscles to water.

'You look about collapse,' said Ma. She put two fingers in her mouth and gave a long, high-pitched whistle.

Two more workers dressed in brown overalls appeared.

'This woman 'ere needs go that van there.' Ma pointed to a somewhat dilapidated vehicle at the back of the little circle of caravans. 'Store animal feed,' she added. 'Feed low now, lots of room for 'er. Fetch rope, tie her,' she said to one of the workers. 'Willie, you go police station, fetch constable.'

'I think I'd better write a note to Inspector Drummond of the Marylebone Station,' said Jackman. 'They can send it on.'

Ursula admired the skill with which Ma organised them all. In no time it seemed Mrs Bruton was incarcerated in the old van, her wrists and ankles tied and the door fastened with a padlock; Jackman had been provided with pen and paper; Willie had been sent off with his note to the police station; and Ursula had been made to stretch out in Ma and Pa's luxurious caravan with her feet up and a glass of Ma's 'special tonic' to revive her.

'Is old, old recipe I always 'ave. Would bring life to Egyptian mummy.'

The drink was slightly bitter, with a complex mixture of flavours that really did seem to make Ursula feel she was no longer going to keel over.

'What did you say in your note to Inspector Drummond?' she asked Jackman, sitting up, swinging her legs down to the ground and trying to neaten her hair into its usual knot. It had come loose in her fight with Mrs Bruton and her hat was still somewhere up where they'd been sitting. Beside everything else that had happened, it didn't seem to matter. Only Jackman was there to see what a mess she was in. Ma had gone, she said, to check on Pa and the lions and tell him about the dog whistle. 'Beasts never act so before,' she said as she left.

Jackman gave Ursula a smug look, sat opposite her and put his bowler beside him. How, Ursula wondered, had he managed to keep hold of his hat through everything that had happened?

'I told Drummond that we had the murderer of Joshua Peters and Albert Pond under lock and key, and suggested he get over here pronto and take her into custody. And that he could release Miss Fentiman and arrange the same for Mrs Peters.'

'It seems that Rachel has already been released. While we were waiting for tickets into the menagerie, I saw her. She was with Lord John. And it's no use looking at me like that, I have no idea why she was allowed to go.'

Jackman ran a hand through his hair. 'Lord John, isn't his father some high-up aristocrat?'

'A duke, I believe.'

'Bet he's used him to pull rank. Gone to the Commissioner of Police, probably. Those toffs all stick together. My, Drummond will be mad as anything. And now I'm presenting him with the real killer.' His smug look suddenly disappeared. 'What is Rachel Fentiman doing here? Is she in league with your Mrs Bruton?' He got up and went to look out of the door as though she might pass by.

'Honestly, Thomas, can't you give up on the idea that Rachel
Fentiman murdered her brother-in-law?'

'It seems a good deal more likely than that Mrs Bruton should.'

'And Alfred Pond?'

He shrugged, came and sat down again. 'Drummond said he
had a witness that saw the Fentiman woman calling on Pond's
house just before he was killed.'

'Ah, now that's what put me on to Mrs Bruton. I was packing up her clothes this morning,' Ursula paused for a moment.
It seemed so much longer ago she had been with her employer
in Brown's Hotel, acting as her maid. 'And I found a cream beret,
identical to the one Rachel Fentiman has. Rachel was wearing
it when she came to Mrs Bruton's tea party. She removed it from
my hand. It set me to thinking. If someone saw a woman wearing a cream beret over dark hair hanging loose, in the vicinity of
Albert Pond's building on Friday afternoon, it could very well be
taken as a description of Rachel Fentiman. She always wore that
beret. It was like an epiphany. That's why I wrote that note.

'What clinched it for me was that, while we were having lunch,
I mistook a woman for Mrs Trenchard because she wore a hat
almost identical to the one she wore at that same tea party. And
I said something about how one had to be careful to look at the
face rather than the hat. Stupid of me, it must have convinced
Mrs Bruton I was on to her.'

'Why did she have a cyanide-loaded syringe in her handbag?'

Ursula had been giving some thought to just this question.
'She wouldn't have wanted me to find the syringe or the cyanide
while I was doing her packing, or Enid doing the unpacking.
Much safer to place both in her handbag. She probably had them
carefully wrapped or in some sort of case. Then, having seen
me with the beret, she decided she had to be prepared to deal
with me if I really did suspect her. She could have made sure the
syringe was to hand after she sent me off to arrange with the
concierge for her baggage to be taken to Wilton Crescent.'

'She kept the syringe loaded?'

'Isn't your revolver?'

'But that has a safety catch.'

'It's a large syringe, probably needs a firm hand to inject
its contents. After I'd made my remark about thinking I saw
Mrs Trenchard because of a similar hat, Mrs Bruton called over

the waiter and made a fuss about needing water. I think that was a deliberate attempt to divert my attention away from hats. And I think that was when my death warrant was signed.'

Jackman didn't seem convinced. 'Is she that quick a thinker?'

Ursula nodded and stretched her legs, thinking how much stronger they now felt. 'Oh, I think so. All along she has behaved as though all it needed was one action to solve her problem. Sending Joshua Peters the poisoned chocolates would remove her blackmailer. It would have seemed the perfect crime. She had no connection with him that anyone knew about, so why should she know of his love for cherry liqueur chocolates?'

'Just as she thinks she's in the clear, Albert contacts her?'

'Exactly. Another problem to be removed and so she sets another plan in motion.'

'Surely he can't have told her where he lived!'

'No, I'm sure he was far too canny. I reckon he arranged initially for them to meet in some public place and I think it was sheer luck, or Albert's bad luck, that one morning she saw him enter *Maison Rose*. Her rooms at Brown's Hotel overlook their building. She is then all ready to follow him when he emerges.'

Jackman looked sceptical. 'Blackmailers very seldom reveal themselves to their victims. All along the fact that Peters met his death because of his fondness for cherry liqueurs meant that his killer knew him.' He thought for a moment. 'If, therefore, Mrs Bruton knew who her blackmailer was, it wouldn't have been a big step to identify Albert as the one carrying on the blackmail after Peters' death.'

'As I said, she is a very quick-witted woman. Far cleverer than she looks. She has built herself a valuable portfolio of properties she rents out. They are yielding her a sizeable income on top of whatever her husband provided for her.'

'So, however she does it, she identifies where Albert is living and immediately decides to murder him?'

'Yes, I think that is exactly what happened. The poisoned chocolates wouldn't work with him, nor would any other comestible, Albert would be far too suspicious of anything he hadn't acquired himself. Mrs Bruton, a long time ago, worked with Mrs Maple in a hospital. She would have known all about syringes and injections. I think she also planned to incriminate Rachel Fentiman by acquiring a beret identical to hers. She would have remembered her from the tea party. She is very friendly with Rachel's aunt, Mrs Trenchard, and after Joshua Peters' appearance in her drawing room, the Fentiman sisters will have been a subject of conversation. Rachel and Mrs Bruton are about the same height and have the same coloured hair. Wearing her very plainest outfit and with the beret worn over her hair loose, from the back she could easily have been mistaken for her. And as far as the police were concerned, Rachel might easily have been being blackmailed by Albert Pond.'

Ursula gave Jackman a severe look. 'After all, you were convinced that Rachel could have killed her brother-in-law, and, even if she hadn't, was capable of killing Pond to save her sister.'

He made a graceful gesture that said she had a point, then gave her a sharp look. 'But what could Peters and Pond, what a devilish pair they made, what could they have been blackmailing Mrs Bruton over?'

Ursula laced her fingers together and stretched her arms out, knowing she had come to the hardest part of her theory. 'This is where I have no evidence, at least, not yet. Remember that tea party where Joshua Peters turned up?'

Jackman nodded. 'He had me with him, waiting outside. He left that party looking as though he'd been mauled by a wild animal.'

Ursula smiled. 'At the time I thought Peters was acting strangely because he was so angry about the disappearance of his wife, and that Mrs Bruton was upset because he had ruined her party. But this morning she mentioned what a terrible fellow he was and I thought it was a little strange of her to bring that up then. But I remembered how shocked each of them had seemed, with Mrs Bruton going quite pale. What if they had recognised each other?'

'You mean, perhaps they had known each other a long time ago?'

Ursula nodded. 'And hadn't expected to meet again.'

'But why not say something? In such circumstances, wouldn't you comment, "Why, Joshua, how amazing that you should visit my tea party", and I would respond, perhaps, with: "How many years is it since we last met? And where was it?" Wouldn't that be how it would go?'

'Well, yes, except there could be a very good reason for not wanting their relationship to be known to any of the people at that tea party. Think of who was there: his sister-in-law, Rachel, and aunt-in-law. Mrs Trenchard, who has a wide circle of friends and moves in society.'

'And that is a good reason not to let them know you have met an old friend?'

Ursula took a deep breath. When this theory had first occurred to her, she had dismissed it as too nonsensical. Trying to respond naturally to Mrs Bruton's light chatter over lunch, though, she had found it coming back to her, and gradually it began to make sense. So much so that by the time the two of them were in the cab going to the menagerie, she could hardly behave in her normal manner. No doubt Mrs Bruton had noticed that as well.

'Suppose,' said Ursula slowly, 'Joshua Peters and Mrs Bruton had once been married to each other and they had never been divorced. That would have made both their subsequent marriages bigamous and invalid.'

'That's your theory?' Jackman sounded completely disbelieving.

Ursula hurried on: 'When Mrs Maple first suggested that Mrs Bruton might like me to work for her, she told me how she had had a tragic early life. Her husband had gone abroad almost immediately after they married, leaving her with child. Then the baby had died in childbirth and shortly afterwards she had heard that her husband had died. Well, when Mr Bruton came along and offered her a second chance of happiness, she might well have thought that she was free to marry again.'

'But didn't have a death certificate to prove it?'

'If the death had occurred abroad, perhaps one was too difficult to obtain, or perhaps she just didn't think she needed one.'

'And what about Peters? Didn't he even think to enquire whether the wife he'd abandoned was still alive?'

'Maybe he did and couldn't find any trace of her, so assumed she was dead.'

'But, wait a minute. How could Peters blackmail her? They were both in the same situation. Revealing hers would mean he had to reveal his.'

'At the time of the tea party, he had nothing to lose. Alice had walked out on him, and they had no issue. Revealing that their marriage had been illegal was not going to do him any harm. Whereas Mrs Bruton ...'

'Was not entitled to any of the comforts her second marriage had brought her! Her wealth could save his company.'

'Exactly!' Ursula said with a touch of triumph. 'There was a situation Peters could make money out of! If her stepson learned that her marriage with his father had not been legal, he would have stripped her of everything. I've met him and I have no doubt he'd do that.'

'What about the property portfolio?'

'Bought with money from sums her husband gave her to run the household on and provide her wardrobe. Wouldn't they be held to belong rightly to her husband?'

Jackman gave a slow nod. 'Leaving her with …?'

'As far as I know – nothing.'

Ursula did not expect Jackman to accept her theory straight away. Not without testing it from every angle, which was what he now proceeded to do, probing all its different aspects.

'You say Mrs Bruton from her hotel bedroom window could have seen Pond being ejected from *Maison Rose* and followed him. Had she ever met him before?'

'I don't know. But she would know it was Peters who was blackmailing her. After that tea party she would have got all his details out of Mrs Trenchard; with her inconsequential way of talking, Mrs Trenchard would not have noticed all she was giving away. I wouldn't then put it past her to go down to Peters' office in the docks to catch him unawares.'

'In his offices?' Jackman sounded disbelieving.

'I don't think so. With all the traffic, both human and vehicular, it would have been easy for her to wait in a hansom until he approached or left his office and encountered him that way. Albert could have come up while she was talking with him and she would have made sure she knew who he was. And she would never have forgotten that waistcoat.'

'And you really think that all this time she has been enjoying a bigamous marriage? Do you have any proof?'

'Thomas,' she cried. 'The only marriage certificate I've seen is the one for her union to Mr Bruton. It describes her state as 'spinster'. She has never mentioned she had a husband before Mr Bruton, dead or alive. Nor has she mentioned an offspring that died in childbirth. She has never talked of cyanide or of working in a hospital. What I know about her background comes from Mrs Maple. Please, you either have to accept or reject this theory as I've presented it.'

He looked slightly amused. 'Surely it is possible to question and look for further evidence? It's certainly going to be needed if we are to pursue a case against her.'

Exhausted, Ursula threw up her hands. 'At least admit that if my theory is right, Mrs Bruton would have known how fond Joshua Peters was of cherry liqueur chocolates!'

'Yes, I'll give you that. As far as Drummond is concerned, though, much will depend on how far Mrs Bruton is prepared to confess.'

'Did I hear my name?' The inspector appeared at the top of the caravan steps. 'I have been told this is where to find Ursula Grandison and Thomas Jackman.'

'You have it right. Good to see you, Drummond.' Jackman rose and offered his hand. The inspector, curly bowler tilted back on his head, a paisley silk kerchief carelessly tied around his neck, his yellow waistcoat almost a match for his hair, ignored the hand and instead removed his hat and tucked it underneath his arm.

'Now what's this I hear about apprehending the killer of Peters and Pond? I warn you, I am in no mood to hear airy-fairy theories without hard, cold evidence.'

Ursula left it to Jackman to present the case against Mrs Bruton. He was concise and lucid. Drummond heard him in silence, looking searchingly at Ursula as the battle with the cyanide-loaded syringe was described. She had a distinct impression that he gave little credence to what he was being told.

'Were there any witnesses to this encounter?'

'As Mr Jackman said, the top rows of the auditorium were empty apart from us and there was too much going on in the ring with the lions for anyone to pay any attention to two women having a fight.'

'Hmm. You have this syringe?

Jackman handed over Mrs Bruton's bag.

'And this woman is being held under lock and key? Then let's see what she has to say for herself.'

'She may not have recovered consciousness yet,' said Ursula.

'Let us find out.'

Jackman, Drummond and Ursula, followed by two large, uniformed policemen, went over to the van in which Mrs Bruton was being held.

Jackman unlocked the door and opened it. Mrs Bruton was revealed sitting neatly on a pile of hay. Nobody looking less like a murderer than this calm, well-dressed figure could be imagined.

'Oh,' she said, looking up. 'I am so pleased to see you. I have been wondering what I am doing here. Why, there are policemen! has something happened?' So innocent she sounded!

'Madam,' said Inspector Drummond. 'You are being accused of assaulting Miss Grandison here, indeed of attempting to murder her with a syringe of cyanide.'

Mrs Bruton looked astonished. 'Murder? Cyanide? Ursula, dearest, you cannot imagine I would want to do you any harm?'

'We have the syringe here in your handbag, together with the dog whistle you used to upset the lions,' Jackman said.

'Upset lions? Oh, dear, I would never want to do that. I do have a dog whistle, I kept it by me to remember my rascally Charlie, who I adored. I do sometimes carry it in my handbag.' Her face wore a sad, contemplative look; the look of a woman who had deeply loved her dog. 'As for a syringe, I know nothing about that. If there is such an item in my bag, it must have been put there without my knowledge.'

'I can show you my bruises,' Ursula said hopelessly. She could see that the inspector was very taken with this quietly spoken, well-behaved woman. Then she remembered a detail that might support her version of events.

'Inspector, I think you can see that Mrs Bruton's jacket is torn. That happened while she was trying to inject me with cyanide. The material caught on a nail.'

Mrs Bruton looked at the rip. 'Oh, dear, it's one of my favourites. Do you know, I don't remember how it happened! In fact, I don't remember anything from the moment I bought our tickets. Did you give me a draught of something, Ursula? Why, no, I think you, or someone, hit me with something very hard. There is an awful lump on my skull.' She felt the side of her head with a graceful gesture.

'Do you need medical attention?' asked Drummond.

'I think it would be as well. I might be suffering concussion. I know that can be serious. But what are you trying to accuse me of?'

'Murder,' said Jackman grimly.

Mrs Bruton gave a little screech, 'Murder? You can't be serious? Do you have witnesses?'

Inspector Drummond looked from Jackman to Ursula. Neither said anything.

'You see!' Mrs Bruton said simply. 'Can you really arrest me on the word of two persons who seem to have very little credibility? I am so disappointed in Miss Grandison. I shall have to check all my records most carefully now in case she has interfered with them.'

Ursula felt a slow burning anger gather in her. Surely the woman could not get away with this attitude? Surely the inspector would not believe that Jackman could have conjured up a syringe full of cyanide and deliberately put it in Mrs Bruton's handbag?

'I saw what happened.'

Ursula turned; Millie was standing behind them.

'I was on duty in the circus and I caught sight of these two women sitting right at the top, in the empty seating. Well, it seemed strange, so I looked more closely and saw this woman,' she gestured towards Mrs Bruton, 'get something out of her bag and put it to her mouth. Then the lions began to behave funny so I looked back at her and that's when I saw her take what looked like a syringe out of her handbag, big bag it was, and a big syringe as well, and she tried to stick it into Miss Grandison, here. I knew it was Miss Grandison because I recognised her coat.'

Ursula gave silent thanks that she had lent the garment to the girl.

'I was going to get someone to stop her,' continued Millie, 'only the audience was in such an uproar and we were all being told to help calm them because they were exciting the lions even more than what they already was.' She looked apologetically at Ursula. 'I reckoned you were able to take care of yourself. I did come looking for you after everything had quietened down, only you had both disappeared. I picked up your hat, though.' She handed it over to Ursula, who took it and found herself speechless.

'So, now you've got your witness,' said Jackman to the inspector.

'Surely you are not going to trust the word of a bitch like that?' For the first time Mrs Bruton's performance cracked.

'You'll all need to make statements,' said Inspector Drummond. 'And I'm taking you into custody, Mrs Burton, or whatever your name is. Officer, cuff her, take her to Marylebone station and put her in a cell.'

Mrs Bruton's eyes narrowed. 'You'll regret this, inspector. I know people. Your career will be finished.'

'We'll see about that. I'll be along shortly to question you. And, Jackman, you hand over that bag, together with its syringe, whistle and all. You and Miss Grandison can come with us to make your statements.'

'Wouldn't you prefer to do that in the morning rather than on Sunday evening?' said Jackman.

'Sunday? What's a Sunday when you're in His Majesty's Metropolitan Police?'

Glad as she was to see Mrs Bruton being taken off to a police cell, Ursula was full of aches and pains. She needed rest, and for the first time since arriving in England six months earlier, she longed for a cup of a tea.

Chapter Thirty-Seven

After they had signed their statements, Jackman insisted on escorting Ursula back to Mrs Maple's boarding house. Not only that, he hailed a hansom cab and overrode her objections.

'The case is solved. Drummond will have to release Alice now and my fee will be paid. Not that I have earned it, I shall insist it goes to you. After you receive it, you can repay me the cab fare.'

Ursula laughed. 'Oh, Thomas, sometimes it's difficult to take you seriously. You were the one who did all the leg work. The fee is yours.'

She couldn't help thinking, though, that she now had no job. She stroked a sleeve of her new coat, blessed the fact that it hadn't suffered in the fight with Mrs Bruton, but wished for a moment that its cost had been placed in a savings account.

'For a moment in that van, I thought Mrs Bruton was going to carry all before her. I told you she was a quick thinker. She must have put that story together the moment she came round from your bash on her head. So simple and so effective. I could see Drummond absorbing it like turkey does gravy. It was only after Millie said her piece that he wavered.'

'And so did she.'

'Do you think Drummond will search Mrs Bruton's luggage for the beret? Surely that will be another piece of evidence against her?'

Jackman put a hand on her shoulder. 'He may well be able to wear her down under interrogation. Right at the end she seemed to be crumbling.'

'But the journey to the police station will give her time to recover. I'm sorry I couldn't produce more hard evidence.'

His hand pressed a little harder and she found it comforting. 'No investigator could have had a better assistant. Without you, I would still be looking at Miss Rachel Fentiman for the part of murderer.'

'Or even Millie?' Ursula smiled at him. 'Let's face it, there wasn't a great deal of evidence against anyone, was there?'

'You know,' Jackman said after a moment or two, 'I'm thinking of asking you to work as an assistant to me. I can probably afford to pay you whatever you were earning with Mrs Bruton and maybe those *Maison Rose* people could keep you on. Maybe working together we could earn enough to afford a proper West End office.'

Before an astonished Ursula could respond, the cab arrived outside Mrs Maple's and Jackman handed Ursula down and paid the fare.

Meg opened the door to them, her face excited. 'You got company, miss. It's Mistress Alice's sister and ever such a nice young man. They are with Mrs Maple in her parlour and you're to go along there as soon as you arrive.'

Ursula's tiredness slipped away. She couldn't wait to find out how Rachel had been freed from gaol and what she'd been doing at the menagerie.

The moment she and Jackman entered the parlour, Rachel came and embraced Ursula. Lord John shook Jackman's hand. Mrs Maple said how pleased she was to see them both and went to get Meg to produce fresh tea.

'Before you ask,' said Rachel, releasing Ursula. 'John got his father to intervene on my behalf. I hated having a duke use his position like that but I have to admit that life in a police cell was dire.' She smiled at the young man. 'I think we're now engaged but I don't expect John will find it all beer and skittles.'

'Really, dearest, where do you get your language from?' said John, laughing.

Ursula sat down. 'Why did you go to the menagerie?'

Rachel went silent for a moment.

'She had a letter from that pretty girl at the circus,' said her fiancé.

'John, it's my story.'

He retired to the back of the room, leaning against Mrs Maple's desk, covered as usual with papers, and remained looking lovingly at Rachel. Ursula wondered how long he would be happy to be ordered about.

'Millie asked me to go and meet her, said I could change her life. I thought first of all she was trying to blackmail me but I think it was just she's unused to writing letters. It turned out that she wants to find another post as a lady's maid and thinks I could recommend her to someone.'

'Would your sister take her back, do you think?'

Rachel looked at Ursula and realisation dawned. 'You mean you've found out who murdered Joshua and Alice is going to be released?'

Ursula nodded. She turned to Jackman. 'You tell them.'

Before he could start, Mrs Maple entered, followed by Meg with a tray of tea.

Once cups had been passed around, Jackman detailed what had happened.

His audience looked stunned.

'Mrs Bruton?' said Rachel. 'The one who held the tea party that Joshua gate-crashed? You mean, that was when it all started?'

Ursula nodded. 'I worked most of it out this morning.'

'And still went to the menagerie with a murderer this afternoon,' muttered Jackman. 'Talk about taking your life in your hands.'

'The way you told it,' said Mrs Maple, putting her cup on to her desk, 'it sounded as though she could be clever enough to get away with it. Even when I knew her, all those years ago, she was a very smooth talker, always thought she was a bit above the rest of us. I suppose with a name like Eugenie she thought she could behave like an empress. We never called her that, though, she was known in the hospital as Jeannie. If it goes to court, she'll put on a good show.'

Jackman nodded. 'If she gets an experienced counsel, he'll make mincemeat of Millie, he'll trash her reputation. After he's finished with her, I wouldn't take a bet on any jury believing she'd actually witnessed Mrs Bruton attacking Miss Grandison.'

'And he can claim anyone can have a cream beret in their wardrobe,' said Rachel.

'A beret doesn't sound like Eugenie's style at all,' said Mrs Maple.

'You said you knew her?' said Jackman.

Mrs Maple nodded. 'A long time ago. We were nurses in a hospital, and quite close at one time.'

'Then she would be able to use a syringe?'

'Indeed. There was a doctor who made sure all the nurses knew how to inject. We were taught to put our fingers either side of where the needle was to go in, and pinch the flesh together; then to insert the needle at an angle and push it gently in. Quite easy really.'

'Mrs Bruton didn't bother with any of that this afternoon,' said Ursula grimly.

'Well, as I said, in those days she acted a bit uppity but she could be very entertaining. We used to get young men to take us to the music hall, she said there was safety in numbers. Not that that counted for anything, as I found out later.' She gave a reminiscent smile. 'I was maid of honour at her wedding to Joe Peters.'

Her words had an electrifying effect. 'Joe Peters?' said Rachel. 'Could you mean Joshua Peters?'

Mrs Maple laughed. 'That was his name on the marriage certificate. We had a good laugh over that, Jeannie and I. She said she'd never call him Joshua.'

'You mean he was married to Mrs Bruton?' Rachel sounded astounded.

'Did he really abandon her?' asked Ursula.

Mrs Maple nodded. 'I don't think he ever really wanted to marry her. Only she was in the family way and she had a nest egg saved up. Well, he took it all and went off, just before the baby was due. Right bastard he was.'

Nobody seemed surprised at such unusual language from Mrs Maple.

'How did she hear that he'd died?' Ursula asked.

'Ah, now there I have something to confess,' Mrs Maple said, not looking at all guilty. 'There was a report in the *Times* one day. A patient used to give me newspapers, he said he was trying to educate me.' She looked almost bashful. 'That was Mr Maple. After he recovered we walked out together. Anyway, I read all the papers, every page; didn't understand half of it, all those speeches from politicians and accounts of what was going on abroad. But I found a story that said an Englishman called J. Peters had been accidentally shot and killed in Cairo. I showed it to Jeannie. She had taken his desertion very hard and she'd lost the baby in childbirth. I thought if she knew her husband was dead, she could start over again.'

'Did you ever find out he wasn't really dead?' asked Jackman curiously.

'Oh, yes! Jeannie decided to give up nursing and trained as a manicurist instead. She offered her services in a big spa hotel on the coast, and that's where she met Mr Bruton. She came back and told me all about him. She seemed really happy and I was pleased for her. They had a small marriage ceremony and went off to the continent on honeymoon.' Mrs Maple paused. Everybody was waiting for more and after a moment she continued: 'By then Mr Maple and me were affianced, but I was still working in the hospital. And one day he turned up, Joe Peters, and asked to see me.'

'Must have been something of a surprise,' said Ursula.

'A breath would have knocked me down. Joe tried to spin me some tale of wanting to repay her the money he'd taken – except he told me she'd lent it to him. Well, I knew that was a lie. It seemed he'd made it big and thought he'd make it up to her.'

'Was he going to try and make another go of their marriage? asked Jackman.

Mrs Maple shrugged her shoulders. 'Never asked him. Never could stand him and the way he'd treated her, I couldn't bear him to ruin her life again. So I told him she'd died having the baby.'

'And you didn't tell her he'd turned up?' said Ursula.

Mrs Maple shook her head. 'He said he was going back to Egypt, he had a shipping business of some sort there, so I didn't think there was much chance of her ever finding out.' She poured herself more tea. 'It wasn't as if she needed Joe's money, Edward Bruton had plenty.'

'Would you be prepared to give a statement as to the marriage between Eugenie whatever-her-name-was-then and Joshua Peters?' asked Jackman.

'Her maiden name was Carson.' Mrs Maple thought for a moment then said, 'Well, I can't see giving a statement would do any harm. And if it means helping to get her convicted, then of course I will.' She turned to Ursula. 'I feel just terrible that she attacked you like that. And to think I sent you to work for her!'

'You thought you were doing me a good turn, and you were. It was a very good job. Tell me, when you ran into her that time, how long was it since you had last seen her?'

'Oh, many, many years. After she married Mr Bruton, she … well … I understood he was a cut above me and Mr Maple.'

It was obvious that Mrs Bruton had dropped her old friend and that it still rankled with Mrs Maple.

'But when I ran into her outside Harrods, we recognised each other instantly and she was charming. We had quite a chat, I told her about this place,' Mrs Maple glanced around her parlour with a touch of satisfaction. 'And she told me she'd just emerged from mourning and intended to build a social life. That was when she mentioned that she would be looking for a secretary.' She turned to Ursula. 'I immediately thought of you. She said you might be suitable and gave me her address.'

'Is there any chance, do you think,' said Jackman to Ursula, 'that the certificate from her first marriage could be in Mrs Bruton's home somewhere? Hidden away? If we had that, the case against her would be strengthened. Or,' he turned to Mrs Maple. 'If you could tell me where and when they were married, I should be able to get a copy.'

'You don't need one,' said Mrs Maple. 'I've got their marriage lines here.'

There was an astonished silence.

'You mean?' said Ursula.

'I mean when Jeannie left the hospital to train as a manicurist, she said she was leaving all her old life behind her. She was fed up with caring for the sick, now she was going where the money was and making sure the rich paid her way through life. She told me to take anything I wanted from her old room and throw the rest away. Well, I found her marriage lines in a shoebox with a letter or two that Joe had sent her at some stage, plus a nursing certificate and some odd bits and pieces. She hadn't given me a forwarding address, so I just took the box and kept it carefully. I should have thrown it away a long time ago but, somehow, I couldn't bring myself to.' She bent down, opened the bottom drawer of her desk and took out a battered shoe box. 'Here it is. Who should I give it to? You, Thomas, or you, Miss Grandison?'

'I'm only the assistant,' said Ursula with a smile, 'You'd better give it to Mr Jackman.'

Epilogue

A week later Ursula went down the basement steps to the Wilton Crescent kitchen, knocked and entered.

Enid was sitting at the pine table, rubbing at a copper pan with a salt-laden lemon half and sniffing. She looked up as Ursula entered.

'Oh, Miss Grandison! I thought I'd never see you again!' She rose and put the kettle on the range. 'You'd like a cup of tea, I'll be bound.' Then her smile vanished. 'Only, Mr Bruton is here.'

'Is he? Well, I expected that he would have been informed of Mrs Bruton's arrest. And I understand that she has now been charged with the murder of Joshua Peters and Albert Pond.' Ursula could have added the attempted murder of herself.

'Oh, miss, it's dreadful. He's fired Cook and Ned, the boy what did, you know? I'm the only one left. And he says as soon as he's sorted out things upstairs, I'll get my marching orders.'

Enid bustled about organising teapot and cups.

'I hope he gave them proper references – and wages in lieu of notice.'

'Cook said he wasn't overgenerous but she couldn't complain. And so long as I get my reference, I shan't be sorry to leave; he's a right little Napoleon, issuing orders and never a thank you.'

'It must have been a shock to discover his step-mama was being charged with murder.'

'You could have knocked all of us down with a fairy cake. Who'd've thought it!'

Enid supplied Ursula with a cup of tea and a slice of seed cake. 'That's the last of it. I'm not to make any more, Mr High and Mighty says. Half for you and half for me.'

As Ursula settled down for a nice chat, the bell rang.

'Lawks, that'll be him wanting something or other. More than my life's worth not to tell him you're here, Miss Grandison.'

'Of course,' Ursula sighed.

Five minutes later she was standing before Mrs Bruton's stepson. He sat at the desk she still thought of as hers. All the files had been taken out of the cupboards and there were neat piles of papers everywhere.

'So, Miss Grandison, you are back visiting the scene of the crime, eh?'

'There are one or two personal items I came to collect.'

He picked up a small carrier bag from the back of the desk. 'Notebook, comb, small scarf and two handkerchiefs? That correct?'

'Thank you, Mr Bruton.' Ursula looked at him a little more closely. He seemed to have aged ten years since she had last seen him, and lost some of his bombast.

He leaned back in his chair and ran a hand over his neat beard in a weary gesture. 'I suppose I should apologise for my step-mother's attempt on your life.'

'It was nothing to do with you.'

He nodded with a return of some of the authority she associated with him. 'Indeed. Yet, if only I had been able to persuade my father she was not what she seemed … well, he would not listen to me.' He put a large hand on one of the piles of paperwork. Ursula recognised a set of monthly bills. 'I suppose you're going to ask for severance pay.'

'Mrs Bruton owes me for two weeks' wages; I was about to write to you.'

'Nothing but outgoings at the moment! And it'll be months before I can dispose of any of the assets. At least that marriage certificate means I don't have to wait for a guilty verdict before I can take possession of my heritage. To think I need not have had to wait all these years!'

Ursula said nothing.

Mr Bruton removed a wallet from an inside pocket and opened it. For a long moment he hesitated, then removed several large, crisp white five pound notes. He placed them on the desk, reached for a piece of headed notepaper and wrote out a receipt.

'If you will sign that, Miss Grandison, I think we shall have concluded all business between us.'

She scribbled her name, received more than three months' wages and tucked the notes into her wallet.'Thank you sir, that is generous.'

He nodded. 'I trust you will be discreet about your employment with Mrs Bruton, as I suppose I must continue to call her. I have written a reference which should meet your needs.' He handed over a brief document that attested to Miss Grandison's abilities to carry out the duties required of a social secretary.

She placed it in her handbag, thanked him again and, with a final farewell to Enid, left Wilton Crescent.

★ ★ ★

Next Ursula called on *Maison Rose*. The previous Monday she had woken feeling wretched. Delayed shock, she decided, and wrote to Count Meyerhoff excusing herself for the rest of the week. She also gave the count the news of Mrs Bruton's arrest for the murder of Joshua Peters and Albert Pond.

As she climbed the stairs to the *Maison Rose*'s salon, Ursula mulled over the details Jackman had given her the previous Wednesday.

After he had enquired if she had recovered from Mrs Bruton's attack, he gave her the news that the woman had been arrested and charged. 'Confronted with the certificate of her marriage to Joshua Peters, she collapsed and confessed all,' he told Ursula. 'She is apparently now a broken woman.'

Then he had taken some highly coloured brochures out of an inside pocket. 'When I went down to Peters' study the evening we were looking for the key to his safe, I remembered seeing these in the front drawer the first time I searched the desk.' He handed Ursula the leaflets. 'They are sales pitches for what looks like some highly desirable yachts. And in the top corner there's a scribbled name: Meyer-something-or-other. At the time it seemed irrelevant; I had never heard of your count. However, now it seems obvious that the name is Meyerhoff. I went back to the shipping office and spoke to Martin Roberts, Peters' partner.'

'A yacht,' murmured Ursula. 'Why should he want a yacht? Austria is land-locked.'

'Roberts told me Meyerhoff used their company to ship ingredients for his beauty salon's preparations. And that he bought a yacht through them. He also told me that the count had taken possession of it but owes them a considerable amount of money on the deal. As to why he might want a sailing boat, wasn't it you who suggested he might be a spy? If he is, maybe he needs a quick escape route. Roberts would dearly like to know where it is currently berthed. He wants to serve a possession notice on it.'

'So Albert could have been dunning the count for what was owing, rather than blackmailing him,' said Ursula.

'We don't know,' said Jackman. 'You've been involved with the salon accounts, any clue there as to how much money is around?'

'The beauty side of the business is quite successful but weighed down with all the personal expenses the Count and Madame Rose charge to it.' She thought for a moment. 'There has been talk of patrons investing money in the business but I have not seen an account for such capital sums.'

Mrs Bruton had not invested in the beauty salon but there would be others who had taken a financial interest.

Hilda Ferguson opened the door to her. 'Oh, Miss Grandison! Come in. We are in a bit of a state, I'm afraid. Madame Rose, look who is here.'

The beautician was seated at the little table where she examined clients, a large notebook in front of her, her hands folded on top of it, her face a mask.

'I know it is not one of my days,' Ursula said hastily. 'I wanted to apologise for not being able to come last week.'

She might not have spoken.

'He's gone,' said Madame Rose.

Hilda Ferguson slipped her arm round the beautician. 'We will survive,' she said stoutly.

Madame buried her face in her hands. 'He's taken everything.'

Ursula wondered if she had heard aright. 'You mean Count Meyerhoff has gone? Disappeared?'

Madame Rose dropped her hands. 'He had hoped Madame Bruton would invest. Then your letter came and told she is in prison. He said that was that and there were no more possibilities for investors.'

'But to disappear!' Ursula could not make sense of this – unless: 'Is it because he's a spy and been discovered?'

'A spy? How can you think that? A spy – who for?'

'For Germany?' suggested Ursula weakly. 'I know he went to the naval dockyards at Chat-ham.' She broke the name into two, the way she had heard the count do, 'The English think Germany wants to invade.'

'Julius went to see an investor who lived at Chat-ham. My heavens, Julius a spy!' She broke into a coarse laugh. 'All Julius cares for is money. Not Austria, not Germany, not me! Not us!'

'We have been to see the bank manager,' said Hilda, sinking into the chair opposite Madame Rose. 'He has taken everything …'

Ursula brought over another chair and joined the two women. 'Please, you must tell me everything.' Gradually she managed to piece the story together.

The count had left the previous Wednesday. At first Madame had had no suspicions. Then, on the Thursday they discovered all his things had gone, together with his personal servant. That was when Madame Rose had gone to the bank. There she discovered that both *Maison Rose* accounts, the day-to-day one for cheques and expenses and a special one for capital sums from investors, had been closed.

'He asked for bankers' drafts,' said Hilda bitterly.

Not only that, but Madame had found that all the cheques Ursula had drawn up to pay their bills had been converted by the count into his own name and paid into his personal account. Ursula remembered that though she had inserted all the payment cheques into their envelopes, the routine had been for them to be placed on a table in the office for a servant to take to the post.

'Everything we have worked for has gone!' said Hilda.

'Do you have any idea where the count would disappear to?'

Madame sighed bitterly. 'Once, we discuss plans for expanding, opening a new salon, Julius said he dreamed of sailing across the Atlantic in his own boat and building an empire in America. He said that that was where the money was and we should look in that direction.'

'I wonder he didn't start there,' said Ursula.

'He said London was where he had contacts. Rich society ladies he had met in Vienna and other capital cities.'

Ursula wondered if there was any chance of intercepting the count's yacht before it reached America. Then realised that would be a hopeless task. He had a wide choice of possible American cities to aim for.

'You have built a fine reputation here in a very short time,' said Ursula. 'Could you not continue? Put all your investors in the picture and say you will work to build up enough money to make their investment pay? You make a very good team.' She looked from Madame to Hilda Ferguson.

Then she took out the letter they had found in Joshua Peters' safe and placed it on the table. 'Nobody knows who wrote this,' she said to Madame. 'Nobody can use it against you.'

The beautician looked inside the blank envelope and for a moment closed her eyes. Then she said, 'Thank you, Miss Grandison.'

Before she left *Maison Rose*, Ursula agreed to continue organising the accounts while Madame explored the possibility of continuing with the beauty salon.

By the time Ursula reached Montagu Place, it was late morning. Sarah answered the door. 'Mrs Peters is not at home,' she said.

Ursula took out a card and scribbled a note on the reverse. 'Perhaps you would be good enough to give her this,' she said.

The maid left Ursula in the hall and a moment later Alice appeared and embraced her. 'I am about to have a light luncheon, you must join me.'

It had taken a little time for Mrs Bruton to be charged with the two murders and for Alice to be released. Immediately she had written to Ursula thanking her for all her help.

'Oh, it is wonderful to see you again,' she said and sat Ursula in a chair next to hers. She was still far too thin but her eyes were shining and her face had colour. 'I had begun to despair of ever escaping from my prison cell.'

'How is Daniel?' Ursula looked around the room, half expecting the young man to be there as well.

'He is fine! He has been commissioned to write an article on Mr Bernard Shaw, the playwright and critic and today he is doing research for it.'

'That's wonderful!'

'He seems to think it could be the first of many such commissions, I do so hope he is right.'

'Are you still thinking of leaving the country, Alice?'

She nodded. 'I have to sell this house. Joshua left nothing but debts. Once they and the mortgage have been paid, there will be very little left.'

'What about your jewellery?'

Alice sighed. 'I took it to the jewellers, Garrard's, on Friday. They almost laughed. Apparently they are all paste copies – and they had supplied them! Joshua's story was they were for security. He must, though, have sold the originals. Garrard's were kind, they said their copies did have a certain value but it is not high. Only my dear mother's locket is real.' She put a hand to her neck and Ursula recognised the little gold heart-shaped piece Alice had worn while staying at Mrs Maple's.

'I may well be delivered of this precious child before everything has been sorted.' Alice gently touched her swelling womb. 'Afterwards, when the house has been sold and Joshua's estate finalised, then Daniel and I will marry and decide where we shall live.'

'If your destination is to be America, I shall be delighted to give you some addresses. And what about Rachel? Are you pleased with her engagement?'

Alice laughed ruefully. 'John Pitney is delightful. I only hope he can accept my sister's managing ways. I dearly love her but there are times ...'

Sarah came in to announce that luncheon was on the table.

Over cold meats and fruit, Ursula asked if Alice had taken back Millie as her maid.

Alice shook her head. 'I could not trust her. I am sorry for we dealt very well together. At the moment Sarah is assisting me to dress and do my hair. I may well take her on as my maid permanently.'

Ursula could not blame her for this decision. 'Millie is a resourceful girl, I am sure she will manage,' she said.

'I have given her a good reference, explaining that I am retiring from social life and have no further need of her.'

'Forgive me for what I am about to ask but now that your husband's activities as a blackmailer are known, would you be willing to say how you found out what he was doing? For surely that was why you wrote those things in your diary that meant you were arrested for his murder?'

Alice looked down at the pear she was peeling and for a moment Ursula thought that she would not answer. Then she pushed away the plate.

'I think you deserve to know. It is a very, very sad story. I had a close friend, Irene. Her husband was a fine man but dull. Even

I, who had known him from childhood, had to concede that. They had a daughter, a darling girl. When she was about five, Irene fell in love and began an affair with another man, one who was handsome and charming. They met at his rooms. In between times, they wrote each other passionate letters.'

Alice rose, walked over to the window and looked at the last few roses in the little garden. 'She told me all about it one day, said she had to tell someone. When I expressed my horror at what she was doing, she said I did not understand and tried to tell me about all the excitement of her meetings with Rupert, her lover. She said she wouldn't dream of leaving George, she was very fond of him and he was the father of her daughter, but that I had to agree that he was not a charismatic man. She brought out a bunch of letters she had received from Rupert and said I must read them. I looked at one but it seemed an invasion of privacy, there was such passion! I had to say I was deeply shocked.' She laughed ruefully. 'How could I have known that later I would find myself in love with a man who was not my husband? I told Irene that George was a good man and deserved a faithful wife. That upset her. She was so upset she dropped the letters; they went all over the floor. I helped her pick them up. Then she left and cut off contact with me.

'Several months later I received the dreadful news that she had passed away. I immediately went round to express my condolences to George. He was ... ravaged was the only word I can think of to describe him. Did I tell you he was a very old friend? Well, he poured his heart out to me. Irene had taken an overdose of laudanum.' Silence followed this.

'Was it suspected to be deliberate?' Ursula asked gently.

Alice came back to the table, sat down and started fiddling with the cutlery. 'George said that for a number of months Irene had been in an increasingly nervous state. He became very worried about her. Finally she came to him and confessed that she had had an affair and said that she was being blackmailed. Someone had got hold of one of Rupert's letters to her and was threatening to send it to her husband unless she paid him for its return. Irene told George she had sent him the money that had been asked for but that her letter had not been returned. Instead, she received another demand for money.' Alice paused again. 'I suppose that is the way of blackmailers.'

'So I understand. How long did she continue to pay him?'

'Until she ran out of funds. That's when she went and confessed everything to George. When he told me this, he broke down and sobbed as he said how devastated he'd been with what Irene had told him, so devastated that he'd lost his temper and told her that their marriage was at an end and she was no fit mother for their child. Then he'd gone to his club for the night. The next day he'd been horrified at what he'd said and had dashed back home to tell Irene he still loved her and they would rebuild their marriage, only to find she had taken the laudanum and passed away in the night.'

'That's the most terrible story.'

Alice nodded. 'George showed me one of the blackmailer's demands. For a moment I couldn't believe what I was seeing. The writing was all in small capitals, as though the blackmailer wanted to disguise it. But all the 'R's were back to front. It was an idiosyncrasy of Joshua's, he never seemed to know he was doing it. I tried to tell myself there must be someone else with such a habit but I couldn't help remembering Irene dropping all those letters on the floor. One could easily have ended up beneath the settee. Albert was sometimes called upon to help move heavy furniture so the maids could brush the carpet underneath.' Alice had no need to say more.

Ursula caught her hand in hers. 'My poor friend, what a burden you have had to bear.'

'I thought I could do my duty, stand by my husband no matter what he had done, but the knowledge of what Irene had gone through troubled me more and more. Then I met Daniel and he taught me what love could be. I had no child, nothing to tie me to a marriage that was more and more hateful. I began to dream of what life could be like if I could be with Daniel, maybe even bring Joshua to justice. But when I knew he had another chance to be a father, I knew I could not deprive him of that privilege or reveal to my unborn child that his father was a criminal.'

'It will have to come out at Mrs Bruton's trial.'

'Perhaps if Daniel and I live abroad, the child need not know.'

Alice looked at Ursula, 'Thank you for being my friend through all this. I hope you will remain one.'

Ursula assured her she would, then said, 'One final question, how was your friend to have paid the money asked for?'

'It was to be sent to a post office box number. The office was not far from us, very near to Marylebone station. George said that if Irene had not passed away, he had determined to send, not a payment, but a note in a striking envelope, to the box number then to haunt the post office until he saw who collected it.'

Was that what Mrs Bruton had done after Albert had continued with the blackmailing of her? Or had she indeed followed him from *Maison Rose*? She was capable of either course of action.

Shortly afterwards, Ursula took her leave of Alice, promising to come again.

★ ★ ★

It was only a short walk to where Ursula needed to be next. Thomas Jackman had sent her a note saying he would greatly appreciate it if she could meet him at three o'clock Monday afternoon. He had given her the address and a little map showing exactly where it was.

Wondering a little at the purpose of this meeting, she had agreed, planning her various calls that morning to end up in the right area. Luncheon with Alice had been a bonus. Originally she had thought to treat herself to a snack from a street seller while she explored the area.

Now the timing was working out perfectly and she found herself in a short road not far from Oxford Street. It had a variety of small shops and No. 8 was a brown door between one that sold flowers and one that offered umbrellas and sticks of all kinds. It had no sign to indicate what business was conducted there but when Ursula tried the handle, the door opened. It gave on to a very small hall and a staircase. Climbing up, Ursula found another door with opaque glass in the top half. She knocked, gently opened it and found herself in what seemed to be a completely empty space, newly painted.

'Hallo?' she said. 'Thomas?'

He came through another door. 'You made it! Good. Come and have a look at this.'

The second room was as empty as the first. It had a handsome window overlooking the street and was of a good size.

'Take a perch,' Jackman said, offering the wide windowsill.

Ursula settled herself beside him. 'I have made some very interesting calls this morning which I must tell you about. I also went job hunting last week and it looks as though I may have found one. A high society lady has just lost what sounds a very efficient secretary. She is involved with a number of charities, runs a large household and seems to think I might suit as a replacement.'

'Hmm! You haven't lost much time.'

'Can't afford to.'

He bent down and drew an envelope out of an attaché case leaning against the wall. 'I have been asked to give you this,' he said.

Ursula drew an inward breath as she recognised the well-shaped, strong handwriting.

'I received a letter from him last Monday. He said he didn't know your direction, by any chance did I? I didn't know if you'd want your details to be sent to all and sundry so said if he sent me the letter, I'd see that you got it.'

Ursula sat and turned it over, wondering whether she should open it there and then or later.'

'I wouldn't wait, if I were you,' Jackman said with a smile.

She tore open the heavy envelope and took out the piece of equally weighty quality paper with its familiar crest and address.

Dear Ursula,

At long last we seem to be on the way to sorting out the estate. Ever since you left, I have been conscious that neither you nor Thomas Jackman were properly recompensed for the very valuable work you carried out for us at Mountstanton earlier this year. Now I am in a position to rectify this situation. No doubt you will say that you didn't do it for money, and I cannot forget that you refused all help in finding a situation in London. You would, though, be doing me a great favour if you could swallow your pride for once and accept the enclosed cheque. I am sending a similar one to Jackman. I am glad that you are in touch, he is a sterling fellow and no doubt would have run you to earth if I had needed him to do so. I send you every good wish and hope London is proving entertaining.

Yours,

Charles

'You dropped your cheque,' said Jackman, bending and picking up a folded-over slip of paper. He handed it to Ursula. 'Colonel Stanhope has been very generous.'

She looked disbelievingly at the total.

'And mine was on top of the agreed fee. But, then, imagine the pickle they'd have been in if we hadn't got it all sorted.'

Ursula was too stunned to say anything.

'For me it means I can fulfil an ambition I have had for some time. As soon as I got the cheque, I went looking and this is what I found.' He stretched out his arms as though to embrace the whole space.

'You're going to open your own office!' Ursula was delighted. 'Somewhere prospective clients can call upon you and discuss their business.' She remembered how rude Rachel had been about his surroundings when they had visited him in Shoreditch. 'And these premises seem ideal. Nice and central, within easy reach of both society and more ordinary clients.' She looked again at her cheque. 'Do you need additional funds? I seem to be rather flush at the moment.'

He fumbled behind the attaché case and brought up a wooden rectangle. 'I was hoping after our chat the other day you might be willing …' He held the sign up. 'I got this painted on Saturday. If you agree, it would go beside the door downstairs.'

The sign read:

JACKMAN & GRANDISON
Private Investigators
Confidentiality Guaranteed

'Can you tell your high society lady you have made other arrangements?'

Ursula took a deep breath. Then she said, 'I think the sign should be in brass.'

THE END

Acknowledgements

The battle for women's suffrage had been joined long before Emmeline Pankhurst raised its level to militancy. An excellent history of the whole campaign and the ideas behind it is *The Ascent of Woman* by Melanie Phillips, published by Little, Brown in 2003. Concerning poison, two books I found most helpful were *Poison and Poisoning* by Celia Kellett, published by Accent Press Ltd in 2009, and *The Poisoner's Handbook* by Deborah Blum, published by Penguin Books in 2011. Helena Rubinstein's autobiography, *My Life for Beauty*, published by The Bodley Head, in 1965, inspired my creation of *Maison Rose*. And Larry Lamb's story for the BBC's series *Who Do You Think You Are* produced the setting for the book's first chapter.

I would like to thank Michael Thomas for reading and advising on the ms, my agent Jane Conway Gordon for her expert help and support, and the Mystery Press editors Matilda Richards and Emily Locke for their care and attention in the publication of this book. Finally many thanks to Shelley Bovey and Georgie Newbery, who have critiqued every stage of the writing of this book and without whom it would not have reached THE END. And to Peter Lovesey for his wonderful tag line. Any resemblance of the characters to actual persons, living or dead, can only be by coincidence, and all mistakes are mine.

About the Author

JANET LAURENCE is the author of the Darina Lisle culinary crime novels and the historical mystery series featuring Canaletto (both Macmillan). She was a weekly cookery columnist for the *Daily Telegraph* between 1984 and 1986, has written cookery books and contributed to recipe collections. Janet was Chairman of the Crime Writers' Association between 1998 and 1999, included in *The Times*' '100 Masters of Crime' in 1998, and was invited to run the crime-writing workshop at the Cheltenham Festival of Literature in 2000. She runs a number of crime-writing courses including at the Bristol CrimeFest conventions. She lives in Somerset.

Also by Janet Laurence

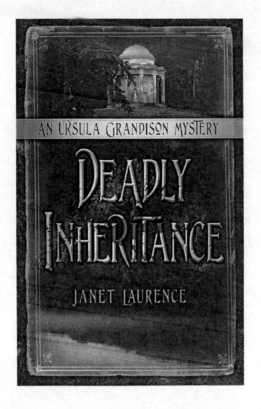

Accompanying American heiress Belle Seldon on a visit to her ancestral family home in Somerset, Ursula Grandison soon discovers that the decaying stately Mountstanton House and its inhabitants has many secrets, including a crumbling marriage and a missing dowry. When Ursula discovers the drowned body of the nurserymaid, she is determined to reveal the killer and, in doing so, reveals a tangled web of deception and adultery that threatens the reputation of the house of Mountstanton.

Find this title and more at
www.thehistorypress.co.uk